A LITTLE PINPRICK

PAIGE DEARTH

ISBN 9781735079677

Dirt On The Author

Born and raised in Plymouth Meeting, a small town west of Philadelphia, Paige Dearth was a victim of child abuse and spent her early years yearning desperately for a better life. Living through the fear and isolation that marked her youth, she found a way of coping with the trauma: she developed the ability to dream up stories grounded in reality that would provide her with a creative outlet when she finally embarked on a series of novels. Paige's debut novel, Believe Like A Child, is the darkest version of the life she imagines she would have been doomed to lead had fate not intervened just in the nick of time. The beginning of Believe Like A Child is based on Paige's life while the remainder of the book is fiction. Paige writes real-life horror and refers to her work as Fiction with Mean-ing. She hopes that awareness through fiction creates prevention.

CONNECT WITH PAIGE:

Find all of Paige's books on her Amazon Author Page
Visit her website at paigedearth.com and sign up for book release updates
Follow Paige on Facebook at facebook.com/paigedearth
Follow Paige on Twitter @paigedearth

For Frank, Patti's husband, who on Easter day 2021 knocked me over. Lucky for me my nephew, Joseph picked me up and dusted me off. Nothing was broken or bruised aside from my ego. You need to be a little more careful around me, Frank, or you may find yourself written into a future novel.

~

Written for all the people suffering because family or friends are addicted to drugs or alcohol. I know you are living the best you can and acting as if everything were normal to the outside world. Having lived with an ex-husband addicted to heroin, I recognize the addict isn't the only one who needs to be understood. Take care of yourself in the aftermath, many of us know your life has changed because of someone else's addiction.

—Paige

~

For my daughter, my love, my life.

—Mom

Acknowledgements

Remo, I'm so grateful that you still *believe like a child*, that makes you the last one standing. Thanks for sticking around now that all the glitz is gone.

Thanks to every person who continues to read my work and encourages me to write more books. I will be forever grateful to all my readers.

Chapter One: Tuesday

Rainey Paxton was only a few hours old. The nurses tried to calm her as her tiny body twitched. Her wail was shrill and steady. Rainey Paxton was in pain, the sound and sight of a child born addicted to heroin.

Rainey weighed less than four pounds. Her arms and legs shook wildly. The baby couldn't sleep, couldn't be comforted. No amount of swaddling, stroking, humming, or cradling could soothe her.

For the first days of her life, she cried for long periods, barely ate because she couldn't keep still long enough to suckle, and vomited when she did eat. The piercing screams didn't stop, so she had to be isolated from the other newborns in the neonatal intensive care unit.

It wasn't a mystery why Rainey was the way she was. She needed a fix—the same drug her mother injected while she was in her womb.

A few nurses who nurtured the infant while she remained in the hospital gave Rainey the love her mother should have given.

One of those nurses, while holding the child, turned to a colleague. "And to think . . . this precious girl will be sent home to her parents soon—the people who did this to her. It makes me sick."

Chapter Two: Four Days Prior

Miranda clenched her jaw and panted through the next labor pain. Her water had broken thirty minutes prior and the contractions were coming more frequently. She knew this meant that the baby would be coming soon. Miranda's long dark hair was held back with bobby pins. The skin on her face was peppered with angry red sores, dug raw by her fingernails clawing at insects that weren't there, a result of hallucinations brought on by her addiction to meth and heroin. Her once-sparkling brown eyes were flat, and except for the bulge in her belly, her bones protruded through her scrawny physique.

Miranda looked over at her boyfriend, Peter. He had wavy blond hair and dull gray-blue eyes. The couple were sitting in their station wagon, an old jalopy a hair away from being just a pile of rusty metal. They were in the parking lot of Bedford Hospital. Barry White's "Can't Get Enough Of Your Love Baby" was blaring from the radio so loudly that the windows vibrated from the bass thumping inside the smoke-filled interior.

Miranda, groggy from the heroin she'd taken earlier, threw her head back and belted a verse of unrecognizable song lyrics, "my garlic eyes, can't 'nough of you lovin' baby." Then she looked over at Peter again, while mindlessly shoving a few fingers inside the torn car seat to feel the cool metal of the springs. The smell of mildew from the leaky rear window was secondary to the rankness of old beer and stale cigarettes. The car's brake lights were duct-taped in place, something Peter was proud to have *fixed* himself.

Grinning at Miranda, Peter tapped white powder from a small bag into a spoon, then squirted water from the end of the needle into the powder and flicked his lighter to cook the mixture. Nodding, Miranda tied off her arm, using her free hand and her teeth to tighten the worn canvas belt. Then she turned the volume down on the radio, and watched her boyfriend expectantly. She wanted her last hit of heroin before going into the hospital.

"Hurry up, Peter," she said with a grunt. "Before I get another contraction."

Peter filled the syringe with the heroin solution, slapped the vein on Miranda's arm, and slid the sharp point under her skin and into her vein. He pulled back on the syringe, waited to see the blood flow into the needle, and injected the drugs. Miranda's shoulders twitched and her eyes rolled back in her head.

"Ahhhh," she groaned, laying her head back on the seat as her mouth dropped open and her slack tongue jutted over her bottom lip.

Peter smiled, knowing how good Miranda felt, and this built anticipation for his high, that would follow. "I'm gonna take you inside before I hit myself," he said. "I don't want you to have that kid in the car."

Miranda fumbled to light a cigarette, took a few sloppy drags, and nodded.

In the emergency room, Miranda's head hung, chin on her chest. Occasionally her head bobbed from side to side.

Peter looked at the intake nurse, "I'm Peter Paxton and this is my girlfriend. She's ready to have that baby," he said, anxious to get back to the car. The intake nurse, appalled, watched Miranda closely, concerned by the pregnant woman's condition.

"Mr. Paxton, she's really out of it. Do you know if she took anything?"

Miranda doubled over and grabbed her stomach as a hiss escaped her.

Peter ran his hand over Miranda's greasy hair. "Come on, babe. Just breathe through it."

His eyes were blazing when he dragged them back to the nurse. "No, she didn't take nothing. What's your problem? Can't you see she's having a baby? She needs you to help her. How about that? How about you do your job?"

Miranda lifted her head, eyes still closed, and let out a wail. "I need this baby outta me."

Pursing her lips, the nurse turned back to her paperwork and asked, "What's her name?"

"Miranda Andersen."

"Yeah, baby?" Miranda said, lifting her head half an inch. "What's going on?"

"Nothing. I'm just telling the nurse your name."

The nurse's lips pressed together tighter. "Mr. Paxton, it's important that we know if Miranda has taken anything . . . for the sake of the baby."

Racked with another contraction, Miranda doubled over and let out a throaty moan.

Peter forced a sigh as he looked into the nurse's eyes. He shook his head slowly in a show of disapproval. "Listen, my girlfriend is tired and in a lot of pain. That's it. Now let's get on with it unless you expect her to have this kid in the wheelchair."

The nurse's eyes narrowed and she turned her attention to the paperwork, jotting down a few more notes. She stood and pushed Miranda into the back, where she was transferred from the wheelchair to a gurney. After needing help to undress, Miranda was covered in blankets, and an oxygen mask was put over her mouth and nose.

With Miranda settled in, Peter went back to his car and mixed himself a brew of heroin and meth. "Something to lift me up but keep me grounded," he muttered to himself.

Forty-five minutes later, Peter stumbled back into the hospital to find that Miranda had given birth to a baby girl.

The medical team in the delivery room was heartbroken for the baby and repulsed by the lack of remorse Miranda and Peter seemed to have for what they had done to their child.

After the juddering infant was laid in her mother's arms, Miranda smiled and glanced up at Peter.

A smile played on the nurses' lips as she touched the baby's fingers. "She's beautiful. What's her name?" she asked, worried about the life the child would have with her parents.

"Rainey," Miranda said dreamily, then winced with pain.

The nurse lifted her eyebrows. "Rainey? That's unusual."

"Yeah," Miranda said, her smile growing. "Rainey ain't no ordinary kid. She's gonna bring me and Peter all kinds of good luck."

Peter chuckled as he rubbed his arms. "Girl, I love that name, and she's gonna love it too."

The delivery nurse leaned away from the derelict couple and stared hard at them. Her expression was mild but her body was rigid, arms crossed. She forced a smile. "Is there a significance to her name?" the nurse asked in the most pleasant voice she could manage.

Miranda's high was wearing off from the intense labor pains. She had a far away, dazed look when she glanced at the nurse, "You ever hear of the blues singer Ma Rainey?"

The nurse shook her head.

"She was born in Alabama. Beautiful black woman. Yeah, was known as the Mother of the Blues. You should check her out. Cool and mellow . . . when I'm high I love to lay back and listen to her voice. I'm telling you that woman sounds like an angel."

The nurse let her hands drop to her sides, trying to ease the tension that had built up in her shoulders. The medical staff had a hard time with drug-addicted moms. So many women wanted babies who couldn't have them, and then there were women like this . . . women who didn't deserve the miracle of motherhood.

The nurse looked at Rainey's tiny figure, then reached over and placed her hand on the baby's back and said gently, "A blues singer, huh? Well, Rainey sounds like a hearty name. However, this little angel is having a hard time, so she'll have to go to the NICU. It's pretty clear she's in withdrawal, but the doctor has ordered tests to make sure."

Peter glanced at the nurse with fiery eyes. "Our daughter will be just fine, okay? Right now, Miranda could use something to ease her pain."

"*Sir.*" The nurse struggled to keep her tone even. "Clearly, your daughter is sick because Miranda took drugs while she was pregnant. There's nothing *fine* about that."

Miranda looked at Peter. "Geeze, babe, she's so uppity," she grunted. She turned back to the nurse. "Who the hell do you think you are to judge me? You don't know nothing about what I've been through."

Peter gave the nurse a strained smile and said, "Give us a minute, will you?"

When the nurse left the room Miranda kissed the top of Rainey's head while the baby wailed in her arms.

Peter grabbed Miranda's hand. "Rainey Paxton," he said letting the name roll off of his tongue. "She's beautiful . . . the most gorgeous baby I've ever seen."

Peter leaned in, kissing the tops of both Miranda's and Rainey's heads. "Miranda, you're so damn hot as a mom, I'd fuck you right here," he said, then pulled down the thin hospital gown and kissed her breasts.

Miranda giggled and pushed her greasy, tangled hair away from her face. "You have to stop it. They ain't gonna let us get it on in here—besides, I'm kinda sore down there. But I can't wait to get the fuck outta this place. It's like I'm in prison with all these wires attached to me and shit." Miranda pulled Peter close. "I need a hit, babe. The morphine they gave me earlier is wearing off."

Peter kissed the little craters on her cheek. "I don't think that's a good idea. Before the doctor left, I heard her tell the nurses she was gonna give you something to help you with withdrawal. So, I think you should hold off for a while. Besides, I only have a little H left in the bag."

The nurse came back to take Rainey to the NICU. Since Miranda couldn't shoot up drugs while she was in the hospital, her doctor gave her methadone to keep her from having withdrawal symptoms. This kept the cravings at bay, and her whining about pain to a minimum.

Within twenty-four hours of giving birth, while baby Rainey fought to detox, Child Protective Services was summoned, and two days after Rainey was born, Miranda left the hospital without her child. If she could prove that she and Peter could stay sober, they'd be permitted to bring Rainey home.

In the car, Miranda turned to Peter. "Look, man, we both gotta stay clean if we wanna bring the kid home." She opened a plastic bag and pulled out a box. "They gave me this stupid pump to use until she comes home. They won't let me feed her until all the dope is out of my system, and if I don't pump, my milk will dry up, and then we'll have to buy shit for her to eat."

Peter lit a cigarette and nodded. "Yeah, it sounds like a whole lot of stuff you gotta do, sucks to be you." He grinned. "Anyway, I found a clinic we can go to near our house. That dumbass doctor told me about it so we can get that methadone shit. But just one thing first." He reached into his pocket and dangled a small bag of heroin from his fingertips. "I say, one last party before we give it up for a while."

Seeing the small plastic bag, Miranda's body was awakened. Her arms tingled and her mind raced with thoughts of getting high. She smiled. "Oh, Peter. I love you so much," she said, taking the bag from him, "Okay, one last time."

Chapter Three

Rainey was diagnosed with neonatal abstinence syndrome and a cluster of other issues caused by illicit drug use by her mother. As a consequence, Rainey spent the first month of her life in the Neonatal Intensive Care Unit. She had frequent seizures while being weaned from heroin and meth. Gradually the baby grew stronger and gained weight.

By the time Rainey was healthy enough to leave the hospital two months later, Miranda and Peter had stayed clean, and after drug testing, were cleared by Child Protective Services. Though the baby might not have known the shift, she was soon taken from the sterile walls of the hospital with loving, round-the-clock care into a rundown home in the heart of Kensington, a small, dilapidated, drug-infested section of Philadelphia. Miranda and Peter lived on a block that had twelve row homes on either side of the street. They rented one of two on the entire block that hadn't yet been condemned uninhabitable by the city.

Peter and Miranda made a bed for Rainey from a pile of old clothing and ripped towels. Although they visited her at the hospital nearly every day, they enjoyed being close to her without the nurses watching them. The first night they sat on the floor next to her.

"She's so beautiful," Miranda said.

"Yeah, 'cause she looks just like her mom," Peter said, leaning in to give Miranda a hard, messy kiss. When they finally parted, he flashed his girlfriend a sly smile. "So I was thinking to celebrate Rainey being home, we could party a little."

Miranda's eyes opened wide. She had been hoping that they could stay clean. They had both committed to a sober life after finishing the initial withdrawal, but the craving for drugs was always there, sitting just beneath the surface.

"Oh, yeah? How little?"

Peter pulled a bag of heroin and two joints from his shirt pocket and waved them at her.

Miranda placed her palms on his cheeks. "I don't know. We've been sober for two months."

Peter took her hand. "You're right. We've been so good. But I miss that buzz, you know?" he admitted, leaning his face close to hers. "It's just a little taste to celebrate having Rainey home."

"It's never a little taste, Peter. You know it," she said looking from his face to the bag of white powder. "Do you have any works?"

Peter bounced his eyebrows, lifted his pant leg, and pulled a hypodermic needle from his sock. "Of course, I have works. Life wouldn't be the same without them," he laughed.

Miranda's right hand slid up and down, over the veins in her left arm. Her lips parted as she made firm eye contact with Peter. "We've waited so long to bring her home," she said, kissing the sleeping child's cheek. "Man, this is the happiest day of my life," she said, grinning.

It took only a moment's pause before she was following Peter, slinking away from Rainey's bedroom, down the steps, and to the kitchen table. With the briefest of thoughts of her baby in her rag pile upstairs, Miranda extended her arm and Peter tied it off with a shoelace.

Peter held the needle up for her to make a toast and she leaned in closer. "Here's to our daughter," Peter said and inserted the needle under her skin. As he pushed the potent fluid in, Miranda's eyes glossed over and she let out a ragged purr.

Peter watched the elation wash over his girlfriend. "Shit, babe. You look so sexy when you get off. I could do you right here on the kitchen table."

Miranda gave him a crooked smile and her eyelids fluttered shut.

A short time after Peter shot himself up, he lit a joint, took in a long drag, and pulled Miranda from the kitchen chair. With her back to him, he unzipped her jeans and bent her over the table. Miranda lazily complied, and when he slid his fingers inside her, she let out a sensuous moan. Dropping to his knees, he pressed his face between her legs. After a while he rose from the floor, letting his jeans drop to his ankles and plunging inside of her.

"This is the best celebration ever," Miranda slurred afterward, her eyelids drooping as she swayed slightly.

Rainey's first night home set off a long heroin binge for her parents. They had held onto the concept that their daughter belonged with them and, no matter how bad their addiction became, the baby was right where it belonged. Before Rainey was born, they'd gotten by on a small inheritance from Miranda's parents. But once they started taking drugs again, they blew through the remaining money. Desperate, Peter came up with the idea of letting other addicts pay to stay at their house overnight.

Within a month, and with the money they collected from squatters, Miranda and Peter were using several times a day. Given the crowds of people, the house became a breeding ground for drug dealers.

Rainey was often left for hours on the pile of clothing that was her bed while her mother and father got high downstairs in the living room. Though she'd been weaned off the drugs in the hospital, the infant was soon back on them through her mother's breast milk.

Chapter Four

Somehow Rainey survived the first several weeks at home. From the tainted breast milk, the child was undernourished, addicted, and manic. Then, when she was not quite three months old, a blessing entered the baby's life: Miranda's older sister Sophie.

Sophie hadn't dated much and never married, preferring to focus on her work as a professional photographer. She traveled most of the week throughout the region, and while she made a modest living, it was enough for her to buy a two-bedroom home in a middle-class neighborhood. Sophie and Miranda couldn't look more different, yet before addiction they were equally attractive.

Where Miranda once had an exotic look with her silky black hair and large light brown eyes, now she was gaunt, with dark greasy hair hanging like clumps of spaghetti around her face.

In contrast, Sophie had blond hair and blue eyes. She was just over five feet, six inches tall, and was slender, with long legs and a tiny waist. Sophie turned heads when she walked into a room. While many men had pursued her, she loved her freedom too much to get tied down. At only twenty-five—four years older than Miranda—she wasn't ready for a long-term relationship.

Sophie and Miranda had never gotten along, and their relationship had turned volatile in their teenage years. Sophie was a well-balanced child who had been pushed to the side by their parents, who were focused on Miranda's drug addiction, which began when she was only sixteen, after she met Peter. Sophie carried deep bitterness for her sister's selfish behavior, and Miranda hated that Sophie didn't understand she couldn't control her addiction and secretly thought Sophie acted the way she did out of jealousy.

Rainey was almost three months old when Miranda called Sophie to tell her about the baby.

"Hey, Sophie. It's me," Miranda moaned into the telephone.

"What's going on?" Sophie asked. "I haven't heard from you in almost three months. I've been calling you. Is everything okay?"

"Yeah, I had my kid. I named her Rainey. Anyway, she had some problems so they kept her in the hospital for a while. But she's home now."

Sophie closed her eyes and pressed her forehead to the wall. "Why didn't you call me sooner?"

"You know, me and Peter have been busy—going back and forth to see her at the hospital and all."

"Why did they keep her so long? What was wrong with her?" she asked, though part of her already knew.

"Ah, you know how it is. She had to get some of that methadone for a while and gain a little weight."

"That's just great, Miranda," Sophie spat. "You couldn't stop getting high while you were pregnant? Classic. Really, it is."

"Whatever," Miranda huffed. "Anyway, Peter and me have been sober for a while now. That's the only way those jerkoffs would let us take the kid home."

"Really?" her sister asked hopefully. "And you're doing okay?"

"Yeah, we're doing fine. Anyways, I'm calling 'cause I gotta buy my baby girl some stuff and I wanted to know if you'd loan me some cash."

"What kind of stuff?"

"You know . . . diapers, clothes, shit like that."

"How much do you need to borrow?"

"I need about three hundred," Miranda said, holding her breath while she waited.

"Are you sure you aren't using?"

"Yeah, of course, I just got done telling you that . . . can you help me out or what?"

"Yeah, sure. I can lend you some money. I'll drive it to your place on Saturday. I can't wait to see Rainey."

Two days later, Sophie got into her car and drove to Kensington. She dreaded going into the area and knew it wasn't safe. She drove through the depressed neighborhoods while hoping her niece was being cared for and thriving. Unable to have any children of her own, Sophie longed to be part of Rainey's life.

Standing on her sister's rotting, uneven porch, Sophie banged on the front door. Nothing. She tried to peer into the front windows, but they were covered with blankets or boarded up. After a few minutes, Sophie kicked the bottom of the door. Finally, Miranda pulled it open and eyed her sister up and down. Then she stepped out onto the porch.

Sophie watched her sister carefully. Her heart lay like clay in her chest. She had wanted to believe Miranda was sober. It pained her to see the familiar signs of her sister's addiction. She stepped closer to get a better look, Miranda's face was washed out, her eyes were bugged, and she had angry fever blisters clinging to her top lip. She looked into her glassy, red eyes, "You look like shit, Miranda. You're not sober—look at you—you're completely strung out. I thought you meant it this time. Come on, you're a mother now."

"I'm sorry I ain't as perfect as you, Sophie. But guess what? At least I can get a man and have a damn baby. That's more than you can do," she snapped.

Sophie felt like she'd been slapped. "You're such a bitch," she said, fighting back tears. "I can't have children because I was born without ovaries and you know that. What the fuck is wrong with you?" She paused and took a few deep breaths. "Look, I didn't come here to argue, I came to see my niece. For the record," she stated, making her voice more authoritative, "You should have called me when she was born; not wait three months."

Miranda rolled her eyes. "Hey, you know where I live. You could've checked on me just as easy."

"Really? The last time I was here you were six months pregnant and Peter, that asshole, threw me out of your house because I was annoyed that you were smoking. Remember that? Do you remember telling me not to call you again?"

Miranda shrugged, not wanting to talk about what happened in the past or fight with Sophie—she wanted her money and for her sister to leave.

"How is Rainey doing?" Sophie asked in a gentler tone.

The tight lines around Miranda's eyes softened, and for an instant she looked more like the girl Sophie remembered growing up. "She's okay. She cries a lot, like, a really high-pitched, never-fucking-stop-crying cry.

Sometimes," she said, gritting her teeth, "I just want her to shut the hell up." She raked her fingers through her hair. "It's annoying as hell. I can't stand it. It gets so bad I wanna toss her skinny ass out with the trash."

Sophie, accustomed to Miranda's erratic behavior, focused on keeping her cool. She knew if she grabbed her sister by the neck of her shirt like she wanted to, she would stop talking. She wanted to know everything about her niece, so instead of reacting just said, "Yeah, I totally get it. One of the women I work with just had a baby and it's colicky. She said he cries all the time and she can't get any sleep."

Miranda snorted. "This ain't about sleep. This is about shut the fuck up, kid. I feed her . . . she cries. I change her dirty ass . . . she cries. I hold the thing . . . she cries. That's all she ever does. That kid doesn't know how to bring me an ounce of joy."

Sophie reached for her sister's hand and lowered her voice to a gentle hum. "Listen, we both know that you're using again." She paused, uncertain how to ask the next question without pissing Miranda off, so she just went for it. "Are you breastfeeding?"

Miranda looked away and Sophie's heart sunk. She pulled her sister in closer. "Really, Miranda?" she said into her sister's hair. "Your kid spent the first two months of her life in the hospital and now you're giving her more drugs. That's probably why she's crying all the time." Sophie rubbed her forehead and gathered her thoughts. "Look, how about if I pay for baby formula?"

"Yeah . . ." Miranda looked up at her sister and smiled. "Yeah, I definitely need money to buy formula."

Sophie shook her head. "What I meant to say is that I'll go to the store and bring some back for you."

"Right, because you don't trust me."

Sophie nodded. "That's true. I don't trust you with money. You're a junkie."

"So what? You think just because I like dope that I don't love my kid?"

Sophie wanted to say, *yes, that's exactly what I think about you when you're high*. Instead, she let out a loud sigh. "No, I think because you like dope you forget about your priorities. You and Peter are twenty-one. You've been doing drugs since you met in tenth grade. It's time to stop."

Miranda lit a cigarette and stared blankly into the garbage-littered street.

Sophie hiked her purse higher on her shoulder. “I want to see Rainey and we can talk more after. Are you going to let me in your house or what?”

Miranda shrugged, opened the rickety front door, and let her sister inside.

Chapter Five

"You live like vampires. You need to let some light into this house," Sophie said, straining her eyes in the dimness of the room.

"We like it this way," Miranda huffed. Then she grinned. "Peter says the best things happen in the dark when no one is watching."

"That's because Peter is a moron," Sophie said. She'd hated Peter since the first day Miranda had brought him home, glassy-eyed and distant, and eyeballed him now as he took a hit from a bong. After hacking from the harsh burn of the pot smoke hitting the back of his throat, he looked up, noticing she was standing there.

Peter stumbled to his feet and made his way over to her. "Hey, Sophie. How are ya?" he said, forcibly pulling her into an embrace she didn't want.

The foul smells of sweat and urine wafting from Peter's body hit Sophie's nose, and she instinctively pulled away from the filthy stench.

"I'm good." She looked around the room. The furniture was old with ripped fabric fraying from the seat cushions of the sofa. People gathered in small groups on the floor, passing joints and sharing beers. The cigarette smoke was so thick it stung her eyes. "I'd be better if you didn't have all these people partying like animals with your baby in the house."

"Ahh." Peter held Sophie tighter. "There's my judgmental, snotty girl. I knew you were in there somewhere."

Sophie jerked her body from his arms. "Knock it off, Peter. It isn't a joke. I mean it. These people shouldn't be here and you shouldn't be acting like a teenager. You have a kid and responsibilities."

Annoyingly, Peter just smiled. His eyelids sagged around his green eyes. "Might do you some good to loosen up a little . . . maybe you'd even get laid. I know some guys here that would screw anything with two legs." Peter leaned closer to Sophie's ear. "I can hook you up with one of them if you want."

"Kiss my ass, Peter. And by the way, you should probably think about a shower and a change of clothes. You reek like the inside of a garbage can. It's disgusting."

Peter shrugged. "See, that's part of your problem. You try to control everyone. No one around here cares what I look like or what I smell like. They're here for a good time. Simple as that."

Sophie was about to lecture him but realized quickly it would be a waste of her time. "I'd like to see Rainey," she said, keeping eye contact with Peter.

One side of Peter's mouth lifted into a half grin. "Fine. Go meet our kid."

Sophie followed Miranda up into a dank bedroom. The once pale pink carpeting had dark stains that resembled large bodies of water on a map. The wallpaper was peeling and water stains streaked the exposed sheetrock. Against the far wall was a scratched wooden dresser with the top drawer missing. In the other corner of the room, the missing drawer was overflowing with old clothes and towels. Lost in the pile of smelly material was Rainey, fast asleep.

When she spotted the baby, Sophie gasped and approached quickly. Her heart sank to her stomach, horrified and nauseated by the filth that covered and surrounded her niece. With her hand covering her mouth, she tenderly knelt next to the dresser drawer and lifted the sleeping infant into her arms. Rainey's eyelids fluttered open, revealing piercing hazel eyes. When she peered up at Sophie, the woman had a sudden thought: *Rainey looks like me, but with green eyes.*

Miranda watched her sister with envy, taking in how good she looked in her tight jeans and well-fitted blouse. Sophie looked healthy and fresh. Even in her altered state, Miranda had noticed the resemblance between her daughter and older sister. For both reasons, a twinge of jealousy ran through her.

Miranda barreled forward. "Now look what you did, she's awake. You're so dumb," she growled. "I just told you that all that pain in the ass does is cry when she ain't sleeping."

Sophie glanced at her sister sideways. It was painful to see her so strung out, and she wished that Miranda could be joyful about having a child.

There was an underlying resentment that she could be so irresponsible and have a child, while she herself had been born barren. Her anger bubbled over. "Maybe she's in withdrawal when she's awake. Has that ever occurred to you?"

Miranda flopped on the floor. "Shut the hell up, Sophie. You're not a mom. Remember? So I ain't taking any advice from you."

Sophie flinched before she looked the baby over carefully. Rainey was pale and her skin was loose. Her lips had no color and her pupils were dilated. Sophie wasn't a doctor, but even she could tell the child was high. She held the baby closer.

"She's beautiful," Sophie said, looking down at her niece.

"Yeah, I know. She looks just like Peter. Right?" she said to torment her older sister.

Sophie shrugged. "I think she looks a lot like me and Mom."

"Whatever makes you happy," Miranda said, lying flat on the dirty carpet.

Sophie looked back down at the helpless child. "Hello, Rainey. I'm your Aunt Sophie, and I'm going to take good care of you."

To Miranda's surprise, Rainey wasn't crying; instead, her child was mesmerized by her older sister. Perhaps it was the sound of her calm voice or the poise and patience she didn't feel from her mother, but it was apparent the baby was soothed and comforted by her aunt. Miranda resented that she couldn't pacify her child in the same way.

Just then, Peter popped his head in. "Hey. Pickle is bringing over some good dope. He said it's as close to pure as he's ever had. You coming?"

"Shit. I forgot he was coming." Miranda sat up quickly, all thoughts of motherhood gone from her mind. She held her arms out toward Sophie. "Give her to me."

She glanced at Sophie, knowing her own eyes were bloodshot, but not caring, and lifted her shirt, exposing her braless chest, ignoring her sister's probing stare.

"Miranda," Sophie said, her voice firm, "did you shoot up today?"

"Yeah." Miranda averted her gaze. "So what?"

"You're passing the drugs to Rainey through your breast milk. I just told you that fifteen minutes ago. Doesn't that mean anything to you?"

She had no interest in taking care of her baby, plus the need for drugs was calling her.

Miranda shrugged. "So, you'd rather me starve her to death?"

"No. I'd rather you used the money you're spending on drugs to take care of your daughter."

Miranda wrapped her arms under Rainey and took the baby from Sophie. "Don't preach to me. I don't wanna hear it."

Hungry, Rainey quickly latched onto her mother's breast as Sophie watched, first in horror, then in shame.

Chapter Six

"I'm as much of an asshole for watching you allow that child to feed from your breast as you are for doing it," Sophie said.

Miranda smirked at her sister. "No, wrong. You're just a flat-out asshole."

Sophie stepped away from her sister. "You say such rotten things to me, Miranda. All I'm trying to do is help you."

"Yeah, well I don't need your help. Besides, you say rotten things to me too. That's how it's always been."

Sophie stood by quietly, hurting inside and wishing their relationship was different.

When Miranda was done feeding the baby, she handed her back to Sophie. "Here. You can take care of her now. There might be a clean diaper in the bathroom down the hall. Change her for me, will ya? She hates getting her diaper changed, so she'll scream so loud that you'll want to choke her."

"There's something wrong with you," Sophie snapped, grabbing Rainey from her sister.

As she was fastening a clean diaper, the color in Rainey's face changed. At first, in the dim light, Sophie thought she was seeing things, but when she looked closer, she saw it was true: the child had turned a shade of light blue. In a panic, she rushed down the steps and into the smoke-filled living room.

"I'm taking Rainey to the hospital. Something's wrong with her."

Miranda, midway through fastening a belt around her arm, stumbled from the sofa and looked into Rainey's face. "There ain't nothing wrong with her. She gets that way sometimes."

Sophie looked at her sister in shock. "Miranda!" she said. "This isn't normal. If you won't let me take her to the hospital, then I'm taking Rainey home with me. I'll get her used to formula and then I'll bring her back."

Miranda walked over to Peter and whispered into his ear, loud enough that Sophie could still hear. "My stick-up-the-ass sister wants to take Rainey home for a while . . . said she's gonna get her used to drinking formula. She said she'll buy it for the little rat from now on. What do you think?"

Peter turned to Sophie and flashed her a quick grin. "I think you let the hag take her. But tell the bitch when you want her to bring Rainey back. She can't have her too long. Your sister ain't getting her hands on our kid—there's nothing she'd like more. She's never liked me and, you know, I ain't that fond of her either. Now get it over with fast because she's killing my buzz."

"Maybe Sophie would be good for Rainey," Miranda babbled.

Peter glared into her eyes.

Miranda sputtered. "I mean, for a while. I know you love our daughter, so do I, but you have to admit having a baby is kind of a drag."

"She's our kid and your sister ain't keeping her," he said, turning his back to her.

Miranda marched back to her sister, who pretended she hadn't overheard. "Okay. Just two days. If you don't have her back here on Monday, I'll send some scumbags we know to your house to burn it the fuck down. Understand?" she said loud enough for Peter to hear.

"I need more than two days. Give me at least two weeks."

"Nah-ah. Too long," Miranda spat.

"Fine," Sophie relented. "One week."

Miranda jutted out her hip and touched Rainey's scalp. "What's in it for me?"

Sophie's mouth dropped open. "Are you serious?"

Miranda maintained eye contact as she puffed on her cigarette, and the smoke floated around Rainey's face.

Sophie, carefully containing her rage, took in a long, silent breath. "What will it take?"

Miranda took another drag from her cigarette and exhaled loudly. "I mean a week is a long time to be without my kid. Plus, I'm gonna have to pump this milk outta me, and that's going to take time away from me being productive. So I think it's fair that if I ain't gonna see my kid for a week, you have to give me money so I can buy something to calm my nerves. It ain't easy for a new mom to be separated from her kid."

Holding Rainey with one arm, Sophie reached her hand into her jeans pocket, pulled out two twenty-dollar bills, and pushed them toward Miranda in a forced motion to emphasize her anger.

Miranda separated the bills. "Forty bucks? Is that all you think my kid is worth?"

Sophie reached in her pocket for her last twenty. "You are truly a rotten person."

Miranda swayed and eyed her up and down. "I really like those jeans you're wearing too."

Sophie glowered at her. "You can forget it."

Miranda grabbed the last twenty-dollar bill from Sophie. "One week. And don't think I'll forget. Mothers don't forget about their kids, but you wouldn't know nothing about that, would you? I mean since you can't have your own."

"Fuck you," Sophie snarled.

"Yeah, fuck you too," Miranda fired back, shoving her sister—still holding Rainey—toward the front door.

***

Sophie entered her bright, clean home and laid Rainey on the floor surrounded by pillows. After filling the tub with a few inches of warm water, she picked up the child, and stripping off her dirty clothes and diaper, laid Rainey into the tub on several towels.

Sophie smiled at the baby. "Yes, baby girl. That water feels good, doesn't it?"

Rainey smiled and cooed. When the bath was done, Sophie wrapped the child in a clean towel and carried her into the bedroom, where she dressed her in a soft cotton onesie. She cradled Rainey in her arms and fed her a bottle of formula before placing her inside a bassinet she had borrowed from her neighbor.

Sophie watched Rainey as she slept and whispered, "I wish you could live here forever."

Working in the living room, to stay within earshot of the sleeping baby, Sophie admired the pictures she'd taken of Rainey. "Grandma and Grandpop would've loved you," she said.

Chapter Seven: Back to Heroin House

One week later, against her will and better judgment, Sophie brought Rainey back to her parents. When she entered the row home, Miranda stumbled toward them and grabbed her daughter from her sister's arms.

Miranda put her nose at Rainey's neck and took a long whiff, "Oh, you smell so good."

Sophie crossed her arms over her chest. "It's called a bath. Something that Rainey needs regularly. Now, listen. She did great on formula and I brought four cases to leave with you. They're in my car. I bought her a few outfits and a box of diapers too."

Sophie watched as Miranda lifted the baby to smell her again. "That's good. I need all that shit, since you didn't give me a baby shower or nothing. I think it's good you bought her that stuff. Especially the formula, I hate nursing. It's a pain in the ass and too time-consuming."

Sophie moved on to her plan and put her arm around her younger sister. "Let's talk somewhere private."

Miranda scowled at her. "Why do you have to be so serious all the time? It's a drag." She stuck her nose in Sophie's blond hair. "But you smell really good too," she said.

"Well, it's crazy what a shower and a dab of perfume will do," she said sarcastically. Sophie lifted Miranda's hair and tilted her head. For a moment, she saw her sister there—who Miranda used to be. "You're a beautiful woman. If you cleaned yourself up and fixed your hair, maybe you could get a job or do something different with your life. It would be good for Rainey."

Sensing what was happening, Miranda tried to pull away from her sister, but Sophie tightened her hold. "Come on," she said. "Let's talk in the kitchen." Sophie pulled her to the back of the house, where they sat at the kitchen table together.

Nervous, Sophie placed her hand at the base of her throat to steady her voice, "Rainey had several seizures the first two days I had her and I got really scared. I didn't know what to do, so I brought her to the doctor. He was very concerned and did some tests. They found drugs in her system. I told them she is staying with me now so they wouldn't try to take her away from you."

"Did you tell him about me?" Miranda demanded.

"I . . . I had to tell him something, and well . . ." Sophie saw no other way out but the truth. "I told him you have a drug problem and that you were letting Rainey stay with me while you try to straighten out your life."

Enraged that Sophie would tell anyone about her or Peter, she grabbed the collar of her sister's coat. Her face was only inches from her, "Are you stupid or something?"

Sophie ripped Miranda's hands from her collar. "What the hell was I supposed to do? Rainey was in withdrawal. At least I told him she's living with me now. Maybe I should've told him the truth . . . that her mother is pounding heroin into her veins every chance she gets." Sophie, realizing her hands were shaking, took a deep breath and sat back in the chair. "Anyway, the doctor wants to see her for regular visits."

Miranda studied her fingertips as Sophie spoke, then munched down on her thumbnail.

"Are you listening to me?" Sophie asked. Her sister had the attention span of a flea.

She glared at her and growled, "Who the hell do you think you are taking my kid to the doctor?"

"Stop it, Miranda. This is serious shit. Rainey is my flesh and blood and I care about her. You need to take better care of her, and she needs medical attention. If you want, I'll raise her for a while and bring her back when she's a little older and easier to manage."

Miranda glared at her sister. "You'd like that, wouldn't you? You just wanna get your hands on her so that you can tell those Child Protective Service assholes that she should stay with you forever. You're trying to steal her from me. You're a rotten bitch!"

Sophie shook her head, but deep in her heart she knew that Miranda was partially right. She would have loved to take Rainey and raise her as her own child.

"I wouldn't do that to you," Sophie said, her voice softer now, humbled.

She might have wanted to throttle her sister most of the time, but she loved Miranda and would never intentionally set out to hurt her.

The two women sat in silence. Then Sophie set the bait. "Look, if you let me take Rainey to the doctor's appointments, I'll help you apply for welfare money. Now that you have a kid it'll be a lot easier to qualify."

Miranda's eyes popped open and a grin played on her lips. "Who told you that?"

Sophie stood and leaned against the kitchen counter. "I did some research, and since you're not married to that loser, you should qualify as a single mom."

Miranda looked into Rainey's face, taking in her daughter's small features. "Yeah, okay. I'll let you do that—but I ain't paying for any of the doctor appointments."

"You don't need to pay, I'll take care of it," Sophie said, a rush of relief coursing through her. It wasn't a perfect solution, but it was a step in the right direction.

Miranda smiled absently as she tapped her lighter on the table. "Besides, welfare *should* be helping me. It's the least they can do. Maybe I can get food stamps too. I know lots of people that get them, and I have as much right to free shit as they do. That's why we pay taxes."

Sophie smirked cynically at her sister. "When did you ever pay any taxes? You've never worked a day in your life."

"I don't know," Miranda snapped. "When I buy stuff from a store."

Sophie looked down at her feet because inside she wanted to shake the stupid, entitled thoughts loose from Miranda's head. Instead, she considered her efforts a small victory.

***

Two weeks later, Sophie picked up Rainey for a doctor's visit. To her and the doctor's delight, the baby's health had improved on her formula-only diet. After the doctor's appointment, Sophie sat with

Miranda at her kitchen table and helped her complete the paperwork for public assistance. In the end, Miranda collected a monthly check plus food stamps.

The money from the state intended to be spent on the things that Rainey needed, unsurprisingly, was used to buy heroin for her mother and father.

Sophie continued to supply diapers, formula, and later baby food every week. She wanted to keep an eye on Rainey. Miranda, having sucked everything out of her older sister, was obnoxious and rude to her whenever she went to the house. The tension between the sisters grew with each visit. Sophie scrutinized her sister's lifestyle, and Miranda, high and paranoid all the time, believed her older sister was trying to steal her child.

Miranda was wrong, Sophie never stole her child. She did everything in her power to make sure that Rainey had the things she needed, and for her, that had to be enough. Even though she longed for a child of her own, she found contentment in her niece.

Chapter Eight

After a few months on welfare checks, Miranda and Peter were drinking whiskey while waiting for their drug dealer to come by the house. Rainey was ten months old by then, and just beginning to crawl.

Miranda took a hit of a joint she was holding and, turned to Peter. "I've been thinking about my sister a lot lately," she said out of nowhere. "I don't want that annoying bitch to spend any more time with Rainey. She's always ragging me about how we live."

Peter popped a Valium into his mouth and choked it down dry. "I ain't worried about Sophie. Look, she brings that kid food and diapers. Who the hell cares what she thinks?"

"But what if she turns Rainey against us?" Miranda asked, voicing the worry she'd been keeping secret over the past several months.

"She won't. Kids love their parents no matter how fucked up they are."

"Not true," Miranda said. "I had that girlfriend, Cassy, in high school and she hated her parents. Remember her?"

Peter rubbed the back of his neck. "Yeah, I guess so, but who cares, Miranda? It ain't like you're up for mother of the year."

"Well, you ain't up for father of the year either," Miranda snapped. She stood and straddled Peter in his chair. "Let's not be mean to each other. Besides, you're right. I don't wanna be mother of the year. I wanna be the best-piece-of-ass-you-have of the year."

Grinning, Peter pulled her tank top down to expose one of her breasts and took her nipple in his mouth, biting on it lightly. Miranda's head snapped back and she grabbed his crotch.

"Anyway," Peter said, slipping his hand inside her jeans, "it's final. Your sister can come once a week like she has been. That way, the kid stays fed without costing us any money."

Miranda shook her head and opened her mouth to protest, but Peter, with his hand in her pants, pressed forward. "I'm the man of the house and I say it's final. Got it?" he said. Then his touch mellowed and he gently stroked her.

Miranda lost all sense of rational thought. Sensation took over. "Oh, God, Peter. I love when you act like you're the boss."

Peter slapped her across the face. "I'm the man of the house, that makes me the boss."

Miranda nodded and moved forward to kiss him, and both of them slid off their jeans. They had sex in the kitchen with five other people standing nearby. But no one cared—it wasn't unusual. When they finished, Miranda and Peter dressed and each took a shot of whiskey.

When Sophie showed up later that day, she entered Rainey's bedroom, and when the child saw her aunt, she cooed and flailed her arms. Her world appeared to lighten, and Sophie was sure she seemed happy. She realized there was nothing more thrilling than having her helpless niece see her as an advocate and protector . . . someone she was happy to see. Sophie wrapped the child in her arms, wishing she could protect the small girl from the fires of addiction. She wanted to let Rainey know she was loved and wanted. That there would be more to her life than the walls of her broken-down home.

Sophie spent one day a week with Rainey. She would pick up the child and drive back to her house to bathe her. Then she would sit in her living room with pillows and quilts around them to read books and play silly games. It didn't matter that the child was too young to understand; her goal was to give her as much normalcy in the time she had with her. When Sophie brought Rainey home, the child would wail at the top of her lungs and cling to her as if her life depended on it. Those were the worst, the hardest moments for Sophie. Rainey continued to cry even after she was gone, desperate for attention that her parents didn't give her. Instead, the child got angry and impatient, frustrated and scared.

The other days of the week, when Sophie couldn't visit, Rainey would cry until she shook from hunger or dirty diapers. By the time Rainey was three years old and speaking nearly full sentences, she understood enough to know that her parents were different people when they shot up, even if she didn't know what they were doing.

"Mommy," she screamed one night, "stop putting that rope on your leg!"

Miranda looked over at her daughter, seeing the disappointment and fear on her child's face. "I need this, Rainey. It's my medicine and it makes me feel better so I ain't sick."

Rainey's face went slack; she shuffled over to her mom and crawled into her lap. "I don't want you to be sick no more. It makes me scared when you take medicine."

"Well, there's nothing to be scared of. Now, you need to get off of me and let Mommy take her needle."

"No! I don't want you to take a needle."

"Come on, Rainey. Get off me. I have things to do."

Rainey defiantly stared into her mother's eyes and didn't budge.

"I mean it, Rainey. Get the hell off," Miranda said, jerking the child's arms from around her neck and shoving her onto the floor.

Rainey, shocked and hurt, put her face down on her arms and cried.

Annoyed by her daughter's wails, Miranda used the tip of her sneaker to nudge the child farther from her. Rainey, frustrated and rejected, slithered farther from her mother and collapsed back into her crying position, where she stayed until a twentysomething woman named Buddy, who stayed at the house occasionally, picked her up and carried her to the sofa. Buddy poured some of her soda into a used cup and handed it to the child. As the two sat together and watched cartoons, it struck Buddy how messed up it was for the child living in a home overrun by a group of spaced-out, blitzed slobs. Buddy decided that she'd keep an eye on the kid if she could continue to afford her daily fee. Because no one stayed at Peter and Miranda's house unless they paid the daily fee.

Chapter Nine

The next Saturday, when Sophie went to get Rainey for her weekly visit, she was hit by a rancid, burned plastic smell she couldn't quite place. Once her eyes adjusted to the dim light, she noticed several people smoking cigarettes and pot, which wasn't unusual. Then, craning her neck, she spotted a group in the corner of the room smoking from a clear glass pipe: crack.

Sophie quickly put her hand over her mouth and nose and moved through the groups of wigged-out people sprawled on almost every inch of flooring throughout, hoping that Rainey was safe up in her room and not somewhere among them. There were beer cans and used red plastic cups everywhere. In the kitchen, she found crushed cigarettes abandoned on top of the burned linoleum floor. She was used to Miranda's house being messy, but this was something else. There were trash, empty cans, and discarded blankets and pillows everywhere. Taking in the recklessness that must have ensued over the past week, Sophie's anxiety grew while she assessed the remnants of excessive partying.

She rushed back through the house, looking for Rainey. Taking the stairs two at a time to the second floor, Sophie barged into the child's bedroom and scanned the room. Under the only window was a plastic milk crate turned upside down to make a table, and she got closer for a better look. Laying on top were half a dozen used needles and two metal spoons that were easily accessible to the child. Her panic soared to new heights as her eyes darted around the clutter looking for Rainey. Then, a few feet away, buried under a pile of clothes and garbage, she saw the top of Rainey's head sticking out. Fearing the child was dead, she dug through the things on top of the child and pulled her from her unfit cocoon.

Her breath caught in her throat when Rainey opened her eyes and smiled. Sophie quickly assessed the child. She appeared intact, breathing fine, and her body temperature seemed normal. Allowing herself a moment of relief while she talked to Rainey, she calmed her shattered nerves. Then she put her on the floor and scurried around the room, grabbing a used grocery bag and carefully collecting the used needles and metal spoons.

Sophie's anger boiled over as she burst into her sister's bedroom. Peter lay on the bed, with Miranda on his left side and a girl with long red matted hair on his right. All three were naked.

"What the fuck is wrong with you two?" Sophie shouted, the door banging into the wall behind it. She held up the bag she had filled. "These are used needles. They were in Rainey's room. What if Rainey had stuck herself with one of these? God only knows what could have happened to her."

The red-haired girl lifted her head and rolled her eyes. "Hey, lady. Can you be quiet? I have a bitching headache and you're making it worse." Then she dropped her head back down on the pillow she was sharing with Peter.

The girl's rudeness set Sophie off even more. Hands on her hips, she snarled, "I'm sorry. Who the hell are you? You're in bed with my sister and her poor excuse of a boyfriend. You need to get your sorry, trashy ass out of that bed and get the hell out of this house." Sophie said unblinking, with rage coursing through her and glaring at the girl.

Miranda and Peter, who had never seen her so angry, stared at her for several seconds until Peter grunted, "Sophie, maybe it ain't such a good idea that you spend time with Rainey anymore. You can't keep your cool with our friends. This girl here," he said, grabbing the red-haired girl by the face and giving her an open-mouth kiss, "she's a friend of ours, her name is Margie. Let me tell ya, Margie gives the best head on earth. Doesn't matter if you're a guy or a girl, her mouth is magical. Plus, she's a pleasure to screw. Margie likes to be loved and give love. I bet she'd even do you if you asked her nicely."

Margie smiled and nodded.

Sophie pointed her index finger at him. "You're a pig, Peter." She turned to her sister. "And it doesn't bother you that your boyfriend, the *father of your child*, is screwing another woman at the same time he's screwing you? Have you gone mad?"

Miranda leaned over Peter and took one of Margie's breasts into her mouth. She sucked on it hard, and the redhead arched her back in pleasure.

Sophie flinched and bile rose to the back of her throat. *How can my niece survive this home? These parents?*

Miranda turned back to her older sister. "Nope. Doesn't bother me a bit. Did you ever think that maybe I'm the one who invited her into our bed? 'Cause I did. I like sex better with Peter when we add another girl to the mix. Ain't nothing wrong with that."

Sophie pressed her fist against her mouth, and her cheeks filled with air suppressing the urge to lunge forward and grab her sister by the throat. Peter's threat of not spending time with Rainey was unthinkable after years of helping to raise her. Without a word, she turned on her heel and headed down the hall to Rainey's bedroom. She kneeled next to the sleeping toddler and gently kissed her forehead.

Rainey gave her a sleepy smile. "Hi, Aunt Sophie."

"Hi, sweetheart. Did you have a good sleep?"

She nodded. "Can I have ice cream?"

Sophie chuckled. "Well, first we're going to my house, and after your bath, I'm going to make you pancakes with a smiley face made out of chocolate chips. How's that sound?"

The child grinned. "Then can I have ice cream?"

"I'll make you a deal. After lunch, we'll go get ice cream and then we'll go to the grocery store and you can pick out food that you want before I bring you back here."

Rainey ran the backs of her small hands over her eyes. "Okay, but I really wanted ice cream now."

Sophie cuddled her. "I'm sure you do. We better get moving."

Back at Sophie's house a few hours later, Rainey kneeled on the velvety soft cushion at Sophie's kitchen table, eagerly awaiting her pancake. When Sophie bent over to place the plate in front of her, Rainey reached up and wrapped her small hand around her hair.

"You and me have the same," she said, pointing from Sophie's hair to her own.

Sophie smiled. "Yes, it's exactly alike," she said, sitting down beside Rainey. "Did you have a good week?"

Rainey shook her head. "No, 'cause when Mommy and Daddy take their medicine, they don't pay attention to me, and then when I'm hungry and thirsty they yell at me 'cause they always have to take medicine."

Sophie's eyebrows met as she tried to think of how best to explain this to Rainey. "I know, honey. Mommy and Daddy are sick. But they still need to take care of you."

"Sometimes Buddy takes care of me."

Sophie's back stiffened and she turned to face her niece. "When does Buddy do that? Does he come into your bedroom when you're in there by yourself?"

"No, silly." Rainey leaned over, slapped her own forehead, and giggled. "Buddy's a girl. I like her. She's nice."

Sophie had never met or heard of any Buddy, and wondered who this girl or woman was. "Does Buddy ever do anything that makes you uncomfortable?"

Rainey grinned and shook her head. "Nah-uh. She's nice. She doesn't have to take medicine."

"When I take you back to the house will you let me meet Buddy?"

Rainey took a bite of pancake and nodded. "But she's only there sometimes."

Sophie wiped Rainey's mouth with a napkin. "Sure, that's fine. If she's there then I'd like to meet her. But if Buddy ever hurts you or anyone else ever hurts you, I want you to tell me. Promise?"

"Why is someone going to hurt me?" she asked, wide-eyed.

"No, no. I didn't mean that someone is going to hurt you. What I said is *IF* someone ever were to hurt you that you have to tell me. Understand?"

"Yeah. Sometimes the people who live at my house watch things on TV that make me ascared."

Sophie let out a loud breath. "Well, if that happens again, I want you to tell your mommy so she can change the channel," she said with little hope.

Rainey shrugged. "Mommy can't hear me. After she takes her medicine, her eyes get closed and when I talk to her, she can't hear nothing."

"Well, when we get back, if Buddy is there, I'll ask her to change the channel for you. Okay?" she asked with the slightest relief that someone was at the house to look after Rainey.

"Yeah. Can we bring Buddy some ice cream too?"

"Sure. Why not?" Sophie said with a sigh.

Satisfied, Rainey began to happily chat about anything and everything. She had so much personality and was exactly how Sophie imagined a child of her own would have been. She longed to raise the child in her home. She wished she could steal Rainey away and give her everything the little girl deserved, but she didn't know if Peter would make good on his threat and not allow her to see Rainey if she continued to push them. The last thing she wanted was to be banned from their house. If that happened, there's no telling what would become of Rainey. The thought of it sent a chill up her spine.

Chapter Ten

On Rainey's fourth birthday, Sophie picked her up for lunch and a movie.

Over a grilled cheese sandwich, Rainey looked up at her aunt, and in a small voice said, "Aunt Sophie? Can I live with you?"

"Oh, Rainey. I would love for you to live with me. But it's not that simple. Your mommy and daddy would miss you if you weren't at home with them."

"Nah-uh. They wouldn't miss me. They yell at me. They never play with me. I gotta stay in my room 'cause Mommy says I bother people. And you know what?" Rainey asked, wide-eyed and serious.

"What?" Sophie said, leaning closer and fearful of what she was about to hear.

"Sometimes they hit me and it hurts."

"Who hits you?" Sophie asked, trying to steady the rage swelling in her chest.

"Mommy and Daddy."

"Well, that's not right. I'll talk to them about it. Okay?"

Rainey pouted. "Okay."

On the way back to Kensington, Sophie and Rainey stopped at a grocery store to buy food to get the child through the week. Sophie had already taught her how to stash her food away in her room so the others wouldn't find it. As a birthday treat, she pushed the grocery cart into the bakery and let Rainey pick out a cake to eat with her chocolate ice cream.

When they returned to Miranda and Peter's, the two of them stood just inside the door, holding hands as Sophie looked around the room. There were three men in the next room arguing and pushing each other. Standing in front of them, there was a young woman with rotted teeth and dilated pupils laughing wickedly, as though she were possessed by Satan. When the woman noticed Sophie staring at her she lunged forward and said, "Hey, lady, you got any change you can spare?" Her crazed eyes fell on Rainey, "I can babysit for you . . . you know, to earn some money."

Sophie's teeth clenched together. "If you ever come near this child, I'll kill you."

"Whoa!" the girl said, backing away. "You ain't gotta be a nasty bitch about it. I'm just tryin' to make a little extra money."

Sophie spun and ascended the stairs. She found Miranda in Rainey's bedroom, sitting on the floor with five other people. She told Rainey to stay out in the hall, that she'd be back in a few minutes, then stepped inside the room and closed the door behind her.

"Hurry up, Sliver," Miranda barked. "We're all waiting to use the needle."

"Shut the hell up, Miranda. My fucking veins are sunk and I gotta find one that works." The man called Sliver looked into her eyes. "Peter's right, you're like a whore in heat when you need your dope."

"Ain't we all? Besides, you and Peter can shove your opinions up your asses."

Sophie, shocked and a little scared, forced out a couple of loud coughs to make her presence known. "Miranda, do you have a few minutes? I need to talk to you."

Miranda looked over her shoulder, and Sophie noticed it took a few seconds for her eyes to focus. When they did, she let out a sigh. "What the hell, Sophie. Can't you see I'm busy?"

Sophie narrowed her eyes and pursed her lips. "It's important," she hissed.

"Fine," Miranda huffed. She stood and took one step away before turning back to the circle of people. "This is my fucking house so nobody better take my turn. I'll be back in a couple of minutes."

Miranda walked up to Sophie. "For fuck's sake, what do you want?"

Sophie leaned in to whisper in her sister's ear. "You do remember today is Rainey's birthday?" she asked.

Miranda's hand shot up to her forehead. "Oh, man. Nah, I lost track of the date. That happens sometimes, you know?"

"No, actually that doesn't happen to me or most other people. Really, Miranda? This is not cool. Rainey's old enough now to know it's her birthday."

Miranda leaned against the broken dresser to hold herself up. "Yeah, because your dumb- ass told her. That kid doesn't know what day it is. I swear you're so annoying. You're always sticking your big nose in my business and trying to make me feel like shit."

"You make it easy because you act like a selfish bitch," Sophie snapped. "Getting high is all you care about. It's nauseating. Get some help with your drug problem. How about that?"

Miranda's mouth hung open, not from shock, but from the drugs she'd been doing all morning. "I don't give a shit what you think about me. I never did and never will. Why did you pull me away from my friends? Huh? What do you want?"

Sophie threw her hands in the air and sighed. "Because it's Rainey's birthday, remember? I just told you that. Anyway, I let her pick out a cake and ice cream. I also bought her two dolls. One can be from me and the other from you and that shit-for-brains boyfriend of yours."

Miranda grinned. "Oh, good. I'm glad you've finally decided to do something to help me with that kid."

The two stared at each other. Then Miranda raised her arms to hug her sister, and as she did, Sophie caught sight of the needle marks on her arms. It looked as though several dozen cigarettes had been snuffed out on her flesh. The track marks were round and black under her fair skin, while the newer marks were red with fresh scabs.

"I wish you weren't such a bitch all the time. I half like you when you act normal," Miranda whispered. "Now listen, it's almost my turn and then we can have cake and ice cream and give my precious baby girl her gifts," she said in a sloppy slur.

Sophie cringed. This was her sister making an effort, but it pained her this was all Miranda could give. "Maybe you can just skip your turn for today and spend time with Rainey and me. We could go to the park. Can you please do that this one time?"

Miranda shook her head. "No. Can. Do. It's not that I don't wanna hang with you guys, but I can't skip my dope. I need my dope and my dope needs me," she said, giggling, and turned to go back to the group.

"Hey, one more thing," Sophie said, grabbing her sister's arm. "Rainey told me you and Peter are hitting her. You can't do that. She's getting older and understands what you're doing—you don't want to get in trouble, do you?" Sophie knew what she was implying with that last statement. Her problem was that she loved her sister and held onto the unrealistic hope that she'd get sober.

Miranda jerked her arm free. "Listen, little love taps here and there ain't gonna kill the brat. She needs to toughen up. She whines and moans all the time. So butt out or I'll tell Peter you're trying to tell us how to raise our kid and he won't let you see Rainey. Is that what you want?"

Sophie suppressed the urge to slam her fist into Miranda's face and just shook her head. She watched her sister saunter across the room toward the group of smackheads preparing their heroin. Something bubbled up in her chest, a sudden feeling of blind rage toward her sister.

"Miranda?" she called out.

Miranda turned and thumped back over to her. "What?" she said through clenched teeth.

"You go on and get your fix. That's the way it has always been with you. When you're finished, your daughter and I will be waiting to have cake and ice cream." Sophie softened her voice even though her annoyance was ramping up. "I mean, I know you have a lot going on. Maybe I can take Rainey home with me for a couple of days since it's her birthday."

Miranda's lips pinched into a straight line. "I don't think so. Today is the day *my* child was born. It's only right that she spends her birthday with her mom and dad." Miranda shook her index finger close to Sophie's face. "I know you think I don't know shit about shit, but you listen here, big sister. Rainey is my fucking kid and you need to keep your goddamn paws off of her. Stop asking me if she can live with you . . . the answer is no. Got it?"

Sophie turned and left the bedroom before she said things she'd later regret. She lifted Rainey into her arms and marched downstairs to the kitchen to get ready for the birthday celebration.

Fifteen minutes later, as Sophie opened the box that held the birthday cake, Rainey pulled on the hem of her skirt. "Are Mommy and Daddy gonna eat cake with us for my birfday?"

Sophie nodded, though it felt as though the wind had been knocked out of her. Rainey grinned and sat on the rickety chair while Sophie went to find Miranda and Peter. As much as she hated it, the fact that Rainey wanted her parents to celebrate her birthday indicated that the child longed to be cared for by them.

Rainey was thrilled to watch her mom and dad sing "Happy Birthday to You" to her. After eating birthday cake, Sophie pulled Peter aside.

In a clear voice, she said, "I have to tell you something, I've already spoken to Miranda."

"Oh, yeah?" Peter said, getting closer to smell her perfume. "What's that?"

"Hey," she said, trying to get Peter to focus. "Rainey told me you and Miranda hit her. I swear, if she tells me you hit her again, I'll go to the police."

"Oh, yeah?" Peter hissed. He grabbed her wrists and pushed her against the wall. Sophie winced from the tight grip he had on her. He put his nose an inch from hers, then growled, "You won't go to the police or child services or anywhere else. Do you know why?" He paused.

Sophie watched him, nervous that he might hurt her—he was so angry that spittle flew from his mouth as he hurled his words at her.

"You won't tell anybody anything because if you do Rainey will disappear and you'll never see her again. In fact, we will all disappear and you won't ever see your sister either. And another thing: Rainey doesn't have bruises and ain't nothing broken on her. She's a kid . . . kids make shit up. You need to mind your own business. You're an angry, crazy bitch that has no life, no friends, and if you keep this shit up, no family."

Sophie's blue eyes were blazing at Peter. She pushed her blond hair over her shoulder, turned, and walked away, appearing more confident than she was feeling.

She found Rainey, who had wandered off to the living room, and took her hand. "Sweetheart, Aunt Sophie has to go. Now, I want you to promise me you'll stay in your bedroom this week and not roam around the house."

"Why?" Rainey asked.

Sophie picked her up, trying to decide how to explain the danger to the child without scaring her. "Well, the people who sleep over your house . . . they're, um, sick. They all take medicine and sometimes it makes them do things they shouldn't."

"Like when Daddy's friend Vice put the couch on fire because his medicine made him go to sleep and he dropped his cigarette?"

Sophie sighed heavily and tried not to picture it. "Yes, that and other things. I want you to promise me that you'll never let anyone in your bedroom with you. That's your personal place."

Rainey stared at her, nodded, and tilted her head to the side. Sophie was heartbroken and knelt and put her hands on her shoulders. "I'm sorry, sweetie. I wish I could say something to make you feel better. You shouldn't have to deal with any of this. But I'll tell you this . . . you and I will spend every Saturday together forever. We can play and go out to eat and do things that you love to do." She placed her nose against Rainey's. "Maybe your mommy will let you sleep at my house sometime. Wouldn't that be fun?"

Rainey's eyes lowered and she nodded half-heartedly. "But I don't wanna live at my house anymore. I wanna live with you."

"Now, you listen to me," Sophie said, lifting the child's chin gently. "You do your best to stay out of your parents' way. You know, like when you and I play hide-and-seek and you have to be really quiet. That's all you have to do."

Rainey sulked, and her eyes filled. Sophie pulled the girl into her and held her close, partially to comfort her and partially so Rainey wouldn't see her tears.

"Don't cry, sweetie. You're going to be okay. I'm going to work this out. Okay?"

Rainey rested her head on Sophie's chest as the woman carried the weight of her anguish.

"I wuv you," Rainey whispered.

Sophie's chest hitched. "Oh, I love you too. I love you more than anything in the world."

Chapter Eleven

Over the next three years, Sophie's weekly visits continued to be the only constant thing in Rainey's life. The one bright spot she could count on every week. Not even school was a relief for the girl. Because she was academically strong, her teachers had little concern and spent most of their time with the children struggling to learn or with behavioral issues. As for her classmates, her shyness and disinterest to engage left her an outcast among her peers. Rainey loved to learn and found solace and a sense of accomplishment in her school work.

It was a Friday night and Rainey, now seven years old, wandered into the kitchen.

"Mommy, is Aunt Sophie coming tomorrow?"

Miranda scowled at her daughter. "Yeah," she said, taking a drag from the joint she was holding. "Why? You want me to tell her you're busy or something?" She cackled at her joke and handed the joint to a man next to her.

Rainey glanced at the man next to her mother and blushed. "No, I'm not busy. I can't wait to see her. I was just checkin'."

Miranda leaned toward her, scrunched her forehead, and said in a mocking tone, "*I can't wait to see her.* Your stupid aunt has you brainwashed . . . you act like she's so great. Well, guess what: she isn't. She is the worst sister ever. Never gave me money when I asked her for it and even turned my mom and dad against me."

Rainey's eyes widened. Hearing bad things about her aunt was uncomfortable for her. She wanted to defend her aunt but knew it would only make her mother angrier. "I'm sorry, Mommy," she mumbled.

"You should be sorry!" Miranda yelled as Rainey left the kitchen.

The next morning Rainey woke early, sticky with sweat in the mid-August heat. Still, she sat up and smiled in the dark room because it was Saturday, which meant Aunt Sophie would be coming in a few hours. She edged out of her makeshift bed and dressed.

A few hours later, Sophie knocked on the front door twice. When no one answered she turned the knob and let herself in to find Miranda standing just inside the door at the foot of the steps. She was bent over at the waist, rocking from her heels to the balls of her feet, somehow not toppling over. Sophie was repulsed to see her sister so blitzed but still approached and put her hand on Miranda's back. Miranda looked up with half-opened, bloodshot eyes, her mouth twisted and pulled up to one side. Sophie's stomach knotted and a surge of acid flowed up to her esophagus as she watched how the drugs had ravaged Miranda, who, once upon a time, was her innocent, delightful baby sister.

"Come on, Miranda. Let me help you sit down," she said patiently.

Miranda allowed Sophie to guide her into the living room and settle her on the sofa. Sophie left the room and a few minutes later she returned with a glass of water. She looked at the open space next to her sister and sat down.

"Here, drink this," Sophie said, handing her the glass and sitting close.

Miranda's head popped up and her chin fell back down to her chest. "Nah, I don't want water, man. How about a beer? I gotta keep my buzz going."

Sophie, with no fight left in her, set the water on the floor. The two sat for a long time in silence. Sophie stared at the filthy wall, covered with marks from years of neglect and carelessness, then fixed her attention on the chaos around her. The teens and twentysomethings kept coming and going, smoking and drinking, popping pills, and injecting needles. Nothing had changed, except Rainey was getting older, and her thoughts turned to worry about the child's future. *Will Rainey eventually succumb to addiction?*

A while later, Rainey came down, ready to go, Sophie told her that their outing was delayed because she had some grown-up things that needed to be handled. Disappointed, the child lumbered back up the stairs.

By early afternoon, Miranda came down from her high enough to know Sophie was there.

She sat forward on the sofa. "What are you doing here?"

Sophie looked over at her sister with red, swollen eyes. "I've been here for a couple of hours. I need to talk to you, so I waited. It's really important."

"If you're going to ask if Rainey can live with you again, the answer is still no. So you can stop asking."

"This has nothing to do with Rainey. It's about me."

Miranda reached for a pack of cigarettes on the coffee table. "Well, spit it out already." She pulled one out and lit it. Then she turned her attention to Sophie.

"I have some news. I haven't been feeling well for a while so I went to the doctor."

"What does that mean? How have you've been feeling? You better not have given any contagious shit to Rainey," Miranda accused her. "I can't deal with a sick kid shitting and puking all over my house."

Tears sprung to Sophie's eyes; it was like she was talking to a stubborn child. She wished that her mother was still alive. Sophie needed someone who could take care of her for a change—someone she could rely on.

"No, it's not the flu, Miranda," she said, taking a deep breath to steady herself. "It's more serious."

"Why are you crying? What the hell? Do you always have to be so dramatic?"

"I have Huntington's disease." Even saying it out loud felt like a death sentence.

Miranda flicked the ash from the end of her cigarette onto the carpet. "And? So what does that mean?"

"It means that my brain is dying. Do you remember how Mom's arms and legs would jerk around and she always lost her balance?"

"Yeah, I remember. When she was in the bathroom twitching all around, I would steal her whiskey before school." Miranda smiled at the memory. "Me and Peter would catch a buzz before first period. A little whiskey . . . a little pot . . . those were the good old days. But then our mom went and got herself run over by a car and left you to do the mothering. Ha!"

Sophie took her sister's hand in her own. She had hoped this would be easier and that her sister would understand. "The reason I'm telling you all this is because I suspect that Mom had Huntington's disease too. She never went to the doctor. She always said it was her nerves because she was so worried about you all the time, especially after Dad died. Now that I know about this awful disease I'm thinking she probably had it. I mean, it's hereditary so I had to get it from someone."

Miranda was still groggy, and the left side of her mouth arched into a half smile while a cigarette dangled from the other side. She flung her arm over Sophie's shoulder. "Did the doctor say you're going to die?"

Sophie's eyes bulged and her mouth fell open. Miranda's reaction was even worse than she had expected. She shook her head. "No. The doctor said I'm going to need someone to take care of me."

Miranda took a quick drag and loudly blew out the smoke. "Well, don't look at me. I ain't got the patience to take care of you or nobody."

Sophie's mind was still. In a momentary reprieve, her thoughts stopped whipping inside her head and numbness took over. She hadn't expected much from her sister, but it was still devastating to know for certain, that she was all alone in the world. "Of course, I don't expect you to be that person because, for one, you'd have to stay sober," she said, annoyed and disappointed. She looked across the room and took a moment to calm herself. "Miranda, I need to know you'll check in on me and bring Rainey to visit. I'm scared about what'll happen. I'm afraid when I die, I'll be all alone."

Miranda rubbed her forehead. "Yeah, that would totally suck to croak all by yourself." She hesitated, trying to think of what to say next. "Look, I ain't making you no promises, okay? I got enough going on in my life. I mean, now that I think about it more, maybe dying alone wouldn't be so bad." She leaned into her sister like she was about to say something serious, something profound. "You need to tell the doctor you want a lot of drugs so you won't even know what's happening."

Sophie leered at her, realizing nothing, not even her death, would come between Miranda and her drugs. "Thanks for the great advice," she snipped.

Miranda nodded, not picking up on her sister's sarcasm. "Do you have to move?"

Sophie took several deep breaths. It was hard to imagine that in a year she could be lying in bed incapable of talking or thinking or moving her body. Her stomach was roiling, and, she wanted so much to be comforted. "Right now I don't have to move. But in a year or so I may need to go into a care facility. I've been having symptoms for several months now. I didn't think anything of it until a month ago when I was on a photo shoot and my hands were shaking and I couldn't capture the pictures. Now other parts of my body jerk uncontrollably too." Sophie lowered her head, and tears dropped onto her lap. "The shaking episodes have become more frequent."

"That's some fucked-up shit. I hope I ain't got it too. So, what're you gonna do now?" Sophie raised her head, feeling her bottom lip quivering. "I don't know. I'm terrified, Miranda. I can't think. I need you right now. I need to know you won't leave me all alone," she admitted, hoping to break through to her sister.

Sophie watched as Miranda looked up just as Peter came into the room. The two made eye contact and he walked over to them. Inwardly, Sophie wished he would go away and leave her to talk alone with her sister.

"What's going on, Sophie?" Peter asked. "Kind of out of character for you to be hanging with us losers this long."

Miranda shrugged. "She's got a disease. It's gonna kill her fucking brain," she said, balling her hair up in her fists.

Sophie gasped. "Christ, Miranda. Is there any kindness in you?"

Peter chuckled. "You wanna know the funny part about it? You always said that drugs would fry our brains. Now ain't that a twist of fate."

Sophie ignored Peter's ignorant comment and rested her head on Miranda's shoulder. "I'm sorry we weren't closer. I hope you'll think about what I've asked you to do."

Miranda placed her hand on Sophie's thigh and looked up at Peter. "Go grab us each a beer and the bottle of tequila in the freezer. We're gonna need them today."

Sophie hoped and prayed that for once in her life Miranda could be the sister she'd always wanted. That for just one day, her sister could think about someone besides herself.

Chapter Twelve

For the next year, Miranda tried to be more kind to her sister, which meant, she didn't say mean things to her as often. She forced herself to hug Sophie before she left the house when she remembered. But as time passed, Miranda forgot about the health issue and left Sophie feeling more isolated.

Shortly after Rainey's eighth birthday, Sophie arrived for her Saturday date with her niece, and Miranda was nowhere to be seen. She went upstairs and knocked on their bedroom door. When there was no answer, she pushed it open slowly. "Miranda? Are you up?"

Peter lifted his head. "No, we ain't up. What the hell's your problem?"

Miranda sat on the side of the bed and rubbed her scalp. She looked at Sophie and rolled her eyes. "Come on. Let's go downstairs so Peter can sleep just like I wanna be doing."

Sophie wrung her hands nervously as she followed her sister.

Down in the living room they stepped over people making their way to the sofa. Miranda shook two people awake and made them get on the floor to make a space for her and Sophie to sit. "What the hell are you thinking?" she said, making Sophie recoil. "You can't barge into our house and expect to talk to me first thing in the morning!"

Sophie held her hand up. "It's not first thing in the morning, Miranda. It's eleven thirty. I need someone to talk to. Is that too much to ask?"

Miranda reached toward two girls smoking a joint on the other end of the sofa, grabbed the joint between her thumb and index finger, and took a long drag. She held it in her lungs and hacked out a cloud of smoke.

"Here," Miranda said, pushing the joint to her older sister.

"I don't want that. I don't smoke pot, remember?"

Miranda shrugged and took another drag. "Sophie, take a goddamn hit. Trust me, it'll do you some good."

Sophie eyed the burning weed, considering her options. She hated the idea of doing drugs but she wanted relief from her morbid thoughts, something to make her escape her problems for a while. "Thanks, but no."

Miranda pulled her legs under her. "Okay. What is so important that you had to drag me outta bed to talk?"

"My symptoms are getting worse, and I've made arrangements to move into a facility that can care for me. I need to talk to Rainey about it, and I was thinking I'd tell her today. I wanted to see if you'd come with us to eat so that you could be there to support her . . . and me."

Miranda shook her head. "I ain't going anywhere. I have shit to do today."

"Like what?" Sophie asked, stunned.

"Like none of your business," Miranda stated. Then she got up and went upstairs to her bedroom, leaving Sophie alone on the sofa.

Sophie sat motionless. She was literally dying, and her sister didn't care for her enough to take the time to help her. Once she realized the illness would hijack her body no matter what she did, talking to Rainey about not being there for her anymore had plagued her with worry. While she equally loved and hated her sister, Sophie had only the purest love for her niece.

Sophie took a few minutes to rise from the sofa and steady herself on her feet. She slowly shuffled up the steps, using the railing to pull herself forward. Inside the bedroom, the girl was in the closet, humming as she flipped through a book.

"Hey, Rainey," Sophie sang, forcing some energy into her voice.

"Aunt Sophie." Rainey rose and rushed toward her, throwing her arms around her waist and almost knocking her aunt over. "Can we get hamburgers and French fries today?"

"Sure," Sophie said. "I thought we'd go to the Oregon Diner. That would be a good place for us to talk."

Thrilled, Rainey quickly slid her bare feet into her shoes and took Sophie's hand.

An hour later, with plates of burgers and fries on the table, Sophie turned serious. "Rainey, I need to talk to you about something."

"What do you wanna talk about?" Rainey asked, chomping down on her burger. Ketchup slid from the side of her mouth, and Sophie reached over and wiped it with a napkin and took a moment to admire the child. Her hazel eyes were full of wonder, and her blond hair, shining like tinsel, hung past her shoulders. She'd always known Rainey looked like her, but now it was like she was almost a mirror image of herself.

"Well, I'm sick and I wanted to talk to you about it."

"Will you have to take medicine like my mom and dad?" Rainey said, scrunching her nose.

"No, sweetheart. There isn't any medicine for what I have."

Rainey's expression turned serious and she laid her burger on her plate. "Then how will you get better?"

Sophie took in a long breath and let it out slowly. Telling Miranda had been one thing, but telling Rainey—this was harder than she'd thought it would be. "That's the thing, sweetheart. I'm not going to get better. I wanted to tell you myself so that if you have any questions, we could talk about them."

Rainey's eyes cast downward. She pushed her plate away. "Are you still going to visit me?"

A sharp pain jabbed Sophie in the chest. Seeing the hopelessness on Rainey's face was almost more than she could handle. She tried her best to hold back her tears, but once the first fell, the others followed in rapid succession. "No. I won't be able to visit you. It's very difficult for me to get around even now."

Rainey's eyes welled and she rested her forehead on her arm as she cried. "But who's gonna take care of me? You're the only person in the whole world that loves me. I don't have nobody if I ain't got you."

A gulping sound escaped Sophie's throat. She focused on her hands to gather herself. Over the past six months, she had beaten herself up for not trying harder to get custody of Rainey since she was a baby. Instead, she believed that by being part of the child's life, if only one day a week, she could make a difference. She never pursued legal action because she loved her sister and, like their parents, she wanted to believe that Miranda would wake up one day and decide to be sober.

"You're going to take care of yourself. You remember all the things we've learned. You have to read as much as you can. And it's very important not to ever take drugs unless a doctor tells you it's okay."

"But you always said if anyone bothers me, to tell you. You said if anyone at my house touches me down there or calls me names or hits me, I have to tell you. Who am I gonna tell if anything bad ever happens to me?"

Sophie rested her chin in her hands. "I'm such an idiot. I should've known you would ask a lot of questions." She focused on Rainey's gaze. "If any bad things happen, you're going to tell your teacher. Can you do that?"

Rainey shook her head. "I'm not allowed to tell my teacher anything. Mom and Dad said so. I don't wanna get a beating."

Sophie's stomach clamped down. There were so many things she didn't know about that Miranda and Peter did and said to her niece. And now that Rainey was revealing some of these truths, she couldn't help but have deep regret for ever having any faith that her sister would do right by her child.

"I'm sorry, Rainey, I don't have all of the answers. But here's what I do know. You're a strong, brave girl, and no matter what happens, you will *always* know what to do. What that means is there may come a time when you'll have to do something your mom and dad don't want you to do. Something that might get *them* in trouble."

"But then I'll get in trouble too," Rainey cried.

"No." Sophie shook her head. "Not if you do what's right and tell the truth."

"How will I know what's the right thing?"

Sophie placed her hands on the table in front of her. "Because as long as you're stopping bad things from happening to you, then it's the right thing. I'm not trying to scare you, but you need to stand up for yourself and never let *anyone* take advantage of you. Do you know what that means?"

Rainey nodded.

"Okay, good." With great effort, Sophie slid out of the booth and sat down next to Rainey, who leaned into her, sliding as close as she could get. There was a long stretch of stillness as the two held each other.

Rainey looked up at her, tears making streak marks down her dirty face. "Will you come and see me after today?"

Sophie bit her lip. This was the worst part, the thing she'd been dreading to tell Rainey the most. Slowly, she shook her head. "I barely made the trip today. That's why we had to take a taxi here because I can't drive anymore. I'm moving into a place tomorrow where people will take care of me."

Rainey's hair hung in her face as she lowered her head and bawled. "I'm never gonna be the same without you. They don't love me like you do. Can I move in with you to the place you're going? I'll take good care of you. I swear."

"Oh, I wish so much you could come with me." Sophie tried to speak without her voice cracking, but failed. "But it wouldn't be any fun. You have your whole life ahead of you. I know you're going to grow up to be something special, someone who makes a difference in this world."

"I don't wanna make a difference. I wanna be with you, Aunt Sophie," Rainey pleaded.

Sophie turned her head and looked into the child's eyes. "I know you do, Rainey, but you wouldn't be allowed. Besides," Sophie said lowering her eyes, "soon I won't be able to do anything but lay in bed and I won't be able to remember much—I probably won't be able to remember your name. I wouldn't want you to see me that way. I don't think you want to see me like that, right?"

"No."

"Good. Because I think we should remember each other just like this. Eating burgers and fries at our favorite place in the whole world. I'll never forget all the fun we had here."

Rainey looked around the Oregon Diner. "Me neither. But I'm scared. I don't have any friends at school, and I don't have anyone to play with at home. You're the only friend I got."

"Oh, Rainey, you'll have lots of friends. Things are going to work out just fine. Better than fine, better than you can ever imagine. You are smart and beautiful and so easy to love. I want you to remember that for as long as you live, but especially when you feel like nothing is going your way."

***

Back at the house, Sophie and Rainey sat together up in the girl's room. Rainey plastered her body against her aunt's as they held each other. When it was time to part, Rainey let out a bewildering moan as her tears fell.

Before leaving, they walked down to the living room and stood at the front door. Sophie took off her favorite straw hat and placed it on Rainey's head.

"This hat will bring you good luck. I want you to always remember how much I love you. Can you do that for me?"

Rainey clung to her aunt as she sobbed, and her chest rose and fell sharply.

Sophie lifted the child's chin. "No matter what you do in your life, remember what I told you. Don't ever take drugs and always tell the truth. Telling the truth will save you a lot of pain and suffering. There will be times when your honesty is tested, and those are the times you need to stay true to yourself. Sometimes it's harder to tell the truth because people want us to believe their lies, but you should always tell the truth. Promise?"

Rainey looked into Sophie's eyes. "I promise."

Sophie smiled. "Okay," she said, forcing a note of cheer into her voice. "Now let me take a picture of you in that hat."

Sophie pulled a Polaroid camera from her purse, and as she took the picture Rainey pulled the hat down over one side of her face, trying to hide her tears. The photo shot out of the front of the camera, and Sophie removed the picture and waved it around. She handed the camera to Rainey. "Now you take one of me that you can keep. Just look through the hole and press this button."

Rainey took the picture of her aunt, and as she held it in her hand, Sophie leaned down and scooped the child into her arms.

Rainey looked into her aunt's eyes. "Please don't leave me here."

Just then, Miranda came up from behind and draped her arms over Rainey's shoulders. "All right, you two said your good-byes and now Aunt Sophie's gotta go. She don't feel good."

Miranda gave her sister a one-arm hug. "See you later. Remember what I told you. Take whatever drugs they give you. I swear you won't even know what's happening."

Sophie kissed her sister's cheek. "Please come visit me."

Miranda gave her a noncommittal shrug.

Sophie looked down at Rainey, who was watching them carefully. Then she dropped to her knees and pulled Rainey close for one last hug. "I'm going to miss you so, so, so much. I'll always love you, always."

Rainey nodded and the two held each other close as sorrow racked their bodies. When they parted, Sophie stood, walked out, and closed the door behind her.

Immediately, Rainey dashed to the ripped screen door and pressed her nose against it. “Aunt Sophie! Aunt Sophie! Come back! Don’t leave me!”

Sophie didn’t look back. She knew she had to walk away with her heart torn in two. She could still hear Rainey screaming for her to come back as she got into the waiting taxi.

Chapter Thirteen

The month following Sophie's last visit, Rainey kept to herself, mourning the loss of her only protector. Her resentment for her parents grew as the month wore on, and she rarely spoke to them. Rainey was isolated; her sadness and anger simmered in her belly, and her bitterness turned to hatred.

One afternoon, Rainey ventured down to the kitchen to hunt for food. It had been a full day and night since she'd last eaten and her empty belly was rumbling loudly. On her way to the kitchen, she saw her mom in the bathroom with the door open.

Rainey paused outside the door. "Mom, I'm hungry, we need to buy food," she cried. "My stomach hurts real bad."

"Okay. Do you really need to cry about it? I mean seriously, Rainey."

Rainey tried to pull her tears back. "I can't help it. It hurts."

"Whatever. Go to the kitchen. In the cabinet below the toaster, I hid a box of crackers way in the back. Don't eat them all."

Rainey left her mother in the bathroom, found the box of crackers, and carried it into the living room, where a small group of people were watching *The Exorcist*. Being alone most of the time, Rainey had a strong desire to be around people. She looked around her and plopped down on the floor with the others to watch the movie. Miranda and Peter didn't have cable, but they had boxes of used tapes for their VHS machine. Rainey sat like a statue, her eyes wide and fearful. Her mouth dropped open when the girl's head in the movie spun around her neck. Terrified, she covered her eyes and screamed. She couldn't help it. The guys laughed at her, but the lady, Buddy, pulled the girl to her feet and led her into the kitchen.

Rainey followed Buddy, who had met her Aunt Sophie twice. And while Sophie wasn't thrilled that Buddy was a pothead and beer drinker who snorted meth occasionally, she did recognize that the young woman was the soberest adult in the house.

"It's going to be okay," Buddy said, patting Rainey on the back.

"I'm scared. What happened to that girl on the TV?"

"Oh, baby girl, that ain't real. It's make-believe. Besides, you're way too young to watch that nonsense. How about if I take you outta here for a little bit? I'll ask your mom if it's okay."

Rainey clung to Buddy's hand, feeling safe with her. "Yeah. I'd like that. Nobody's taken me out for fun since Aunt Sophie was here."

Buddy wrapped her arm around Rainey and held her close. The young girl returned the embrace and then pulled back to look into Buddy's smooth, brown face. Her tight, curly hair was cut two inches from her scalp, which Rainey thought looked just perfect with her full lips and light brown almond-shaped eyes.

Rainey stared at the young woman's face. She took in all of her features and the warmth in her eyes. "You're pretty," she whispered.

Buddy grinned. "Aw, sweetie, thank you. I think you're pretty too."

Buddy took Rainey's hand and pulled her along until they found her mom sitting on the floor of the pantry, alone. Miranda's upper body was folded over her outstretched legs. Beside her, Rainey recognized a crack pipe.

She hung back as Buddy reached down and gently shook her mom's shoulder. "Hey, Miranda."

Miranda lifted her torso a few inches up but her head still hung by her knees. She turned sideways and looked up. "Hey, Buddy."

"I'm gonna take Rainey for a walk. We're gonna get some ice cream or candy or something. She got real upset and she's hungry. Is that okay?"

"Yeah, yeah, sure it's okay." Miranda held out her arms unsteadily to Rainey, who didn't want to go to her mother, but concerned she'd change her mind, went to her anyway. She placed a sloppy kiss on her daughter's cheek. "See you later."

Rainey turned her back to her mother with her face puckered and wiped the saliva from her cheek.

Buddy reached for Rainey's hand again and they left the house. "Little girl, you need to get some sun," she said, touching her finger to Rainey's snow-white forearm.

Rainey looked up at her and smiled. She realized it was nice to have an adult to talk to again. "I stay in my room. Because I don't wanna get in anyone's way."

Buddy frowned and nodded.

Rainey pulled at the hem of the shirt she was wearing that was two sizes too small for her and didn't cover her belly. "Buddy?"

"Yeah?" Buddy said, looking down at her.

"I'm really hungry," she whispered, hoping Buddy wouldn't get mad at her like her mom had.

"I know you are, baby girl. That's why I'm taking you to get something good to eat."

Rainey's mouth watered at the very mention of getting food to eat. Her stomach rumbled, but a feeling of gratitude washed over her. The clouds around her seemed to lift as the two walked to a restaurant.

Buddy and Rainey sat next to each other in a booth at a pizzeria several blocks from the house. The restaurant was crawling with strung-out people, which was nothing unusual, but now with the young girl sitting next to her, Buddy noticed it more. Kensington, she knew, had once been a bustling city, but for as long as she could remember, it was where the lost roamed the streets, hopelessness growing like untreated cancer. Kensington was overflowing with people with nowhere to go. People who preferred life on the streets to life in a home. So they flocked to Kensington to live among other lost people and find comfort in a chemical that made them feel magical. Buddy put her hand over Rainey's hand to let her know she was safe.

The man behind the counter yelled Buddy's name, signaling their food was ready. The young woman quickly went over and grabbed the box of pizza and two sodas, while keeping an eye on Rainey. Back at the table, the child pulled the plate toward her, eyes wide, and took bite after bite of the cheesy goodness.

"Whoa there, baby girl," Buddy said, laughing. "You need to slow down or you're gonna get a bellyache."

Nervous that Buddy wouldn't take her out to eat again, her eyes bulged and her bottom lip turned downward. "I already have a bellyache. That's why I'm eating fast 'cause I'm really hungry." The child placed the remaining pizza on the plate. "I didn't mean to make you mad," she said quietly.

Buddy felt her heart break a little, and she moved in closer. "What are you talking about? I ain't mad at you. You ain't in trouble. You didn't do nothing wrong."

Buddy knew that Rainey was accustomed to being yelled at by her parents for everything. It was only the day prior that she'd witnessed Peter demoralizing the child.

Peter had whacked her on the side of the face. "Stop being a fucking mouth breather!" he yelled.

"Sorry," Rainey muttered, trying to breathe more quietly.

The memory made Buddy sick to her stomach and weak for not intervening, but she forced herself to focus on Rainey.

Buddy took a small bite of pizza. "See, you need to chew it slowly. Nobody's gonna take your food from you, and if you want another slice, I'll give you one. Yes, indeed, I'll give you a second and even a third, for sure."

"'Cause you love me?" Rainey squeaked out, and the look on her face was so earnest that Buddy's breath got caught in her throat.

"Well . . . yeah," Buddy said, smiling. "I love you . . . I mean, I love everyone until they fuck me over. It ain't your fault that your parents don't have a brain between them. Don't get me wrong, I like your mama and all, but she's one messed-up lady. I'd never let my kid be around all those stoners like she does with you."

Buddy's only brother was serving a long sentence in prison. She had no family of her own since her mother died but had been loved completely when she was alive. She couldn't imagine how hard it was to be Rainey's age looking for someone to show her the love and affection normally found in the arms of a parent.

Rainey asked, "Can I tell you a secret?"

"Sure you can. You and me are friends now and friends tell each other stuff. Ever since your aunt left, I've been wanting to spend more time with you," Buddy assured her.

Rainey leaned in closer and whispered, "I wish I didn't have to live in my house. I hate it there. I hate all the people that stay there, and I think that my mom and dad wish I wasn't there. I could've lived with my Aunt Sophie but they wouldn't let me." She looked at Buddy expectantly.

Buddy grabbed a napkin and wiped her mouth, wondering how best to handle this. "Well, first of all, your house ain't no place to raise a kid.

But you shouldn't be so hard on yourself. The way your parents act isn't about you, it's all about them."

Rainey looked at the girl and tilted her head. "What do you mean?"

"Look, it ain't that complicated. Drugs make people do things that they shouldn't. It's really that simple. Someday, when you're older, I think you'll understand what I'm telling you."

The girl nodded. "I guess so," she said, taking another bite of her pizza. She gave Buddy a side glance. "Do you know my Aunt Sophie's sick and that's why she doesn't come to see me anymore?"

"Your mom mentioned something about your aunt. It's a damn shame . . . for her and you."

"Maybe I can stay with you. You don't stay at my house all the time," Rainey suggested, waiting with raw desperation for a response.

Buddy blinked a few times, trying to compose herself. The sadness in Rainey's eyes was almost too much for her to bear. "No, baby," she said gently. "I don't have a place where I can take you. That's why I'm at your house once in a while. When I ain't there, I'm sleeping on someone's sofa or in an alley or wherever I can lay my head. But listen," she said, forcing cheeriness into her voice, "whenever I *am* at your house, I'll try to take you out once in a while. Like we're doing now. Okay?"

Rainey nodded, wrapped her hands around the can of soda and pulled it toward her until the straw was between her lips.

"Can we go to the park?" she asked after a sip of soda.

Buddy looked behind her to the window. "I mean, it's gonna be dark soon. But we can stop by, and if there ain't a bunch of thugs there I'll let you play for a little. But then I need to get you back home because it ain't safe on these streets."

When the two were finished and had spent a little time at the park, which was already crawling with addicts, prostitutes, and pushers, Buddy took Rainey back home, where the girl immediately ran up to her bedroom. Buddy went to find Miranda and talked her into letting her go upstairs and read with Rainey before bed. After the child had read a few chapters out loud of the book her aunt Sophie had given her, Buddy pulled out a pack of cupcakes she'd been keeping in her purse. "See these?" she said.

Rainey's eyes lit up. "Yeah."

"I'm gonna put them under this sweatshirt, and in the morning, if I'm not here, you can eat them for breakfast."

"Why don't you stay here with me?" Rainey pleaded. "We can share my blanket."

"Because I have to go out and work so I have money."

Rainey nodded and nuzzled down on her makeshift bed. Then she patted the sweatshirt on top of the cupcakes. "I'll eat those cupcakes tomorrow."

"That's right, baby girl." Buddy bent over and kissed the girl on the forehead. "Night, sleep tight, don't let the bedbugs bite."

As Buddy closed the bedroom door behind her she thought of her childhood. Being brought up in Kensington by a single mother—although more attentive than Miranda—she understood the grueling road Rainey would travel. Her thoughts wandered to the morning her mother had died, the image of her lifeless form when Buddy had identified her body in the morgue.

When Buddy was only seventeen, her mom had been killed by a gang member. She'd been in the wrong place at the wrong time when a stray bullet hit her in the head and killed her instantly. The young teen had been devastated by the sudden loss of her protector. Five years had passed since her mother was stolen from her, and not a day went by that Buddy didn't wish she was still alive.

With her mom murdered and her only brother in prison, Buddy took the first drink. The only thing that kept her from using a needle or smoking crack was her mother's voice warning her it would ruin her life. Even though Buddy hadn't finished high school and had settled for a minimum-wage job at a nearby convenience store, she had avoided the temptation of hard-core drugs. Still, she knew that her use of alcohol had morphed from a want into a need. Buddy had thought about using drugs just so she could drink less but was deterred again by seeing most of the drug addicts she knew turn to prostitution to support their habit. She understood the high cost of feeding an addiction.

Leaving Rainey in her room that night, she went downstairs and into the living room. Buddy and Miranda made eye contact as she walked into the room and sat on the floor by a guy she had casual sex with whenever the mood struck them. Buddy pulled a quart of beer from her sack and lit a joint. She looked around her and quietly hoped a miracle would happen for Rainey, and that she would get away from the recklessness of her home.

Chapter Fourteen

Over the next two months, without her aunt to fight for her, Rainey had become more daring, challenging her parents' authority more often.

Rainey also spent time with Buddy whenever the young woman came to her home. When Buddy wasn't around, she kept to herself and focused on doing well in school, just as her Aunt Sophie and Buddy had told her to do. But that wasn't hard for Rainey because her love for learning just grew over time.

It was the beginning of October and the weather was just turning chilly when Miranda and Peter walked into Rainey's bedroom.

"Hey, Rainey, whatcha doing?" Peter asked, more pleasantly than usual.

Rainey held up a book, one she'd borrowed from the school library. "Reading."

"Well, your mom and I have some news for you."

Rainey sat up expectantly. "Is Aunt Sophie better? Can we go visit her?"

Miranda huffed. "No, this ain't about Sophie. Jeez, Rainey, everything isn't about *her*."

Rainey slumped against the wall, not even caring that she had made her mom mad. "I miss Aunt Sophie."

"Whatever. Anyway, we wanted you to know that I'm having a baby."

Rainey froze, then she looked from her mother to her father. "Why?" she asked, the first question that came to her mind.

"What do you mean, why?" Miranda barked. "Because I got knocked up. Why the hell else would I have another kid?"

Rainey got up on her knees. "Mom, you guys don't even take care of *me*," she said. "All you two do is hang out with your friends. Now you're gonna have a baby, and who's going to take care of it?"

Miranda shrugged. "You're such a spoiled brat. It looks to me like you're turning out just fine."

"Yeah, well, that's because Aunt Sophie was here to help me," Rainey bit back.

"You're an ungrateful little bitch," her mom snapped.

"Come on, babe," Peter cooed. "You don't have to answer to her—she's a fucking kid." He turned back to Rainey. "We're having a baby. You don't need to like it but you do need to get used to it. And you'll be expected to help . . . since you're the big sister."

Alone in her bedroom, Rainey pulled a worn blanket over her head. She gagged at the smell of sweat and feet and pushed the blanket away from her face to breathe. In a quiet voice, she cried, "I wish you were here, Aunt Sophie. I don't know anything about babies."

There was a painful void left by the absence of her aunt, an unbearable sorrow and loneliness set aside for those living a life where they have no one to love them.

As Rainey cried, her shoulders shook and snot dripped onto her upper lip. She fell asleep resentful and angry that her parents didn't care enough about her to do and give her the things she needed. Now there would be another person expecting, but never receiving, the love of Peter and Miranda.

A sibling was forced upon Rainey, like everything else in her life. She was nine years old by the time Miranda gave birth to her second child. They named their second daughter Ivy. Like Rainey, her life was fragile, and immediately following her birth she had to be slowly weaned from the drugs in her system.

When Miranda returned home from the hospital Rainey was anxiously waiting in the living room. By that time she'd not only accepted there would be a baby but also had looked forward to having someone else to share her life with. When her parents entered empty-handed, Rainey was confused.

"Where's my sister?" she asked.

Miranda huffed. "Oh, she's gotta stay in the hospital for a while. Ain't nothing to worry about though; she'll be home soon."

"Will you take me to see her?"

"No, you ain't going to see her. I ain't going back for a few weeks either. I gotta go to the clinic and get on some other medicine so that when she's ready to come home there ain't nobody that gives me a problem."

"So you're not going to take your medicine anymore?" Rainey was confused but hopeful.

"Oh, girl, stop with all the questions. I just need to go on a different kind of medicine so they'll let me bring Ivy home."

"Ivy. I like that name," Rainey said, picturing a baby that looked just like her. "How long will she stay in the hospital?"

Peter pushed the back of Rainey's head, and her feet clumsily pounded a few steps forward. "Your mom already told you to stop with all the questions. Ivy will come home when she's ready. Now go out back and grab me a beer."

Rainey rolled her eyes and flounced from the room, found the beer outside the back door, and returned. She held it out for her father, waiting for him to acknowledge her. When his eyes didn't meet hers she pushed the beer against his chest. "Here," she stated.

Peter took the bottle without even looking at her, deep in conversation with a teenage girl. Insulted by his lack of attention to her, Rainey's bottom lip quivered as she slowly made her way to her bedroom.

For the next two months, Rainey got to live with two miserable parents as they weaned themselves from heroin just long enough to take custody of their infant daughter. They were less tolerant of her and each other, always snapping and arguing over every little thing. Even when they weren't focused on taking drugs, they obsessed about when they could take them again.

Rainey retreated into her shell, occasionally going to the pizzeria with Buddy, but for the most part her life was going to school and staying in her room. She was doing her homework when her parents burst through her bedroom door. The girl flinched at the sudden noise and looked up to see her mother holding a blanket with a small face peeking through the top. Excited, she sprang from the floor and flew over to them.

"Is that her?" she asked, desperate to see her little sister's face.

Miranda smiled and bent down so Rainey could get a look at her sister. Rainey pulled in a quick breath when she looked into Ivy's light brown eyes. She was only a baby, but she could tell Ivy looked more like their mother. Rainey pressed her hand over her own heart and leaned in closer.

"Can I hold her?" Rainey breathed.

Miranda smiled at the baby one more time and pushed the bundle toward her. Rainey awkwardly took the baby in her arms. "Yeah, you got her until I come back up," she said, then plunked down a plastic bag. "There's formula and diapers in the bag. The nurse at the hospital was such a bitch. I asked for enough shit to hold this kid for a week, but she only gave me enough for a couple of days. Anyway, you can figure it out."

"Wait!" Rainey yelled, panic-stricken, terrified she'd hurt Ivy.

Miranda spun on her daughter. "I said you can figure it out. You ain't dumb, are ya?"

Rainey shook her head and wondered if this was the same way they had treated her when she had first come home from the hospital.

"Then don't be such a drag," Peter added.

"But I thought the bottles need to be warmed up," Rainey argued. She'd taken a book out of the school library about babies and tried to remember as much as she could.

Miranda waved her hand in the air. "That's all bullshit. She'll be fine drinking them at room temperature. She'll probably need to eat like every three or four hours."

"Is it three or four?" Rainey asked with waves of anxiety flooding her body.

"Whatever it is, it is. When she's hungry, she'll cry," her mom said, then followed Peter to the bedroom door. Miranda stopped and looked over her shoulder at her older daughter. "You'll learn as you go along. I don't want to see your boney ass downstairs bugging me every minute. Remember," Miranda said, pointing her finger at her daughter, "don't fuck this up. Got it?"

Rainey's mouth hung open as she glared at her mother. "You don't want to be bothered by *your baby*?" she said, keeping her voice low not wanting to wake Ivy. "Why can't you be like other moms? Like the kind I see on TV?"

Miranda beamed. "'Cause I ain't like those old hags. I'm unique and I love it."

When her parents left, Rainey used her foot to close the door behind them. Then she sat on the floor with her baby sister. Ivy was asleep and she laid next to the baby, counting her fingers and watching her breathe. As she did, her thoughts drifted to aunt Sophie and a pang of sadness washed over her. Etching Ivy's nose and forehead with her index finger, she wished her aunt was with them.

Rainey's thoughts lingered and she fantasized about her aunt busting through the door and rescuing the two of them.

Rainey was a child without hope and that was the saddest thing about her life. Rainey Paxton was tired of fighting the endless battles that no one ever knew about.

Rainey clutched Ivy closer to her and quietly cried until her own eyelids were too heavy to hold open, and after drifting to sleep, she found an escape from her pitiful life.

Chapter Fifteen

From that first night together, Rainey became Ivy's protector. All of her anxiety about not knowing what to do subsided whenever the baby smiled or made funny little noises at her. She now had a real purpose for existing—Ivy was everything to her. It gave her joy to have someone to love again.

Rainey, still a child herself, fed, bathed, and changed the baby's dirty diapers. When she went to school during the day all she could think about was getting home to her sister. She was in a constant state of agony believing that something awful would happen to the baby while in the care of her parents. Rainey knew firsthand that her parents wouldn't look out for the baby, and by the time she returned home from school, Ivy would invariably be howling in the upstairs bedroom because she was hungry and needed her diaper changed.

As Ivy's main caregiver, Rainey was forced to grow up quickly, and with that, she rapidly learned more of her parents' limitations. She'd come to detest them for lying to her about their drug use, still calling it medicine, but she knew the truth. She knew that Peter and Miranda never considered their children when they made decisions. But Rainey was determined to look out for Ivy's well-being, and she put her annoyance aside and focused solely on her sister.

At ten, Rainey was the most dependable person in eight-month-old Ivy's life. In all ways, she had become Rainey's child. The sisters shared the miserable feeling of going to bed with hunger pains every night and waking up to an empty stomach every morning. One morning, as Rainey laid on her side with her knees pulled up to her chest, she breathed through spasms that felt as though her intestines were being turned inside out. Once the worst of it had subsided, she glanced at her sister, still asleep, before she snuck out of the bedroom. She stood at the bathroom sink and caught her reflection in the mirror. Pausing, she moved closer and cringed at the thin, gray skin on her face and how her hazel eyes bulged in their sockets. Rainey stepped back so she could get a look at her upper body. She lifted the bottom of her shirt and gasped at the sight of her protruding ribs. Scared by the skeleton in the mirror, her breathing quickened. She turned to look at her boney back just as Ivy wailed from their bedroom. Rainey ran to her.

"It's okay," Rainey soothed as she held her close. "I bet your belly hurts too. Let's go see if we can find Mom."

Exhausted, irritated, and hungry, Rainey stomped out of her bedroom with Ivy in her arms.

"Mom!" Rainey yelled when she reached the kitchen. "We need food. We're hungry and we have to eat. You need to do something. You and Dad spend all of your money on drugs. And I don't care anymore, but you guys need to take care of us too or we're gonna get really sick."

Miranda spun on her. "Who do you think you're talking to, Rainey Paxton?" she snarled, grabbing a handful of her daughter's hair and jerking her head around. "You don't get to tell me how to spend my money. If you weren't such a snotty brat, maybe some of the people around here would give you a little food or money. But you think you're too fucking good for everybody. You're just like your aunt Sophie."

Rainey's lips pinched together into a tight line, willing herself not to cry despite the pain. Then she ripped her head away from her mother, leaving Miranda with a fistful of long strands of hair. Her adrenaline surged with such force she barely flinched at the hair being torn from her scalp.

"There's nothing wrong with me being like Aunt Sophie!" she screamed. "I love her. At least she cared about me and she would've cared about Ivy too. But Ivy will never know her because you won't take us to visit her." Rainey's breath was rough and jagged. "And the stupid people who sleep here aren't even normal. They are either laying on the floor moaning or standing around bent over at the waist so high they don't even know where they are."

Miranda put her hand on her hip. "They're our friends. So stop talking shit. You're so stuck up it makes me sick." Miranda reached into her pocket and threw a five-dollar bill at her. "Take the goddamn money and buy yourself food . . . since you're so hungry and deprived."

Miranda moved closer and flicked Rainey's forehead with her index finger. She did it with such force that she almost dropped the baby, but she kept herself steady, never letting her eyes leave the five-dollar bill at her feet. Ignoring her mother, she snatched the money off of the floor and rushed to the sink. She filled a bottle with water from the faucet and took the baby up to their bedroom.

Rainey fed the baby most of the water in the bottle and laid her on the pile of clothes while she pulled on jeans and a shirt. Then, with Ivy in her arms, she went into the bathroom to dig through the closet for a clean diaper. Finding none, she slumped to the floor for several minutes, exhausted from fighting with her mother. When she hoisted herself up and went back to her room, she grabbed a pair of old raggedy underwear and pulled Ivy's gangly legs through the holes. Then she packed the underwear with old rags as carefully as she could.

After dressing them both in layers to keep warm, Rainey bent over and kissed the tip of Ivy's nose. "Come on. We need to go out. We're gonna buy some food."

Ivy, satisfied for the moment with her belly full of water, stared into Rainey's eyes and gave her a gummy smile.

Rainey ran her hand over the baby's head. "I know you're hungry. I'm hungry too. We have five dollars." Rainey showed her sister the money. "We're gonna go to the store and get some food. They have lots of good stuff for us to buy there."

Ivy gurgled at her older sister and wiggled her arms and legs.

"We have to get out of here quick before Mom remembers she gave me five bucks and tries to take it back," Rainey said, picking up the baby and rushing down the stairs.

Rainey walked with Ivy in her arms through the cold to a bargain dollar store. Inside, Rainey looked around for the best deals. She grabbed a box of no-name cereal and a six-pack of unrefrigerated Parmalat milk. Moving through the aisles, she picked up four cans of Vienna sausages, four cans of pumpkin pie filling, and four cans of green beans because all were on sale: four for one dollar. With a basket of food on one arm and Ivy in the other, Rainey made her way to the cash register. As she walked, she spotted a box of cupcakes and stopped dead in her tracks. She looked at them with longing—cupcakes were one of her favorite treats.

"No, I can't buy those," she whispered to herself. "We can't afford cupcakes. This food needs to last us a while." She looked down at the baby in her arms smiling up at her.

"What do you think?"

Ivy let out a soft giggle.

"You don't care, do you?" she said, brushing her nose against Ivy's. The baby just smiled and cooed.

Rainey put the basket of food on the floor and readjusted her hold on her sister. As she did, she felt the wetness seeping through Ivy's outfit.

"Oh, noooo. I forgot you need diapers."

Ivy looked up at her sister, her face quickly turned bright red and she farted.

Rainey cracked a smile. "Well, no cupcakes today, that's for sure."

Ivy laid her head on her older sister's shoulder.

"Next time we'll get cupcakes," she said.

Now she had to decide which of the food items were the least necessary. After careful consideration, Rainey removed the green beans, since pumpkin pie filling would be easier for her sister to eat. Then she looked at the small pack of diapers and considered her alternatives to save another dollar. *There are plenty of old T-shirts in my bedroom,* she thought and grabbed a pack of large safety pins instead.

While loading the stubby belt with her items, Rainey's stomach rumbled and she knew everyone standing near them heard it. She blushed deeply.

The cashier looked Rainey over. The woman took in her greasy hair and dirty fingernails and gave her a warm but uncomfortable smile. "You all doing okay there?"

"Yes, ma'am," Rainey said, averting her eyes. She hated lying to anyone, even strangers, especially since Aunt Sophie had told her to always tell the truth.

"That your sister?"

"Yes, ma'am."

"Where's your mother?"

Rainey fidgeted. She reached into her pocket and pulled out the five-dollar bill and handed it to the cashier. "My mom is waiting for us in the car . . . down the block."

"I see," the woman said. "Now, you listen here. My name is Rosemary. See? You can call me, Miss Rosemary." The woman pointed to the name tag on her red smock.

Rainey looked up and nodded.

"I don't want you to take no crap from nobody. Out here you stand tall. Fight if ya have to, but don't put up with no disrespect. We clear?"

"Yes, ma'am."

"Good. Now I want you to turn around and grab one of those chocolate bars on the rack. That candy bar there is gonna be my treat."

"Really?" Rainey asked, her chest filling with hope. "You would buy me a candy bar? You don't even know me."

"Sure, I'd buy you a candy bar. And don't worry, I know you. You're every child that lives in this godforsaken town."

Rainey picked up a chocolate bar, took her bags, and walked toward the door. As she pushed it open, she turned back. "Thank you, Miss Rosemary."

"Ain't no problem, sugar. You be good now and get that baby home quick because it's colder than a polar bear's ass outside."

Rainey giggled and gave the woman a quick wave.

On the streets, as Rainey walked back through the bitter cold she thought about Miss Rosemary. A stranger had been more kind to her than her parents. *Why would she give me something and not ask for anything in return?* she wondered. *Why can't Mom and Dad be that nice?*

Chapter Sixteen

When the sisters arrived back home with their food, Rainey raced upstairs with Ivy. She laid the baby on the bedroom floor and quickly filled a bottle with milk. She cradled the hungry child in her arms while Ivy attached to the bottle nipple and took long, hard sucks. Rainey's eyes locked in on the baby, and sadness washed over her. Her heart broke watching hunger possess Ivy to where her eyes glazed over and she greedily drained the milk from the bottle.

"I'm sorry we have to live like this. If Aunt Sophie was here, it would be better," Rainey said. "Someday you and me are gonna leave here and never come back. I promise."

While Ivy finished the bottle of milk, Rainey pulled the tab off the top of the Vienna sausage can. The smell of the canned meat hit her nose, and her eyes narrowed as she waited out the initial stench. Then she plucked a sausage out with her fingertips. She nibbled on it, taking small bites to make the link last longer.

When they had both finished their meager meal, Rainey moved to the closet and pushed aside cardboard boxes, clothes, and a broken laundry basket until she cleared a spot on the floor. Then she shoved their food in and buried it with the same junk.

Satisfied that their stash was hidden well enough, Rainey laid down next to Ivy, who was almost sleeping. "I bet your belly feels a lot better now," she whispered. "Guess what? Tomorrow you're gonna have pumpkin pie filling. How's that sound?"

Ivy met her gaze heavy-eyed, and a moment later she was asleep.

***

Over the next two years, Rainey frequently battled with her parents over money for food and diapers. She became braver, more forthright now that she was standing up for someone else. The sisters were deprived of their most basic needs, but that didn't stop Rainey from being resourceful. She did whatever was necessary to make sure they survived.

Rainey's life consisted of going to school, rushing home, and taking care of Ivy. She'd wake before the sun rose, while the house was quiet, cram her feet into sneakers too small for her, and slink quietly downstairs. Then she would tiptoe into the kitchen. When she flicked the light switch, the bulb hanging overhead would shine, and cockroaches would scatter. It happened every morning and, after many years, numb to sharing her home with bugs, the roaches no longer bothered Rainey. They were disgustingly gross, but she knew the roaches wouldn't hurt her or make her suffer.

One morning, Ivy had cried for hours from hunger pains. Desperate to ease her sister's discomfort, Rainey moved quietly from her bedroom down into the kitchen. But when she threw on the light switch, the kitchen bulb remained dark. Cursing her parents for not paying the electric bill again, she walked across the kitchen floor in the dark, crunching the cockroaches under her sneakers. She moved toward the sink, where the moon shone through the window. She looked down at the filthy water filled with dirty dishes. There were drowned bugs floating on top, and two cockroaches stood on the windowsill, as though they were gathering strength from the moonbeams that shined on their glossy, brown backs. Rainey watched another pair of roaches that sat on an old, partially ripped sponge floating in the backed-up sink water, antennae wiggling at her as if to say, *Kiss my ass, bitch, I ain't running from you. This is our kitchen too.*

Rainey stared at the bugs a moment longer, her stomach spinning as she came to a tragic realization. "My life is no better than yours. How did that happen?" she said to the bugs. Then she lifted her hand and smashed it into the filthy water until she caught one and squeezed her hand closed. She felt the gooey ooze of bug guts between her fingers and looked at her palm covered in a thick, white, frothy mucus. Coming to her senses, Rainey's skin crawled and she ran to the back door, gagging until she caught her breath.

Pulling herself together, she rinsed out two plastic cups from the mound of mess on the kitchen counter and filled them with tap water.

Then she moved to the living room, where she scrounged for something to eat. She'd be happy with anything, even small scraps of food that were left over or tossed to the side. She quietly stepped over people, moving around them, while she poked through takeout containers and fast-food bags. She found nothing edible, and her stomach rumbled as she grabbed a white paper bag on the floor. Inside were two pizza crusts. Feeling an overwhelming sense of gratitude, she grabbed them and the two cups of water and rushed up to her bedroom to share the rare findings with Ivy.

In the bedroom, Rainey soaked one crust in water. When it became mushy, she spooned the pizza crust out with her fingers and fed it to Ivy as she chomped on the other crust.

"I know it's not much," she told her baby sister, "but at least we got to eat something. I think this is going to be a good day."

Chapter Seventeen

By the time Ivy was four years old and Rainey was thirteen, she had established herself not only as the older sister but also the authority figure in the child's life. Rainey didn't mind being responsible for her sister, but she never stopped resenting her parents for their active disinterest. The child was tender and loving, and her favorite thing to do was cuddle with her older sister. Rainey did everything she could to make sure Ivy was fed and clothed. She gave everything to her sister, and in return, the child gave Rainey a sense of purpose.

Once, after an entire day when the two girls hadn't eaten, Rainey walked to a convenience store and meandered through the aisles. When she was certain no one was watching, she shoved a jar of peanut butter into her coat pocket. In the other pocket, she hid a box of saltine crackers and left the store, trying to look as casual as possible. She and Ivy sparingly ate peanut butter crackers for breakfast, lunch, and dinner for two weeks.

Once that food ran out, Rainey crept down the stairs from her bedroom and slunk into the living room, where several grown-ups were partying while her parents were in the next room smoking crack.

"Hi Joanie," Rainey said to one of the few women in the room. Joanie was a sarcastic eighteen-year-old, but Rainey liked that about her. The girl had confidence.

"Oh, hey there," Joanie said, picking at one of the scabby sores on her lips.

Rainey averted her eyes from the painful-looking sores. "Um, me and my little sister are hungry. Do you think you could give us some money?"

Joanie laughed. "Nah, I ain't got none to spare. But I'll help ya out a little."

Rainey smiled, and although she'd learned by now not to expect much, she couldn't help but anticipate getting something that they could eat.

"Hey, everyone," Joanie announced loudly, "the kid here is looking for some money to buy food for her and her kid sister."

"Money?" one guy Rainey didn't recognize yelled. "Go ask your parents for money. We already pay them to stay here. Maybe they ought to stop selling their food stamps."

"Food stamps?" Rainey asked, dumbfounded. She'd never heard of such a thing.

Joanie snickered and turned toward the loud guy. "Miranda and Peter are so fucked up they have kids begging for money from junkies. They expect everyone else to take care of 'em. This is why I ain't got no crumb snatchers. I ain't never having kids."

Annoyed at Joanie's sarcasm now targeted at her, she realized there would be no help coming her way. "You suck, Joanie," Rainey barked before she backed out of the room and up the steps to her bedroom. She sat on the floor and pulled her sister onto her lap.

"We need to go out for a while. I want to go check out the library."

Ivy put her head on her sister's chest. "I wanna go out too."

"Of course you do. Let's get going."

Rainey and Ivy left the house hand-in-hand. They entered the library, and Rainey walked them up to the counter where a woman with short black hair stood.

"Hello, girls," she said warmly, looking Rainey up and down. "How are you today?"

"We're fine," Rainey answered, gripping Ivy's hand tighter.

"Are you here by yourselves?"

"Yeah," Rainey stated. "I have to look up some stuff for school."

The woman leaned her elbows onto the counter. "Well, then you've come to the right place. My name is Sandy. Is there something I can help you find?"

Rainey nodded. "I have . . . I have a school project," she lied. "I'm writing a thing on food stamps. So I need to find out what they are."

Sandy rubbed her chin with her thumb and index finger. "Well, food stamps are something that the government gives to people who need them so they can buy food."

"You mean, people can buy food without money?"

"Well, sort of. Grocery stores let people use food stamps in place of real money."

"So everyone can have food stamps?" Rainey's mind was working a mile a minute.

"No. Not everyone, just people who need them. In other words, when a family doesn't earn enough money, the government will provide food stamps so they can buy the things they need. It's intended so that people can feed their families." Sandy walked around the counter and stood next to the girls. "I can show you a few books where you can research the whole history of food stamps and other government programs. Is that what you're looking for?"

Rainey looked at Sandy and bit her bottom lip, wondering how much to tell her. She seemed nice, and the young girl tried to make a habit of not lying, so she shook her head. "I'm trying to find out if my family gets food stamps."

"Oh, I see." Sandy winked at Rainey. "Well, in that case, there's a new program in place. The grocery store will have an account where the government sends the money for food stamps." Rainey was hopeful until Sandy sighed and leaned on her desk. "Unfortunately, you'd have to know which retailer it's going to."

"Retailer"? She didn't know the word.

"Yes, I'm sorry. Which grocery store."

Rainey was disappointed; her shoulders dropped forward, and her long, greasy hair covered her face. She knew it was unlikely to ever get that information from her mother.

"I'll tell you what," Sandy said in a perky voice. "I brought way too much food for lunch today. I know the two of you must be very busy, and probably don't have enough time to stop at home and eat lunch."

Rainey listened intently, not letting herself hope too much.

"How about if I give you the extra food I have with me so that you can get all of the things done today that you set out to do? You and your little sister can sit at one of the tables over there and eat," she said, pointing at the children's section. "How does that sound?"

Rainey beamed at the librarian. "That sounds good because, like you said, we have a lot of reading and stuff to do today."

Sandy left the two girls and went into the back room and came back shortly with a large brown bag, which she handed to Rainey. Cautiously, the girl took the bag from the librarian and sat Ivy at the table before sitting down next to her. In the bag was a turkey sandwich, chips, carrots, and a banana. To most, it was an ordinary lunch, but to the Paxton sisters, it was a meal at a five-star restaurant.

Later in the afternoon, when they arrived back at their home, Rainey found her mother.

"Mom. Do we get food stamps?"

"Who wants to know?" Miranda snapped.

"I do. If we get them, then you should let us buy food. Do we? Do we get them?" Rainey held her ground firmly, even as her mother's eyes raked over her. The girl could feel Ivy's grip tighten on her thigh as the exchange escalated, and the child stared at their mother as though she was a stranger.

"What your dad and I get is none of your business. How many times do I need to tell you, it ain't right to ask your parents about their financial situation?"

Rainey held Miranda's glare until it became too much and she broke eye contact. She knew better than to expect her mother to give up anything to her.

"You know what your problem is, Rainey?" Miranda said. "You're a whiner. You know there are kids out there that don't even have a place to live. You need to count your damn blessings. It ain't like you're starving."

"Yes, we are! We *are* starving!" Rainey yelled. She pulled her shirt up so her mother could see her ribs pressing out from under her pale skin.

"You always gotta be so dramatic. You're a bad influence on your little sister."

"I'm tired of hunting for food," Rainey said, just as Ivy let out a moan. She bent down and picked her up. "It's okay, Ivy. I'm just mad at Mom because she needs to help us more so we can eat better," she said defiantly.

"Don't say that to my child!" Miranda yelled. She moved forward and grabbed Ivy under the armpits. She attempted to take her from Rainey's arms, but the child held tight to her sister's shirt collar and turned her head away from her mother. Rainey pulled Ivy in closer.

When Miranda's hand met her arm, Ivy let out the sound of a wounded animal and she immediately withdrew it.

"You've ruined her," Miranda said, slapping Rainey in the face. "You ruin everything you touch. I swear they gave me the wrong kid at the hospital. Now you've turned my baby against me. You're a rotten bitch."

Rainey held a hand over the burning flesh on her face, her eyes stinging with tears. "I didn't turn Ivy against you," she seethed through clenched teeth. "Ivy doesn't go to you because you've never paid any attention to her. I've been raising her since she was born. I'm the one who does everything for her. You and Dad . . . all you two know how to do is get stoned. That's all you care about. When are you going to start caring about us, Mom?"

Miranda pulled back her arm and backhanded Rainey on the side of her face. This time the force knocked her back on her butt. Ivy went down with her and thudded against her chest. Shaking it off, the young girl rose to her feet and took Ivy's hand, turned on her heel, and left the room, Miranda screaming for her to come back. When the girls got to the living room, coming through the front door was Buddy.

Seeing Rainey was distraught, Buddy rushed over to her quickly. "Are you okay?" she whispered, gently touching the side of Rainey's face where she'd been hit.

Rainey jerked her head away and stared at her. She straightened her back and looked Buddy dead in the eyes. "Where have you been? I haven't seen you in almost five years. You just left. You were here and then one day you were gone and never came back. So why don't you just leave me alone?"

Buddy looked away and her head hung as she shook it gently. "I'm so sorry. Really I am. I had some issues, but I always thought about you and hoped you were doing okay."

Rainey's eyes narrowed. "Well, this here," she said, looking at Ivy, "this is my little sister, who was born after you left. Take a good look at the two of us. We aren't okay. So just move outta the way. We are going out. I need to make some money so we can eat."

She put her hand on the doorknob, and Buddy touched her shoulder. Rainey flinched. Her instinct was to turn and throw herself into the woman's arms, but she feared being abandoned again.

"What can I do to help?" Buddy asked.

"You could've stayed around a long time ago instead of disappearing. I was a little girl, and I had to take care of a baby all by myself. I know it's not your fault, but you were the only person I had in my life. So unless you have the money to feed us and buy the things we need . . . then there's nothing you can do to help us."

When Buddy didn't reply, Rainey opened the door and stepped outside. She took in a long breath and, with Ivy by her side, headed toward Kensington Avenue.

Chapter Eighteen

The sisters stood at the corner of Kensington Avenue and Westmoreland Street. Rainey pulled her shoulders back and kept a visual of everything going on around them, trying to formulate a plan. When she'd told Buddy she was going out to make money, it had just been a thing to say, but now she really wanted to do it. Noticing a drug deal taking place across the street, she instinctively put her arm around Ivy and pulled her closer.

"What's wrong?" Ivy asked, looking up at her sister with wide eyes filled with fear.

"Nothing is wrong. We just have to be careful because there are lots of people around and you need to stay close to me."

Rainey waited until the drug deal ended, then shifted her gaze to the other side of the street. Her curiosity piqued as several older girls dressed in skimpy clothing pranced around the sidewalk as cars cruised by slowly. A car pulled over and one girl bent down and looked into the passenger window.

Rainey's couldn't pull her eyes away. Of course, she knew they were prostitutes, but she had never actually seen them working like they were now.

Rainey gawked as another hooker approached a man on the sidewalk. She pressed Ivy's face against the side of her body to keep the child from seeing the scene as the man looked the hooker over, grabbing her ass and sniffing her.

"Hey, baby, I got what you're looking for," the girl purred. After a few seconds, the girl opened the car door, slipped inside, and the car drove away.

Rainey paused and took in the heart of Kensington. People filtered in and out of the run-down stores and buildings like sleepwalkers—all seemingly searching for their lost souls. Some were high or drunk but others were trying to live among the chaos. There were sounds of raised voices and car horns blaring. In the distance, she heard glass smashing against the pavement. Trash thrown from car windows and left behind by those who didn't care snuggled the edge of the sidewalks. Time stood still as the grimy elements mixed to create an unwelcome world for the children of Kensington.

Several people buzzed by the two girls with no acknowledgment, like they were ghosts, invisible to other humans. After about ten minutes, a man stood beside them waiting to cross the street. Rainey sized him up and thought he looked kind—or, at least, he wasn't scowling like a lot of the other guys around.

She tilted her head back and looked up at the man, widening her eyes to look extra innocent. "Hey mister?"

The man glanced down at her. She noticed that he was wearing a uniform with a patch sewn over his chest that said, *Dan*. He looked from Rainey to Ivy.

Rainey realized this was her shot. "Hey Mister," she said again. "Do you have any money you can give us so me and my little sister can eat?"

Dan stooped in front of them. "When was the last time the two of you ate?"

Rainey looked down at her sneakers. "I'm not sure . . . a couple of days ago." That was a lie, but she justified it because food was essential.

"When's the last time you had a bath or put on clean clothes?"

"Why does that matter?" Rainey asked, trying not to let her impatience be heard. "We're hungry, mister."

Nodding, Dan reached into his pocket and pulled out a five-dollar bill. "You're right. I didn't mean to be rude. But looking at the two of you . . . I mean, neither of you look well. And your clothes aren't warm enough for this weather. It's winter and it's going to get even colder soon. I'm sure your parents are worried about you two."

Rainey looked into the man's face. "Our parents are dead," she said solemnly. "We live with our older sister. And I know how we look. We're poor, that's all."

Ivy moved closer to Rainey and laid her head on her shoulder. "I wanna go home," she cried.

Rainey stood. "Thanks for the five bucks, mister."

This was the first time Rainey had begged for money on the streets. She realized quickly that begging in Kensington would be hard. It had taken a long time for Dan to wander by them. Since the streets were infested with drunks, addicts, and prostitutes, it made panhandling much more difficult.

"We're going to have to find another way to make money," she said to Ivy, who nodded, too young to understand what her sister was saying.

When Rainey and Ivy got back to the house, there were more people there than usual. Music was blaring, and people stood around with cans of beer. A couple in the living room was having sex while others around them prepared needles and smoked joints. Rainey's stomach bubbled with acid as she looked at the adults scattered throughout. She took Ivy up to their room and barricaded them in by pushing her old dresser against the door.

Over the past few years, Rainey had learned which squatters were rowdy, and that night, they were all there. Drugs were sold and used. People got too drunk and too high and the entire house became alive with a reckless vibe. Then all hell would break loose and there would be fights and sex and louder music. When this happened Rainey worried that the partiers would hurt her or Ivy. She worried they'd set the house on fire or bust into their bedroom.

As Rainey laid on the floor that night, with the volume of the music turning up every hour, she hunkered down farther under the pile of clothing. Carrying the burden of keeping Ivy fed was hard on her. She wouldn't dare complain to anyone about their situation because she was afraid the authorities would come and separate her from Ivy—at least that's what Peter had drilled into her head. She drifted to sleep thinking about her aunt Sophie and wishing she were there now to help her and Ivy live a better life.

Chapter Nineteen

Rainey was consumed with the safety of her sister more than anything. While she was at school, her four-year-old sister ached for independence and would wander the house looking for entertainment.

One day when she returned from school, she found Ivy in the living room where two teenage boys had forced her to sit with them while they took turns blowing cigarette smoke in her face, laughing as the child gagged. Rainey was furious, and that anger quickly turned to determination to make a drastic change before her little sister was hurt. That night, she did the only thing she could think of to protect her sister. She went into the attic, found an old typewriter, and pecked away at the keys.

Dear Principal Warner,

This is to inform you we will be homeschooling our daughter Rainey Paxton. We believe the home and family environment will make it a much richer learning experience. Please let us know if you have questions.

Sincerely,

Miranda Andersen and Peter Paxton

Rainey waited until just before midnight to make sure her parents were plastered, to get them to sign the letter.

"What the hell's this?" Peter grumbled when Rainey put the letter down and handed him a pen.

"It's a note saying that I'm going to be homeschooled. I can't leave Ivy here by herself anymore. She's getting in . . . in the way. Someone has to take care of her so unless you or Mom are going to step up and do it then it has to be me. She won't start kindergarten for a while and, even then, she only goes in half a day," Rainey explained.

Peter grinned. "Well, you sure as hell know it ain't gonna be me. And we know it's not your mom because she's got things to do during the day too."

"Mom gets high all day and night. That's what you both do."

"Yeah, getting high takes money. So she's busy. Just wait until you start to get high. You'll see."

"I'm never going to get high," Rainey said. "I see what it's done to you."

"You think you're so much better than us because you don't party," Peter scoffed. "Someday, when you're a little older, you'll understand that getting high is what helps you get through this shit-fuck life."

Rainey ran her fingers through her long, blond hair and rolled her eyes. "There's something else we need to talk about. I'm going to need money every week so that me and Ivy can eat and buy things we need."

"Every *week*?" Peter chuckled. "That's excessive."

Rainey shot her hand forward and held her father's chin with her hand so she could look into his eyes. "That's not excessive. We're kids. We need to eat."

Peter tapped his head with his index finger. "*You're* a pain in the ass. How much are you talking?"

"I need at least forty bucks a week."

Peter laughed. "You're out of your mind. That's way too much. I'll tell you what . . . I'll give you ten bucks a week. If you shop at the dollar bargain store that'll be more than enough."

Rainey held out her hand. "That's a promise then?"

Peter took his daughter's hand. "Yeah, fine. But I don't wanna see Ivy roaming around here without you—not even once."

Rainey knew that in her house promises were made to be broken, but she hoped that this time her father would finally be true to his word.

Chapter Twenty

The following week Rainey, dragging Ivy by the hand, found her father in the living room. He was sprawled out on a broken recliner with his arms hanging off the sides. She pushed her open hand toward him.

"Dad, I need ten bucks for this week."

Peter gazed up at her with glassy, bloodshot eyes. "What ten bucks?"

"The money you promised to give me every week. Remember? We talked about it last week."

Peter stared at her with heavy-lidded eyes and coughed. "You're crazy. I never agreed to anything. You think money grows on trees."

Rainey crossed her arms tightly over her chest. "You agreed to give me money every week for Ivy and me." She watched his face, waiting for the lightbulb to go off. When she got only a blank stare, Rainey adjusted her stance. "It's so I can buy things that we need . . . like food. Come on, Dad, just give it to me. We're both hungry."

Peter jabbed his cigarette into the ashtray on the table in front of him. "Listen, girl, you don't tell me what to do."

Rainey ground her fist into her open palm in frustration. "I'm not telling you what to do. We talked about this and you agreed. We shook hands on it. I know you remember."

Peter looked into her eyes and pursed his lips. "I don't remember shaking hands, but if I did, it's only because you tricked me." Peter paused and handed his friend a pack of rolling papers. "I'll tell you what. You go over there and hug Freddy and I'll give you the ten dollars."

Rainey looked at the man her father had pointed to. He was as old as her dad—and had long dark hair, except he was bald on top. He had bushy eyebrows and the skin on his face was pitted with pockmarks. His shirt was dirty and torn in various spots like he'd gotten stuck on barbed wire. His jeans looked as though they hadn't been washed since the day he put them on, and as Rainey's eyes moved to his face, Freddy gave her a stained-tooth grin.

Rainey grimaced, then glanced back at her father and raised her eyebrows. She knew Freddy; he was a permanent fixture at their house. He gave her the creeps the way he stared at her butt and small boobs. The weight of Freddy's stare always made the little hairs on the back of her neck stand up.

Rainey shook her head. "I'm not hugging Freddy. He has nothing to do with you giving me money so that we can eat."

Peter shrugged. "Then I guess you don't want ten dollars."

Ivy, who'd been quiet the whole time, looked up at Rainey and whimpered, "I'm hungry." The sadness in Ivy's eyes pulling on her sister's heartstrings.

Steeling herself, Rainey turned back to her father. "One hug. That's it."

She dropped Ivy's hand. Then she slowly moved to the chair where Freddy was sitting. She bent down, put her arms around his neck, squeezed lightly, and tried to pull away, but Freddy overpowered her and pulled her onto his lap and kissed her neck.

"Get off of me!" Rainey screamed, but Freddy tightened his grip.

She looked at her father, desperate for help. But Peter gave her a sloppy grin.

Rainey's heart pounded and her hands shook. She kicked and swatted at Freddy. "Let me go!" she shrieked loudly.

Buddy, who had been in another room and heard her screaming, rushed in at the sound of Rainey's cry.

"What are you doing?" she yelled at Freddy, grabbing Rainey's wrist. "Get the fuck off of her!"

Freddy glared at Buddy. Then he pushed Rainey off of his lap and she fell to the floor with a heavy thud.

"You got a feisty one there, Peter. I like 'em like that."

Rainey flinched when she saw her dad grin.

"You owe me now," he said. "Let's call that a deposit."

Freddy licked his lips. "Okay. A *small* deposit."

Rainey glared at her father, her heart pounding wildly. "What are you talking about?"

Peter turned toward her. "Am I talking to you? Or am I talking to Freddy? That's your problem. You don't know how to mind your own damn business. You need to stop asking so many questions and do whatever the hell I tell you to do."

Rainey was about to argue with him when Buddy pulled her up, wrapping her arms around the girl's shoulders in a protective stance. "Come on, Rainey," she said. "It's time to go."

Determined to get her money, Rainey stomped closer to her father with her hand out. Grinning, he reached into his pocket and pulled out a ten-dollar bill.

Rainey snatched the money from his hand and looked him in the eyes. "There's something wrong with you. How could you make me do that? You're disgusting. Don't *ever* try to make me do something like that again." Grasping for straws, she threatened, "I swear I'll tell Mom what you made me do."

"Be my guest. Your mom knows damn well that you don't get nothing for free. You want money, well then, you'll need to do something for it. You'll learn soon enough this ain't no free world we live in."

"Dad! It's not for nothing. You're supposed to give me money to buy food, remember? You're supposed to feed us. It's not a favor or a handout for you to buy your kids food."

Peter lifted his hip, pulled a bag of weed from his pocket, and handed it to Freddy. "Roll a few up." Then he glanced at his daughter. "Don't be so uppity. You sound just like your aunt."

"*Good*," Rainey seethed. "At least she cared about me."

"Listen, you little shit. Get the hell outta here before I beat your ass."

Hot tears burning her eyes, Rainey grabbed Ivy's hand and left the room. She didn't stop walking until she reached the front door.

Before leaving, Rainey looked back at her father and caught Freddy staring at her. His disgusting gaze made her insides run cold. Freddy's eyes were hungry and fixed on her in a way that made Rainey want to leave and never return. Whatever Freddy was thinking, she knew it couldn't be good. Dread trickled down her spine as she pulled Ivy along, shutting the door to the dangerous place she called home.

Chapter Twenty-One

Outside of the house, Rainey put her arm over Ivy's shoulder, and Buddy came out right behind them. The three of them walked into the center of Kensington.

"What happened with Freddy?" Buddy asked.

"I don't know," Rainey mumbled, pushing back shame. "I asked my dad for money for Ivy and me to eat, but he wouldn't give me any until I hugged Freddy. I hate that guy. He's always smiling at me. He makes my skin crawl." Rainey's cheeks flushed and she looked away from Buddy.

"There's nothing for you to be embarrassed about. You didn't do anything wrong. Your father is an asshole."

Ivy smiled. "Daddy's an asshole . . . Daddy's an asshole," she sang.

Rainey cocked her mouth to the side. "That's not a nice thing to say. It's a bad word. Don't say that anymore. Okay?"

The smile vanished from Ivy's lips. "I sorry, Rainey."

Rainey stopped walking and knelt in front of her sister. "It's okay. It's just that I don't want you saying bad words. Do you understand?"

Ivy pouted and clasped her tiny hands together. Her head hung as she gave her sister a confirming nod.

As Rainey stood, she glanced at Buddy. "No cursing in front of her. She repeats everything."

Buddy pressed her palms to her cheek. "That was stupid of me. I should've known better."

Rainey shot her a quick smile. "It's okay."

Buddy placed a hand on the girl's shoulder. "Did . . . did Freddy do anything to hurt you?"

Rainey shuddered at the memory. "No, but the dirtball wouldn't let me go and kept kissing my neck. I was scared of what else he was going to do, and my dad just sat there watching."

"Is that the first time your dad made you do something like that?"

Rainey pushed her hair from her face. "Yeah. Why? Do you think something else is going to happen to me?" she asked, suddenly nervous.

"No, I mean, I hope not," Buddy said quickly.

Rainey's stomach spun.

Buddy added, "You just need to be careful. Keep your guard up. I know you're young and you're smart, but you're beautiful, too. Those people shooting up drugs . . . it's hard for them to understand boundaries. Most of them don't even think, they just act. I'm worried someone will try to take advantage of you."

Rainey looked down at her sister, then back at Buddy. "Yeah, I know. That's what I'm worried about too. I hate living at my house." She paused and took in a deep breath. "Thanks for making Freddy stop. It scares me to think about what he would've done to me if you hadn't come into the living room."

"It's cool. I'm happy to help out," Buddy said. "Back to Freddy though, maybe you should tell someone."

"Who? The only person I ever felt like I could confide in was my aunt Sophie—and you. After my aunt was gone, I couldn't tell my teachers because all they would do is report it to someone else. Then the school would call child services and they'd take me and Ivy from my parents. That wouldn't be so bad, but I can't take the chance that they'd separate us. Besides, now that I'm thirteen there ain't any foster parents that would want me." Rainey bent down and buttoned Ivy's sweater. "I stopped going to school so I could take care of Ivy, and I'm not about to leave her now. So the way I see it, there isn't anyone I can trust, so I ain't saying a word."

Buddy rubbed her forehead. "How about telling the police? I can go with you and make sure they understand that you two need to stay together."

Rainey's jaw clenched. "No! We can't tell the police anything. I already know what they'll do. I've read about stories in the newspaper at the library where kids are taken from their parents and bad things happen. Not only that, but in the five cases I read about, they separated the kids because people wouldn't foster more than one kid at a time."

"Maybe it would be different for you," Buddy said. "There might be a family that would be happy to have both of you live with them."

"No way, Buddy. I can't risk that. You need to promise me you won't say anything to anybody."

Buddy patted Rainey's shoulder. "It's fine. I promise I won't say anything. Okay?"

***

Later that night, Buddy was sitting in a diner at the edge of town, far away from where anyone knew her.

"Hey, Buddy."

She looked up at the man approaching and gave him a faint smile. "Hi, Agent Lindquist."

The undercover detective sat in the booth across from her. "So, do you have any new information to share with me?"

Buddy's lips pressed together and she stared at her hands on the table in front of her. She'd been meeting Agent Lindquist, a drug enforcement officer, monthly for the past year, reporting anything suspicious she saw in and around Kensington, any information she thought might interest him. In return, the detective had promised to help her brother, who was in prison serving time for murder.

Buddy looked up and locked eyes with the detective. "There's this thing I need to talk to you about first."

"Oh, yeah. What's that?"

"In that house on West York Street, there are two little girls. One is thirteen and the other is four. I'm nervous the thirteen-year-old is gonna start using dope just to escape the shit that goes on in her house. So I have to know that they'll be okay. You know, like, if their parents get busted, you'd keep them together," Buddy said.

Agent Lindquist rubbed his fingers over his mustache. "This is where it always gets messy." He gave Buddy a sympathetic smile. "I'd like to help, but I can't promise you anything when it comes to kids getting placed. Sometimes these things are out of our hands." Lindquist leaned across the table. "I can promise you this—if we ever raid a house with little kids, I'll do the best that I can to keep them together, but I'm not going to lie, it's very difficult once these kids are removed from their parents and placed into foster care."

Buddy studied the detective. She trusted Agent Lindquist. He'd already done good things for her brother—most importantly, getting him a little extra protection in prison.

Lindquist sat back. "Hey. Buddy. I've always been honest with you. Here's the thing you need to consider. I've seen kids like the ones you're talking about. They live in houses overflowing with addicts. They're exposed to things that no kid should witness and are usually too young to understand. They're often neglected, hungry, and dirty. Most times we find they've been verbally, physically, or sexually abused. Bad shit can happen to them in that environment. Now, you need to ask yourself if those things are better or worse than these kids being placed in separate foster homes."

Buddy leaned back and looked up at the ceiling. "It's not that simple. This kid, the older one, she's special. I've known her for years. It'd kill her to be away from her sister. She's the only mom her little sister knows, and I promised her I wouldn't tell the cops anything about them."

"I get it, Buddy. But the work my department is doing is much bigger than two kids. What about all the kids dying from overdoses? What about all the corruption and prostitution in the city being caused by drug abuse?" He leaned forward across the table. "This isn't just about kids. This is about stopping these drug dealers from having safe places to move their dope. Dope that's killing people and ruining this city."

Buddy lifted her mug and took a mouthful of cold coffee. "I know, I know."

Agent Lindquist looked down at his hands and back at her. "Now, get me some information we can use to get these drug dealers off the streets. The DA is counting on us."

Buddy nodded and looked into Lindquist's face. She took in his green eyes and pale, white skin. He was a handsome man with a round face and brown hair almost to his shoulders. She placed her hand on top of his and took in the contrast of her brown skin against his whiter-than-white skin. A smile played on her lips as she met his gaze.

Buddy lowered her voice. "I know you're a good person. Please don't let me down with this one. These kids are caught in the path of destruction and I don't want them to go through any more shit. The older one is young and pretty, you know? Things can happen to her there. Like today, I walked in on that fucker, Freddy, groping her with her father sitting right there watching."

Lindquist cringed. Then he laced his fingers through hers. There had been sexual tension between them since the first time they met, right after Buddy's brother was arrested, but she knew Lindquist never would have acted on it on his own, and she wasn't too keen on getting romantically involved with a cop—it wasn't as though she lived the cleanest life either.

"You did the right thing telling me. I don't want you to worry." Lindquist gave her a steady smile. "We make a good team."

Buddy gently pulled her hand away and grabbed her purse. "I'll see you back here in a month?"

"Yeah, call me if anything comes up sooner."

Chapter Twenty-Two

Rainey was sleeping when a thumping downstairs woke her. She crept from her bedroom after making sure Ivy was still asleep and hesitantly went downstairs to find out what was happening.

She found a party spinning out of control. A group of people were standing in a circle around a keg of beer. Most were talking and laughing, while one girl in her twenties stood with her head hanging and an unlit cigarette dangling from her mouth. The sofa was overcrowded with people. Next to the sofa, she saw two men brawling over money. As she moved through the house, she passed clusters of people sitting in small circles. Some held lighters at the end of crack pipes. Others were injecting drugs directly into their bloodstream.

Rainey, who had grown used to the constant partying, was taken back by the sheer number of people in the house. She hurried to find her parents. Inside the kitchen, Peter and Miranda sat at the small table with men she'd never seen before.

"What are you doing in here?" Peter asked.

Rainey looked at her father. His hands were shaking and his forehead was moist with sweat. She knew the look. He needed a fix. Her eyes moved over to the three men; all of them had muscles bulging from their arms and necks. Rainey shrunk back and crossed her arms over her chest.

The largest of the men leaned forward and pointed his finger in her dad's face. "What the fuck's going on, Peter? Who's this kid and why is she still standing there?"

Rainey stood, frozen, as Peter got up and walked with jerky movements toward her while Miranda picked at her forearms.

"Hey, sorry, Jiggy," Peter babbled. "This is my kid and she was just leaving."

Rainey was surprised when her dad put his hand around the back of her neck and pushed her back toward the door. He leaned close to her ear. "Go back upstairs before you find yourself in a heap of shit," he breathed. "Do *not* fuck this up for us."

Rainey, more terrified by the man called Jiggy than the threat her father had made, rushed out of the kitchen, down the hall, and back up the stairs toward her bedroom. When she got to the door it was slightly ajar and she paused in the dark hallway, her heart hammering in her chest. She never left Ivy in the room unless she was certain the door was shut. She pushed the door open slowly and burst through it when she saw Freddy inside holding her sister in his arms.

The music from the first floor hammered in the background.

"What are you doing in here? Give me my sister," Rainey growled, adrenaline pumping through her veins.

Freddy wheeled around and stared at Rainey. His eyeballs were bulging beyond their sockets and he didn't blink. Rainey sucked in a loud breath and her hands flew up to her throat. Freddy's gaze left her eyes and wandered down to her bare feet.

"You're high. Give me my sister," Rainey said, trying to steady her shaky voice as she stepped forward. "Ivy doesn't like you near her. You're not allowed to touch her."

Freddy said nothing, and Rainey's insides ran cold, but she didn't back down. With a small space between them, she stretched out her arms to take Ivy from him. In one swift motion, he lifted Ivy higher and licked the child's cheek.

The little hairs on the nape of Rainey's neck stood tall. She crossed her arms over her chest to control the involuntary shaking working its way down her body.

"What do you want?" she asked, keeping her eyes on the child.

"Ah, finally the question I've been waiting for you to ask," he said. "See, the answer is simple. I want you and me to be friends. Special friends that trust each other and can keep each other's secrets. Do you think you can be that person?"

Rainey clutched her stomach and her breathing burst in and out. She didn't know what was happening, but given the whole hugging incident, she feared he wanted something sexual with her. "I . . . I . . . have no idea wha . . . what you're talking about. Just give me Ivy and leave us alone. Pleeease," she begged.

Rainey could no longer hide her fear, and her limbs shook uncontrollably. She reached her arms out again for Ivy, who had somehow, mercifully, stayed asleep during their exchange.

"What I'm talking about is you and me being together." He looked into Ivy's sleeping face. "Unless, of course, you'd rather your little sister be my special friend."

Rainey reached behind her and gripped the wall as the room spun. She steadied herself. *I will die before I leave Ivy alone with this monster. Pull yourself together,* she thought.

After several seconds Rainey found her footing again. Her chin trembled as she made eye contact with Freddy. "I'll be your friend, but only if you put my sister down and promise never to touch her again."

"That's what I thought," Freddy said in a flat voice. He laid Ivy back on the mound of clothes and turned back to Rainey. "Come over here."

Rainey looked at Ivy and took a few steps toward Freddy. The shaking was getting worse.

"Don't be scared," Freddy hissed in a low, steady voice.

Rainey took another step toward him and stopped. He quickly closed the gap between them, grabbed her around the waist, and pulled her body into his before she even realized what was happening. Instinctively, she twisted and jerked her body to break free from his embrace.

Freddy landed a hard slap across her cheek. Stunned, she froze. It was as though her brain couldn't control her body any longer.

He raised his eyebrows and sneered at her. "I don't mind it rough if you don't. My guess is you haven't done this before so you may want me to go easy the first time." He ripped her shirt in half, stuck out his tongue, and ran it between her developing breasts. "No more resisting tonight. We can get into the harder stuff another time."

Rainey had been overexposed to sex since she was a child. She often saw people having and giving oral sex in her house. She knew what Freddy wanted, and she was horror-stricken. Pressing her palm against his chest, she pushed him away, but he didn't budge.

"Leave me alone. Please, just let me go. I swear, I'll tell my parents if you try to do anything to me," she threatened, hoping to deter him.

Freddy threw his head back and let out a sinister laugh. "Who the hell do you think told me to come up here and take what I want? Your *parents*, as you call them. They owe me money . . . a lot of it. This is how they intend to pay me for *some* of what they owe."

Rainey blew out several short breaths. "They wouldn't do that," she said, her mind reeling.

"Well, I hate to be the one to tell ya, they did."

Chapter Twenty-Three

Freddy pushed Rainey to the ground and ripped her pajama bottoms and underwear off with one fierce tug, keeping his hand firmly over her mouth. She tried to scream, but it came out muffled.

In response, he pressed his hand over her mouth tighter and he forced himself inside of her.

Sharp, excruciating pain took over her body, she scratched and clawed until he slammed her head against the floor. Her whimpers and begging fell on deaf ears. Rainey withdrew inside of herself. Her mind plunged to a dark place where there was no light, no sound, and no feeling at all.

Freddy raped the teen for twenty minutes. They were the longest twelve hundred seconds of her life. When he finished, he laid his deadweight on top of her. The weight and width of his body, consuming hers, constricted her chest, and she labored to fill her lungs with air until finally Freddy heaved himself off her and she leaped up. She ran to the other side of the bedroom and pressed her back against a wall. He cackled, watching her fearfully scurry to put distance between them. It seemed to Rainey like he deliberately took his time dressing. She slid down the wall, closed her eyes, and pulled her knees up to her chest, trying to ignore the burning between her legs.

"What is it, little girl?" Freddy said, startling her by how close he'd gotten. "You wanna go again? I think you like me."

Rainey just looked away and shook her head. When he left, still laughing, she rolled into a tight ball and wept. She reached down and her fingers glided over the swollen area, checking that he hadn't torn her in two. Rainey pressed the palms of her hands to her eyes to ease the pain behind them. The shrill ringing in her ears from having her head smashed against the floor was piercing. The inability to fight off her rapist made her feel inadequate, weak, and ultimately violated. She felt used and dirty and damaged. Her thoughts were not formed or cohesive—she moved from one negative thought to the next.

Unable to process what had happened, she lay in a zombie like state, cold and naked until she heard movement. Her heart started thumping, thinking Freddy was coming back again, but when she opened her eyes, Ivy was standing over her. Rainey had almost forgotten she was there. The child's eyebrows were raised and pulled together, and her mouth hung open as if a scream had tried to pass but nothing could escape.

"No, Ivy. Turn away, don't look at me," Rainey cried.

Ivy moved a few feet to her right, grabbed a T-shirt from the floor, and draped it over Rainey's shivering body. She sat down at Rainey's head and leaned into her older sister. "Are you sick?"

Rainey's face was wet with anguished tears. "Yeah," she managed. "I'm sick."

"You need medicine?"

She shook her head. She forced herself to sit up, pulled on the T-shirt, grabbed her pants, and pulled them on quickly. "Something bad happened to me and I got hurt."

"You need a Band-Aid?"

Rainey covered her face. "No, Ivy. I need to lie down. Will you lay with me?"

She moved toward the pile of clothing and Ivy snuggled in against her.

"You got hurted?" Ivy asked.

"Yeah, I got hurt," she mumbled.

"That man hurt you?"

Rainey's eyes opened wide as another round of nausea circulated through her system. There was no way Ivy could process what just happened, and she hoped the child didn't witness her being raped as she asked the next question. "Did you see him hurt me?"

Ivy nodded.

"Oh, I'm so sorry," Rainey sobbed.

As the two sisters lay together, Rainey replayed the rape over in her head. The more times she played it the less human she believed herself to be. For her, being pinned down and raped was like ripping her soul from her body. After a while, she forced herself to stop. *I have to take care of Ivy,* she thought.

With Ivy's steady breath against her chest, she cried silent tears, steeped in loss and sorrow. Because of Freddy and her parents, Rainey had lost the only thing that had ever belonged to her. But even worse was the thought of Freddy doing it to her again.

Chapter Twenty-Four

The next morning, Rainey hobbled into the bathroom. Her body was stiff and she had a burning pain while she urinated. When she wiped and saw blood on the toilet paper, her heart quickened.

Not knowing what else to do and desperate for help, she rushed from the bathroom to her parents' bedroom. She threw the door open so hard it banged into the wall.

"What the fuck?" Peter yelled jumping out of his bed, glaring at his daughter.

Rainey glowered at him with disgust unable to fully believe her parents could be that evil.

"Freddy raped me last night! He said you two let him, and now I'm bleeding!" Rainey yelled.

Peter gave Miranda a shove. "Get up and deal with your daughter."

Miranda grunted as she heaved her body up. "What's wrong now, Rainey?" she asked in a sleepy, disinterested tone.

"Like you don't already know? Freddy raped me last night," she sobbed. "I'm bleeding."

Miranda ran her fingers through her greasy hair. "Stop being so dramatic. Freddy didn't *rape* you. We owed him some money and we told him you'd give him a spin. It ain't rape if he had permission."

Rainey's mind spun—there was no escaping her parents' depraved decisions. "You don't get to say he can have sex with me. Nobody gets to do that except me."

The couple gave her blank stares, unaffected by her sorrow and outrage.

Her arms were flailing as she screamed, "You're both rotten and you never should've had kids! All I am to you is a way to buy your drugs! You're sick, you're both sick in the head!"

Miranda laughed. "Oh, stop it! Look, you were gonna lose your damn cherry at some point. We may as well get some money for it."

Rainey sucked in a breath and shook her head. Hate for her mother surged through her. "You're crazy," she bawled.

"Listen to me, *Rainey*. You're not a baby. You're thirteen years old. I lost my virginity at fourteen. It's not a big deal. If you had played it right, Freddy would've probably given you a few extra dollars for your time."

Rainey brought a shaky hand up to her forehead. Her mouth moved, but the words wouldn't form. She let out an unsteady whimper and, looking down at the floor, took calculated breaths. "I'm your kid. How do you sell your kid to some dirtball?"

Miranda flopped back on the bed next to Peter. "We're done talking. I need to get some sleep."

Hopelessness washed over Rainey. Her mind was jaded with disturbing thoughts as she walked out of her parents' room and back into her bedroom, where Ivy was playing with her doll.

"Rainey," Ivy called out happily, "I hungry. I wanna eat now."

Rainey's heart lightened somewhat as she took in Ivy's pure joy at seeing her. A reminder she was still human and, more importantly, loved. "Yeah, okay. Let's get something to eat."

As Rainey and Ivy headed for the front door, Buddy rushed from the sofa. "Hey, Rainey. Wait up."

Rainey stopped and looked at Buddy with a blank expression.

"Are you okay? You look like you've been crying. Did something happen?"

Ivy looked up at Buddy. "Rainey was sick last night. She got a boo-boo right here," the child said, pointing between her legs.

Buddy moved closer and ran her hand gently over Rainey's hair. "What happened?"

"What does it matter?" she asked, feeling distant and, worthless. "There's no one who can change anything in my life."

"That's not true," Buddy said. "Tell me what happened."

She looked down at her little sister. "She already told you—Freddy raped me last night."

Buddy gasped. "Fuck me. All right, listen, there are places you can go. People you can talk to." She studied the girl for a moment, and Rainey's cheeks were on fire under her gaze.

Buddy opened her arms and pulled the girl to her. "I'm so sorry this happened to you. We have to stop it from ever happening again." She put the girl at arm's length and looked into her face. "You have to tell someone. I know it sounds scary, but I'll go to the police with you."

That Buddy believed her sent a ripple of relief through Rainey. But she bristled at the suggestion of telling her story to the police.

"No . . . no cops. I won't take any chances with Ivy—you know this already." She looked down at her little sister as tears fell from her eyes.

"Don't cry," Ivy said, patting her sister's leg. "It's gonna be okay," she soothed, repeating the words Rainey often said to her.

Rainey bent down and put her arms around her little sister. "Don't worry . . . nothing's going to happen to you." She looked up at Buddy, lifted her brows and opened her eyes widely, trying to convey a subtle message to stop talking in front of Ivy. "Just let it be. It's over."

"We can't let it be. He needs to be punished for what he did to you," Buddy said with more persistence.

Rainey looked away, stood, and took Ivy's hand. "The only thing I care about is getting away from him. That's all."

Buddy's chin dropped to her chest. "I wish I could take care of you two. I just don't have the money I . . . I have to do something to help you. This isn't right."

Slowly, Rainey reached for the young woman's hand. She knew it wasn't Buddy's fault and that she was trying to help them.

Rainey sighed. "I know you want to do something to make it stop. If I think of anything you can do, I'll tell you. Okay?"

Without waiting for a response, Rainey led Ivy out the front door. As they ambled along the crumbled sidewalk of their block, the small child chatted away.

"Where are we goin'?" she asked.

"We're going to the library. Remember, the nice lady who gave us her lunch?" Rainey asked.

Ivy's eyes lit up and she nodded. "I liked her."

"Yeah, I liked her too. I hope she's there today. If she is, maybe she'll give us something to eat."

Inside the library, Rainey took a quick scan as they entered. Sandy wasn't behind the counter, and her heart fell in her chest.

"Oh, no, Ivy." Rainey screeched. "Sandy isn't here."

Ivy looked around and her eyes lit up. "There she is," the child said, pointing to a table across the room.

"Good catch," she said, then pulled her sister toward the woman.

As they got closer, Rainey realized how awful they both looked. Neither of them had bathed in more than a week because the gas to the house was shut off for nonpayment and there was no hot water. She could still smell the rank odor of Freddy on her and was paranoid that Sandy would smell it too and know what it meant. Still, Sandy was her only hope of getting Ivy fed that day. Hungry and exhausted, Rainey pushed her tangled hair behind her ears and walked up to the librarian.

"Hi. Sandy, right?"

Sandy turned to look at them and the smile fell from her lips. Her eyes widened as she took in the gaunt, ashen faces of the neglected Paxton sisters.

"Oh, look who it is," Sandy said in an uplifting voice. "How have the two of you been?"

Rainey pulled on the hem of her shirt. "Actually, we haven't been doing that great. We're . . . we're really hungry and thought maybe—"

Sandy held her palms up. "Say no more. You two sit down and I'll be right back."

This time Sandy sat with the girls as they ate. Rainey kept quiet, lost in the dark remembrance of the previous night, while Ivy yakked away.

When they finished eating everything Sandy had given them, Rainey stood, feeling suddenly awkward, as though the librarian could read her mind and see the memories of Freddy raging in her head.

"Well, thank you for the food," she said stiffly.

Sandy pulled at the bottom of her hair. "Um, you know, if you'd like to use the bathroom to wash up that would be okay. I'm not saying you *need* to or anything, but if you wanted to clean up in there that would be fine."

Rainey's cheeks flushed. "That would be nice."

As the two young girls disappeared into the women's bathroom, Sandy watched them. Then she whispered to herself, "You poor babies."

Chapter Twenty-Five

Inside the library bathroom, Rainey undressed Ivy, washed her in the sink, and redressed her. Then Rainey washed her own face, hands and arms. Soaking a mound of paper towels with soap and water Rainey turned to Ivy. "You stay right here. Don't move."

Rainey went into a stall and took her clothes off. She looked down at the bruising on her hips and thighs. The night before flashed through her mind again. She closed her eyes and shook her head trying to loosen the memories, hoping to make them vanish. With the soapy paper towels, she gently attempted to wash Freddy off of her. Every stroke was like sandpaper on a brush burn. The soap stung at the swelled skin, but she didn't stop until she was clean. Then she sat on the toilet and cried, feeling that no matter how hard she scrubbed, she'd never get him off of her.

When the girls left the bathroom, Rainey tried to leave quietly, but Sandy rushed over to them before they made it to the exit.

"Girls?" she said. "Hold on. I wanted to mention a place where you can get food."

Sandy held a pamphlet out and Rainey took it, grateful, but too wrapped up in her thoughts to care. "Thank you."

"I don't want you to misunderstand," Sandy said. "I'm more than happy to help you out. Anytime you need something to eat, you can come and see me. But this is a way for you to have more consistent meals."

"Okay, thanks," Rainey said, wanting to leave.

Sandy crossed her arms over her chest. "Look. I'm sorry. But I have to ask. Are you and Ivy safe? Do you have a place to live?"

Rainey nodded, not about to divulge any secrets to the kind woman that she barely knew. "Sure we do. We live in a house with our parents."

Ivy stood on her tiptoes to get closer to Sandy. "My mommy and daddy have to take medicine 'cause they're sick. They have to take lots of needles. I hate needles."

The hair stood up on the back of Rainey's neck, and there was a sudden urge to flee.

Sandy's mouth dropped open and her eyes shot from Ivy to Rainey. The librarian turned back to Ivy. "I'm sorry to hear that. I hope your mommy and daddy feel better soon."

Ivy nodded.

Sandy looked at Rainey again with sadness in her eyes. "Are you two going to be all right?"

"Yeah. Of course. We'll be fine. Thanks for the food and for letting us clean up. It's just that . . . well, my father just lost his job and we're having a hard time right now."

"I understand. When parents lose their jobs, it can be hard on the whole family. But I'll tell you what. How about if you and Ivy come see me tomorrow. I can bring in a change of clothes for you?"

Rainey shook her head. "No, thanks. If we show up at home in new clothes it'll make my dad feel bad and my parents will wonder why you got them for us and all. It . . . it wouldn't be good."

"Are you sure?" Sandy asked.

"Yeah, I'm sure. My parents would be embarrassed and wonder what I told you that made you bring us stuff."

"Right, I see. Well, if there's anything else you need, you let me know."

"Sure. I'll let you know. Come on, Ivy."

At the door, Rainey looked over her shoulder at Sandy. "Thanks again."

***

Rainey stayed out of the house for most of the day. She didn't want to go back. If she never had to see her parents again, she would consider herself lucky. As she and Ivy walked miles across the neighborhood, her thoughts drifted to Freddy, and her anger was replaced with fear. *What will I do if Freddy tries to come after me again?* The question buzzed around her brain and filled her with terror. Before Freddy had raped her, she didn't think her life could get much worse, but now she knew she'd been wrong.

In the late afternoon, as the sun was setting, Rainey knew they had to go home. From the outside, the house looked dark and cold, with its boarded-up windows. Once inside, she took her little sister up to their bedroom, where they quickly buried themselves under a pile of clothes. Rainey pulled out a book and read it to Ivy until the child's eyes grew heavy.

Once Ivy was asleep, Rainey put her hands behind her head and stared at the ceiling. Her mind raced with thoughts of Freddy, wondering if he was coming back that night. *Don't be afraid,* she told herself, but the inner dialogue fell short.

Since she hadn't started her period yet, Rainey believed she couldn't get pregnant; she had learned that much when she was in school. But then her thoughts turned to worry about sexually transmitted diseases she'd read about in a health book. After breaking into a cold sweat, she kicked the pile of clothes off of her and turned onto her side. Needing to stop the morbid thoughts, she closed her eyes tightly, trying to shut out the darkness that filled her entire being.

In the blackness of the bedroom, Rainey listened to the intense buzz of noise downstairs. She was focusing on the sounds when a bang on her door made her jump. She sat up quickly and her heart hammered in her chest.

"Go away!" she shrieked, watching in terror as the knob turned slowly and the door creaked open.

When Buddy's face peeked around the door, the air in Rainey's lungs gushed out of her mouth.

"Can I come in?"

Rainey nodded as tears in her eyes spilled over.

"Oh, I'm sorry. I didn't mean to startle you," Buddy said, turning on the lamplight and moving toward Rainey. "Freddy just got here, and I, um . . . I thought maybe I could just sleep in here with the two of you tonight."

Rainey leaped out of her spot next to Ivy and threw herself into Buddy's arms. "Yes. You can sleep in here. I was so scared that you were him."

"I know. That's why I came up here."

Rainey laid her head on Buddy's chest and allowed herself a mournful cry.

Buddy rocked her. "You're going to make it through this."

Rainey nodded as her tears of shameful distress soaked the front of Buddy's shirt.

Chapter Twenty-Six

Still in Buddy's embrace, Rainey let herself relax. She looked up and gave the girl a weak smile.

"Buddy," she said softly, averting her gaze, "thanks for coming up here."

"Hey, it's totally fine. I want to ask you a question if that's okay."

Rainey nodded.

"Did Freddy use a condom?"

Rainey shook her head. All of her thoughts of worry flooded back. "Why?"

Buddy's brows pulled together. "He's a fucking asshole." She hesitated for a few seconds to check her anger. "Is it safe to say you ain't on birth control?"

"No, I'm not. I haven't gotten my period yet."

Buddy nodded. "Good. I didn't know for sure. I got my period when I was twelve. So at least we know you can't get pregnant yet."

"I would die if I got pregnant from that mutant asshole. I hate him so much," she cried throwing her head back and grimacing.

Buddy shook her head, then leaned back against the wall. "I know, baby, I know. This ain't something you ought to be worrying about, but we gotta think this through. I'm still a little worried about STDs. Do you know what those are?"

Rainey bit her bottom lip, scared to hear the words out loud. "Yeah, I'm worried about that too."

"Hey, look, there are things we can do. I'll take you to one of the clinics in Kensington and see if we can have some kind of test done."

"Won't we need my mom or dad there?" she asked.

Buddy bit at the cuticle around her index finger. "Oh, yeah. You're probably right. I'll talk to your mom about it."

"Don't bother. My parents told Freddy he could have sex with me. If they cared about me at all they would've never let him do it." Rainey, agitated talking about her parents, stood and walked to the other side of the bedroom. "My mom said I was being too dramatic and that I can't say that asshole raped me because her and my dad gave him permission."

Buddy's head jerked back as if she'd been slapped across the face. "Is that true?"

"Yeah, Buddy. I wouldn't lie to you."

Buddy nodded again. "Of course you wouldn't lie. I didn't mean it that way. All I mean is . . . your parents are big, fat fucks. I'm sorry to say that to you, but they're disgusting. I ain't talking no shit either, I mean it."

Rainey placed both hands over her heart. "Thanks for looking out for me and Ivy tonight. I'm really glad that you're mad at my mom and dad for what they did to me. It makes me feel like somebody cares."

***

Over the next two months, Buddy slept in the girls' bedroom with them. Freddy had stayed out while she was in with the girls, but he was becoming more aggressive with his words. One morning, on her way to the kitchen, Rainey stopped abruptly at the sound of Freddy's voice.

"Listen, Peter," he was saying. "I don't know what the hell is going on here but we had a deal. You either pay me the money you owe me or you pay me in another way. That bitch who sleeps in your kids' room every night needs to go."

Peter let out a sigh. "Yeah, all right, don't get yourself all worked up." There were a few seconds of silence.

Rainey hoped her father was reconsidering.

Then he said, "Miranda, take care of Buddy. Unless you wanna go out and earn the money we need to pay Freddy, you need to fix this."

"Yeah, yeah," Miranda grumbled. "I'll take care of it. But listen, Freddy, this ain't no free-for-all. We gotta figure out how many times you get to have Rainey to pay off our debt. Understand?"

Rainey could have barfed in the hallway. She turned quickly and tiptoed back upstairs.

Later that night, when Buddy showed up in her room, Rainey shoved her hands into her front pockets, knowing she had to tell her what she'd overheard.

"Things are about to get worse," she said. "I heard my mom and dad talking this morning. My mom's gonna do something so that you can't stay in here every night."

"I swear I'll do everything I can to be here," Buddy said.

Rainey shook her head softly. "Freddy's coming for me again. We both know it." The girl's hands shook and she paced the room. Her anxiety had turned to sheer panic. The only thing she wanted to do was get as far away from the perverted man as possible. "I was thinking that you could take me and Ivy away from here. I can get a job to help pay for things."

Buddy squeezed Rainey's shoulder. "It's not that easy. I can barely take care of myself. Even if I could provide for all of us, that would make me a kidnapper. I want to do more. I really, really do. We talked about this before, but we have to consider going to the police."

Rainey's shoulders slumped as she gave Buddy a bitter smile. "No, I can't. I have Ivy to think about."

Buddy forcibly pulled her lips into a smile. "Hey," she said. "Ivy is gonna start school this September. Right?"

Rainey looked away as her eyes welled. There was nothing left for her to do but accept that Buddy couldn't help them.

"Well," Buddy said. "I was thinking you could go back to school too since she'll be away from this shithole all day. That's good news, right?"

"Yeah. Sure," Rainey muttered, knowing that was only a temporary solution to her ongoing nightmare that didn't provide any immediate relief.

Ivy spoke up from behind them. "I'm gonna go to school," she said.

Buddy leaned over and gently touched Ivy's cheek. "You're going to get so smart in school."

Ivy removed her thumb from her mouth and yelled, "I already smart, Buddy!"

Buddy giggled. "Yes, you sure are, but when you go to school, you're gonna get even smarter."

"Rainey told me I get to eat at school."

Buddy beamed at the child. "Rainey's right. You will get to eat at school, you'll get dessert every day too." She turned to Rainey. "Honestly, this whole thing is sickening. I don't know how you two can keep going on. I know it's horrible for you to live here."

"It's not like we have much of a choice," Rainey mumbled.

Buddy drew in a deep breath through her nose to steady her anger. She had strong feelings for the kids, a need to nurture them, and only wanted the best for the girls.

"Yeah, you guys weren't very lucky, that's true," Buddy said. "Hey, listen, I've been meaning to ask you if you've noticed Jiggy here when I'm not around. You remember him?"

Rainey ran her fingers through the ends of her tangled hair. "Yeah, how can anyone forget him? He's so gross. Mostly he sends those other two big guys and like one day a week he comes with them. They're such goons. They never talk other than to tell my dad how much money he owes Jiggy."

"Have you heard your parents talking about him? Like . . . where he lives or anything?"

"No. Whenever I know they're in the house I take Ivy to the park. Those guys scare me even more than Freddy. Jiggy looks at me the same way."

"It's probably good that you're scared of them. They're bad people. The only thing they care about is making lots of money from other people's hardships."

Rainey tilted her head to the side and gazed at the older girl. "Do *you* ever talk to Jiggy?"

"Oh, hell, no. I don't want nothing to do with him. I don't take the hard drugs that he's pushing. Dealing with Jiggy is scary shit and no one that stays here feels safe around him. He's like a volcano ready to erupt . . . he's unpredictable."

"Right. So, of course, my stupid parents are buying their drugs from him. You know what really scares me?"

"What?"

"Well, I heard Jiggy tell my parents if they don't pay him on time, he'd make their lives miserable. He said he'd cut off my father's fingers and all my mother's toes. My mom and dad were so high I don't even think they heard him say it. If something bad happened to my parents, I don't know what is gonna happen to me and Ivy."

"Really?" Buddy crossed her arms over her chest. "Because they do so much to help you now?"

"No, but at least I get to keep Ivy and take care of her. She's all that matters to me."

Buddy's arms dropped to her sides. "You have too many things to worry about for a teenager. I know it sucks, but I think you're one tough girl."

Rainey pulled on her sneakers and tied the laces. "Hey. I was thinking. Is there any way you could help me get to the place where my Aunt Sophie is living? I found a paper in my mom's top drawer with the name and address where she's living. I got some bus schedules and mapped out how we can get there. I just need money for the bus."

Ivy glanced at Rainey. "I wanna go on a bus. Can I come on the bus with you, Rainey?"

Rainey snatched her baby sister up and hugged her tightly. "Of course you're going with me. I'd never leave you here alone, silly."

Ivy giggled. "Yeah, I silly."

Rainey turned back to Buddy. "So can you help us?"

"I'll do my best." Buddy placed her hand over her heart. "I swear."

Chapter Twenty-Seven

The next night, Buddy knocked on Rainey's bedroom door before waltzing in. She gave the teenager a huge smile. "Today was a good day," she said, holding out a wad of cash. "Here you go."

Rainey took the money from her. She counted it and hugged Buddy. "Wow. Thank you so much. But this is more than we need. The bus won't cost this much."

Buddy swung her hips and nodded. "That's right. It took me some fast talking, but I managed to get more. There's extra money so you two can get something to eat."

"I'm lucky to have you as a friend," Rainey breathed. "You're the best."

***

The next day, Rainey and Ivy stepped onto the first of three buses that would take them to the care facility in Ridley Park, a small town about twenty miles from Kensington, where their aunt was living. After an hour and a half, the two girls arrived at the facility. Inside the front entrance, they were met by a cheery woman with gray hair and wearing bright pink lipstick.

"Hello, girls. Can I help you?" she asked.

"Yes. We're here to see our aunt Sophie," Rainey said. her voice quivering.

The receptionist pursed her lips. "Okay. What's your aunt's last name?"

"Andersen," Rainey said. "Sophie Andersen."

"Oh! I didn't know Ms. Andersen had any family."

Rainey was confused, and her eyebrows met. "My mom has been here to visit her, but she wouldn't let me come."

The woman stared at the girl and shook her head gently. "No, I'm sorry. There must be some confusion."

Rainey thought back to the times she had asked her mother to visit her aunt, and Miranda had said Sophie was doing fine but wasn't up for visitors. "It's true. My mom told me she's been here to see her . . ." Her voice trailed off, realizing her mother lied.

"Yes, well, I'm certain Ms. Andersen will be happy to see you," the woman said, smiling again. "All of our patients are happy to have visitors. You can go through the door behind me and stop at the nurses' station. Someone will bring you in to see her."

Grateful she had asked no more questions, Rainey led Ivy through the door and toward the nurses' station. It was empty when they arrived, and as they waited, Rainey thought about how rotten her mother had been by never coming to see her aunt. Worse, how stupid she'd been to believe what her mother told her.

"Hello, girls. I'm Monica," a nurse said in a high-pitched voice as she approached. "Can I help you?"

"We're here to see our aunt," Rainey said. "Her name is Sophie Andersen."

Monica rubbed her chin with her thumb and index finger. "Oh, how nice. You two can follow me and I'll take you to see her."

Rainey followed Monica down a long hallway, trying not to look inside the rooms as they passed. When they reached Sophie's room, Rainey's excitement mounted as she imagined how happy her aunt would be to see her. Rainey was hopeful she and Ivy could live with their aunt. In Rainey's mind she dreamed of taking care of Sophie so she would not need to stay in the nursing home.

When Monica stopped midway down the hall at one of the rooms, they all entered, and Rainey gawked at the frail woman lying in a fetal position. She moved closer, fixated on the spot where the neck of her nightgown hung low and her collarbone protruded. Was this really Aunt Sophie? The vibrant and beautiful woman who had once been her savior? Rainey shifted her gaze around the room at all the pictures her aunt had framed of her and hung on the walls. She spotted a picture she recognized and walked up to it. It was the last picture her aunt had taken of her, wearing the straw hat. *That was the day we said good-bye,* Rainey thought. She touched the frame, recalling the pain and anguish of those final moments.

"Is that you?" Ivy asked.

"Yeah." Rainey pointed to the three walls. "These are all me." She turned and looked at the nurse, who smiled at her.

Rainey stepped closer to the bed and looked into her aunt's face. The skin around Sophie's eyes and mouth hung loose. Her hair was thin and her scalp was peeling. Rainey looked closer to be sure it was her aunt. A twinge of nausea stuck in the girl's belly.

Monica stood at the bed next to Rainey. "Sophie, there are two gorgeous girls here to see you. Can you open your eyes?"

When Sophie's eyes remained shut, Rainey's expectant smile vanished. The anticipation of her aunt rescuing them was diminished.

"So you're Rainey," Monica said, glancing at the pictures on the walls.

"Yeah. I'm her niece, and this is Ivy, she's my little sister. She was born after Aunt Sophie came here."

Monica smiled warmly. "It's nice to meet you both." The nurse pulled the covers over Sophie's shoulders and flattened down her hair. "When Sophie first came to live here, she spoke of you all the time. You were like her own daughter. She loved looking at your pictures."

Tears pricked Rainey's eyes. "How is she?"

Monica rubbed her hand down the arm of the sleeping woman. "She's had a rough time. She's lost so much of herself."

Rainey held onto Ivy's hand tighter while she leaned over the bed.

"Sophie?" the nurse said. "Rainey's here to visit you."

There was no response.

Rainey wiped her free hand on her jeans to dry the sweat before she looked at Monica.

The nurse continued to rub her hand gently up and down the woman's arm. "Sophie? You're going to want to wake up, sweetie. It's your niece Rainey."

Sophie's eyes fluttered open, and a smile spread over Rainey's face. "Aunt Sophie. It's me."

Sophie's eyes were open but unfocused.

"Can she see me?" Rainey asked Monica.

"I don't think so. Your aunt Sophie hasn't spoken in a long time. Within two years of coming here, her speech was gone. But maybe if you just let her look at you for a while, she'll recognize you." Monica pulled a chair next to the bed. "You two sit here and I'll come back and check on you in a bit. You should talk to her. I think she would like that."

Alone with Sophie, Rainey studied her face. She sat on the edge of the chair while Ivy scooted in behind her.

"You look different, Aunt Sophie. Your hair is shorter and you have lots of lines on your face now, but not in a bad way; they make you look smarter."

Rainey kissed the top of Ivy's head, stood, and held onto the bars of the hospital bed.

"Aunt Sophie? Can you hear me?"

Sophie stared straight ahead.

Rainey put her arms around her sister. "This is your niece Ivy. She was born after you came here." She leaned over the side of the bed as Ivy scooched off of the chair and stood beside her sister. She slid her small hand inside Rainey's and stuck her free thumb in her mouth.

"Rainey, I scared," Ivy whispered.

Rainey bent down and looked into Ivy's eyes. "You don't need to be scared. This is our Aunt Sophie, and I know she would love you very much. She took care of me when I was little . . . like how I take care of you, but better."

Ivy pulled her wet, wrinkled thumb from her mouth. She put her face closer to the older woman. "Aunt Soapy?" she said, then turned to Rainey. "How's come she won't talk to me?"

Rainey gave her a gentle smile. "Aunt Sophie's sick."

"Oh." Ivy sighed, putting her thumb back in her mouth. She stopped sucking, and still watching Sophie, she said, "Is she gonna get better, Rainey?"

"No, Ivy. She can't get better. But you know what?"

"What?" the child asked, her eyes widened.

"Aunt Sophie was the best. She was fun and always held me tight when I was scared. She's Mom's sister just like I'm your sister."

"Oh. Did she take medicine like Mommy?"

Rainey shook her head. "Aunt Sophie didn't need any medicine. She was perfect without medicine."

Rainey pulled the plastic chair closer to the bed and sat down. "Aunt Sophie, I wish you were still here with me. Things have gotten really bad.

Anyway, I had to come and see you. I wanted you to meet Ivy. Aunt Sophie, I was raped by some guy my parents owed money to."

Just then, Sophie's eyes widened and Rainey stopped speaking.

"Can you hear me?" Rainey asked, daring to hope just a little bit.

Chapter Twenty-Eight

"Aunt Sophie? Can you see me? Can you hear me?" Rainey asked breathlessly. "Blink once if you know I'm here."

There was no response; Sophie's eyes stayed open.

"Come on, Aunt Sophie. You can do it. Me and Ivy need you. Our life is all messed up. It's awful at home. You have to help us."

Rainey closed her eyes and sobbed while Ivy looked up at her with wide eyes and a thumb in her mouth. "Don't cry, Rainey," she mumbled. "I want you to feel better. Okay?" the child said, grabbing her sister's hand.

Rainey pulled herself together and lifted her head. "I'm okay. I just need Aunt Sophie to know what's happening because I've been really sad lately. Why don't you sit in the chair? I'm almost finished."

Ivy climbed onto the plastic chair and Rainey gave her an old baby doll she'd picked from the trash a few months prior. The doll's hair had fallen out and the previous owner had poked holes in her eyes. But it was Ivy's baby, and she hugged the doll to her chest as she plugged up her mouth with her soggy thumb.

Rainey stood over her aunt. She had a burning desire to let Sophie know everything, even if she wasn't certain her aunt could hear her. In a shaky voice, she said, "Since that man raped me I'm scared all the time, and I don't know what to do. I'm afraid he's going to come back and do it again." She lowered her mouth to her aunt's ear and whispered, "I'm so scared he'll do the same thing to Ivy."

Rainey brushed her aunt's hair with her fingers. "I was thinking of taking Ivy and going to find somewhere else to live, but I don't have any money and I'm not sure where we'd go."

She sat next to Ivy again and, slumped against the back of the chair. She closed her arms around her little sister. "It's no use. She can't hear me."

"'Cause she's sick," Ivy said.

"Yeah, you're right. Are you ready to get going?"

The child nodded vigorously, slid off the chair, and walked toward the door.

Rainey stood over her aunt, then leaned down and kissed the top of her head. "I love you, Aunt Sophie. I'll come and visit you again, I'm not sure when, but I'll be back . . . I promise."

After eating dinner at a deli, the girls got on a bus for their journey home. Ivy was sitting next to the window and pointing things out. Rainey smiled and nodded, but all she could think about was how her strong, vibrant aunt had become fragile, weak, and unresponsive. Sadness filled the space in her stomach usually reserved for fear.

"Rainey?" the child said, pushing her older sister's leg.

"Yeah?"

"Will you always take care of me?"

"Of course I will."

"'Cause Mommy and Daddy don't?" she asked.

"Nope. It's because I love you more than anything in the world," she told her.

Ivy beamed. "And 'cause I love you back?"

"That's right. You and me are stuck together forever. Because we love each other and we wouldn't have it any other way."

"Rainey, how come we can never play downstairs at our house?"

Rainey ruffled Ivy's hair. "Because too many people live there with us."

"Why does so many people have to live there?"

"Because Mom and Dad are selfish. They only care about doing things for themselves, but that's okay because you and me can do our own thing. Right?"

The child grimaced. "Does that mean Mommy and Daddy don't love us no more?"

Rainey wanted to reiterate that her parents were selfish pricks who didn't even love each other let alone their children, but she knew better. "Of course they love us. Especially you. Everyone loves you because you're adorable and happy and smart and strong."

Rainey gently pressed her fingers in Ivy's armpits and tickled the child until she shrieked with delight.

***

That night, when the girls were almost asleep, the bedroom door opened. In the darkness, Rainey breathed a sigh of relief that Buddy had finally gotten there. It was always impossible to sleep, at least deeply, until she showed up.

Rainey turned onto her side and opened her eyes, allowing them to adjust to the dark. "Hey Buddy," she whispered in a raspy voice.

A few seconds passed and Rainey leaned up on her elbow.

"Buddy? Buddy? Is that you?"

Rainey listened intently, but she was met by an eerie silence. Then she heard heavy breathing followed by the sound of a belt being unbuckled. She jumped from the floor and darted toward the door, but before she could make it a fist smashed into her face and she was lying on the floor, unconscious.

Chapter Twenty-Nine

When Rainey came to, the first thing she felt was the weight of his body on top of her, how his pelvis was jabbing her into the floor. Searing pain shot through her groin. Once she regained clarity of what was happening, she punched his hairy, sweaty back as hard as she could, but it didn't seem to bother him. Then she clamped her teeth down on his shoulder until she tasted his blood. He stopped long enough to clamp his large, thick fingers around her throat, squeezing until the flow of air to her lungs was closed off.

"You fucking bite me again and I'll kill you and that stupid kid over there," Freddy growled. Then he released his hand from her neck and she gasped for air. "Now I need to start all over again, 'cause your little tantrum made me lose my rhythm. Stupid bitch."

Rainey's eyes were bugging out of her head in panic. "Just leave me alone. Please," she said, trying to look around for Ivy but unable to move her head. "Buddy's coming and she's going to catch you."

Freddy grunted. "Your little friend Buddy ain't coming tonight. I made sure your parents turned her away. Took me a while to strike a deal with those two idiots, but I finally did."

Anticipating the horror that would follow, Rainey swallowed hard to push her bad feelings into her gut. Knowing she had no chance, she relented, went limp, and laid under him without yelling or moving or begging. Her thoughts and emotions slipped deep inside her body, where she hid until Freddy finished with a loud, gurgled grunt.

When Rainey was alone again, she stared up at the ceiling of the dark, eerie room until she fell off into a deep, dreadful sleep. She dreamed of being trapped under a fallen building. She couldn't get out and no one could hear her screams for help. She clawed and pushed at the cement blocks but couldn't move them. Then a feeling of finality draped over her and it was clear there was no escape from her fate. She woke with a start and a few frightening minutes passed before Rainey slid into a dreamless state.

The next morning, Rainey woke in the same spot where she had stopped fighting her predator. She sat up slowly and found her underwear. Ivy was still sleeping as she slipped out of the room and set out to find her parents.

"Mom?"

Miranda jerked her head toward the door. Her arm was tied off with a belt and Peter was slouched over her, sticking a needle in her arm.

"What's your problem, Rainey? Can't you see that me and your dad are busy?"

"Damn it," Peter huffed. "I need to try your leg. The fucking veins in your arms suck."

Rainey moved farther into the room. "Mom. We need to talk. I need you to tell Freddy to back off. Please. I'll go out and get a job or something if you need money that bad."

Miranda ignored her, tilted her head back, lifted her hand with a cigarette between two stiff fingers, and took a long drag. Then she reached down and pulled her pant leg up, kicked off one shoe, and plucked her sock off as Peter stood by, waiting.

"Go ahead, babe," she said. "If you can't get a vein in my leg, try my toes."

Rainey cringed. Her parents looked like they were part of a freak show. "Can you two just stop for a minute?"

Peter held the syringe in midair.

"Oh, for fuck's sake, Rainey. What? What do you want?" Miranda barked.

Tears fueled by anger trickled down her cheeks. "I just told you. I want you and Dad to tell Freddy to leave me alone."

Miranda snorted. "He paid Buddy's fee for the night and he wanted to sleep in her spot in your room. That's a lot of dough—I don't think you'd be able to get a job making that kind of money."

"Mom, Look at me. He punched me in the face and then he put his hand around my neck and squeezed until I couldn't breathe. He almost killed me."

Miranda glanced at her daughter's face. "Stop being so theatrical. He didn't kill you or even almost kill you. He wouldn't do that. Freddy's a slob, but he's a decent guy."

Bewildered and aggravated, Rainey clenched her fists. "A decent guy doesn't have sex with teenagers. Do you get that?"

Miranda put her lit cigarette into an empty beer can. "You and me don't think nothing alike. You get that whiny shit from your aunt Sophie. I let you spend too much time with her when you were young. Anyway, you ain't got your period yet so there isn't anything to worry about."

"Yes, Mom, there is!" Rainey screamed as she rushed toward her mother with an urge to throttle her. "He's a disgusting pig. He's hurting me. What if he does the same thing to Ivy?"

Miranda's head rolled to the side and she glared at her daughter. "As long as you keep Freddy happy you ain't gotta worry about him touching Ivy."

Rainey planted her feet wide and breathed loudly through her nose. "I hate you," she roared. "Why did you ever have children if you weren't going to take care of us?"

Without waiting for an answer, she turned on her heel and stomped out of the room. She limped down the hall, her inner thighs stiff and bruised again. In the bathroom, Rainey stood in front of the sink. She ran the cold water and rubbed a bar of soap over an old T-shirt. Then she scrubbed her entire body. When she was done, Rainey turned on the shower and got under the cold water, thinking that she'd rather freeze to death in a cold shower than smell that disgusting pig on her again.

When she went back into the bedroom, Ivy was no longer there. Panicked, Rainey threw on an oversized shirt and hurried as best she could, down to the first floor.

"Ivy! Where are you?" she screamed.

Rainey raced from room to room. Finally she found her in the kitchen, sitting at the table holding onto her baby doll.

"Where were you, Rainey?" the child cried. "I couldn't find you."

Rainey scooped her up. "I was in the bathroom. Don't ever come down here without me again. There are too many people here and I don't want anything bad to happen to you. Do you understand?"

Ivy's bottom lip quivered. "I'm sorry. I not gonna be bad anymore."

Rainey held her sister and kissed the top of her head. "You're not bad. You're a good girl. But we need to be careful because everything in this house is all wrong, and there are bad people you need to stay away from."

"Freddy's bad. Right, Rainey?"

Rainey gave her sister's hand a light squeeze, worried about how much the child had seen and heard. "Freddy is very bad and you are never to go near him. Ever."

Chapter Thirty

Nearly three weeks had passed since Buddy had stayed with the girls at night. Without her, Rainey and Ivy had no protection from the evil that lurked within the walls of their "home." Thankfully, Freddy didn't go to Rainey's room every night, but he still showed up a couple of times a week.

Fed up and desperate for something to change, Rainey dragged a whining Ivy out of the house and headed into the heart of Kensington. With no one to turn to for help, and feeling like a sitting duck for Freddy to devour, the only person who could help was Buddy. After several blocks, Rainey stopped and squatted in front of her sister.

"Listen, I know you're tired and hot. But we need to find Buddy. Me and you can't live in our house without her sleeping over anymore. We have to figure out somewhere else to go."

Ivy brushed the back of her tiny hand across her brow. "But why can't we live at our house without Buddy?"

Rainey looked to her left, thinking of how to explain her circumstances to her now five-year-old sister. "You know Freddy, right?"

Ivy's lips turned down and she nodded.

"Well, Freddy hurts me."

"I know. I saw him hurt you last night. It made me really scared and I was crying but you didn't hear me," she said.

"Oh, Ivy, I'm sorry. I didn't want you to see anything. I want you to listen to me, it's going to be okay."

But Rainey was a young kid herself and she couldn't hold back the emotions caused by the abusive trauma she was enduring. Unable to stop herself, Rainey broke down and cried.

"Don't cry no more," Ivy said, wrapping her arms around her older sister's neck and squeezing.

Rainey nodded but couldn't keep her tears from falling. To comfort both of them, she pulled the child to her and they embraced for several moments.

Ivy pulled her head back and looked into Rainey's face, "We can live somewheres else. K?"

Rainey sniffled and stood. "Yeah, okay. We'll figure everything out."

She reached for Ivy's hand and looked around them, taking in the sights and sounds of Kensington. Even on a bright, hot summer day, the buildings and streets of Kensington were dark and filled with an energy of desperation. She looked up at the sun sitting high in the deep blue sky, but even its rays of light couldn't reach through the buildings to brighten the shadowy crevices of the gloomy and threatening city streets. The underbelly of Kensington reflected the debilitating despair that held Rainey captive. Her eyes didn't deceive her and she understood what roamed the streets was just as dangerous as the predators that lurked within the walls of her home.

With no promise of escape, Rainey plugged along trash-strewn Kensington Avenue with Ivy in tow, searching for Buddy. An hour later with her feet screaming in pain, she sat on the curb at Somerset Street and pulled her sister onto her lap.

"Rainey, I'm hungry!" Ivy bellowed.

"I know. Don't worry. We'll find Buddy and I'll ask her to buy us something to eat."

Stroking the child's hair, Rainey watched the people around them as she tried to figure out what to do next. Women in seductive skirts with low tops and, high heels yelled into cars at men who drove past. Rainey knew they were prostitutes, but Ivy was fascinated by them.

After a little while, one hooker approached the two girls. "Hey, girls. How's it going? You gettin' a good show today?" she asked.

Rainey turned her head away, hoping the woman would just go away, but Ivy engaged.

"Hi. I'm Ivy and she's Rainey."

"Well, now. Aren't you a friendly little princess? My name's Ramona, but you can call me Mona."

"Mona, we're hungry," the child offered.

Mona jutted her hip out and took in the grunge that covered the two young girls. "Sweet child, everybody out here is hungry for somethin' so you ain't alone in that."

Rainey pulled on Ivy's arm. "Stop it. She doesn't have any food to give us." Then she stood and looked directly into Mona's eyes. "We're fine, actually. We're looking for our friend Buddy. Do you know her?"

Mona shrugged. "She a white girl?"

"No, she's black."

Mona tilted her head. "She a prosti?"

"What's that?"

"Is your friend Buddy like me?"

Rainey stared at her.

"A prostitute," Mona said, throwing her arms out, inviting Rainey to look closely at her Daisy Duke Shorts and the bra she was wearing.

"Oh, no. She works at a convenience store somewhere in town. We stopped at a few on our way here but nobody knows her."

Mona tapped her forehead with her index finger. "Little girl, there's about twenty convenience stores in walkin' distance."

"Right." Rainey sighed, looking down at her feet. "Okay, well, we have to go. Thanks for your time."

Rainey took Ivy's hand and walked away.

"Hey, now. Hold up," Mona said, shuffling up to the girls in her high heels. "No need to get your ass all tied up in knots. I was just messin' with ya . . . *honey*."

"It's Rainey," she said, annoyed that Mona thought she could call her "honey."

Mona looked into a passing car, then turned back. "I remember when I was your age and I first came out to the streets, ya know before I was a prosti. I was the black version of you. Anyway, I was dirty, too skinny, and hungry as fuck, but I sure was a looker."

"What's your point?" Rainey huffed, losing her patience. "Are you trying to make me feel worse than I already do?"

"No, no. I wouldn't do that to nobody who's been where I've been. My point is I understand what you're going through." Mona reached into her pocket, pulled out two one-dollar bills and held them in her hand. "My pimp Rock, has some motherfucker named Jiggy watch over me on the streets. He sees every damn thing I do out here and he don't give me much money. Let me tell you somethin'," she ranted forgetting herself,

"Jiggy and Rock, are selfish pricks. I'm out here all day and night making money so they can live good."

Seeing Mona's anger surface and her voice getting louder, Rainey backed away from the woman not wanting to draw attention from any of the people passing by.

When Mona realized she was scaring the girl she lowered her voice. In a kind tone she said, "Sorry about that it's just that those two men are evil. Look, I can spare ya two bucks. Go on and get somethin' to eat. I hope you find your friend," she said, pushing the bills toward the girl."

Rainey's expression softened. "This is really nice of you."

Mona said, "Do yourself a favor. Don't fall into the prosti business to eat. Once you start you can never get the fuck out unless you get too old or die."

Rainey held up her hand holding the money. "Thank you. Maybe we'll see you around again." She gave Mona a weak smile and walked away.

As the two girls stepped into a convenience store, Rainey thought about Mona's warning, realizing that her parents had turned her into a prosti in her own home.

Chapter Thirty-One

After the girls shared a soft pretzel and carton of chocolate milk, they walked back toward their house. The sidewalk seemed to sizzle. and through her worn sneakers, Rainey could feel the heat on the bottoms of her feet. Blisters had formed on the backs of her ankles from the tight sneakers rubbing, and she gimped along before picking up a discarded paper cup. She tore the cup into a few small pieces and shoved them into the back of her sneakers for relief.

They had just crossed a street and started down a block when Rainey heard music pouring out of an open bar door ahead. She glanced inside as they passed, and what she saw inside made her stop abruptly. There, slouched on a stool, was Buddy.

Leaning toward the door, Rainey hissed, "Hey, Buddy!" but the woman didn't look in her direction. After a few more attempts, Buddy finally turned. Her head wobbled and her eyeballs rolled as she tried to focus.

Rainey's stomach spun at Buddy's condition. After searching for the woman, she was disappointed to find another incoherent adult. All hope for help was put on hold. "Buddy, it's me. Rainey," she said louder.

Buddy stumbled from the barstool sideways, lost her footing, and fell onto her hip. "Fuckin' bullshit," she mumbled as she pushed onto her knees in slow motion, then grabbed the edge of the bar to hoist herself to her feet. She staggered, almost falling again, to the door. Rainey watched in horror as Buddy stumbled out.

"Hey, you guzzz," she slurred. "How ya been doin'?"

Rainey's eyebrows bunched together. "What the hell is with you, Buddy? You're drunk. Like gross drunk."

Buddy swatted the air. "You don't know nothing 'bout having to deal with grown-up shit." She stepped over the threshold and the girls backed away. Then she steadied herself on the graffiti-covered wall and leaned her cheek onto the hot stone. "What are yous guys doin' here?"

Rainey put her arm over Ivy's shoulder. "We came here looking for you because we thought you could help us. But now I see that you can't even help yourself. You were the only adult in our lives that we could count on. And now you're ruining yourself. What's going on with you? Maybe you need my help more than I need yours."

Buddy raised her index finger into the air. She swung away from the wall by accident, took a few clumsy steps, and grabbed onto the wall again. "Now, wait for one, shingle minute," she garbled. "Just 'cause I got a little drunk today don't mean I ain't in catrol."

"Where have you been? Things have gotten really bad with Freddy. You said you'd protect us and then you stopped coming," Rainey fired. "You were my only hope."

Buddy ran her fingers over her cornrows. "Well, first off, your dumb parents wouldn't let me in. Then," she said, leaning her whole body closer to the wall, "I had some problems. Lost my job at the convenience store because the owner's cousin needed a job. How's that for loyalty? People don't care 'bout nobody but themselves. I ain't had a place to live and now I can't even afford the money to squat at your parents' dump even if they let me . . . so here I am. Been living on the streets mostly. Got a couple of friends that let me shower at their place once in a while. So maybe you're right, I can't help myself. And I'm almost outta money so I can't help you out there . . . in case you was gonna ask."

Rainey's eyes dropped and landed on Buddy's hands. There was black grime under her fingernails, rings of black in the creases of her brown neck, and a sweet-urine smell that wafted from her clothing. It was clear that the woman was struggling with life.

There were stress lines around Buddy's eyes that weren't there before. They told a story of hardship. Rainey's hands clamped over her stomach to settle it down. She could see Buddy was in bad shape and hoped she hadn't turned to drugs.

Guilty thoughts emerged for being harsh with the woman, and Rainey adjusted her footing. "Why don't you look for another job?"

"It ain't that easy being out here on the streets all the time. There ain't no jobs for people who don't have skills. Hell, there ain't jobs for people *with* skills in this messed-up town."

"Maybe we can help each other," Rainey said. She lowered her eyes to the broken sidewalk. "Freddy's really been hurting me. You know?" She glanced at her little sister, hoping she wasn't scaring her.

"Oh, man. That's some fucked-up shit." Buddy leaned farther into the brick wall and slowly slid to the ground. She sat with her back against the wall, looking up at Rainey. "I have an idea how we can help each other."

"How?" Rainey asked, sitting on the ground next to the woman, hoping she had a good idea.

Buddy lowered her voice to a whisper and Rainey leaned in, straining to hear her. "If I can get more information on Jiggy I can sell that shit to the cops. We could split the money."

"I don't understand. What kind of information about Jiggy? That guy is nuts. I don't wanna mess with him. I heard him yelling at my parents the other night that they better pay him what they owe, and they better start selling his dope and stop using it."

Buddy put her index finger over her lips. "Shhhhhhh. You can't be talking about Jiggy in the open. You need to keep your voice down. You wanna get us killed or somethin'?"

Startled by the remark, Rainey pulled Ivy closer to her. "Killed? What are you talking about?"

"See," Buddy said as she sloppily leaned into Rainey, "Jiggy is a big-time drug dealer in Kensington. Anyway, I been talkin' with this cop for a while and he helps me out when I give him information about Jiggy or other shit happenin' on the streets."

"You mean be a narc?"

"Well, you ain't gotta call it that. It's more like helping to clean up the streets."

Rainey inched away from the smell of the liquor on Buddy's breath. "What would I have to do?" she asked, interested in the idea of punishing those people pushing street drugs.

Buddy touched the tip of Rainey's nose with her finger and the girl withdrew, repulsed by the drunkenness of the young woman she had been so fond of.

The woman explained. "You just need to find out the name of the dude who Jiggy gets his dope from. Then the cops can bust Jiggy and the other guy. Can you do that?"

Buddy's request sent off warning signs. Rainey instinctively knew it would be very dangerous for her to do what she was being asked. She was annoyed and insulted that Buddy would suggest she put herself and Ivy in such danger.

Rainey stood and looked down at Buddy, then closed her eyes and dropped her head. She briefly covered her face with her hands. "Are you nuts? You know there's no way I can do that. I don't want anything to do with those people. You can count me out. You can do your own dirty work."

Rainey took Ivy's hand and turned to leave but stopped short. "And another thing, you need to stop getting drunk. It's gross and you're not the same person. It's not a good look for you. I hope you can get yourself better."

Chapter Thirty-Two

Rainey led Ivy away from the bar, ignoring Buddy as she called for them to come back. The woman was a snitch for the cops, and she knew that bad things happened to people who gave information about what went on in her house. It was better to keep her distance. She thought back to a guy named Skeeter, who'd stayed in the house when she was seven. He must have been in his early twenties. He was tall and thin with blond, curly hair. His eyes were blue and kind. She remembered liking him and finding comfort in his demeanor. Skeeter had always been nice to her, and she thought about the first time they had met.

"Hey, little lady," Skeeter sang.

"Hi," Rainey replied, turning away in shyness.

Skeeter had kneeled in front of her to be eye-to-eye with the child. "Hey, guess what?"

Rainey's hands were clasped together and she shrugged. "What?"

He pulled a Lollipop from his pocket. "I brought this especially for you."

Rainey's eyes lit up. "Wow. For me? Is it grape?"

Skeeter pretended to study the purple paper. "Yep. I think you're right. It's grape. Do you like grape?"

Rainey nodded feverishly. "Grape's my favorite. One time my aunt Sophie took me to the store and bought me a grape soda, and I loved it so much."

"Well then, I'm happy that I picked the right flavor for you. Here you go," he said, handing her the Lollipop.

The child took the candy, ripped the wrapper off, and shoved all of its sugary goodness into her mouth. Skeeter sat on the floor Indian style. Rainey plopped next to him and mimicked his position.

He watched as the child sucked on the candy as though she were having her first drink of water after a long walk in the desert. "You're pretty hungry, huh?"

"Yeah. We don't have a lot of money and so there ain't too much to eat."

From then on, every time Skeeter went to the house, Rainey would race over to him to see what he'd brought her.

Skeeter was a drug addict but had been raised by kind parents who'd imparted him with compassion and understanding. And, through his heavy addiction, he'd hung on to his inherent kindness.

One day, when he brought Rainey a burger and a pack of bubble gum, he sat with her while she ate. "I have a little sister your age. Her name is Fawn. You remind me of her," Skeeter explained.

"Where's Fawn? Maybe I can play with her," Rainey said. She lowered her head, "I don't have friends. Nobody likes me."

Skeeter put his right hand over his chest. "What are ya talking about? I'm your friend." He gave her a warm smile and the tension in her shoulders eased away. "Anyway, Fawn lives in Texas with my mom and dad. But I know that if Fawn lived around here, she would love to be your friend."

"Really?" the small girl asked.

Skeeter reached into his pocket and pulled out a deck of cards he always carried. He often gambled with the homeless that lived on the streets. "Yeah, really. Anyway, do you wanna play Go Fish?"

Rainey pouted. "I don't know how to play."

"I'll teach you, silly," Skeeter said playfully.

For Rainey, Skeeter was the kindest person she knew aside from her aunt Sophie. She hoped they could stay friends forever. Skeeter and Rainey built a special bond over the months that followed. The two always played Go Fish before he would buy his dope and get high. The young girl enjoyed the company and positive attention he showered on her.

One night, Rainey was in the kitchen when she heard banging in the living room. She could hear bottles shattering against the wall. Cautiously, she eased into the hall and peered into the living room.

Skeeter was lying on the floor, covering his head with his arms and hands while four men kicked him.

Peter stood with his arms crossed over his chest and watched. Then he said, "What did you tell the cops, Skeeter? We know you said something about Johnny D." Rainey's father pointed to a tall, heavyset man standing next to him. "Yes or no. Did you tell the pigs you bought crank from him?"

Still, in a ball with his head covered, Skeeter cried, "No, I didn't say anything. I swear, Peter."

Peter raised his chin to the four men, and they all kicked him again. One man bent down and, with his massive fist, pounded on Skeeter's covered head and ribs.

"Stop it!" Rainey screamed from the doorway.

Peter looked over at his daughter, then over to Miranda. "Get her the fuck outta here. Can you act like a mother for once?"

"Fuck you, Peter," Miranda said and went back to smoking a joint.

Ignoring his daughter and girlfriend, Peter looked down at Skeeter again. "You're a liar," he barked. "There was a hooker in the holding cell while you were being processed by the cops. She heard you tell them you copped your shit from Johnny D. So you brought the heat down on him to save your own scrawny ass."

Peter held his hand up to the thugs beating the young man. He squatted and looked Skeeter in the eyes. "Here's the deal. You're gonna tell the cops you lied because you were scared, and if you don't, I'll let Jiggy know what you've done, because you know he kills any narc that dimes out one of his dope runners."

Peter grabbed a handful of Skeeter's hair and pulled hard. "That's what you're gonna do. Right?"

"Yeah, yeah. That's what I'm gonna do, Peter. I promise."

"Good. Now get outta my house and don't ever come back!" Peter yelled.

Skeeter stumbled to his feet. Holding his ribs, he gimped to the front door and noticed Rainey standing off to the side. The girl gasped at the blood coming from his mouth and nose. Then their eyes locked, and Skeeter gave her a slight nod.

Rainey, fearful of never seeing him again, ran to him and threw her arms around his legs. "Don't go, Skeeter. Who's gonna play Go Fish with me?"

Skeeter patted the top of her head, then pulled her arms away from his legs. He leaned down and whispered into her ear, "I'm sorry, Rainey. Someday you're gonna grow up and get outta here. Make sure you do something great with your life." Then Skeeter straightened up as best he could, and still holding his ribs, handed her his deck of cards and walked out the front door.

Rainey turned back to her father, standing in the middle of the living room with a couple of dozen people around him. "I hate you!" she screamed. "Skeeter was my only friend in the whole world!"

Peter chuckled. "Get over it. You'll make other friends. Besides, you don't ever wanna be friends with a narc. Remember that."

Peter turned away from her, the vein in his forehead protruding from the blood pumping through his body. "To be clear," he announced to everyone within earshot, "we don't put up with narcs around here. You open your fuckin' mouth to the cops and you better expect acid rain to drench you to the bone. And trust me, what you watched happen to Skeeter is nothing compared to what Jiggy will do to you."

Rainey pulled in a loud breath in the silenced room, scared by the gruffness of her father's voice. Peter's eyes darted toward the only noise in the room, and making eye contact, he scowled at his daughter.

That was how Rainey was educated about narcs. She was old enough to know that what her father threatened the others with applied to her too. From that day forward, Rainey knew she'd never open her mouth about the things that went on in her house.

Chapter Thirty-Three

After losing all hope that Buddy would help them, Rainey struggled to think up other ways to keep herself and Ivy safe. But how, when she couldn't even fight off Freddy?

Rainey was a rational teenager, despite her parents' inability to act like adults. At fourteen, looking beyond the dirt and shabby clothing, a beautiful young woman was emerging. A beauty that Rainey herself didn't see when she looked in the mirror. When she stared at herself, she saw a helpless girl trapped inside with no way of getting out.

On a stormy evening a few days later, Rainey was sitting at the kitchen table mixing ketchup and tap water to make a cold soup for Ivy and her to eat with the last of their saltine crackers when Miranda walked in.

"What's going on?" Miranda asked.

Rainey scowled at her. "What does it look like? We're eating. I'm making ketchup soup because there's no food for us."

"You know, you're very unattractive when you act so arrogant. I'm your mother and you need to talk to me with respect."

The girl laughed. "When you act like a mom then I'll treat you like one. What do you want?"

"Your dad and me need you to do something for us."

"What?" Rainey huffed, pressing back the fear rising in her at what was about to come. "I can't believe either of you would ask me for a favor."

"We need you to sleep with Jiggy."

Paralyzed with fear, Rainey choked on her cracker and pushed herself away from the table. "Are you out of your mind? You've sent that slimebucket Freddy up to my room and he hurts me. This is not who I am and you can't make me do things I don't want to do."

Miranda slapped her across the face so quickly that Rainey had no time to react.

"Just so we're clear," her mother growled, "if you so much as *hiccup* when we tell you to do something you'll be the sorriest girl alive."

"You're sick!" Rainey cried, holding her blazing hot cheek. "I'm your kid. Your flesh and blood. These are grown men. I don't understand why you don't love me enough to protect me."

"See, that's your problem. This isn't about love, baby. This is about being part of a family and everyone pitching in to do what's needed. I love you and Ivy. Loved you girls since the day you were born—so I need you to do what's asked of you."

Rainey's thoughts circled her brain like a hurricane. She was mortified to think that her parents believed they loved their children. Disgusted, the girl abruptly stood and her chair banged to the floor. "This isn't about us being a family. This is about you and Dad and drugs. You use me, Mom. You sell me so that you can get high. Let that sink in. I can't take it anymore. I *won't* take it anymore!" she screamed, trying her best to argue her way out of the situation. She crossed her arms over her chest and glared at her mother.

Miranda got closer and kicked the fallen chair into the wall behind her daughter. "You aren't the boss here, so shut your fucking mouth. You're gonna do what we need you to do. Jiggy's got the hots for you and you're gonna take care of it. I'll tell your father that Freddy can't *visit* you until further notice."

Rainey, ready for her mother to strike her again but willing to fight, stepped back and shook her head. "I won't do it."

Miranda lunged forward and grabbed the collar of Rainey's T-shirt and leaned in so close their noses touched. "You can and you will do it or you better run as far away as you can get." She lowered her voice to a sharp whisper. "There's plenty of interest in Ivy too."

The girl shook her head, not comprehending what she'd just heard. "She's five years old. I'd rather die than let anyone touch her. If you were any kind of a decent mother, you'd feel the same way about both of us."

Miranda gave Rainey a grin that turned her stomach. The girl knew that her mother understood that the threat of anything bad happening to Ivy would make her submit. It was the one surefire weapon she had over her.

"Jiggy's coming here tomorrow night," Miranda said. "Make sure you take a shower."

Rainey's nose wrinkled and she averted her mother's steady gaze. "Right. Take a shower in cold water, really?"

Miranda poked Rainey in the sternum with her index finger. "Yeah, really."

***

Rainey laid awake all night thinking about Jiggy. She sunk into a morbid place where there was no light and no end to her misery. She envisioned Jiggy's hands grating at her body. She tried to force the thoughts from her mind, but it was impossible to avoid the abuse that awaited her. She shivered under the layers of clothing resting on top of her. With Buddy no longer coming around, she wondered how to get herself out of the situation. Finally, in the early morning hours, an idea popped into her head.

The next day, she took Ivy and set out to Somerset Street hoping to find Mona, the prostitute she'd met on the streets. The sisters sat on the corner until early afternoon when she spotted the woman.

Rainey got to her feet. "Hey, Mona," she called out.

"Hey, little girl."

Rainey's eyes narrowed and put her hands on her hips. Mona stopped short, threw her head back, and laughed.

"All right, all right," the woman said, holding her hands up in front of her. "Hey, *Rainey*. You sure do have a thing about your name, huh?"

Rainey shrugged. "Look, I kinda need your help," she asked, crossing her fingers.

Mona hoisted her large purse up higher on her shoulder. "My help? What the hell do you think I'm gonna be able to do for you?"

"Remember when we met and you told me never to be a prosti?"

Mona's backbone slipped and she held one open palm up to the teen. "You listen real good. This ain't no place for a girl like you. Don't tell me you're thinking 'bout turning out."

Rainey shook her head. "It's my parents. They're making me have sex to pay for their drug debts."

"Lord have mercy, child. Who the hell are your parents? Mr. and Mrs. Satan? I mean shit, don't get me wrong, my parents weren't much better. No siree, they were no saints. They loved their alcohol. Both of them would get all liquored up and fight like two boxers going after the heavyweight title. Anyway, once they started pounding on me, I up and left that hellhole and ended up here. That's some messed-up shit, ain't it?"

Rainey put her hand on Mona's arm, but she jerked it away. "Hey now, I don't like to be touched!" the woman's voice roared.

Rainey was left stunned. "I'm . . . I'm sorry. I didn't mean anything by it."

"Yeah, well, I'm a little jumpy about being touched without knowing it first. I got a bunch of slobs handling me all day and night."

"I understand," she said. "There's this gross guy that comes to our house and he forces me to have sex. My parents let him sleep in my room."

Rainey noticed Mona kept looking around, "What are you looking for?"

"Just making sure my pimp ain't in sight. He'll whoop my ass if he catches me yapping with a kid instead of working. So what do you want with me?"

"There's this guy that my mom told me I have to . . . sleep with tonight." Tears sprang to her eyes, and a burning ember ignited in her chest. "His name's Jiggy."

Mona's hand flew to her mouth as she pulled in a jagged breath. "Jiggy? Oh, child, you in a bad, bad way."

Rainey's heart dropped into her stomach and she stared at the woman. Her fear grew more intense, Mona's words swirling in her head. Things in her mind were moving far too fast for her to process.

Chapter Thirty-Four

Mona's reaction to Jiggy unnerved Rainey, and the blood drained from her face. Shaken, she rubbed her sweaty hands on her pants, then wrapped her arms around herself to control the trembling. She squirmed and finally grabbed onto Mona's forearm, remembering too late that the woman didn't like to be touched. However, sensing the teen's intense panic, she let the girl hold onto her.

Rainey had to know everything now. "How do you know Jiggy?"

Mona looked left and right. "Jiggy's got lots of power out here." She tapped her index finger against her forehead. "That man ain't right in his head. You understand what I'm sayin'?"

"No. No, I don't understand. What do you mean?" she asked, noting that her voice had turned into a shrill tone, like a bad karaoke singer trying to belt out a Whitney Houston song.

"Jiggy likes to see his bitches suffer. Especially the women he screws. The sick fuck got a thing for pain. Don't get me wrong, he don't like no pain on himself, he likes to do the hurtin'."

"Hur . . . hurt me, how?" Rainey's terror was almost too much to bear as her eyes darted around as though looking for a place to hide.

Mona steadied her eyes on the girl, and her heart ached as she fumbled for the right words. "Look, I know I'm scaring ya. But I gotta tell you straight up. He, um, he bites and slaps and punches. He's rough and doesn't have no regard for how he's making you feel. Some men are tender even with a prosti, but that ain't Jiggy. That motherfucker takes what he wants, exactly how he wants it. You ain't got no say in the matter."

"What am I gonna do? You have to help me. Please," the girl begged.

Rainey could see that the woman was trying to help and, in an odd removed way, she thought the woman cared. But now, with the new information, she wasn't sure if she felt better or worse. She went there thinking Mona might have been able to help her—hoping the woman knew Jiggy and could talk him out of it.

Mona reached into her purse, pulled a cigarette from a pack, glided it between her lips slathered in bright-red lipstick, and lit it, taking a long drag before answering. "Look, I'd love to help you out, but ya see, Jiggy works for my pimp. He's beat my ass a couple of times when a john complained about me. And when I say beat my ass, I mean one time, he bent my wrist back so far, he broke it. That was a bad night, as soon as I got outta the hospital, that asshole made me work the streets. I had a goddamn cast on my arm and I was still out of it from the pain killers. You think Jiggy cared? Nope, he expected me to make up the money I lost while I was getting my wrist set that *he* broke."

Mona sighed. "Anyway, Jiggy is a ruthless pile of horseshit. I've seen him beat some of my prosti friends until they couldn't walk no more."

Tears sprung to Rainey's eyes. "You have to tell me what to do. Please!"

Mona looked deep into the girl's eyes, and the Rainey could see her terror. "Run."

She gasped, her entire world collapsing in on her. "Run? Where am I supposed to go? And I have Ivy," she hissed, pulling the child into her. "We don't have anywhere to go." Her face twisted with fear as a sob broke free. "Please, please, you have to help us."

Mona was almost moved to tears. She saw her younger self in Rainey when she first ran to the streets to escape her parents. Back then, Mona had prayed for someone to come along and help her, but the only person who rescued Mona was her pimp. She embraced his offer to be loved and protected by him. It had been the biggest mistake Mona made because people who set out to use you are incapable of giving love and protection.

Mona's frustration boiled over and she stomped her foot. "This is damn bullshit!"

Rainey recoiled at the intensity. "What's wrong?"

"I always get myself involved in stuff I don't belong in. Look, kid, I don't have all the answers. You think I'd be out here selling my ass to a bunch of smelly, creepy dudes if I had answers?"

Rainey's mouth dropped open and her chest hitched. "I . . . I just need to figure out what to do." She walked in a small circle and stopped suddenly. "Maybe we can sleep at your house tonight?"

Mona sucked in a quick breath. "You done lost your damn mind. I don't live in no house by myself. I live in a house run by my pimp with thirteen other prostis. Ain't no place there for you and certainly not for that baby of yours. My pimp would take one look at you and turn your pretty, white ass out quicker than looking at ya. You'd be better off giving yourself over to Jiggy and begging for his mercy than getting involved with my shit!" she ranted with heated enthusiasm.

Just then, Ivy spoke up. "What's wrong, Rainey? Are you guys mad?"

"No, sweetie. Me and Mona are just trying to figure out some things." Rainey turned back to Mona. "You have any other ideas? Anything?"

Mona fumbled around in her purse for a few seconds. "Open your hand."

Rainey did as she was told.

Mona dropped a small orange pill on her palm.

She squinted at the pill. "What is it?"

Mona sighed. "It's hydromorphone. It's a small dose . . . only two milligrams. That shit is potent so I'm only giving ya one. Take it before Jiggy comes to see you. It'll put you out of it enough so you won't give a crap. But remember, you gotta plead with him to be gentle. Tell him it's your first time. Don't resist him. Make him think you like him."

Rainey closed her fingers around the pill. She'd do just about anything to flee the raging storm headed her way, but taking drugs was almost as repulsive as having sex with Jiggy—not quite, but close.

Chapter Thirty-Five

Rainey took her time getting home that afternoon. She kept her eyes glued to the sidewalk as an ache pounded inside her skull. She dragged her feet over the pavement like she was marching to her death. Her thoughts were dreary, imagining what awaited her at home. Her thin, frail body was heavy. It seemed like the blood in her veins had been replaced with a murky, thick substance that weighed her down. Her heart beat in double time until she was short of breath. With a few blocks to go, she stopped walking, pulled Ivy onto a bench, and tried to calm herself.

A little later, when the girls arrived back at their house, Rainey looked around the living room, and not seeing Jiggy gave her a false sense of relief. She took Ivy up to their bedroom, trying to pretend everything was okay. She gave the child two crackers with a light coating of jelly from a couple of partially used packets she'd picked out of the trash behind a small greasy-spoon restaurant on their way home.

Then her body seized and her limbs shook when she heard the boom of Jiggy's voice downstairs. Afraid of what her sister would see, and more so, what he might do to Ivy given the chance, she quickly changed her and brought the child into her parents' bedroom. She lay with her until the child fell asleep, then she snuck out. She went back to her bedroom and prepared herself, as best she could, for the deviant pedophile coming for her soon.

Rainey's stomach clamped down tightly as she lay in her darkened bedroom alone. She rolled onto her side and lifted the small pill that Mona had given her. She'd almost thrown it out on the way home, but something had told her to keep it in her pocket. Now she placed it between her fingers and stared at it. It was almost nine at night, and she had no idea when Jiggy would come up to her room. She'd dressed in layers, hoping it would deter the sick man. But now, with trouble pending, her blood ran cold and she laid on her back and covered herself with more clothing to help melt the ice in her veins. She tried her best to erect barriers between herself and the cold and the cruel ghost of dark anticipation. As time passed, she drifted into a light sleep from sheer exhaustion. It was close to eleven when she was awoken by her bedroom door being thrown open.

Through the curtainless window, the moon shone in and lit the room with a yellowish glow. In the moonlight, Rainey could see Jiggy's form in the distance. He was of medium height and stocky, with a belly that protruded well beyond his hips and hid his belt. His hair was the color of carrots, and the white, flabby skin on his face bounced when he walked. He wore sideburns to the top of his double chin. But what made him grotesque was not so much his slovenly appearance as his rotten demeanor. Jiggy was the guy who wore all the gold he owned around his neck every day because, for him, it screamed status. His large socked feet were jammed inside his rubber sandals regardless of the time of year.

Jiggy hacked up phlegm and spit it on the floor. Then he let out a loud burp that rumbled off of the walls as he approached the girl, who tried to do as Mona had advised and not resist. As he lurched closer, the moon glinted off the orange of his hair. Rainey shuddered and sat up quickly.

"Please don't do this to me," she said, the urge to resist taking over. "I'm only fourteen and I've never done this before. Just get out. Get outta my room!" she shrieked.

Jiggy gave her a wicked grin and stomped farther into the room. He dropped a large duffel bag on the ground next to her, then he removed his handgun and put it on a milk carton next to the bed of rags.

Sneering at her, he said, "Listen, you little slut, you need to pick which way you want this to go. It can be rough or brutal. They're the only two intensities I got, that's the way I like my sex. I'm only giving you the choice, because, as you said, *you're only fourteen*," he mocked in a high-pitched little girl voice. "As if I give a shit how old you are." Jiggy was standing over her by now. "Lose those clothes," he barked.

Rainey reared up on her knees, holding an old coat tightly against her chest, looking up with bulging green eyes set back behind the blond hair that had fallen across her face. She was crazed and ready to pounce, fight for her life . . . fight to save her body and soul.

Jiggy leaped on her quickly. He snatched her wrists with his strong hands and squeezed tightly, pulling them down and back slowly, watching the agony on her face as pain shot up her arms and into her shoulders.

Remembering Mona's broken wrist, Rainey knew he would break her arms if she didn't stop struggling. She was waiting to hear her bones snap. Unable to withstand the agony, she let out a scream so shrill that surely her parents and the partiers downstairs must have heard. But no one came.

Jiggy released Rainey's wrists and in a flash gave her a backhand across her face. Her head flew to the side. Left dazed and confused, she tried to slink toward the bedroom door until the ogre smashed his foot down on her spine.

Jiggy put his face close to hers and let out a gruff chuckle. "Don't matter to me one bit how much you scream, but to be clear, when you scream it gives me the urge to hit you. Next time you yell I'll let you find out what my fist feels like hitting your face instead of the back of my hand." He clasped his hand around her throat and pulled her closer. "You got that?"

Rainey's mouth was forced open and her tongue was dangling to the side. Quickly her face was turning red from the lack of oxygen. She nodded in jerky movements.

Jiggy let go of her neck. "Stand up," he ordered.

Rainey staggered to her feet, heaving deep breaths, and stood before him.

"What the hell are all those clothes you got on?" Jiggy threw his head back and let out a deep, chest-pumping, grisly laugh.

She instinctively backed away from him. *I'm in my bedroom with the devil. He's probably gonna murder me while he rapes me.*

Jiggy's laughter ended sharply. His eyes narrowed and he lifted his shirt over his head, dropping it to the floor. Her eyes quickly scanned the hairy mound of flesh-covered fat in front of her. His large breasts hung from his chest like two water balloons, and his round, white belly spilled over his jeans covering his black, silver-studded belt. Just above his hips, purple stretch marks looked like spider webs crawling over his torso.

Repulsed, and in desperate need to get away from the disgusting man, Rainey's eyes darted around the room looking for an escape. Finally she spotted the pill she'd never taken, the pill she couldn't take because she'd rather live through the nightmare that Jiggy had planned for her than be anything like her parents. Inside, a tiny surge of courage plowed through her, and she looked up at him, eyes blazing. She could do this.

Jiggy pulled a switchblade from his pocket and it sprang to life with the press of a metal button. "You can take all that shit off or I can cut it off. You should know, though, that if I have to cut them off I ain't gonna be delicate."

Rainey bit her lower lip, her courage bleeding out of her body. She fidgeted under his vile stare. Then she fussed with her clothes. She fumbled with the buttons on her sweater, her fingers unable to receive the commands she was giving them. Jiggy let out a low growl that gurgled from his throat, sounding more vicious than a junkyard dog.

With her sweater off, Rainey scrambled with the buttons of a long-sleeved blouse she'd worn underneath. Jiggy stalked closer to her. She clawed at the buttons on her jeans and quickly pushed them down around her ankles and stepped out of them. Her guts were twisted, and her bladder seemed like it was being squeezed until she had an uncontrollable urge to pee. Standing in ratty long johns and an undershirt, she looked up at the man. He jutted out his chest and strutted toward her. Almost upon her, Rainey lost control of her bladder and her long johns were quickly soaked in warm, yellow liquid. The relief of her bladder lasted a millisecond as he leered at her, his eyes bouncing from her face to the yellow, wet stain between her legs. He made a clicking sound with his tongue in mockery as he seized her shoulders.

Rainey's pulse jittered and her breath caught in her chest. Her jaw locked and, try as she might, she couldn't move from the spot where she was standing. *This is it. This is where I die. In this shabby, dirty room with my baby sister across the hall, the only person in this world who loves me.*

Jiggy lifted Rainey by her shoulders until her feet dangled in midair. He turned and threw her onto the pile of clothing. He ripped off her pee-soaked long johns and her panties in one swoop. She quickly covered her privates with her hands. He undid his belt, and Rainey closed her eyes, forcing her mind to withdraw from her grim reality and to find that place deep inside herself where she could hide, where she was safe until it was over.

There was a knock at the door, and Jiggy turned his face in that direction. "What? I told you I'm busy."

He stomped over and pulled the door open. One of his associates, Lars, was standing in the hallway. "Hey, Jiggy. I know you said not to bother you but Brooks is downstairs. He's looking to buy forty bags, and I figured you'd wanna know. I mean, that's a lot of blow, man."

Jiggy huffed. "Fine, wait right here." He shut the door and scowled at Rainey. "Open that duffel bag and pull out the big plastic bag," he said, lighting a cigarette.

Rainey sat up and scurried over the floor, pulling the duffel bag onto her lap. She looked over as he glanced at her.

"Now, count out forty of those little bags. Don't fuck up the count, either. Every one of those bitches means money to me."

She dumped a quarter of the contents out of the larger bag onto her lap. With trembling hands, she counted the bags.

"Dude!" his associate yelled and banged on the door. "Get the hell out of here, man! The heat's out front!" a frantic voice yelled.

Jiggy took long strides to the door and pulled it open. "What happened?"

"I don't know, man. We was all hangin' out and then all of a sudden our lookout saw the blue and red turn onto the street. You gotta come now if you wanna make it out."

Still reeling from what was about to come after the bags of white powder were counted, Rainey froze from all the commotion, with her brain unable to process what was happening. Her heart thudded in her chest and, as much as she wanted to run from the room after Jiggy was gone, her body denied the commands her brain was making. She reached to her left and grabbed Jiggy's gun he'd left behind and held it up, facing the open bedroom door.

Chapter Thirty-Six

Rainey was panting. Her mind was filled with questions, none of which she had the sense at the moment to answer. Acting on instinct, she stayed still, pointing the handgun forward. There was a lot of yelling downstairs and then she heard the pounding of feet running to the second floor. A few seconds later a man stalked in, shining a flashlight around the room.

"What the hell . . ." he said, swinging the beam of the flashlight over her.

Rainey willed herself not to move. She was sweating, and her pulse was pounding. As the man drew closer, she saw the silver badge hanging from his belt.

The cop pulled his gun and aimed it at her. "Drop the gun."

Rainey looked at the gun in her hand and quickly lowered the weapon to the floor.

The cop stepped closer. "I need you to push the gun to me, slowly."

She followed the order. The cop squatted next to her, still pointing his gun at her while lifting Jiggy's gun from the floor. Handing it to an officer behind him, he waved his flashlight over her and stopped when he saw all the bags of heroin in her lap.

He looked Rainey in the eyes and she shrank away. "I need you to stand up and face the wall."

When she stood, he realized she was naked from the waist down.

"Dear God," he breathed, turning to his partner. "Throw me a blanket or something."

With a thin blanket in hand, the cop holstered his gun.

"Are you high?" he asked.

Rainey's eyes were wide with fear and she shook her head. "No," she eeked out.

"I'm going to cover you with this blanket now. Okay?"

"No," she yelped, not wanting another man near her. "Just give it to me."

The cop handed her the blanket and stepped back. "What's going on here, kid? Where'd you get all this dope?"

Confused by the question, she looked down at the floor and all the bags of powder around her bare feet. "That isn't mine!" she shrieked, jumping away from the drugs.

Her mind raced as her heart hammered in her chest. She saw the agent watching her closely and knowing he must have thought she was a drug addict too. She considered how she looked, naked . . . gun in hand . . . bags of heroin around her. The situation seemed hopeless as she reached on the floor and grabbed a pair of sweatpants.

The agent was watching her to make sure she didn't try to run. "I'm Agent Lindquist. What's your name?"

She gave the cop a hard look, wondering what would happen to her next. "Rainey."

"Do you live here?"

"Yeah."

"Where are your parents?"

"I don't know," she squeaked out.

The agent stared at her, then tilted his head, recalling Buddy telling him that two kids lived in the house.

"Are there any other kids living here?" he asked.

"Oh, shit!" she yelled, springing forward and, darting past the cop.

Lindquist pulled his gun and pointed it at her back. "Stop! Get on the ground now!"

Charged by adrenaline Rainey barreled forward into her parents' room with Lindquist on her heels.

Rainey snatched Ivy off of the floor and held her tightly.

The agent grabbed the girl's shoulder. "Don't run off like that again and when I tell you to do something, you do it. Understand?" he said in a scolding tone.

Rainey's eyes widened and she nodded. "I'm sorry."

The agent looked at the child she was holding. "Who is this?" he asked.

"This is my sister, Ivy," she said, hugging the child closer.

Lindquist lowered his hand to her forearm and walked her into the hallway, where Peter and Miranda were standing with another police officer. In each hand a third officer held up clear, large bags filled with smaller bags of heroin.

Agent Lindquist said something Rainey couldn't hear to his partner and then turned to her. "What were you planning to do with the drugs?" he asked, pointing at the plastic bags.

"I told you already. The drugs aren't mine. They belong to someone else," she cried. Lindquist turned to Miranda and Peter. "Do either of you know where these drugs came

from?"

Miranda laced her fingers through Peter's. "We don't—" she said, but Rainey noticed Peter squeeze her hand tightly so she wouldn't finish.

Peter stepped forward. "Can I get a minute with you in private?" he asked Lindquist.

The agent gave him a curt nod and they walked away from everyone. "The dope belongs to our daughter. We knew something was wrong with her and suspected she's been dealing," Peter stated.

Lindquist lifted his chin. "Does she use too? Does she seem high to you right now?"

Peter shrugged. "I'm not really sure. She's been acting strange lately."

Lindquist added, "She was pretty strung out when we got here. She looked like a rabid dog when I found her in the other bedroom. She had a gun too. Does that belong to you or your wife?"

"No. We don't own guns."

"Any idea where she got it?"

Peter shook his head.

Lindquist said, "We found her sitting in her room with the bags of heroin spread out around her. How old is she?"

Peter almost smiled at the convenience of the information being given to him. "She's fourteen. She got caught up with some kids in Kensington and then, all of a sudden, she was rolling in the dough. We asked her if she was dealing, but she kept denying it."

"Anything else you can tell me?"

Peter looked down at the floor and put on his most pitiful face. "She's been out of control for about a year now. What's gonna happen to her?"

"Well, we will need to take her down to the station along with you and your wife until we understand what happened here," he explained.

Peter rubbed his forehead so the agent didn't see his annoyance that they'd be required to go to the station too. "Okay, look, can you give me a minute to talk to my kid privately? I'll explain what's happening. I could tell she's terrified."

"Yeah, go ahead, but make it quick."

While Lindquist watched, Peter took Rainey, still holding Ivy, by the hand and walked into his bedroom, with Miranda following. He walked his daughter over to a corner of the room and Miranda stood next to him. He kept his voice to a low whisper so no one else could hear. "So here's what's gonna happen. You're going to tell those pigs that the dope they found is yours. I mean, they did find you sitting with a bunch of bags around you," he smirked.

Rainey wanted to smash his face into the wall. She held Ivy tighter and shook her head frantically. "No, they're not mine. You know it too. They belong to Jiggy."

"You listen to me. If you so much as breathe Jiggy's name he will kill you and then he'll kill all of us . . . including Ivy. Unless you want her murder on your conscience, then you better keep that trap shut."

Her eyes bulged and she couldn't figure out a comeback or a way out of the situation. She knew the way the cops found her made her look guilty. She opened her mouth but no words came out. Instead, a sob escaped her.

Peter pointed at the door. "That copper is gonna come in here in a minute. He's taking us all to the station for questioning. You try to remember that Ivy will suffer if you open that big pie hole of yours and say one fucking word about Jiggy, me, your mom or anyone else in this house."

Just then, Lindquist stepped inside the room and said, "We have to get going."

Miranda wrenched Ivy from Rainey's arm as the child screamed.

Peter looked at Rainey. "Well, we warned you that drugs would only bring you trouble. How can you do this to us? What if your little sister got into those drugs? You could've killed her."

"Yeah," Miranda piped up from behind Peter. "We warned you about this."

Agent Lindquist gave Peter and Miranda a scathing look. "That's enough. We can sort this all out when we get to the station." He put his hand on Rainey's elbow. "We need to go now." The agent glared at her parents, partially blaming them for Rainey's behavior. "Is there anyone who can keep your daughter?" he asked, gesturing to Ivy.

Peter shook his head. "No, unfortunately, we don't have any family that lives nearby. Is it okay if we just bring her with us?" he asked, faking concern for his younger daughter.

When Lindquist didn't answer quickly enough, Peter added, "Look, we're disappointed with our daughter, but we'll stand by her. I think we all can agree that Rainey needs help."

Miranda cooed at Ivy. "Oh, my sweet baby . . . are you okay? Rainey could've hurt you."

Ivy pushed off her mother's chest and bent at the waist. "Rainey, I want Rainey!" she cried.

Miranda said, "It's okay, sweetie. I know you're upset, but Rainey's gonna be just fine. These nice policemen are going to get your sister the help she needs."

Rainey stood dumbfounded. She hadn't seen this one coming. Of all the things she worried about over the past years, she never thought that she'd be stupid enough to be set up in such a way. All she could think about was Jiggy fleeing the room and her sitting there like an idiot surrounded by a mound of drugs.

Agent Lindquist turned Rainey around gently, pulled one wrist behind her back, and closed the cold, metal cuff. Then he did the same with her other wrist. He turned to Peter and Miranda, "You can bring your daughter. Rainey will ride with me and you'll drive with Officer Ackerman."

As the agent led the girl from the bedroom, Ivy let out a loud shriek. "Rainey!" she screamed, lunging toward her big sister.

Rainey turned back to Ivy. "I need to say good-bye to her. Please. She doesn't understand, and she's scared," she pleaded to Agent Lindquist.

Lindquist nodded and guided the girl over to Ivy. The two put their foreheads together. "I love you more than anything in the whole world," Rainey said, trying to keep her voice steady.

"I wanna come with you," Ivy wailed.

"You can't come with me right now. You be a good girl. You're going to ride with Mom and Dad, but I'll be back for you. I promise."

Tears ran down Rainey's face as she turned back to Agent Lindquist and walked out of the room with him.

When Rainey reached the bottom of the stairs, she turned her head to the side to look at the man. "Agent Lindquist, nobody takes care of my little sister like I do. I'm scared about what's going to happen to her now."

The agent gave her a curt nod. "Well, your parents are going to have to handle things." Then he pulled her forward and escorted Rainey to the waiting police car.

Chapter Thirty-Seven

Rainey was confused, scared, and vulnerable in the back of the police car. She leaned her head against the coolness of the window, catching Agent Lindquist glancing at her through his rearview mirror a few times.

"Rainey, I recognize you're young, but those drugs we found you with in your room . . . that's serious. So is the gun you were holding. The most important thing you can do now is tell us who your supplier is."

A heaviness settled on Rainey's chest, limiting her breathing. She met his eyes in the mirror and remained silent.

"Anyway," he continued, "you're going to need legal representation. If you don't have an attorney the court will appoint one for you."

She leaned forward. "This is all a mistake," her voice cracked out in a demure tone. Agent Lindquist stopped at a red light and turned to face her. "I want to help. You seem

like a nice girl, but there's more to it than that."

Rainey nibbled on her bottom lip and broke eye contact. She considered spilling her guts but all the evidence was stacked against her, plus she knew her parents weren't lying, Jiggy would hurt Ivy to get even with her.

"I understand you don't want to discuss this with me. That's your right. But you'll have to tell the judge everything when the time comes," he said, trying to get her to talk.

Rainey looked out the car window. Maybe this would work out okay. It had to. She'd never touched a drug in her life; she was nothing like her parents. Surely the judge would see that and let her go. "What are you going to do with my parents?"

The traffic light turned green and the officer pressed his foot on the gas. "We're bringing them in for questioning—we hope they can fill in some of the blanks for us."

"You don't know my mom and dad. I hate them," she said, sulking.

"Lots of teenagers think they hate their parents. Here's the thing, Rainey, we received a tip that there was a large quantity of drugs at your house. If you'd be willing to provide us with information about who you're working with, the judge would be much easier on you. Can you tell me who you're selling for?" Agent Lindquist asked.

Rainey's head hung. She would not get herself in any deeper than she already was. "I don't have anything to say."

Rainey looked out of the side window at a woman staggering and tripping over her own feet as she crossed the street, and even though she looked awful, at that moment she'd switch places with her in an instant. At least she was free.

Lindquist broke the silence. "You're going to make things harder on yourself," he said. "It'll be important to tell us who you're working with to make things easier on yourself."

She continued looking out the car window. "I'm not working with anyone," she grumbled.

Agent Lindquist tapped his fingers on the dashboard. Rainey pressed her shoulders back into the seat, thinking that she'd rather rot in prison than put Ivy in harm's way. She knew her parents would neglect the child, but that was better than Ivy being killed.

The agent's voice turned gentle. "We're almost at the station. I'll bring you inside and they'll process you. Have you eaten today?"

"I had a couple of crackers with jelly," she mumbled.

"Well, that isn't very much. You must be starving."

Rainey shrugged and thought, *I'm used to being hungry. That I can handle, but this situation, I don't know how to handle it.*

"I'll make sure to get you something to eat," he said with a big smile.

Rainey couldn't care less about food at the moment, and his smile irked her even further. This wasn't a joke—what was happening to her was real. She slouched farther into the car seat to stabilize her trembling legs. She couldn't believe what was happening to her. She didn't want to believe it.

When the squad car pulled into the station on Girard Avenue, Rainey lifted her head from the window. Her eyes darted around the dark parking lot, looking for something familiar, something to ease the fear scratching deep wounds on her insides. She peered at the cinderblock building, stoic and uninviting. There were a few cars, sitting alone, desolate and ominous, parked in the lot. Two metal poles towered above the lot, casting down yellow light. Her eyes searched the eerie, darkened haze and she imagined there was evil lurking between the beams of yellow light—waiting to feed on her. Rainey's heart pitter-pattered a million beats a minute as her anxiety turned into terror.

"I don't wanna go in there," Rainey said, hating the weakness in her voice.

Agent Lindquist parked, got out of the car, and opened the back door. He bent down to look at her. "I'm sorry but you don't have a choice. I'll be with you the whole time."

Scorching, salty tears pushed against the backs of Rainey's eyes, and with her hands still cuffed behind her, she couldn't swipe them away. She was embarrassed to let Lindquist see her cry, but with no choice she let the tears fall. In a small act of mercy, the agent pulled a handkerchief from his pocket and wiped her tear-stained face. In that little time and space, Rainey had the sense of being cared for, the way her aunt Sophie and Buddy had once done. She leaned into the terrifying moment of being fourteen, scared, threatened, and lonely, yet comforted by the agent.

"Let's get you inside so we can get those handcuffs off you," Lindquist said, helping her from the car.

The inside of the police station was bustling with cops and people in handcuffs, and Rainey was thankful when hers were removed. She rubbed her wrists where the metal had bit into them as she watched scantily dressed young women slouched on the benches, waiting for intake. One girl looked no older than she was. There were two drunk men handcuffed to a bench off in the corner arguing with each other, and police moving about mechanically as they processed everyone.

"Agent Lindquist?" she asked, hearing the fear in her voice.

He looked down at her. "Yeah?"

"What's gonna happen to me now?"

"Well, we'll get you processed, and then you'll be put in a holding cell for a while."

"Am I going to jail?" she asked, terrified to hear the answer.

The officer's eyes clouded over and he bit his bottom lip. "Well, yes, but I'm not sure for how long. It was a very large quantity of heroin you had in your possession. We'll have to wait and see what happens."

Rainey's breathing quickened and she blew out several short breaths to steady her nerves. She didn't want to lose it in front of so many people, especially the ones who'd been staring at her since she walked into the building. Rainey rubbed her arms and looked around, then back up at the agent.

"I'm worried about my sister."

"Look, there's not a whole lot I can do, but I'll check on her when your parents get here. Right now you need to worry about yourself."

***

Rainey spent more than an hour being processed. Her last step for intake was to provide information to an older, balding police officer while Agent Lindquist stood nearby, watching.

"We'll be referring you to the juvenile court system to start," the balding man said. "The agents at the scene stated that they found you with bags of drugs in your control and that you were pointing a gun at them." He looked up at her. "Is there anything you'd like to add?"

She gazed at him, trying to decide how to say it best. "That's what happened, but it's not the way it looks. I swear, I've never sold drugs to anyone and, the gun wasn't mine."

The man looked away and rolled his eyes. Then he leaned forward. "Right. Of course not. Miss Paxton, we are going to keep you based on the evidence that was found and you'll have your say in court." He looked over at Lindquist and back at the girl. "Given the quantity of drugs found there's a chance you'll be tried as an adult."

Rainey's eyes grew twice their size. "What does that mean, 'tried as an adult'? I'm only fourteen. I'm a kid!"

"Now," the officer said, "let's not get ahead of ourselves. I'm hoping that since this is a first-time offense, you'll stay in the juvenile system. The juvenile court judges tend to focus on rehabilitating minors, not giving them serious jail time. Agent Lindquist and I think there is a good likelihood it will remain a juvenile case, but of course we can't know that for sure."

"But I just wanna go home," she said, frantically looking from the officer sitting in front of her to Agent Lindquist. "I don't want to stay here."

Agent Lindquist was beside her by then and placed his hand on her shoulder. She looked up at him and he gave her a tender smile, which did nothing to ease her nerves.

"Let's just take this one step at a time. Being referred to the juvenile court system is a good thing. Your case will be presented by a lawyer who represents you. You should not say too much without an attorney with you. Remember your rights . . . anything you say can and will be used against you in a court of law," Lindquist explained.

Rainey squirmed on the plastic chair as an overwhelming need to flee descended upon her. "Well, can someone ask a lawyer to come and talk to me now so I can go home?"

Without commenting, Agent Lindquist escorted Rainey to a private cell. Her thoughts were a scattering of fear and regret. If she could do it all over again, she would have run from the house when Jiggy did. Everything happened so fast it didn't register that the police had entered her home while she was holding a bunch of heroin. Now there was no way she could tell the police about Jiggy and take a chance with Ivy's safety. And that gun, the stupid gun, why did she pick it up? It wasn't like she would use it. Her hatred for Jiggy grew, and she wished him dead.

"Your parents are giving their statements in a few minutes," Lindquist said. "I'll be present while they're interviewed. They've been informed you need a lawyer. You sit tight and I'm gonna grab you a sandwich and soda from the vending machine. Any special requests?"

"I'm not hungry," Rainey said, despite the hollow pit in her stomach.

Agent Lindquist leaned back on his heels. "Well, you have to eat something. You can have anything you want as long as it's in the vending machine."

"Are there potato chips?"

"Sure are. You want a bag?"

Rainey nodded but didn't make eye contact with him. "Yes, please."

Lindquist shoved his hands into his front pockets and gave her a genuine smile. "I'm gonna get you a candy bar too. How's that sound?"

Rainey's hands pressed against her empty belly. "Whatever you bring me will be fine. Thank you" she said in a joyless, monotone voice.

As Lindquist left Rainey alone in her cell and locked the heavy metal door behind him, she thought about Ivy, scared and hungry. A fresh dose of panic flowed through her body. It didn't seem fair she would get to eat, but her sister, hungry and confused, was left with her parents.

As she sat with regret for never running away from home and taking Ivy somewhere safe, the acid in her stomach bubbled up and she ran to hang her head over the toilet.

Chapter Thirty-Eight

Rainey was leaning against the green wall in her cell when the lock on the door unlatched a few minutes later. Lifting her head, she watched as Agent Lindquist walked in with his arms filled with food.

"I bought a few extra things," he said, smiling at her. "Some cookies and peanut butter crackers. You know, just in case you get hungry later and I'm not around."

"Thank you for being nice to me," Rainey said, sitting on the edge of the cot. "But I'm okay here. Could you go see my parents and check on Ivy? You can bring her some of this food," she said, handing him the peanut butter crackers.

He nodded. "Sure, I'm going in there anyway," he said, taking the crackers from her. "You should eat too."

Rainey glanced at him. "I can hardly eat when I'm worried about what's going to happen," she said.

"All right. Now listen to me, Rainey. I know you're worried about what's going to happen to you and your sister, but it's not going to help anything if you don't eat."

Rainey's posture sagged as she opened the turkey sandwich and took a bite.

Lindquist sat next to her. "When you're done eating, give a holler and the female guard sitting out there," he said, pointing to the window in the door. "Will bring you to the showers and get you something clean to wear."

Icicles ran up Rainey's spine. There was something permanent about showering and changing. "Why do I need to take a shower?"

"It's standard procedure. We just need to make sure you're okay . . . you know, no lice or skin problems . . . things like that. You'll shower and put on a uniform so that when you're transferred to juvenile detention, you'll be all set."

"But I . . . I don't wanna be transferred. Where is juvenile detention? Is it far from here? Are you gonna be there too?"

"No, Rainey. I won't be there. I work in Kensington. They're going to take you into Philadelphia. That's where the detention center is."

Rainey shook her head and stood from her cot. She had considered her options and it seemed to her that she would have to take the fall, hoping, by some miracle, that something would change. "You don't understand!" she yelled. Her face snarled as she unleashed her silent frustration. "You don't know what I'm going through. You don't know what it's like to grow up in my house with my parents."

"Whoa, now. I've been doing everything to help you. I'm just trying to be open and honest so you know what's happening. I thought it might be easier on you if it wasn't a mystery."

Rainey pushed all the food to the floor, threw herself on her cot, turned her back to Agent Lindquist, and curled up in a ball. She wrapped her arms around her head. "Just leave me alone. I hate you. I hate everyone."

Struck with a wave of empathy for the helpless teen, he said, "I don't claim to know anything about you or what you're feeling. But what I can tell you is to be patient and wait until you see what your lawyer says. I'm sure he or she will have some answers for you."

Rainey glanced at Lindquist and thought she saw a glimmer of kindness in his eyes. The agent didn't know how to comfort the fourteen-year-old girl. He was only in his mid-thirties, wasn't married, didn't have children, and had one younger sister who was highly independent and hadn't suffered any significant adversity as a child. Everything he knew about kids dealing with trauma he had learned in books and at the police academy. He looked at her with concern and compassion, but she couldn't know all of this about the man. She crossed her arms and turned away from him again.

"I'll be back to check on you," he said with a sigh. "Since you aren't eating, I'll take you out to the guard now for your shower. But you should eat when you get back here."

Rainey rolled over on her cot, and like a robot stood and followed him out of her cell. The policewoman wasn't as friendly as Agent Lindquist—she didn't even break a smile. Instead, escorted her by the elbow through a door on the left, down a short corridor, and into a shower room where she leaned against the wall and crossed her arms over her chest.

"Go on and get undressed. Leave your clothes on the bench," she said. "There's a basket on the counter with soap, shampoo, and conditioner you can use. Towels are on the shelf to the left of the sink. Let's get moving; you're not the only person who needs to be processed tonight."

Nervously, with shaking hands, Rainey walked toward the inner room where the open showers stood.

"Hold up. You need to undress here. Then you can get into the shower."

The young girl's insides clutched. She didn't want to undress in front of someone she didn't know. But understanding that she didn't have a choice, Rainey filled her lungs with air. Looking away from the guard, she quickly stripped off her clothes and darted toward the basket of soaps, grabbed a towel, and rushed toward a showerhead. Once the water was hot, she stepped under and allowed herself to be comforted by the warmth. It had been a long time since she'd had a real shower, and the hot water falling on her was a light in the midst of all of her darkness.

Rainey rubbed a bar of soap on a washcloth and scrubbed at her filthy skin. At first the water ran black around her feet. She continued to wash until the water from her body was clear. Then she focused on her long hair. It took three washes with a palmful of shampoo before it lathered. She watched the shampoo bubbles slide down the drain before she added conditioner and worked it through with her fingers. She allowed herself to forget where she was for a moment, and be consumed by the calming caress of the water on her skin.

"Let's get a move on!" the guard yelled, yanking Rainey from her moment of peace.

Rainey doused her face in the water one last time, then wrapped a towel around her body. She dried off as best she could before going to the next room.

"Those clothes on the bench are yours," the guard said. "Put them on and I'll take you back."

Rainey lifted a pair of white cotton underwear. Her mouth dropped open. The underwear was brand new. It was intact with elastic around the waist and legs. She'd never had underwear this pristine before. She slipped them on, put on a white cotton undershirt, and then dressed in the matching top and bottom yellow uniform she was provided. She picked up a pair of socks, slid her feet into them, and put on the sneakers.

Back in the holding cell, Rainey pulled the remainder of the turkey sandwich from its cellophane container and stared at all the food Agent Lindquist had brought her. While eating, she looked down at her jail-issued sneakers. It was the first time she could remember wearing a pair of shoes that hadn't been worn, thrown away, and picked out of the trash. Her jail sneakers were bright white and clean, and for a few seconds she felt lucky to be in jail. She was momentarily lost in the illusion of being cared for. *Prison isn't so bad*, she thought.

As Rainey sat on the bunk in her clean clothes and eating junk food, she was torn between getting back to Ivy or having a life where all of her basic needs were met, plus a bed to sleep in . . . even if it was a jail.

Chapter Thirty-Nine

Agent Lindquist entered the room to question Peter and Miranda. He was joined by his partner, Agent Roper.

After quick introductions, Roper took lead in the interview. "So, we'd like to discuss all the heroin your daughter had and the gun she was pointing at us when we entered. What can you tell us about them?"

Peter put his hands up. "Hey, we were worried something like this would happen, but we never expected it to be this bad. We are just as surprised as you guys."

Roper leaned forward on his elbows. "Look," he said, steadying his tone. "Your kid is in a lot of trouble. She had *a lot* of heroin. Any leads you can provide to us would be helping your kid."

Peter rubbed his forehead. "Yeah, man, of course. My wife and I still can't believe it. What do you wanna know?"

"We need to find out who Rainey is selling for," Lindquist said, holding Peter's gaze. Lindquist's mouth was in a straight line. His eyes unblinking until Peter squirmed on the plastic chair. He didn't like him or his wife. The condition of the house told the agent a story. He knew there were a lot of impoverished people in Kensington; it wasn't about that, it was about the filth and neglect of the place.

"We have no idea," Peter said, looking at his wife. "If we knew we'd totally tell you."

Roper's eyes locked on Miranda scratching at the marred skin on her arms. "Miranda, why don't you start? What happened with Rainey? Do you know who she's been hanging out with in the neighborhood?"

Miranda's head twitched to the side and her eyes focused on the opposite wall. "Look, Rainey's a normal teenager. She doesn't talk to me about much, you know, she's in that phase where parents aren't cool enough. That kid has been hard to control since she was little. Me and Peter have tried to talk to her about staying out of trouble, but once she gets her mind set on something there's no stopping her."

Roper rubbed his chin and sat back in his chair. It was clear to him that the parents had a drug problem, but that didn't make them drug dealers, it only made them bad examples for their kids. In fact, he wondered if Rainey hadn't met someone that Peter and Miranda partied with and they convinced her to sell. "So you didn't know she was selling drugs or that she had a gun?"

Miranda shook her head. "Nope."

"Have you specifically talked to her about drugs, either using or selling them?" he asked, intentionally staring at the arm she was scratching raw.

Following his eyes, Miranda pulled down her shirtsleeve. "Yeah, lots of times. She knows we would never let her sell drugs. Ever."

"Okay," Roper said. "Is there something I can get you for your arm? It looks pretty bad. What's wrong with it?"

Roper caught Miranda's frantic glance over at Peter.

"She's got eczema," Peter answered.

Roper smirked. "Eczema, huh? That's the worst eczema I've ever seen. You should take care of that."

"See, we don't have the money for the medicine. That's why it looks bad," Miranda said.

Roper nodded. "I understand. Now, just a few more questions. We know Rainey had drugs to sell. Do you know if she's using drugs?" he asked Peter.

Peter shook his head. "You know, we ain't got no idea. But I'd have to say she isn't." He glanced at Miranda, who nodded like a bobblehead. "We've never seen her look high or smell like alcohol or anything. Look, we don't have the information you're looking for, so if you don't mind, we're going to head out."

Roper nodded. "You're right, but one more thing. We looked into Rainey's school records. We understand that you homeschool her."

"Yep, we do," Peter said.

"Why is that? She went to public school, and then you pulled her out in the eighth grade to homeschool her." Roper glanced over at Lindquist. "We're just wondering why you did that."

Peter crossed his legs. "Rainey doesn't do well in social situations. She hates being around other kids. Never made any friends, so she doesn't take after me or her mother," he laughed.

The two agents sat stone-faced.

Roper looked at Lindquist. As with all drug busts, they both knew there was more to the story than either Rainey or her parents would share. That only meant they had to try harder to trip them up and get the information they wanted. "You know, Agent Lindquist, what's interesting is that I looked at Rainey's school records—she was a very good student. Pretty much straight As in the classes that matter."

Lindquist nodded. "Yeah, I didn't have to talk to her for too long to know she's a bright kid. Plus she cares a lot about her sister, Ivy."

Roper gazed at Peter. "You *didn't* remove her from school because she was acting out or cutting class? And, as you just mentioned, Rainey didn't have any friends. How do you think she got involved in selling drugs? I mean, she's homeschooled, and it sounds like she doesn't have a crowd she hangs with. What's your take on that?" he asked.

Not liking the line of questioning, Peter pushed his chair back. "Look, Officer Roper. Rainey is a wild child. Just because she's not in school and doesn't have friends doesn't mean she stays in the house all the time. She sneaks out and roams the streets. You ain't gotta be friends with a drug dealer to sell for 'em. You ought to know that better than anyone. What's more important is that Ivy will be safer without all those drugs in our house," he said, glancing over at the chair next to him where Ivy had fallen asleep.

Roper looked at Lindquist. "You want to explain what will happen now?"

Lindquist nodded. "Rainey will be held in juvenile detention until she can see a judge. She's doing okay right now. You should know that with the large quantity of heroin we seized there's a possibility she'll be tried as an adult. So if there's anything you can tell us about who she's selling for, you'd be helping your kid."

"We told you what we know," Peter said. "Look, Rainey needs to learn this is what happens when she screws up and does things that are illegal."

Disappointed not to have any new leads from the couple, Roper leaned back in his chair. "That's it. Rainey will be transferred in the morning. She's going to need an attorney. Do you have one?"

Peter smiled. "No, we don't have a lawyer. We never needed one."

Lindquist let out a sigh. "Well, if you can't hire one, we can have one appointed to her case."

Peter stood and put his hand out to Miranda. He would need to talk to Jiggy before committing to anything. "We're gonna have to get back to you on that."

***

Roper and Lindquist sat in the interview room after Peter and Miranda were gone.

"So what do you think?" Roper asked.

"I think they're both stoners, and it doesn't seem like they know much about their fourteen-year-old kid. My gut is telling me that even if the parents know who the kid is selling for, they aren't going to tell us—maybe they're worried that whoever it is will go after them."

"How did it go with Rainey?" Roper asked.

Lindquist raked his fingers through his hair. "It's weird. All she cares about is her little sister. She doesn't sound like a troubled teen. I mean, she's closed off and wouldn't give me any real information. She's making it harder on herself but she doesn't know it yet. I feel bad for her."

Roper huffed. "You feel bad for her? Since when do you have a heart for someone pointing a gun in your face while holding a hundred grams of heroin?" he quipped.

Lindquist gave him a sad smile. "Since we busted a kid and not the actual drug lord, I want to catch the bad guys, the top of the food chain. Problem is, these guys move from one drug house to the next. They don't stay still long enough to catch them in the act. That's why we went there, right? This house was on the list where at least two of the drug lords have people selling. Don't get me wrong, that's a lot of heroin to have off the street, so I'm happy about that part."

Lindquist paused. He knew how devious drug lords could be. "I'm gonna go talk to Rainey again. In the meantime, you check around with people in the area to find out if they saw anything that would help us. This kid is in a heap of shit. If there's anything that helps her out, we should bring it forward through the investigation. I get tired of these kingpins using young kids to do their dirty work."

As Lindquist walked to the other part of the building where Rainey was being held, his heart broke for the young girl. Her parents never even asked to see her. *Sad*.

As he stood outside the door of Rainey's cell, he couldn't help but wonder what would happen to this poor kid later in life after she was done serving her time.

Chapter Forty

Rainey was lying on her side in the fetal position, staring vacantly at the wall, startled when she noticed Agent Lindquist looking through the small, triangular Plexiglas window. She sat up quickly, and the metallic scraping sound of the door made her blood run cold.

"What did my mom and dad say?" she asked when Lindquist entered.

The agent shook his head. "They weren't very helpful."

"I figured. Listen, I know it looks bad but it's not what you think. It . . . it . . . was just a mistake," she stated, trying to make up a story as she went along. "I found the drugs in a Dumpster and I should've never touched them. That's all."

"Oh, yeah?" Lindquist huffed, not liking being played for a fool. "And the gun?"

Rainey groaned and jerked her body backward.

Lindquist sat on the cot next to her. "Look, I know you're confused and you want all the answers about what happens from here. Sometimes we do things that we shouldn't, and when that happens, we need to pay the consequences. You're not giving us any information and your parents told us they do not know who you got your drug supply from or that they were aware of you selling drugs."

Rainey slumped back onto the cot, feeling empty. Of course, her parents wouldn't say anything to help her; Jiggy would probably kill them if they did. "What else did they say?"

Lindquist looked down at his hands. "Your parents will decide if they can get you a lawyer on their own or if we need to appoint one to you. That's something, right?"

Rainey shrugged. "Sure." She knew that everything was stacked against her. And with that, she still received kindness from this man. It was confusing why he wasn't angry with her.

Lindquist drew in a long breath and exhaled slowly. "I know this is hard, but is there anything I should know about your parents or the people that they know?"

She pinched her lips closed and lower her head. She quickly weighed her options. If she told him about Jiggy, then bad things would happen to Ivy. The very thought terrified her and she knew it was best to say very little. She looked up and shook her head. "I mean, they have a lot of weird friends, but that's all," she said dismissively.

Lindquist stood. "I wish you hadn't put yourself in this situation. You seem like a nice kid, and it's a shame you made poor choices—you'll need to consider if protecting your drug supplier is worth spending your time locked up. But for now, you'll move to the detention center and your lawyer will build a case to defend you."

Rainey put her hands over her face. Until then, she kept everything at arm's length, hoping for a magical way out of it. But now, hearing a rational adult give her sound advice, the reality of her situation crashed in on her. It was as though someone were standing on her chest. Her sobs were stuck between her gut and her throat, internally stuck by fear.

"What's it like in juvenile detention?" she asked.

Lindquist paused before answering. She looked up at him, but he avoided her gaze. He flexed his fingers, curling and uncurling them several times. "Juvenile detention is a jail for young people. It can be rough, and some of the other kids there can be mean. You need to keep your head down and mind your own business, and you should be fine."

Rainey raked her hand through her hair. "That doesn't sound so *fine*. I know kids that were assholes and bullies from my school. I hated the ones who picked on kids for no reason." She could hear the defeat in her voice. She looked up at him, "I ain't afraid to fight. I've been in fights before with my mom. I used to let her knock me around, then one time I swung back. I whacked her right on the chin and knocked her on the ass." Her face flushed and she looked away from the agent. "I'm not proud of it. It was just something I had to do so my mom didn't think she could get away with hitting me."

A look Rainey couldn't read passed over Lindquist's face. She couldn't tell if it was sympathy or impatience as he stood and moved toward the steel door. "Well, I hope there won't be any fighting in juvenile detention. Like I said, keep your head down and mind your own business. Okay?"

Rainey nodded. *At least I won't get sold for sex in there*, she thought.

Lindquist's posture stiffened and he held out his hand to shake hers. "Best of luck to you. I'll be seeing you sometime soon."

He stopped and turned around before leaving. Lindquist faced her again. "Can I ask you a question?"

"I guess so."

"How come you stopped going to school? Is it because kids bullied you?"

Rainey shook her head and looked into Lindquist's eyes. She decided to tell him the truth, but just about this. "No. It was my idea to stop going and be *homeschooled*," she said, putting air quotes around the last word. "Once Ivy got older, she was a lot to handle. I didn't want to leave her in the house alone. My parents don't pay attention to us and they have a lot of friends coming and going all the time. I was afraid something bad would happen to her. So I decided I couldn't leave her, and I got my parents to agree to let me take care of her. The plan was I'd go back after she was in first grade full time."

"I'm sorry, Rainey."

"For what?" she asked.

"Because like a lot of kids in the area you live in, it's a difficult childhood. There's nothing wrong with being poor, and it's not so much the lack of money, but adults get depressed, and often it's the children who bear the burden." He looked at his watch. "Look, I need to go, but I promise to check in on you," he said.

"Thank you."

After Lindquist left her cell, Rainey laid back on the cot. She had been so brave over the past years in protecting Ivy, but she knew she was weak when it came to protecting herself. She told herself that everything would work out and that she'd be back with Ivy soon. But she suspected that the little voice inside her head was lying to her.

Fearful of the unknown dangers that waited for her in juvenile detention, all of Rainey's senses were on high alert. Then she considered her victory in escaping without Jiggy raping her. There was a slight bit of relief that in juvie she wouldn't have to worry about him coming for her.

Her relief was quickly replaced with guilt, thinking about Ivy at home alone with her parents, and the danger her sister would face without her protection.

Loneliness and uncertainty settled over her like a wet blanket. She wished just one person in her life cared whether she lived or died. Being unable to do something as important as defending her baby sister was insufferable, and she didn't know how she would go on living.

Chapter Forty-One

In the morning, Rainey was escorted to a police van and transferred to the Juvenile Detention Center in Philadelphia. She entered the unwelcoming beige structure through a side entrance, her eyes roaming and taking everything in. A woman in black pants and a green shirt approached.

"Hi, Rainey. My name is Rita. I'm going to check you in and help you get settled. There's a lot of information I need to go over with you. Once we're done, one of the correctional officers will take you to your cell. You can follow me."

Rainey stood, but her feet wouldn't move; she was frozen in place. She stared at the woman but couldn't respond. Suddenly, the move to the detention center seemed formal and permanent. Rainey's words were stuck somewhere between her fear and anxiety. It was only when Rita touched her arm and led her into a room with a round table and three chairs that she finally managed a "Thank you."

"Have a seat," Rita commanded.

Rainey nervously followed the order, sitting on her hands so as not to fidget.

"Let me say first that as long as you do what is asked, you won't have any problems here. I'll start with the most important rules. Remembering them will keep you out of solitary confinement. First and most important is FAD, which makes it easier to remember. That stands for fighting, alcohol, and drugs. We don't tolerate any of those here."

Rainey nodded but she heard the emphasis on the word "drugs." "I don't do drugs," she said defensively. The woman looked down at the paper on her clipboard and pursed her lips.

"Right," Rita said, and the girl reddened, knowing the woman didn't believe her. "Now, second, there's absolutely no bullying. If you find yourself being bullied, either verbally or physically, you're expected to tell one of the guards immediately. Do you understand?"

"Yes. But . . . but are there girls in here who will want to bully me?"

Rita shrugged. "Perhaps. Third, do not steal from the other girls; that's one of the biggest causes of commotion and violence in here."

Rainey nodded; her thoughts still stuck on the possibility of girls bullying her.

Rita glanced at her wristwatch and back at Rainey. "Fourth, all inmates are expected to treat each other and all employees who work here with respect. Fifth and final, do what you are instructed to do by the corrections officers and do not question their authority."

Rita held eye contact with her. "Do you have any questions about what I've told you?"

"Yeah. Can I read them again?"

Rita smirked. "You'll get a copy of them in your inmate handbook. I suggest you read the book as soon as possible. It'll help you better understand what's expected of you."

Rainey fidgeted on the chair. She pushed her hair behind her ears and leaned into Rita. "I'm a little nervous. I've never slept anywhere but my house. And I'm not used to being around a lot of other kids."

Rita gazed at her unsympathetically. "Well, I did notice you haven't attended school recently, so I can understand your concern. I suggest that you be courteous to the other girls, and as I said, if anyone bullies you, then you tell the guards."

"My mom and dad are supposed to get me a lawyer. Has anyone talked to them? To find out when my lawyer will be here to help me?" she asked, still clinging to hope that a miracle was in her near future.

Rita paused before answering, as Rainey anxiously waited for her to say something hopeful. The woman leaned back in her chair and weaved her fingers together over her protruding belly. In a flat voice she said, "Rainey, you need to focus on acclimating to your new environment. You're nervous and that's understandable, but things aren't as simple as you believe. A lawyer doesn't waltz in here and swoop you out. There's an entire process, which includes court proceedings."

A wave of panic passed over Rainey, and she placed her hands flat on the table. Her mouth hung open slightly as she tried to breathe through her growing apprehension. When the woman didn't say anything of comfort, the girl's belly almost purged itself.

Rita looked at her wristwatch again and said impatiently, "I'd advise you to settle in and get used to what's expected of you. I'm sure your parents are working on a lawyer. When your attorney is ready to talk with you, one of the officers will let you know. If you plan to get along here, you need to focus on following the rules and acting like a young lady. Now, we'll need to figure out which grade you should be in. Once that's determined, you will attend classes regularly. You'll also need to be an active member of our drug abuse group."

Rainey pushed back from the table. "But I'm not a drug addict!"

Rita leaned up on her elbows. "Let me be clear, Rainey. This is not a debate between the two of us. Nor do I want to learn that you are debating with the correctional officers. The more you fight us, the harder you'll make it on yourself. I hope we understand each other."

Rainey studied the woman. Rita's back was erect, her facial expression stern, and the high pitch of her voice cut through her. This unleashed a new round of nerves on Rainey, and terror coursed through her. She was understanding that Rita was a taste of how she'd be treated in juvie. "Yeah, I get it."

The woman nodded, then took Rainey through a gated door and gave her over to a female officer on the other side. This corrections officer wore her brown hair in a tight bun; had a sturdy build; and to her relief, a friendly smile.

"You must be Rainey. I'm Officer Fernandez. I'll be taking you to your unit. How are you doing?"

Rainey looked through the glass of the door and into the detention center. Her eyes bloated with tears and her bottom lip quivered. She tried to steady herself, not wanting to cry so soon.

Officer Fernandez moved closer. "I know you're scared. Most of the girls who come here are scared at first. But you must try not to let the other girls see you crying when I walk you in because then they'll think you're weak and that won't be good for you. Now, you and I will walk through fast. Keep your eyes on the ground so the others can't see you were crying. If you're ready, clasp your hands behind your back and follow me. Whenever you walk anywhere in the detention center your hands must be clasped behind your back, like they're in handcuffs. Got it?"

"Yeah. Thanks, Officer Fernandez."

"No worries, Rainey. You're gonna be just fine."

As she followed the officer down several cell blocks and up a flight of metal steps, the other inmates yelled comments. Some made remarks about her being young. But Rainey did as Officer Fernandez told her. Her outward appearance was stark, with her eyes glued to the ground, but inside of her, there wasn't a single piece that wasn't falling apart.

Chapter Forty-Two

Officer Fernandez guided Rainey to the intake showers, which she explained were more private than where she would be taking her daily shower. This set a whole new wave of panic in motion for the girl.

"You'll need to take a shower before I bring you to your cell," Officer Fernandez said.

Confused, Rainey grabbed the collar of the uniform they had given her at the police station the night prior. "But I took a shower yesterday. They said I would be all set when I got here."

Fernandez nodded. "Yes, and now you'll take another one. Daily showers are mandatory here. So get a move on." She handed her a plastic crate. "These are your clothes. You can keep the sneakers you're wearing, but I'll have to take the uniform."

Fernandez gestured to a metal bench a few feet away, and Rainey placed the crate down and looked at the items. Inside were socks, underclothes, sweatpants, a T-shirt, and a sweatshirt. All the new things gave the girl an odd sense of comfort and excitement.

"Is there soap and shampoo in the shower?" Rainey asked.

"No. I'll hand you everything you need through the shower door. Soon you'll be able to keep your own shower necessities, but not until we feel comfortable that you can have those types of things in your possession. Come on. You need to hurry. Take your clothes off and get into the shower."

Rainey flushed deeply and put her hand on her cheeks to cool the fire below her skin. Reluctantly, she stripped with Fernandez watching and handed her clothes over as instructed. Then she walked into the shower and the officer handed her soap and shampoo. The girl showered in the open stall with Fernandez at her back, watching her.

"Do you have to watch me?" Rainey asked, covering her developing breasts.

"I'm sorry Rainey, but there's no room for modesty here. You'll be showering with twenty-three other girls at the same time each day. So this is something you'll need to get used to."

"What? I . . . I don't want to shower with other girls," she cried.

"Of course you don't. None of the girls wants to shower with a group of people."

Rainey lifted her face up to the streaming water to wash away her salty tears.

Officer Fernandez gave her a small smile. "I imagine this is all very scary for you. But once you settle in, things will get better."

Rainey worked quickly, washing her body and hair. She could feel Fernandez's watchful eyes at her back. There was a tightness in her chest that at first she had hoped was a heart attack—then they'd take her to the hospital. Anything to leave juvie. Being held captive was, to her horror, not much different from being at her home under the crushing weight of being pimped out to Freddy and Jiggy. Both situations terrified her and made her feel trapped.

After dressing, Rainey was taken to her new home, a twelve-foot-by-twelve-foot concrete cell with thick metal bars. There were two bunk beds built into the wall, a stainless-steel toilet, one sink with a fake mirror made of reflective metal, a small desk bolted to the floor, and a stool. Her heart sank looking around the confined space. Overcome with terror, the girl looked at the officer hoping for mercy, but Fernandez gave her a curt nod. *This is it. I'm stuck in here,* Rainey thought.

The bottom bunk had been made with a sheet and blanket and she noticed books on a short shelf hanging on the other wall of the cell.

Rainey turned to Fernandez. "Is there someone else staying in here with me?" she asked in a shaky voice.

"Yes, your roommate's name is Phoenix. She arrived yesterday. Maybe the two of you can learn the system together. She's at breakfast right now, but will be back afterward."

Rainey's eyes were downcast. She'd never had any friends her age. She was nervous the girl wouldn't like her and a little excited that maybe they'd get along. "Oh. Is she . . . is Phoenix nice?"

Fernandez put her hand on Rainey's shoulder. "This is a place where girls who can't behave are sent. I'm sure that Phoenix is a decent person. I haven't had the chance to get to know her too well. My advice to you is to take it slow, and don't push anything that doesn't come naturally."

"So then you don't think that Phoenix and me are going to get along?" Rainey asked nervously. Surely if Fernandez *liked* Phoenix, she would have said so. She pictured some girl much bigger than her, stomping into the cell and taking all the new things juvie had just given her.

Fernandez avoided her eyes, which to Rainey felt like an answer in and of itself. "Okay," the officer said, "so I'll leave you to it. I'll be back in about thirty minutes with a breakfast tray. You'll eat in here this morning, but will go to the cafeteria with the others for your lunch. It'll give you a little time to settle in and put away your things from your crate."

"Okay," she said in a flat tone. "When will Phoenix be back?"

"Soon," the officer said as she slid the bars over and locked them in place. "You'll want to get your bed made first thing."

Alone again to face her unknown demons, Rainey moved about making her bed, which was a thin, flimsy mattress on top of a solid steel platform but *still better than the bed of rags she had at home*. She laid on the top bunk and closed her eyes. In the unnerving quiet of her confinement, with the only noise being distant voices and steel sliding against steel in the background, her thoughts wandered to Ivy again. Rainey hugged herself tightly as she imagined Ivy's small arms wrapped around her neck. When the two sisters cuddled it was their way of telling each other there was someone in the world that loved them.

When the door to her cell slid open Rainey sat up quickly. Standing with her arms crossed over her chest was a girl wearing a scowl that set deep lines across her forehead. The first thing she noticed about Phoenix is that she was very unattractive.

"Hi," Rainey said, sounding vulnerable.

"Who the hell are you?"

"I'm Rainey. I just got here."

"No shit. I already know you just got here."

Rainey swung her legs over the bunk. "You're Phoenix, right?"

"Yeah, who told you that? Fernandez?"

Rainey nodded. "Why are you in here?" she asked, which to her seemed like a normal first question. Apparently not.

"Why are you asking?" Phoenix said, her face snarling into a tight knot.

Rainey flinched. "I don't know . . . no reason. Since we're in here together, I . . . I was trying to get to know you, I guess."

Phoenix advanced on Rainey like a gazelle. "Yeah, well, that's not a question you ask somebody you just met. It ain't none of your business why I'm in here." Phoenix stared at Rainey through narrowed eyes, still scowling, hands now firmly on her hips.

To Rainey, it was as if the air in the cell had turned rancid, filled with hate and disgust seeping out of Phoenix.

With a heavy heart, Rainey slid back on her bunk until she was against the wall, her palms held out in front of her. She hadn't realized how much she'd been hoping the two of them would be friends, but now she knew.

"I'm sorry for asking you why you're in here. Okay? I get it. You don't wanna be friends. I was just trying to be nice. That's all. I didn't mean to get you upset." Rainey slumped against the wall and slowly laid on her side, facing away from Phoenix.

Phoenix didn't budge for a while. Then, after a few minutes, Rainey heard the girl grabbing a book from the shelf on the wall and climbing into the lower bunk.

Rainey lay on the top bunk with her eyes open. She was scared that Phoenix would hurt her. And, after her first encounter, her nerves were frazzled about having to meet the other girls housed in the detention center. *What if they all hate me like Phoenix does?* After an hour, unable to drag her thoughts away from all the bad things that could happen to her, she began to cry. She no longer cared what Phoenix thought about her. She was alone and scared.

***

Phoenix listened to the girl trying to muffle her sobs, but she knew all too well, how hard it was to stop those tears from falling. It brought her back to when she first fled to the streets on her own. She'd lived in alleyways and bus stations for the most part. She'd cry herself to sleep every night. It was the scariest time of her life much worse than being in juvenile detention.

Phoenix said nothing; she just listened. Thirty minutes later the crying stopped. Rainey had fallen asleep. *Sleep well, little girl,* she thought, *it won't be long before you have to walk these halls, the halls of the devil's castle.*

Chapter Forty-Three

"Chow time in fifteen minutes. Chow time in fifteen minutes." The announcement came over the speakers, stirring Rainey from her uneasy sleep.

Rainey's eyes popped open and she jumped from the bunk, glancing over at Phoenix, who seemed to be asleep. Frightened, Rainey stood at their door, looking out into the detention center. She didn't even know where to go for food. Some of the other girls yelled to each other from their cells. Rainey realized she was about to be thrown into the full population within minutes. Her breath quickened as she drew in shallow, sharp breaths.

"You need to chill out." The voice was deep and serious from behind her.

Rainey turned and Phoenix sat up and rolled her eyes. "You look a wreck. Pull yourself together."

"Why? What do you care?" Rainey asked with a glimmer of hope that the girl *did* care.

"I heard you crying," Phoenix snapped. "If you keep blubbering like a two-year-old, two things are gonna happen. One, it'll bring attention from the other girls to our cell, and two, I ain't gonna be able to sleep with you bawling all night."

Rainey looked up at the ceiling, blinking away fresh tears. She remained silent, not wanting to piss off her cellmate anymore.

"We're heading down to lunch soon," Phoenix said. "If you don't stop crying, you're gonna get your ass beat before you have your first meal in the cafeteria."

Rainey ran her hands over her hair. "Okay. Thanks. That's helpful," she remarked sarcastically.

"So you're scared?" Phoenix asked in a softer tone, sensing the girl's fear.

Rainey shrugged. "A little. I've never been in a place like this. I'm just hoping all the other girls are nicer than you are."

Phoenix turned away, but Rainey thought she saw a smile. When she turned back, her face was set in a hard scowl again. "I ain't in here to be nice. I'm in here to survive."

"Yeah, well, maybe it would be good if we got along with each other, since we have to share this tiny space," Rainey said, waving her hand around their small confines.

Phoenix was quiet for a moment. Then she stood and faced Rainey. "How old are you, anyway?"

Rainey turned her head and met the girl's gaze. "Fourteen. You?"

"Just turned fifteen last week," she answered. She pulled the stool out from the desk and sat down. "You get your class assignments yet?"

"Nah, not yet. I have to take some tests later today so they can figure out what grade I should be in."

"Why? You live locked up in an attic before you came here or something?"

Rainey shook her head. "I stopped going to school so I could stay home and take care of my little sister."

Phoenix looked down at her hands. "I have a sister too. She's older, though."

Hopeful that the girl was finally letting her guard down, Rainey moved closer. "You do?"

"Yeah, I do. The bitch didn't do shit for me after my parents died. She was never nice to me. I've taken care of myself for a long time. There ain't much I'm afraid of anymore." She looked up at the ceiling, and Rainey thought maybe she was trying to fight back tears.

Rainey let out a soft chuckle. Maybe she and Phoenix had more in common than she'd thought. "I've taken care of myself too. My mom and dad are useless. I had an aunt who took care of me for a while, but she got sick when I was eight. Been on my own ever since."

Phoenix glanced back at her. "Your parents dead now?"

"Ha!" Rainey surprised herself by the harshness of her laugh. "No, they're not dead. They're heroin addicts. Well, they're heroin addicts, meth addicts, crack addicts, and alcoholics . . . depending on the time of day."

"You ever use?" Phoenix asked.

"Hell, no." Rainey shook her head firmly. "I'd rather pluck my eyeballs out with a toothpick. I've seen what it does and there ain't nothing nice about it. It's disgusting to watch people who use—they do the grossest stuff. It makes me sick to my stomach. I never want to be like them."

"I never used either. I thought about it when things were rough, but I can't stand not being in control . . . I'm like my mom." Phoenix went silent and took a few deep breaths as Rainey watched. "My parents died in a freak boat accident when they were on vacation. I've been in and out of foster homes since I was nine. I haven't had a place where I belonged since they died. One day I had a regular life, and the next, it was all gone. There was this one kinda cool foster family, but that didn't work out and I had to leave."

"Where did you go?" Rainey asked.

"Look, maybe I'll tell you all about it someday, but today ain't that day."

Curiosity gnawed at Rainey. "Come on. At least tell me where you went after you left."

"Man, you're a pain in the ass," Phoenix mumbled, standing abruptly. "I just told you—not today.

"Why?" Rainey asked, unable to stop herself. She couldn't remember the last time she'd had a conversation with someone her age.

"If I tell you, will you stop bugging me?"

Rainey nodded, trying to hide her excitement at making a real friend.

Phoenix huffed. "Okay, when I split from that foster home, I asked my sister if I could live with her because she was already eighteen and had gotten out of the system, but she told me I needed to learn to take care of myself. She's a piece of shit . . . was always jealous of me because I was the baby. You know? So I went back into another placement, and those people really liked me."

Rainey grinned. "Why didn't you stay with them?"

The girls were interrupted when Officer Fernandez appeared at the barred door.

"Let's get moving, girls," she said. She placed her hand on Rainey's shoulder, looking from her to Phoenix. "I take it you two are getting along?"

Both girls mumbled, didn't commit, and nodded slightly.

"Good. Make sure it stays that way," Fernandez said, a smile pulling at her lips.

Inside the cafeteria, Phoenix turned to the girl. "Don't sit near me. I don't want any shit from these bitches."

Disappointed, Rainey sat alone at a table and looked at the tray of food. Sloppy Joe, a roll, string beans, and a carton of orange juice. She had been so nervous she'd hardly touched the breakfast that Fernandez had brought her in the morning. Now her belly growled as her eyes moved over all of the food she would have been so grateful for when she lived at home.

Chapter Forty-Four

Phoenix slyly watched Rainey from one table over. When the bell rang, Phoenix moved quickly to the trash can and tossed her uneaten food. While standing there, she jumped when Rainey tapped her on the shoulder.

"Where's your class?" Rainey squeaked in a panicky voice.

Phoenix spun around. "I told you not to talk to me—that I don't want to get involved in your shit. Do you see how all the girls are watching us?" she asked through clenched teeth.

Rainey's head jerked back and she moved her eyes around the room to see who was watching them. "I was hoping we could walk together, you know, so I don't get lost. Do you know where the art class is? That's where I have to stay until I take my placement test later today."

Phoenix snickered. "All the classrooms are in the same area. So how was your lunch?" she asked as they walked.

Rainey's eyes were distant. "It's weird how when I lived at my house I spent every day scrounging for food. I fought to keep me and my little sister fed. But now, a tray full of food doesn't mean anything to me without having her to share it with."

Phoenix looked away, thinking that the girl provided way too much information about her life.

"Whatever. You need to get over the whole *my life is a sob story* because nobody, especially not me, cares about how hard things were for you. Things were hard for everybody in here. Get that through your head real fast."

Rainey crossed her arms over her chest.

Phoenix got closer. "Don't tell me you're gonna cry again."

"You're mean. I didn't do anything to you."

Phoenix turned and left leaving Rainey walking alone.

Rainey, petrified of what was to come, tried to appear casual as she walked quickly behind Phoenix to her first class. The hall was swarming with girls laughing and yelling at each other.

As she turned a corner, Phoenix stopped abruptly. Rainey stood back a few feet as a petite, dark-skinned girl approached her cellmate. Three larger girls, with their arms crossed over their puffed-out chests, stood behind her.

"Oh look, the ugly *el puta* is here," the small girl taunted.

One of the girls standing behind her laughed and pointed at Rainey. "Yeah, Phoenix the whore has a new cellmate. You must be a stupid slut just like your friend here. Huh?"

"Get the hell out of the way, Martina," Phoenix roared at the girl blocking her.

The girl called Martina stepped to the side, moved past Phoenix, and stood close to Rainey, who had broken into a cold sweat.

Martina placed her hands on her hips and jutted her head forward. "It ain't gonna help you in here to be friends with *la niña*," she said, pointing to Phoenix.

Rainey's shoulders pressed back as her spine stiffened. "She's not a little girl, she's my cellmate." She immediately wanted to protect Phoenix, not for a favor, but because it seemed the right thing to do.

"Oh, look at this," Martina sang, glancing at her friends. "The white girl knows Spanish. Were you the teacher's pet in school?" She looked back at her friends and laughed before returning her deadpan gaze to Rainey.

Rainey stood with her feet spread apart. She wasn't about to be pushed around on her first day in juvie—she understood enough to know that once you become a victim it's hard to break the pattern. Her stare was piercing. She didn't blink. Her face was like stone. "Actually, I learned Spanish from some badass bitches that hung out with Jiggy. If you're from around here I'm sure you know who he is."

Martina weakened, and when she spoke, her voice was quieter. "Yeah, I know him. Everybody knows Jiggy."

Rainey formed a temple with her fingertips and pressed them to her mouth. Her lips turned up at the corners. "I was with him last night when I got busted." She tilted her head back and narrowed her eyes at the girl, willing to use whatever she had to make the girls back down.

"Yeah, well, it still ain't good that you're hanging out with this bitch. Just 'cause you know Jiggy doesn't mean *she* does," Martina said, waving her boney index finger in the air at Phoenix. "Did your little cellmate tell you that she likes to sleep with guys who have girlfriends?"

Phoenix stepped forward with her arms at her sides and her hands balled into fists. Her nostrils flared. "Shut up, Martina! Just because your man wasn't loyal doesn't mean you can put that on me. How was I supposed to know he was your boyfriend? And if I knew he had a girl *and* that it was you, I definitely wouldn't have had sex with him. Makes me want to puke thinking that he touched you before he was with me."

Rainey had wanted to put on a tough front, but suddenly, hearing the exchange, she realized she was in way over her head. Something bad was about to happen.

Martina's lips tightened and she moved into Phoenix's personal space. Their noses practically touched. "Maybe your new friend would rather hang out with us. We think you like being a loner anyway."

The two girls stood so close together that Phoenix could smell the sugary sweetness of Martina's lip gloss. "Her name is Rainey," Phoenix said, "and she can hang with whoever the hell she wants. It doesn't matter to me. Understand? I don't need to be surrounded by a pack of bitchy girls to feel safe. I'll fight any of you, anytime."

Martina moved away from Phoenix and placed her arm lightly over Rainey's shoulder.

"Any friend of Jiggy's is a friend of mine," she said. "You can hang with us if you want. How 'bout it? Probably be a lot safer than hangin' with this trash. Besides, ain't gonna do you no good to be acting like you're her friend. I'd say it's dangerous for you, even if you do know Jiggy—'cause, you see, he ain't here."

Rainey could feel the nervous energy rolling off of Phoenix so she lifted Martina's arm from her shoulder. If she had to choose sides, it was going to be the girl she shared a cell with.

"The thing is, I'm a loner too. I appreciate you asking me to join your group and all, but I just got here. Besides, Phoenix is my cellmate. How would that be if I turned on her? Doesn't seem right. So I'll have to pass on your offer. Oh, and one other thing: I wouldn't be so sure about crossing Jiggy . . . *even if he's not here.*"

Phoenix gave what Rainey thought was a genuine smile, which thrilled her.

"Let's go," Phoenix said. "We're gonna be late for class."

Rainey turned to face her. "Yeah. We better get moving."

As the two walked to C Building, Rainey noticed that Phoenix watched everyone near them—as though she were expecting something bad to happen.

"Are you okay?" Rainey asked.

"Yeah. Why wouldn't I be?"

"Because Martina and her friends were mean to you," Rainey said, a little annoyance coming through in her voice. She had just put herself out for the girl and believed they'd share a bond now.

Phoenix was thoughtful for a few seconds. Then she said, "Yeah, well. I only got here yesterday and I've already had a full day of Martina being a pain in my ass. It'll all work out or I'll just have to fight. Thanks for not turning on me, though. I appreciate it."

Rainey, proud she stuck by her, nudged Phoenix with her elbow. "I have a feeling you're not as grouchy as you want me to believe."

Phoenix nudged her back playfully. "Whatever. You have no idea how bitchy I can be. I don't talk to anyone in this place unless I have to." She grinned. "So what's that shit you were talking about Jiggy? I heard about him on the streets but never had anything to do with him."

Rainey glanced at her sideways. "Jiggy is the biggest asshole who ever lived. He was about to rape me right before the cops showed up at my house. He ran out of my bedroom before they got there. I hate his guts."

Phoenix's eyes bulged. "So you bullshitted Martina about being friends with him?"

Rainey's smile stretched across her face, shrugging. "Yeah, I guess I did. I was convincing too, huh?"

Phoenix smirked. "Oh, man. Martina looked like she was gonna shit her pants when you said his name."

"Jiggy isn't someone to mess with. He's powerful on the streets. Everyone is afraid of him, including me," she said, reflecting on her fear from the night before.

Phoenix's forehead creased. "Yeah, I heard that about him. I guess any douchebag that was going to rape you would be scary."

Rainey looked in the direction of a wave of chirping young girls locked up in jail, the squeaky sounds of sneakers and flip-flops making their distinctive echoes in the halls. The unsettling noises of a disorderly place. Her nerves were already frazzled. She hoped the sweat clinging to her stomach and back didn't show through her flimsy prison outfit. As she stepped in time with the racket all around her, Rainey kept her eyes from wandering.

Chapter Forty-Five

At the end of her first day, Rainey grabbed a tray and went through the dinner food line behind Phoenix. There weren't many choices, but Rainey didn't care. She wasn't a picky eater, not like some of the other girls she overheard complaining.

Phoenix moved swiftly into the seating area and led them to the far end of a table, where they sat alone. Rainey lifted her fork and dug into the food on her tray, shoveling it into her mouth, pausing only when she noticed Phoenix's open-mouthed stare.

"Did your family starve you or something?" she asked.

Rainey shrugged, then rammed a spoonful of applesauce into her mouth and gulp-swallowed. "I've been starved for most of my life. Starved of food, love, parents—you name it and I've been deprived of it." She lifted a forkful of macaroni and cheese and put it into her mouth. Rainey closed her eyes. "Mmm. This is so good."

Phoenix put a forkful of macaroni and cheese in her mouth. "I mean, I guess it's okay. I don't think it's as great as you're making it out to be."

Rainey opened her milk and poured in a mouthful. She tilted her head and smiled. "How long do I have to wait before I can ask you why you're in here?"

Phoenix pinched her lips together and banged her hand on the table dramatically. "I already told you it's none of your business!"

Rainey's heart plummeted to her belly. Her eyes bugged out as she set her milk carton back on the tray. The girls sitting closest to them stopped eating and watched. Rainey thought they had bonded, made progress because of what happened with Martina in the hallway. She slid her palms over her cheeks slowly with both hands and cleared her throat.

Phoenix leaned across the table. "Relax, I'm playing with you. I'll tell you after you tell me your story. But not now, we need to finish eating. We'll talk when we're alone."

Rainey nodded, chuckling awkwardly, and swallowed the lump that had formed in her throat. She wondered if she and Phoenix were becoming real friends, even if she was learning quickly that there were no guarantees in juvie.

That night, Rainey was lying on her bunk when Phoenix returned to their cell.

"Hey, where have you been?" Rainey asked.

"Why do you care?" Phoenix said coldly, avoiding eye contact. "I was in the bathroom, okay?"

Confused and insulted, Rainey slid off of the top bunk. "Jeez, Phoenix. One minute you're nice and the next you're mad at me. What's going on? Did something happen with you and Martina again?"

"No. Why do you have to ask so many questions all the time? It's annoying," Phoenix spat.

Rainey backed away and leaned on the bars of the cell door, reminded of how her father yelled at her for the same thing. She traded her hurt for annoyance and said, "You know, you don't have to be so nasty. You're not the only person going through a hard time. My sister is home alone with no one to protect her, and I have no idea what's going to happen to me. I'm just trying to make the best of things. I wish you'd lighten up."

Phoenix rolled her eyes. "Yeah, I know." Her voice was softer. She was quiet for a moment, then sighed. "You're right. I didn't mean to take my shit out on you. Nothing happened with Martina, I didn't even see the bitch."

"Then what's wrong?"

Phoenix let out a deep sigh. "I have to appear in court tomorrow and I'm worried about what's going to happen. I'm in here because I was caught stealing money."

Rainey raised her eyebrows. "Who did you steal from?"

"A convenience store . . . I, um, I held up the guy behind the counter with a knife."

Rainey gasped. "You put a knife in someone's face?"

"Yeah." Phoenix grunted. "I did . . . stuck the pointy tip right against his throat. The problem is it's the third time I'm being charged with armed robbery . . . so I don't expect things to go so good."

Rainey plopped down on the stool by the desk and her shoulders slumped over her chest. "Why would you do that?"

Phoenix shrugged. "I needed money."

Rainey chuckled. "So you decided to grab a knife, go to a store, and threaten some guy you don't even know?"

"When you say it like that it sounds dumb," Phoenix admitted.

Rainey looked up and widened her eyes at her. "It *was* dumb. You're way smarter than that."

"I told you I was in and out of foster care."

Rainey kept her voice even. "Just because things were bad for you doesn't mean you need to make things bad for other people. It's not fair."

Phoenix sat on her bunk. "You don't get it. My last foster was super cheap . . . like crazy cheap. They said I had to learn how to provide for myself. That doing things on my own would make me a better person, even though they were getting money from the state to take care of me. They beat me for the stupidest things. I had to get away from them, so I stole money from my foster mother's purse and hopped on a train to Kensington. I heard it was a sketchy town and figured they'd never look for me there."

"What does that have to do with stealing from a store? Why didn't you get a job?"

"I had a job, but I wasn't making enough money," Phoenix said.

"Well, you could've asked your boss for more money," she offered.

Phoenix snorted. "You don't know shit. I was a hooker. I had lots of bosses."

"A hooker?" Rainey repeated in disbelief.

"Yeah, it wasn't like I planned it or anything. It just happened. I'd been on the streets for a week, maybe longer. I was hungry and cold and tired. Anyway, one night this guy came up to me and offered me twenty bucks to jerk him off. That's how it started." Phoenix blushed deeply at the memory.

"Shit! I'm sorry you went through all of that. I would've been so scared," she said.

"Yeah, it totally sucked. There are some nasty-ass guys out there, but if you're selling, then you gotta take whatever comes your way—as long as they have cash. Anyway, I learned the more I was willing to do with the guys the more money I could make."

Rainey remembered her conversation with Mona. "Did you have a . . . pimp?"

Phoenix bit her bottom lip. "In the beginning, I didn't. I even had enough customers to rent a room from this scumbag landlord who had a beat-up house. But it was better than the streets. At least I could lock my door."

"How many people lived there?" she asked.

"I don't know. I guess there were about a dozen rooms. I didn't pay much attention to the others. Anyway, I worked the streets for a while longer on my own. I made decent money too. Then I met this pimp. He pretended to love me, but that didn't last long. Before I knew it, he was beating the hell outta me and made me hook for him. He said . . . said if I didn't prostitute, he'd make sure I never saw the light of day again. Anyway, one night, Martina's boyfriend paid me to have sex with him, and she found out about it. I avoided her until I landed inside this place." Lowering her eyes, she said, "Dumbass Martina thought he was dating me, she's that stupid. Anyway, I never told her that he paid me to be with him."

"Why not?"

Phoenix looked at Rainey. "Because I hate girls that blame other girls for their boyfriend cheating on them. I don't get why chicks do that and give their cheatin' ass boyfriends a pass."

Rainey stood and moved next to the girl. "This is crazy. I mean, you're a prostitute?"

"Hey Mother Teresa, sometimes you gotta do what you gotta do. Being a prostitute isn't the worst thing in the world. It was something I had to do to survive. I fucking hated it too. That's why I started robbing stores—to get extra money. Besides, I got arrested a couple of times for hooking; those were proud moments," she said sarcastically.

"How did you get out of jail with no money?"

Phoenix raked her fingers through her hair. "My pimp bailed me out twice, but both times when he got me back to the whorehouse, he beat me so bad I almost died. He didn't care. The prick locked me in a bedroom with nothing . . . no water, no food. I just laid on a filthy mattress waiting for the swelling to go down and the bruises to fade, hoping that nothing was broken. He didn't let me out for days. I thought for sure I was gonna die."

Rainey jammed her hands under her armpits. "Will your pimp be at court tomorrow?"

Phoenix shook her head. "No. I didn't call him this time. I mean, I'm sure he knows that I'm in here from one of his bitches . . . he's got prostis everywhere. Anyway, I'd rather stay in juvie than go back to working the streets for him."

"So then you shouldn't care what happens in court since you'd rather be in here than on the streets again."

Phoenix raised her eyes to meet Rainey's. "Yeah, I guess you're right. But there's one thing that scares the hell outta me."

***

The next day, when Phoenix returned to their cell after her court appearance, her eyes were steady, the way a wolf fixes its gaze on his next meal. She didn't look at Rainey, but it was easy to see something had gone wrong.

"Things didn't go well?" Rainey asked. "Are they making you leave juvie?"

Phoenix shook her head. "Nah. Third offense. I got sentenced to eight years with the possibility for parole in five."

Rainey's mouth hung open. Her heart hammered against the walls of her chest. "So you would stay here for three years then be sent to adult prison?"

Phoenix's bottom lip trembled and she shrugged. "Yeah, even if I get paroled in five, I'll have to spend two years in a women's prison." She looked up at the ceiling. "I was hoping to serve all my time here, in juvie. I was worried this would happen."

The hopelessness in her cellmate's voice made Rainey's heart shatter as she tried to think of something positive to say. Rainey knelt in front of the girl and looked into her face. Phoenix wouldn't make eye contact.

"You have three years before you're eighteen. Maybe, by then, you'll figure a way out of here. Maybe a lawyer can help you. I know one thing: I'll be out of here in no time and then I'll help you when I'm out," Rainey said.

"Yeah, right. Why the hell would you wanna help me?"

Rainey smiled. "I know how it feels not to have anyone willing to help. Maybe you and me can learn to count on each other."

Phoenix put a hand on Rainey's shoulder. "Thanks. I don't know you yet, but I think you're okay. Just don't disappoint me. To be clear, if you tell anyone anything that I've told you—I'll kill ya."

Rainey grinned. "See that? You're an asshole," she sang jokingly.

Phoenix gave her a small smile. "Well, it's better than being a cheap whore."

Chapter Forty-Six

The next morning, in the cafeteria, Martina sat next to Rainey while two of Martina's followers stood behind the girl. Rainey's back stiffened and she kept her eyes glued on Phoenix, who was sitting across from her.

"Get lost, Martina," Phoenix said evenly.

"Shut the hell up, you piece of dog shit," Martina growled through clenched teeth. Then she reached over and touched Rainey's hair. "You know, you're so pretty—way too pretty to be hanging out with *her*. They say hangin' with ugly people makes you ugly too. You should consider joining our group."

Rainey laid her fork on the table as she tried to steady her shaking hand. She couldn't believe Martina wouldn't let the grudge go. Anger surged through Rainey's body, and she turned toward Martina. "It sounds like a great offer, but I'm good here. Thanks."

Martina chuckled. "You seem like a cool girl, and I mean we assume that you're smart. Thought you'd want to come over here and give you a chance to get away from this bitch," she said, lifting her chin in Phoenix's direction. "Just so you know this is the last time I'm gonna ask you to join us. So unless you plan to stay with Phoenix for, like, forever, then you best walk away from her now."

Rainey glanced at Phoenix. Under the tight lips and flared nostrils, she could see the sadness smoldering below the surface. She suspected the anger was not only Martina trying to turn her against Phoenix, but also because she called her ugly. Phoenix wasn't the prettiest girl she'd ever seen, but still it was hurtful.

"You know what? You're rude. Phoenix isn't ugly, and oh, by the way, I don't think you're all that pretty. So, I appreciate your dumb offer, but I'm good staying here with Phoenix."

Martina looked into Rainey's face and forced a smile. "Okay, well consider yourself stuck with her then. I suggest you start watching your back too." With that, Martina stood up and walked away, the other girls following behind like she was the Pied Piper.

Rainey sat with her hands folded in front of her. Her greatest fear of coming to juvie was getting into physical fights with the other girls, and now, here she was with a group of girls that already hated her. All she knew was that she couldn't sit by idly and let someone else be pushed around. She understood what it was like to be alone, to have no one to help you in battle, and she didn't wish that fate on anyone. She shoved a grape into her mouth. "You know, Martina just wants to hurt you because she's jealous of you."

Phoenix lifted her chin. "Yeah, sure. Look, I don't need your pity, okay? I don't care what Martina thinks. I know I'm not pretty. I totally get that. Been dealing with it my whole life. So what? Pretty don't mean nothing when you're a rotten, heartless bitch."

Rainey leaned forward on her elbows. "I think you have a unique look," she said.

Phoenix rolled her eyes. "My face is too long. My eyes are too close together. My teeth are crooked, my nose is too big, and I'm blind without these nasty state-issued glasses."

Rainey looked down at her hands resting on the table. Those things that Phoenix said about herself were true, but there was still something attractive about her. She had a killer body and a serious don't-mess-with-me attitude, but more than anything else, she thought it was Phoenix's hidden vulnerability that made her attractive. She was as mean as a rattlesnake, but below the facade of a sharp-toothed serpent was a young girl let down and left broken-hearted just like herself.

"I think you're being too hard on yourself," Rainey answered.

"Whatever. You know, I always thought that if I was beautiful my life would be so much better. But I know lots of beautiful girls just like you and your life is as fucked up as mine, maybe even worse than mine."

Rainey adjusted on the plastic stool. "Hey, to be honest, the only thing my looks ever got me was the attention of some perverted old guys. We all think if we get something we don't have our lives would be better—you always thought being pretty would make you happy, and for me, it was always believing if my mom and dad loved me more, my life would be better. Now all I care about is them getting me out of this place and going home."

"That's your problem. You don't see things so clear."

Rainey's lips pursed and she sat up taller. "What does that mean?"

Phoenix took a bite of bread. "Well, take your parents, for example. You told me that you can't depend on them and that they've done nothing to make your life better. You just said you wished they loved you more. Then you tell me that you still believe they're going to help you get outta here. It doesn't make any sense."

Rainey flushed and looked away, knowing she sounded foolish. "I know all of that, okay? But if I don't believe they'll do something to help me, then I have nothing. Don't you understand that there's no one else out there for me? Do you think I don't know what they've done to me? To my life? To my sister's life? You have no idea how much I hate them. And I'm certain they'll never get me out of this place—I don't know what my problem is, I just wanna feel normal and have hope."

Phoenix, surprised by the outburst of honesty, looked at her with wide eyes. "Yeah, I get it. I'm only saying that maybe if you stop talking about them that way it would be easier for you to accept that you got fucked. And, the truth is, every time you say it, whether you mean it or not, you're opening yourself up for disappointment. Your parents are shitbags—that's all there is to it."

With that, Phoenix grabbed her tray and walked away.

Realizing the truth in what Phoenix told her and, calling her out for her bullshit, Rainey lifted her tray and followed. Her cellmate was right, of course—she sounded delusional talking about her parents like they cared about her. Yes, it scared her to admit to herself she was on her own, but she knew it was her reality.

In the hall, before heading in separate directions to their classes, an officer approached them. "Rainey, I need to talk with you for a minute."

Butterflies fluttered in Rainey's belly. "What is it? Did something happen?"

The officer shook her head. "No. I've come to let you know that your parents will be here tomorrow. Your new attorney has requested time with you."

"That's a good thing, right?" Rainey asked the officer.

"Sure. Having an attorney beats not having one. They'll be here in the morning. I wanted you to know so that you're ready." Then the officer turned and walked away.

Rainey turned to Phoenix with her hand over her mouth. Her face was bright red and tears filled her eyes.

"Why aren't you happy? You have an attorney. That's what you wanted," Phoenix said.

"Because something isn't right. My mom and dad don't have the money to pay for one. I thought they were just trying to act like concerned parents by saying they needed to figure it out, but I totally thought I'd get the free lawyer. Something isn't right," she said.

Phoenix patted her shoulder. "We'll talk later. I can help you make a list of questions to ask your attorney."

Rainey's stomach burned with acid when she gave Phoenix a quick hug. "Thanks. I'll see you later."

Rainey walked down the hallway toward her classroom. While having a lawyer gave her some hope, she doubted her parents would show up. She'd work with Phoenix later on questions so she could handle it on her own.

Chapter Forty-Seven

"Rainey?" Officer Fernandez said softly, waking her from a sound sleep.

Her eyes fluttered open and closed again.

"Come on. Wake up. Your parents are here with your lawyer. They showed up earlier than we expected. Get out of your bunk and get ready. I have to take you down to meet with them in ten minutes."

"Okay, I'm up," Rainey said groggily, rubbing sleep from her eyes.

"Come on, Paxton. Get a move on," Fernandez said, raising her voice when the girl didn't move from her bunk.

Rainey moseyed the few steps to the sink and splashed her face with water.

Phoenix laid in her bunk and watched. "Are you excited to meet your lawyer?"

She rolled her eyes. "Not really, I'm more relieved. Look," she said turning to Phoenix, "everything you've told me about acting like my parents are gonna help me is true. I've been dealing with their shit since I was a little girl and I know nothing is going to change now."

"Yeah, sorry about that. I don't mean to be the bringer of bad news."

Rainey dried her face. "You're the bringer of real news. I appreciate it, you know? Plus, now I know you really listen to everything I tell you. I'm excited to meet my lawyer. I mean, *he's* the guy who is gonna help me with my case. Maybe find a way to get me outta here. That's what lawyers do. Right?"

Phoenix shrugged. "I guess so."

***

When Rainey walked into the interview room, relief trickled through her core looking at the tall gray-haired man wearing black-framed glasses. *This is my lawyer,* she thought.

The man's eyes followed her from the door until she sat across from him. Dread replaced relief as the silence in the room grew thick and awkward.

"Hi," Rainey said looking at her parents. "Nice of you to come and see me. Why did it take you five days?" she asked, her voice laced with anger.

Miranda shrugged. "We were busy. Needed to get you a lawyer and that shit takes time."

Rainey had the urge to spit in her mother's face. "Yeah, okay. How's Ivy?"

Miranda scoffed. "Ivy's fine. You're not the only one in the world that can take care of her."

Rainey's eyes narrowed, insulted by the comment. "I only asked how she was doing. I miss her. Okay?"

Miranda waved her hand in the air, dismissing her daughter.

Rainey paused for a moment. This already wasn't going well, and she feared it was about to get worse. She turned to her father. "Hi, Dad."

Peter lifted his chin in her direction without making eye contact.

Officer Fernandez, still standing at the door, said, "I'm going to leave you all to it. Rainey, when you're done, give a knock on the door, I'll be waiting on the other side."

After Officer Fernandez left the room and closed the door behind her, Rainey turned to the three adults on the other side of the table. She looked at the man.

"Hi, I'm Rainey. I'm really happy you're going to help me."

"I'm Brice Culler. Good to meet you," the lawyer said mechanically, not making a move to shake her hand.

Rainey picked up on the tension and coldness. She could sense that she was going to get bad news, and her nerves unraveled. "You're my lawyer, right?"

Brice held eye contact and shrugged. "That all depends on you."

"I . . . I . . . don't understand. What does that mean?" Rainey asked. Confused, she looked to her parents. Her mother ignored her, but Peter stood and walked around the table, stopping next to her.

"Well, Brice is a very expensive attorney," he said, looking down at her.

"Really? Where did you get the money to pay him?" Rainey asked, holding her breath as she waited for an answer.

"Brice is an attorney that works for Jiggy."

Rainey sucked in a breath. "Why would you bring Jiggy's attorney here to help me?"

Peter leaned closer to his daughter. "That's a good question. See, here's the thing . . . if you want Brice's help to get you a lesser sentence, you'll do what he tells you to do. Sometimes bad shit happens. And, that's when you just gotta suck it up and take one for the team."

Rainey whipped around and faced her father. "I didn't do anything. Yeah, I was stupid because I should've run out of there when Jiggy did, but you know I'm not a dealer. I was counting bags 'cause he told me to it. And the gun . . . I didn't know the cops were coming. I was scared and picked it up. But I shouldn't go to prison for it."

Peter shrugged. "You were caught red-handed. You're not going to just walk out of here; get real. But here's the thing, you better start listening to what Brice tells you to do . . . we don't wanna drag more people into this. Those dumb cops were asking me and your mom about where you got all the drugs to sell. We're sure they're asking you the same thing. Did you tell them anything?"

She shook her head. She was overwhelmed with anger. "No, you threatened that if I said anything Jiggy will hurt Ivy."

"That's right, he will. So keep your fucking mouth shut and do what's best for your family."

Rainey's face reddened. She looked at him with her green eyes blazing. She turned quickly to Brice, who confirmed Peter's story with a nod of his head.

She turned back to her father. "You don't have to worry. I haven't said a word but you better know that's only because of Ivy. If anything happens to her, I'll tell the cops everything I know about him and you and all those other scumbags at our house." She turned to Brice with a scowl. "What is it that you want me to do? Huh? What do I gotta do for you to help me?"

"It's fairly simple," Brice sneered. "You will go to court and tell the judge you made a big mistake. That you intended to sell the drugs you were caught with when the cops arrested you." He pointed his index finger at her. "Keep in mind that you were sitting in a sea of little bags filled with heroin when they found you. You will also tell the judge you bought the heroin from a girl you've never met before in Center City. That's all there is to it. Then you'll serve your time, and when you get out, you'll go on with your life."

Tears sprang to Rainey's eyes. "You're asking me not to say anything to the judge so that Jiggy doesn't get in any trouble." She glared at her parents. "And, so you two can protect yourselves."

Brice placed his pen on the pad in front of him. "Just to make sure we're clear, Rainey. I'm not asking you to do anything, I'm telling you."

Rainey grimaced; it was as though she were their hostage and there was no way to escape the nightmare that kept getting worse. "Why are you all so worried about protecting Jiggy? I say he can go fuck himself."

Brice leaned farther across the table. "Well see, that's going to cause a bit of a problem for you. If you won't do what you're told then there are other things to consider besides your sister's well-being."

"Like what?" Rainey spat, but his statement made her squirm.

"Well, for starters, Jiggy knows enough inmates in here to make your pathetic life more miserable than it already is. The kind of young women who will make you wish you were never born, trust me. You don't want to cross Jiggy and his boss. They aren't the kind of men to let things go. For your safety, I suggest you do as you're told."

Rainey shook her head.

"Oh," Brice said, "you have no idea how the girls in here can make you suffer. Things will get so bad for you—you'll have a level of pain that you never knew existed."

Rainey stood and slammed her fists on the table. She glared at her mother, then her father. "You two make me sick. I know you never took care of me or Ivy but I never thought you would take things this far to protect some lowlife drug dealer. I hope someday you two get everything you deserve."

When neither parent acknowledged her outrage, Rainey turned on her heel and banged on the metal door, not caring that her tears had begun streaming down her face.

Brice stood. "Rainey, I'm going to give you some time to think about it. I'll be back in one week. Hopefully, by then, you will have realized that sometimes you have to do things that are unpleasant if you want to have peace in your life. You need to think about your next step very carefully, little girl."

Officer Fernandez opened the door and, without a word, took her by the elbow and led her away. She was silent until they entered the guts of the prison, when she asked, "Are you okay?"

Rainey kept her eyes to the floor and shook her head gently. Mercifully, Fernandez left it at that. As the two continued back to her cell, neither of them uttered another word. Rainey's mind raced. She tried to wrap her brain around what she'd been told to do. *How did this happen?* she wondered. *Did I imagine all of that? This can't be real.*

Rainey had held hope that her lawyer would fight for her, at least for a lesser sentence. But now she had no idea how to help herself—and was certain that the only way to keep her sister safe was never to talk about Jiggy to the police.

Chapter Forty-Eight

Rainey walked into her cell with red, watery eyes, purposely not looking at Phoenix, then glanced at Officer Fernandez, who gave a nod and slid the barred door closed.

"Breakfast in twenty minutes, girls," Fernandez said.

Rainey stood next to the bars, with both hands clinging to the metal posts.

Phoenix slowly approached. "How did it go?"

"It was awful," she said, unable to steady her quivering voice.

Phoenix stood so close to Rainey she could feel her breath on the back of her neck. "If you want to—you can sit down and tell me what happened. I mean, if you need someone to talk to. You know?"

Rainey glanced at Phoenix and knew the girl was genuine. She was grateful to have a cellmate that cared about her. She was alone and scared, and more than anything, she needed someone to listen to her. She nodded, then sat on the stool and crumpled into herself. "My mom and dad just threatened me."

"What?" Phoenix asked, leaning in closer.

"Okay, so I'm in here because the police found me with a shit-ton of heroin in my lap. Oh, and pointing a gun at them when they stormed into my room. Anyway, Jiggy had been batting me around and had ripped my pants off. Before I knew it, there was a knock at the door and I was counting out forty bags of heroin. Honestly, I didn't even care because I would've done almost anything at that point to stop him from raping me. So when the police showed up, I was holding the gun and had dope everywhere," Rainey explained.

"Soooo, then you're fucked. I mean, the cops found you with the drugs and all. Why did your mom and dad threaten you?"

"Because the cops keep asking me who gave me the drugs to sell. And those two morons said if I even mention Jiggy that he'll kill Ivy and kill the two of them, which I don't care about."

"Holy shit," Phoenix breathed. She shook her head. "I guess I'm not the only one whose life is fucked up. But . . . I gotta ask, is it true that you don't use dope? You don't have to lie to me, I ain't gonna tell no one."

Rainey rested her elbows on her thighs as her index fingers kneaded her temples. "I ain't lying to you. The dope was Jiggy's. I just made a huge mistake, that's all. I've never used or sold drugs in my life. My mom and dad have partied for as long as I can remember. You can't even mention the word 'addiction' to them, though; they freak out. They believe that drugs allow them the freedom to think better and be more creative so that they don't get caught up in *what the rest of the world thinks they should be doing*. It's just an excuse so they don't have to be responsible for anything. They live to get high. It's all they've ever cared about."

"Did your lawyer say anything good?" Phoenix asked.

She shook her head, picturing Brice's sneering face in her mind. "He's rotten to the core."

Phoenix sat on the floor at Rainey's feet. "Well, what *did* he say?"

"That I have to tell the judge that I was going to sell the drugs and that I bought them from some girl I've never met before, in Center City."

Phoenix squinted at her. "I don't understand. Why would your lawyer tell you to say that?"

"Because my lawyer works for Jiggy. He told me if I open my mouth about him that there are girls in here that will make me wish I was dead."

"So Jiggy is a pedophile *and* a drug dealer?"

"Yes, Jiggy is the most horrible person I've ever met. He's a fucking animal. He does anything he wants to do and gets away with it," she said. She bit her lower lip, wishing she had a superpower that could stop him.

Phoenix raised her eyebrows. "Okay, let me get this straight—your lawyer was hired by Jiggy and isn't going to help you with your case. He wants you to keep your mouth shut about who the drugs belong to. So you have to take the fall for everything . . . the drugs and the gun, do your time, and don't complain about it. Do I have that right?"

"It sounds more ridiculous hearing you say it. But yeah, you just summed it up." Rainey pressed her palm on the back of her neck. "Here's my problem: I have no idea what will happen to me if I lie about where the drugs came from, and I'm too scared to find out." Her eyes burned into Phoenix's. "What would you do if you were me?"

Phoenix dragged her hand across her forehead. "Well, I would find someone who can tell me the worst sentence I could get. I'd keep my mouth shut about Jiggy and just do the time."

Rainey's head jerked upright. "Really?"

"Yeah. Look, the way I see it is you're not going to get away with the drugs because they found them on you. You're not getting away with the gun 'cause you were holding it. It doesn't do you any good to say anything about Jiggy . . . it'll only make your life in here worse."

Just then, the bars opened. Phoenix walked toward the cafeteria while Rainey sat on the stool and thought about who she could call. She couldn't think of a single person who would help her. Sighing, she lifted herself from the stool and hurried to catch up to Phoenix.

Sitting across from Phoenix, pushing food around her tray, Rainey had an idea. "I think I know someone who might be able to help me," she said.

***

The next afternoon, Rainey walked into the interview room, feeling nervous but, grateful that he had agreed to meet with her. She sat in the chair and pulled it up close to the table.

"Hi, Agent Lindquist. Thanks a lot for coming to see me."

"Sure thing. What's going on?"

Rainey looked him in the eyes, and as he met hers, a calmness washed over her and the rapid beating of her heart slowed. "I didn't have anyone else to call. I need your help."

The agent lowered his gaze and exhaled a long, slow sigh. "Rainey, I'm not sure I can help you. That's what lawyers are for. What is it that you need?"

Rainey let out a nervous cough. "I'm really scared about what's going to happen to me in court. And . . . well, I was wondering if you knew how long the judge will keep me in here. Like, what's the longest time?"

"Well, a hundred grams of heroin is a big offense. With that much, the judge would probably sentence you to five years."

Rainey's mouth dropped open. "*Five years?* I can't be locked up for that long. I couldn't get out early for being good or anything?"

"There's no telling what can happen down the road," Lindquist said, leaning forward. "But Rainey, I think telling the judge the *truth* about who your boss is will be the right thing to do regardless of the consequences."

She turned her head away and shrugged, afraid that if she kept looking into his eyes, he would read her mind and would know that the drugs belonged to Jiggy. "This place is scary and the girls are mean. That's why I wanted to know the worst that can happen to me," she said.

"I may have misunderstood. I thought you were talking about juvie. Honestly, it will be much worse if the justice system decides to try you as an adult. Because of the quantity of heroin found in your possession that's not out of the question."

"What if the drugs were never mine?"

He shook his head and looked at her with deep concern. "I'm sorry, Rainey. We found you with the drugs and with a gun. There's no getting around that."

Tears dribbled down Rainey's cheeks as she shook her head. He had no idea how much she wanted to tell him everything about her life. Rainey knew that even if she gave Jiggy up to the police it wouldn't do anything to remove Ivy from her parents.

"Rainey, is something else going on that you want to tell me?" Lindquist asked.

"No, but do you think you could tell the judge I should stay here and not go to adult prison? Could you do that for me?"

"I don't have all of the facts yet. I'd like to say yes, but I can't make any promises until I have all the information I need. I'm sorry." Lindquist paused and looked at her with concern. Rainey stared back at him, welcoming the empathy in his expression. "There's *nothing* more you can tell me? Like who your supplier is?"

Rainey looked away. "I don't know," she mumbled, lacking conviction.

His brows pulled together. "You don't know?"

Walking toward the door, she said more definitively, "No, I don't. Anyway, thanks for coming to see me today."

Chapter Forty-Nine

Over the next three days, Rainey struggled to assimilate into living in juvie. She hated the rules and restrictions. Having lost the freedom of taking care of herself to having to listen to people telling her when to eat, shit, and sleep was unbearable. Every minute of her day was planned, but worse was never having a time of quiet, of silence, to formulate her thoughts and think about her future.

The guards were mostly okay, but she hated being told what to do all the time. When to wash her clothes or take a shower. The library was limited, so her choice of books was meager and unexciting. And she was sick and tired of all the fighting among the girls. A day didn't go by when either fists or angry words were being thrown. In some ways it was worse than walking down the dangerous streets of Kensington alone at night. She was in a constant state of readiness to be the target of an unruly inmate. But she did her best not to appear intimidated and paid close attention to the guards, the teachers, and the meanest inmates.

That night, Rainey laid on her bunk while Phoenix paced.

"Have you decided what you're going to tell the judge?" Phoenix asked.

Rainey rolled onto her side to face her. "You have no idea how much I want to tell him the drugs came from Jiggy. I still don't know what to do. I keep telling myself it's only five years, but what if they try me as an adult because I won't give up a name? Then I'm screwed. I don't think I would survive a real prison. The girls here are our age and some of them are real assholes. I can't even imagine how much worse the older women would be."

"You're right. I've heard some bad shit from other hookers who spent time on the inside. Makes this place seem mild."

Rainey put her hand over her forehead, as if trying to hold her thoughts together. "I swear this is the hardest decision I've ever had to make. Whether I choose to give them Jiggy's name or not, I'm not gonna go home anytime soon. Let's say I get sentenced to five years . . . there's no telling what'll happen to Ivy during that time. She'd be ten by the time I got outta here. That's a long time for her to live in that shithole without anyone there to protect her. I hate thinking about what it's like for her without me there."

Phoenix stopped pacing and stood in front of Rainey. "You know, Ivy is lucky to have you. I always wanted a sister like you. I wish I had just one person in the world that gave a damn whether I lived or died. It's lonely sometimes, you know?"

"Yeah, I do. I was happy when my parents brought Ivy home from the hospital. She gave me . . . I don't know what to call it . . . a reason to wake up in the morning. I like taking care of her. She's more my kid than theirs. Before Ivy, I had an aunt that used to take care of me, but she got some stupid disease and lives in a place where they take care of her now."

"Do you ever just want to make it all end?" Phoenix asked.

"Sure, I wish I had magic powers to change my life."

Phoenix shook her head. "That's not what I mean."

Rainey propped herself up on one elbow. When she realized what her cellmate was saying, she gasped. "You mean, like kill myself?"

Phoenix nodded and averted her watchful eyes. As hard as life had been, Rainey had never thought to end her own life.

"No," Rainey said after a moment. "I never thought about that, ever, no matter how bad things got." Her voice softened. "But you've thought about killing yourself. Why?"

Phoenix shrugged. "Loneliness, fear, sadness, hopelessness . . . all kinds of reasons. I bet a lot of people think about it at least once in their life."

"You're not thinking about killing yourself now, are you?" Rainey asked tentatively.

Phoenix gave her a sad smile. "No, I haven't thought about it in a long time. It's kind of amazing, with all that you've been through, that you never once thought of death as an escape."

Rainey pushed her hair back from her face and had a great sense of sadness for her new friend. "I'm not looking to escape my life. I want to make it better. I need to do something that I can be proud of. Giving up would be giving in to the people who hurt me. It means they would win, and one thing is for sure, they ain't gonna win. Not against me."

"I wish I was more like you," Phoenix mumbled.

Rainey sighed. "I grew up around addicts and alcoholics. I've seen what real pain looks like. They were always chasing the next high—that's their main goal in life. It's sad because nothing else matters—not family or friends—and while they're chasing it, their entire lives pass them by. That ain't me. My life is gonna matter."

Phoenix nodded. "How can you be so sure?"

"I'm not," she murmured. "But I have to have something to look forward to. Otherwise my life would totally suck even more than it does now. I want to help people someday. I don't know how, but I know I will."

Phoenix huffed. "But that's kinda the point. There's all this nasty shit around us. Whores, bitches, assholes . . . people hurting people. People benefiting from another's pain."

With a surge of awakening and purpose, Rainey jumped from her bunk. "That's exactly why we need to be better than what we've gotten. See, since I was little, I've watched my mom roll on the floor for hours in pain because she needed heroin so bad it hurt. And I guess ever since then, I knew I didn't want to be like her or my dad. Seeing my parents and their friends, well, it made me realize I want a real life and a real family. Coming here just makes me want it more, even if I don't know exactly what 'it' is or how to get it."

Rainey turned on the water and washed her hands in the small sink. She dried them on a towel and nudged Phoenix with her shoulder. "You know what?"

"What?"

"You're going to do something great with your life too," she assured her.

"Oh, yeah. How do you know that?"

"Because you're awesome. Don't let anyone beat you down. You were born to do something way bigger than you can ever imagine."

Phoenix grinned. "I sure as fuck hope you're right. I want you to know, I don't hate you as much as I did when you first got here," she teased.

***

The next evening, when Rainey was walking back from the shower, she was stopped by a tall, athletic-looking white girl with her black hair in a tight braid down the center of her back.

"You're Rainey, right?" the girl asked.

Rainey gave her a nervous smile, knowing this probably wasn't a social visit. "Yeah, I am. Who are you?"

"They call me Tootsie," she snarled, pulling a Tootsie Roll from her pocket and flinging it into Rainey's face.

"Why did you do that?" she asked.

Tootsie grabbed Rainey by the collar of her shirt and slammed her head against the wall with force. Her face was twisted as she stared Rainey down. "I did it 'cause I wanted to do it. What are you gonna do about it?"

Rainey opened her mouth, but no words escaped. She was too shocked.

Still holding Rainey firmly in place, Tootsie let out a menacing chuckle. Then the girl thumped her against the wall again, knocking the air from her lungs. When Rainey slid to the floor, Tootsie pounced on her, punched her several times in the face, ripped a handful of hair from her head, and slammed her elbows into her breasts. Tootsie's fluent and blatant moves left Rainey dazed. When the girl was finished, she stood, straddling Rainey, who was by now crumpled into a ball, breathless and scared she was going to be beaten to death.

Tootsie leaned down and hissed into Rainey's ear. "Jiggy wanted me to give you a message. You better do what you're told or what just happened now is just the beginning. I'm the highest-ranking bitch in this place and I have a small army that will destroy you."

Rainey gaped at Tootsie wide-eyed. "I . . . I . . . have a little sister."

Tootsie grabbed her chin and forced it back. "Bitch, I don't care what you got. See, you don't know me, but the reason I'm in here is 'cause I suffocated my little sister to death 'by accident,'" she air quoted. "It wasn't on purpose, of course, and had nothing to do with the fact that my asshole sister was talking to the neighbors about me and the shit I was doing for Jiggy," she said with a smile.

"So you see, I'll be outta here in a year. Just think how much pain I'd cause your little sister now that you know what I did to mine. I'll torture that little shit to death. So I suggest you make the right decision.

Trust me, if you don't, I'll know about it and I'll be your worst fucking nightmare. Got it?"

Rainey didn't respond. She lay still as pain and adrenaline collided inside of her.

Tootsie yelled, "I asked you if you got it!"

Rainey's eyes were wide open and her lips trembled as she said, "Yeah."

When Rainey entered her cell, Phoenix got a look at her swollen face and rushed toward her. "What the hell happened?"

"It's nothing," she mumbled.

"Really? Your face is messed up but nothing happened? Come on. Spill it. You don't have to be scared. I ain't ever gonna turn on you," Phoenix said in a commanding voice.

"I just got my ass beat from one of the girls that lawyer warned me about," Rainey said.

Phoenix's chest puffed out. "Who? Who was it?"

"Tootsie."

Phoenix flopped down on the stool. "Shit," she mumbled. "Of all the damn bitches in here it had to be Tootsie. Look," she said, grabbing Rainey's hand, "that chick is bad news. She ain't got no heart inside her chest. You need to keep your mouth shut about Jiggy. You gotta do what you gotta do to stay alive."

Phoenix wet a towel and pressed it to Rainey's swelled lip. She lifted the girl's bruised chin gently.

"You don't know this, but I knew about Tootsie before I got locked up in here," Phoenix said. "That girl . . . she's ruthless. I heard rumors about her when I was working the streets. Heard she slit a girl's throat for flirting with her man and apparently her man flirted with every girl he laid eyes on. She's a strong fighter, but she's a dirty fighter too. The decision you make about what to tell the judge is either going to end you or protect you in here. Shit, think about your sister. Think about what they'll do to her."

Rainey's head hung. "I know, I know."

"Tell me what happened."

Rainey shook her head. "She caught me by surprise. I never knew how much it hurt to be punched in the face," she babbled through her swollen lips.

"You're not gonna tell the judge shit then, right?"

Rainey took the wet towel from Phoenix and pressed it against her forehead. “Right. I can’t see what good it’ll do me if I tell,” she conceded.

Chapter Fifty

Rainey clomped into the interview room, flopped down in a chair, and glared at Brice. After a moment she glanced at her father, then her mother.

"Those bruises look like they hurt," he said with a smirk.

Rainey sat back and shook her head at him. "I hate you," she said.

Disinterested in her drama, Brice looked down at his wristwatch and then at Peter and Miranda. Rainey crossed her arms over her chest and continued to glower at Brice, hoping that her eyes would burn a big, fat hole in his head and his dumb brain would ooze out. They had her trapped like an animal in a cage, and she hated it.

Brice yawned. "So you met Tootsie. She's a good little girl. Does whatever she's told to do. You could learn something from her."

In the silence, the disturbingly loud buzz of the fluorescent bulbs in the ceiling above filled Rainey's ears as she thought about Tootsie. She would have rather chewed glass than be anything like that girl. Tootsie was a thug who had no mind of her own. She was only a puppet, and her strings were strummed by Jiggy.

On the table that separated them, Brice laced his fingers together and lifted his shoulders. "Well? What's it gonna be?"

Rainey's eyes narrowed and she lifted her chin. "I'll tell the judge whatever you want, but I need something too."

Brice looked down and his lips curled into a cruel smile. "You think this is a negotiation?"

Rainey leaned forward. "No, but I think I have a right to ask for something that I need."

Brice raised his eyebrows. "Indulge me. What is it that you need?"

Rainey turned toward her parents. "I want you to bring Ivy to visit me once a week."

Miranda, clearly high, was useless as her head bobbed up and down, but Peter was coherent. He adjusted on his chair. "I don't think so," he said.

Rainey looked down at the table and back at her father again. "Once a month then."

Peter shrugged. "Yeah, you tell the judge everything that Brice tells you to say and I'll make sure you see your sister."

"Promise?" Rainey said.

Peter sneered. "I said I would."

Rainey grabbed a handful of her hair and played with the ends, trying to keep her cool and not celebrate prematurely. She focused on Brice. "My father makes promises that he doesn't keep. He's done it to me before. I need you to promise too."

Brice chuckled. "I won't promise you anything."

Rainey lowered her eyes, playing the odds against the adults in the room. "Okay, no deal."

After a few moments, Brice said, "Here's what I'll do. I'll have someone remind your dad to bring your sister to see you. I can't promise that'll do any good, but if it makes you feel better, I'll do it."

"Thank you," Rainey said, trying not to seem relieved that he agreed. She turned to her father. "Bring Ivy to see me this Saturday, okay?"

Peter glanced at Brice. "Yeah, sure. This Saturday. But we ain't staying long."

Rainey turned back to her lawyer. "When am I going to court?"

"In two weeks."

"You'll tell me everything I need to say before I see the judge. Right?"

Brice stood and grabbed his briefcase. "Yes, that's right. In the meantime, keep your mouth shut about Jiggy. You understand?"

Rainey fought the burning behind her eyes as the beating from Tootsie ran through her mind. "Yeah, sure, whatever."

Brice snickered and took in her bruises. "I see Tootsie taught you a lot in a short amount of time. Remember what you learned from her if you want to stay out of trouble. You keep one thing in mind: Tootsie will do anything for Jiggy. And"—Brice paused, leaning in closer—"I mean *anything*."

With that, Brice walked toward the door. Peter grabbed Miranda's hand and pulled her along, but Rainey stood and blocked her father from leaving.

"Dad, you know that someday I'm going to get out of here, and when I do, I'm taking Ivy to live with me."

Peter poked Rainey in the sternum. "Don't you ever tell me what you're gonna do. Ivy is my kid, not yours. Get that through your thick head," he growled, tapping his index finger on Rainey's forehead.

Rainey swatted his finger away and leaped backward out of Peter's reach.

"All right. No fighting," Brice seethed.

"Sure, as long as she stops acting like she's all high and mighty," Peter stated.

Rainey ignored her father's comments. Instead, she said, "Can you do me a favor? On your way home, stop and buy something for Ivy to eat. She's a little kid and can't do things for herself. Will you do that? Please," she begged.

"Not sure. We'll see how it goes." Peter walked past Rainey and left without looking back.

Rainey was dizzy. The bruises on her face were on fire and her lips were throbbing. She slid down the wall behind her and crouched as she was overtaken by grief.

"Please help me," Rainey whispered to no one.

Chapter Fifty-One

Two days later, Rainey woke with excitement. It was Saturday morning and, Ivy was coming to visit her. She jumped from the top bunk and her feet hit the floor with a thump.

Startled, Phoenix sat up. "What the hell is going on?"

Rainey grinned. "Sorry. I jumped from my bunk without thinking. I'm gonna see Ivy today. I'm so excited."

Phoenix rolled over, putting her back to the girl. "Well, can you be excited in a couple of hours when it's time to wake up?"

Rainey sat on Phoenix's bunk. "Oh, come on. Today is visiting day. Ivy's coming."

Phoenix peeked over her shoulder. "That don't mean shit to me. Ain't nobody gonna visit me. It might sound all exciting, but when you're sitting there waiting for someone who never shows up, it sucks worse than just knowing that no one is ever coming."

Rainey and her cellmate were almost the same; Phoenix had no one in the world she could count on either. She let out a loud sigh, "Yeah, I guess you're right."

Phoenix leaned up on her elbows. "Look, I ain't trying to bring you down. You should be excited that you're gonna see your little sister today. All I'm saying is you don't know how long it'll last. You know, how long your parents will keep bringing her here."

Rainey laid beside Phoenix on her bunk. "I know. My parents don't do what they say they will, so I'm going to try and enjoy this visit," she said sadly. The girls lay in the bunk together until the breakfast announcement came over the intercom.

Inside the cafeteria, Rainey sat down with her tray and ate quietly. Her excitement had dwindled.

"What's wrong with you?" Phoenix asked.

"I was thinking about what you said this morning. You know, how people don't show up. My parents are those kinds of people."

Later that afternoon, Rainey and Phoenix were sitting in the prison rec room playing cards when Fernandez approached. She tapped Rainey on the shoulder.

"Your dad is here with your sister," she said.

Rainey's smile lit up her face. She looked over at Phoenix, who gave her a thumbs up, then followed Fernandez to the visitors' room. When Rainey saw Ivy through the window, the older girl lifted her hand to wave. As she did, her shirt lifted and Fernandez noticed something in her waistband.

Fernandez gripped Rainey's arm. "Put your hands on the wall and spread your feet."

"What? Why? I didn't do anything."

"Paxton, do what I say. Put your hands on the wall and spread your feet," Fernandez barked.

Rainey did as she was told and the officer reached forward and removed the object from her waistband. "What's this?" The officer opened the napkin and found two slices of white bread. She had slathered peanut butter between the slices of bread at breakfast that morning.

Officer Fernandez sniffed the sandwich. "Well?"

Rainey cowered. "I'm sorry."

"Rainey, you know you aren't allowed to take food from the mess hall. That's a violation of the rules. I'm going to have to write you up for this."

"You can write me up, Officer Fernandez. But please, let me bring the sandwich to my little sister," she pleaded.

Fernandez looked down at the sandwich in her hand and back at Rainey. "What do you mean?"

"My family . . . well, we're poor. Like really poor. And, Ivy and me didn't get to eat all the time. Now that I'm in here I'm worried she's eating even less. So I know it was against the rules but I wanted to bring her something to eat. I know she has to be hungry," she explained.

Fernandez sighed and wrapped the sandwich back up in the napkin. She held it out to Rainey. "Go on and take it, but I better see you give it to your sister. And don't ever do this again."

Rainey placed her hand on her chest. "Thank you so much. It means a lot to me."

Fernandez gave her a stiff nod. "Go see your family."

When the door opened, Ivy squealed and slid off of the chair, running to Rainey with arms spread wide. She lifted Ivy off the ground and held her tightly.

"I missed you so much," Rainey whispered. She set the small girl back on the ground.

"How come you left and didn't take me with you?" Ivy asked.

"I didn't leave on purpose. The police made me leave."

Ivy pouted. "But you left me all alone and nobody talks to me."

Rainey led her sister to the table where her father was sitting.

"Hello, Dad," Rainey said sharply.

"I ain't got time for no bullshit today. Get your damn visit in 'cause we gotta get on the road soon," Peter snapped.

She clenched her teeth, but she turned her attention back to Ivy. "I brought you a peanut butter sandwich," she said, laying it on the table in front of the child.

Ivy smiled and bounced on her chair. She picked up the sandwich and took two bites before chewing it.

"You're hungry, huh?"

The child nodded. "Yeah, I'm hungry."

Rainey looked at her sister. Her hair was tangled and knotted. There was dirt on her face and under her fingernails. Ivy was dressed in a stained T-shirt, a pair of ripped leotards, and shorts too small for her. She turned to her father. "Dad, somebody has to take care of her while I'm in here. Maybe if you talk to Mom. Just ask her to buy food, at least."

Peter glared at his daughter. "Shut up. You're always making things seem so much worse than they are. Your sister is fine."

Rainey glared back at her father. "My sister is starving. She's filthy and she just said that no one talks to her."

"Oh, please. We talk to her."

"Nah-uh," Ivy quipped. "You only talk to me when you're yelling at me to be quiet. I'm never allowed to do nuffin' or say nuffin' or nuffin'."

Rainey studied her sister and turned back to her father. "Do you have a couple of dollars so I can get Ivy a soda or something?"

Peter huffed, reached in his pocket, and slapped two one-dollar bills on the table.

Rainey took Ivy by the hand and they stood in front of the vending machines. "Rainey, can I have 'tato chips and . . . and . . . candy?"

The older sister looked at her. "Sure." She helped the child put money into the machine and watched in delight as Ivy bounced on her toes while the items fell out. The child couldn't contain herself waiting for her sister to open the bag of chips.

Back at the table, Ivy gobbled the chips and stuck her nose inside the empty bag to lick all the crumbs.

"You see your kid, right?" Rainey said, looking at her father. "She's starving. How can you live with yourself? I mean, seriously, you and Mom must eat at some point every day or you'd be dead by now."

Peter's face reddened and he grabbed the empty chip bag, crushing it into a ball with his fist. He stood abruptly. "Let's go, Ivy. Your sister doesn't know how to act civilized, so I don't want you around her."

Ivy looked up from the candy bar she was eating and wailed, "Noooo, I don't wanna go with you. I wanna stay with Rainey."

"Yeah, well, that's too damn bad. We need to leave," Peter said, grabbing the child's wrist.

"Wait! Wait! No!" Rainey cried. "Please don't leave yet. You just got here." She pulled Ivy closer to her, and the girl attached to her sister like Velcro.

Peter stepped closer and wrenched Ivy's hands from hers. As Ivy kicked and screamed in her father's arms, all the prisoners and visitors stopped to watch. Peter leaned close to Rainey and said, "You wanted to see Ivy and now you did. Don't expect me to come back here again."

Rainey rushed after them and took Ivy's face in her hands. "I love you so much. Be a good girl. Okay?"

Ivy pulled away from Peter's grip, and Rainey took the child into her arms and kissed her neck, cheek, and forehead. "I want you to remember two things," she said to the crying child. "First, one day you and me will be together again, and second, I'll never love anyone more than I love you."

Ivy sobbed as Peter led her out the door, leaving Rainey to watch the shadows of her life slip away. She hoped that one day she'd be able to do for Ivy what no one had done for her: create a family that cared for, loved, and protected her.

Chapter Fifty-Two

Fernandez had watched the interactions among Rainey, Ivy, and Peter. She unlocked the heavy metal door and with a quick flick of her head motioned for Rainey to follow her.

Rainey, deflated and sullen, allowed herself to be led into the belly of the prison, tears dripping from her chin.

"You need a minute to pull yourself together?" Fernandez asked before they reached the final door.

"No. The girls in the visitors' room probably saw me crying anyway." Rainey lifted her chin. "I know by the way they stared at me. They saw my dad treat me like I'm a worthless piece of shit."

The officer nodded. "You're probably right. But all the girls have their moment. You're not the only girl here who comes from a messed-up family. Don't dwell on what the other girls think about you. This will pass."

"I don't care what they think of me—the person I care about is Ivy. I'm scared for her and I can't do anything to protect her while I'm in here," Rainey grumbled.

Fernandez was silent as she made a quick turn, gesturing for her to follow, walking in the opposite direction of her cell.

"Where are you taking me?" she asked.

"Just follow me," the officer said. She led her into an office with a desk, chair, and computer. Once they were seated the officer asked, "Are you going to be okay?"

She shrugged. "What do you mean? My parents have been this way my whole life—this ain't nothing new."

"That may be true, but now that you're in here you need to have some sort of support network on the outside."

The girl shrugged. "Like you just said, there are other girls here that don't have anyone."

Officer Fernandez nodded. "That's true, but I know how much you love your little sister, and that separation must be hard. While you are in here, the least we can do is make sure you're holding up and working toward a better future. That means not only providing rehabilitation but also, in the process, helping you to grow so that when you're released, you're more prepared for the world than when you arrived here."

"Yeah, I get it," Rainey huffed impatiently.

"Good," Fernandez said, sitting back in her chair again. "Let's talk about your sister—since that's what's really bugging you. Tell me about it."

"There's not that much to tell," she said in a grim tone. "My parents just suck. They have other interests besides their kids. You saw how Ivy looked, right?"

Fernandez nodded. "Yes, I saw a child who was a product of poverty. Being poor doesn't make your parents bad. There are a lot of poor children in this country, that's nothing new. I imagine it would be painful to be a parent and know that I couldn't provide the very basics for my children. Have you ever thought of it that way?"

She shook her head. "No; you don't know my mom and dad." Rainey went deadly quiet, realizing she was saying too much. Fernandez was a nice lady but she'd never understand or believe the stuff that went on in her house. *Who would believe a teenager caught with one hundred grams of heroin*? she thought.

"Back to my original question; about if you are doing okay, I wasn't just asking about the visit with your father. I'm also concerned about those bruises on your face."

"What about them? I fell. So what? Why does everyone keep asking me?"

"Because while you're in here you are our responsibility. That means we must keep you safe. No one who works here wants to see a girl getting hurt."

Rainey turned her head away from the woman. "Okay, so what do you want me to do? Make up a story about someone kicking my ass? I already told you what happened. Just drop it."

"Hey, Rainey, it's not okay for you to speak to me that way. It's clear to anyone watching that you love your sister. I can see you're frustrated with the visit you just had but that's no excuse to talk to me with disrespect." She leaned forward. "Do we understand each other?"

Rainey's head was down and she moved her eyes up to meet Fernandez's. "Yeah, I understand. I didn't mean to take it out on you. I'm sorry and it won't happen again."

The silence stretched on until Fernandez patted Rainey's hand. "I'll tell you what. Let's go grab pudding from the mess hall and then I'll bring you back to your cell."

Her stomach soured from the visit, Rainey said, "I'm not hungry. I'll just go back to my cell."

"Are you sure?" Fernandez asked.

"Yeah. I'm sure."

***

After taking Rainey safely back to her cell, Officer Fernandez returned to her office, opened the desk drawer, and pulled out a card. She dialed the number and waited while the phone rang.

"Lindquist," the voice burst out from the other side of the line.

"Agent Lindquist, this is Officer Fernandez from the Juvenile Detention Center. You told me to call you if any issues came up with Rainey Paxton."

"Shit," Lindquist mumbled. "What happened?"

"Well, her father brought her little sister to see her today. The little one looked ragged, and that affected Rainey. The father treated her terribly and left in a hurry. It was disturbing to watch, to be honest with you, and I've seen a lot working here. Anyway, something happened to Rainey. Her face is bruised and she insists she fell. She's also worried about her sister, and I think a visit from you may do her good. I know it's a lot to ask but she needs a little boost right now. Maybe you could see if her little sister is okay and you'd be able to tell her that."

Lindquist sighed heavily. "The only thing I can tell you right now is that I drove by Rainey's house several times and did see her sister, Ivy, once. Unfortunately, I have no authority to go into the Paxton house to check on her sister. We've added some extra police patrols on the street, but let's face it, we're in Kensington and every street in the city could use more patrolling."

"Right. Of course. I understand." Officer Fernandez said, disappointed that her one idea to help Rainey wouldn't work out.

"I'd be happy to stop over and have a visit with Rainey. That's in my control," Lindquist said.

At this, Fernandez smiled. "That would be great. I think she would appreciate it. She's a good kid. She has her trial next week and I'm sure after what I just watched, that it would make her feel good to know someone, besides me, cares about her."

"Yeah, I'm aware of her upcoming trial. I have to be there, since I was the arresting narcotics agent," Lindquist explained.

"Right; of course you do. Look, I feel for this kid. She doesn't talk back or pick on the other girls. We get all kinds in here, but there's something different about her . . . in a good way."

Agent Lindquist said, "Yeah, I know. But I'm sure you've read the arrest report. There's no way she'll get off on the charges that are pending against her."

"I know, I read the report. It is a shame what she did to her life. Seeing Rainey with her sister today was heartbreaking. She's a decent kid and, I get it, she made a big mistake, but this kid is in real turmoil."

"Yeah, that's what happens. Look, I can get there in a couple of hours. Can I see her then?"

"Of course. That's fine. I'll see you later," Fernandez said.

Before they hung up, Lindquist spoke again, "Wait!"

"Yes?" Fernandez asked.

Lindquist's voice grew deep and serious. "We need more people like you caring for these youths. I appreciate you getting in touch with me, and I want you to call me anytime you need me."

"Will do."

Chapter Fifty-Three

Rainey collapsed on the stool in her cell and laid her head on the small desk. Her shoulders shook as her sadness broke free.

"Hey," Phoenix said softly, coming up behind her. "What happened?"

Rainey shook her head.

"Come on, girl. Tell me what happened," she coaxed.

She looked up at her. "My father was a total asshole. And Ivy was so hungry she practically inhaled the sandwich I brought her."

"How come you're back here so soon?"

Suddenly feeling exhausted, she looked up at Phoenix with sad, tired eyes. "Because my dad's a dick. I asked him to take care of Ivy, make sure she was fed—you know, normal things parents do for their kids. My parents never did those things for us—I knew better than to expect anything different. Anyway, he got all pissed off and stormed out."

Phoenix's forehead creased. "He walked out because of that?"

Rainey straightened her back and grinned. "Well, I might've told him he was a horrible father and that he should feed his kid."

Phoenix's lips turned up at the sides, feeding the other girl's courage.

"All right, and I *might've* said that he eats every day but somehow he can't feed his kid."

Phoenix rested her hand on Rainey's shoulder. "Anything else you *might've* told him?"

She smiled. "I might've asked him how he and my mother can live with themselves."

"So basically you said a lot of things to your dad that have been bothering you. Ain't nothing wrong with that."

"Yeah, but then he got up and stormed out, pulling Ivy along. She was freaking out. He ripped her away from me. I don't think he's gonna bring her back to visit. He pretty much said so," she said, bursting into a sob. "I feel so bad for her."

Phoenix stood and walked to the bars of their cell. "So what are you gonna do about it?"

Startled, she looked in her direction. "What do you mean? There's nothing I *can* do."

"Exactly," Phoenix said. "The only thing that's left is for you to go on, protect yourself in this place, and think about how you can help your sister when you get outta here. Like you said, make something of yourself."

Rainey, now calmer, twirled a long strand of hair in her fingers. "Yeah, I guess you're right."

***

Rainey was lying on her bunk almost asleep after the long morning when Fernandez rapped on the bars. Startled, Rainey sat up quickly.

"Come on, Paxton. You have a visitor."

Surprised, she jumped from the top bunk. "Who?"

"Agent Lindquist."

Rainey tucked in her shirt and ran her hands over her hair as she followed Fernandez. Inside the visitors' room, all the tables were empty except for the one where Lindquist sat. He smiled when he saw her.

"Hello, Rainey. How are you?"

She pulled a chair out and faced the man. "Oh, I'm doing fabulous. I'm here in prison just having a ball. Oh, and this place has a bunch of wonderful girls . . . one who beat the shit outta me," she cracked, gesturing at her face.

"Did you tell a corrections officer that someone beat you up?"

Rainey's mouth tightened, annoyed that she'd said too much. "No, I didn't, and neither can you. Do you know what happens to girls who snitch in here? It'll be safer for me if I keep it to myself. You don't need to worry about me it's my baby sister I want you to look out for."

Lindquist let his head drop back and his eyes scanned the stained tiles of the ceiling. "Okay. I wanted to tell you that I saw Ivy several days ago—I only got a glimpse of her but she seemed fine. The way the law works is unless I have a reason to go into the house, your parents don't have to let me in. I drove by in the mornings, around the time kids leave for school. I thought maybe I'd talk to Ivy then, but the kid never leaves the house."

Rainey leaned into the center of the table with her fingers laced together. "Ivy is five. She can't leave the house on her own. You have no idea how annoying this is. And do you know I go to court next week?"

"Yes, I'm aware that you're going to court. That's one reason why I came to see you. The judge would be more lenient if I can say you told me who your drug supplier is. Also, I wanted to tell you that I'll be at your hearing since I was the arresting agent."

Rainey, vulnerable, shrunk away from the man. "Oh, I didn't know you'd be there," she said, ignoring his statement about the drug supplier.

"Well, I won't be testifying this time. I'll only be there to answer any questions the judge might have about the night you were arrested. I'm letting you know because it seems as though you're already going through enough hard stuff. I know you like people being honest with you. Besides," Lindquist cast her a smile, "I also came because I thought you could use a visitor."

Rainey let out an uncontrolled moan. "Yeah, it's nice having a normal adult to talk to."

"Hey," Lindquist said, reaching below him and pulling up a brown bag. "There is one more thing. I told my sister about you and she went shopping a few days ago to get you something nice you can wear to your hearing." He slid the bag across the table toward Rainey.

Unanticipated excitement ran through her blood as she opened the bag and pulled out a pale green dress. She quickly stood and held the dress against her body. It had a slim bodice with an A-line bottom. "Wow. This is so pretty. Thank you."

"There's more." Lindquist motioned toward the bag.

Rainey pulled out a black button-down sweater, a package of pantyhose, and a pair of flat black loafers. She touched the clean fabric and ran her fingers over the shoes. "I haven't had new clothes since I was little and my aunt Sophie bought me things. It's been a long time. Anyway," she said meeting Lindquist's gaze, "thank you. I would've had to wear this ugly uniform if you hadn't bought these for me. Tell your sister I said thank you."

Rainey put everything back into the bag and sat silently, looking down at her hands resting in her lap, touched by the agent's kindness.

"Is something wrong?" he asked.

"No. Well, it's just that I'm not used to people doing nice things for me. And it's pretty cool."

"I'm doing my best to help you however I can." Lindquist stood. "I have to get going. I'll see you next week in court. You've seen your lawyer and everything?"

"Yeah. I've seen him a couple of times."

Lindquist put out his hand and Rainey shook it. "Take care. And good luck in court next week."

As a female officer escorted Rainey back to her cell, she reminded herself that luck rarely visited her. She prayed that this time luck would brave the darkness and find her.

Chapter Fifty-Four

Three days before Rainey's trial, Brice Culler met with her. Inside the interview room the lawyer was standing, looking out the window. Rainey sat down and waited.

A few seconds later he turned and faced her. "So today we are going to review what will happen on Friday with the judge."

"Okay." Rainey squirmed, feeling suddenly nervous about the whole thing.

"Once your case is announced, you and I will go up to the table in the front. At that point, your charges will be read and the judge will ask you if you're pleading *guilty* or not guilty," Brice said, emphasizing the first plea.

"You mean I have to talk?" She hadn't expected that. She'd thought Brice would do all the talking.

"Yes, you have to talk. Specifically, you have to tell the judge you're pleading guilty to the charges of possession of drugs with intent to sell and having a firearm. All you need to say is one word: "guilty." Then you will tell him that you're sorry. You will also admit to having bought the drugs from a girl in Center City whom you don't know. You never got her name. That's what is most important for you to get right. It's very simple. Do you have any questions?"

"Yeah," she said. "What happens after I say all that?"

"Well, if the judge doesn't decide to try you as an adult, he or she will either sentence you right there or want to take time to consider everything in your case and come back with a decision in a few weeks."

"Oh," Rainey breathed. "What are you going to say about me?"

Brice shoved his hands into his suit pants. "Well, I'm going to tell the judge your parents are distraught over what you've done and that they're hoping he'll keep you in juvenile detention so that you can focus on rehabilitation."

"Is that it?" Rainey asked.

"Yes."

She stood and walked toward the door, then turned back. "By the way, my dad brought Ivy to see me but we got into a fight and he ran outta here. Do you think maybe you could talk to him and tell him he has to let Ivy visit again?" Rainey placed her hands on her hips. "You know, to help with my rehabilitation and all."

Brice hesitated a couple of seconds too long. "Sure. I'll see what I can do."

"Sure you will," Rainey mumbled under her breath as she knocked on the door to be let out of the room.

At lunch, Rainey told Phoenix everything that happened during her meeting with Brice.

"I forgot to ask him if my parents will be in court," Rainey stated.

Phoenix gulped her juice. "I'm sure they'll be there if he's gonna talk about how down and out they are about what you did."

"They make me sick," Rainey said. "I hate seeing them."

"Then don't look at them."

"I can't help it. They only pay attention to me when they need something from me. I bet once I'm locked up in here, they'll forget I ever existed."

***

On the morning of her appearance in court, Rainey woke up nervous about lying to the judge and seeing her parents. She got out of bed and sat on the edge of Phoenix's bunk, squirming around, her leg bouncing.

Phoenix sat up and pressed her hand on Rainey's knee. "It's going to be okay," she soothed. "There's nothing to be nervous about. You already know what you're going to say and your lawyer told you everything that's gonna happen. So just relax."

Rainey gave her a weak smile. "This is super hard for me."

"I know, girl. It's hard on all of us locked up in this place. You ain't alone."

A few hours later, after showering, Rainey put on her new clothes and shoes. When she walked into the hallway, Officer Fernandez gave her a broad smile. She looked like a respectable young woman with her hair pulled back into a tight ponytail and dressed in her new outfit.

"You look very pretty," Fernandez commented.

Rainey blushed at the officer's compliment. For the first time she could remember, she *felt* pretty. "Thank you. Now what?"

"There's a van waiting to bring you to the courthouse. I'm sorry, but I'll need to cuff you here."

Rainey put her hands behind her back, and the officer locked the steel cuffs on her wrists.

"It's hard to be pretty in handcuffs. It kinda takes away all the magic," Rainey said.

"Yeah, sorry about that, kid. They're the rules."

Inside the courtroom, Brice sat between Rainey and her parents. Neither of them acknowledged her, but she did notice they both seemed more sober than usual. She knew it was to make the judge think they were responsible parents.

Rainey's was the second case to be called that day. When it was her turn, she moved to the table at the front of the room with Brice, where the judge could address her. After a few routine questions and verifying that Brice was her attorney, the judge looked up from his papers.

"So, young lady. You've been charged with possession of one hundred grams of heroin with the intent to sell and possession of a firearm that was unregistered and had no serial numbers. That's a big charge for a young person like yourself. It also comes with serious consequences. Tell me, how do you plead? Guilty or not guilty?"

Rainey turned and glanced at Brice, who gave her a slight nod. Then she looked over her shoulder at her parents, who were watching her with anxious expressions on their faces. A few rows behind them was Agent Lindquist, who gave her a reassuring smile and a quick nod. Rainey's lips pinched together and she turned back to face the judge.

Rainey's breathing quickened and blood rushed to her face. She wanted to get all of this over with as she made eye contact with the judge and took in a long breath through her nose. "Your Honor . . ." she said.

Chapter Fifty-Five

"Your Honor," she repeated nervously, "I want to tell you something before I give you my plea. Am I allowed to do that?"

The judge leaned forward, seemingly interested. "Yes, I'd like to hear what you have to say."

Brice leaned into her ear, and in a husky voice whispered, "What the fuck are you doing?"

Rainey whispered back. "I just have to tell him something."

The judge's voice boomed. "Counselor, your client wants to say something. Is that a problem for you?"

"Yes it is, Your Honor. As her legal counsel, I need to be informed of what my client is going to say in advance for me to protect her best interests."

"Miss Paxton, your attorney is right. I suggest you speak privately with your lawyer before addressing the court."

Rainey shook her head. "No, Your Honor. I know what I'm doing. It's okay." She turned toward Brice. "It's going to be fine," she said, nerves rattling in her chest knowing that what she was about to say was risky.

She saw Brice's brows gathering and his lips pinching tightly, but that didn't stop her.

Rainey turned back and looked at the judge. "Your Honor, when I was little my Aunt Sophie, she's my mom's sister, took care of me a lot. She got sick and now she lives in a nursing home where they take care of her. Anyway, on the last day that she spent with me, back when she still knew who I was, she told me there were two things I had to remember to live by."

Rainey paused and wrung her hands together, hoping the judge would realize she wasn't a bad person.

The judge nodded. "Go on."

"Well, the first thing was that I should never take drugs. She said that was the most important rule I had to follow. Because drugs ruin lives and"—Rainey gave a small laugh—"I know she was right about that."

The judge nodded. "Good advice."

"The second thing she told me, and taught me, was if I wanted to save myself pain and suffering, I should tell the truth. She would say the world has enough liars, and what the world needs are more people who aren't afraid to be honest." She studied the judge, hoping the next part wouldn't make her look too bad. "Well, I haven't always told the truth about every little thing, but I have told the truth about things that are important."

The judge's lips puckered, watching her, waiting for her to finish. "Well, I can't argue with that one either. I'd say your aunt Sophie is a smart lady. But lying is lying."

She nodded. "I know, but when you're hungry or people are being mean, sometimes you have to say things that aren't true." Rainey put her shoulders back and lifted her chin in an attempt to steel herself against the backlash she suspected would follow. "Your Honor, I plead *not* guilty."

As Brice flinched and threw his arms in the air, Rainey thought he was going to grab her by the hair and smash her face into the table.

Brice put his mouth close to Rainey's ear. "You dumb girl. You have no idea the pain you've just brought on yourself."

His threat made the blood drain away from her face. She looked to the judge for comfort, but he was scowling at her. Rainey's hands were sweaty, yet a chill settled over her.

"Your Honor," Peter yelled, "she's a drug dealer! You gotta believe us. Just ask my wife. Our daughter needs help. I'm sure you can see that now."

The judge cracked his gavel, silencing Peter. He looked at Rainey dead on, and his eyes revealed a quiet concern. "Thank you for your plea, Miss Paxton. I don't see how this will help you given the strong evidence that the Drug Enforcement Agency has against you. We'll schedule a time one week from today for the facts of your case to be presented. Your lawyer will help you prepare."

Brice turned to her. "You'll need to find yourself a public defender. You've just blown the best chance of a decent life in prison. Good luck living in juvie."

As Rainey stood alone quietly, her head was spinning. When she'd chosen to plead not guilty, she'd felt powerful, justified. It had seemed like the right thing to do. But now she wasn't so sure. She wasn't sure she'd thought it through thoroughly. There was no way she'd convince the judge that the drugs and gun were someone else's—that it was all a big mistake. Now it would look like she was making it up to save herself. Then an image of Tootsie floated across her mind and she shuddered. Would Tootsie really try to kill her?

An officer put her hand on Rainey's shoulder, distracting her from her thoughts as she was escorted toward the exit of the courtroom. On her way, her mother and father stepped into the aisle. Peter gave her a bitter smirk.

"You've just blown your chance to see your sister." He looked at the officer holding Rainey's elbow, then back at her. "Your mother and I *definitely* can't have Ivy around someone who sells drugs and lies to a judge. You would be a bad influence on your little sister. Right, Miranda?"

"That's right," Miranda sneered. "You've always been a handful. You and drugs and drinking, but I'll tell you something, Rainey, this takes the cake. I'm so disappointed in you for not taking accountability for your actions."

Rainey's mouth fell open and it took a moment to regain her wits. She eyeballed her father, then her mother. "Someday you're both going to be sorry for everything you've done to me. You are rotten people and I'm embarrassed that you're my parents."

Peter pulled his arm back, but before he could slap his daughter in the face, Agent Lindquist grabbed his arm from behind. "Unless you want to blatantly commit child abuse in front of us, I suggest you keep your hands off your kid."

Rainey made eye contact with Lindquist, grateful to have one person in the room on her side. She gave her parents a tense smile and walked away. She was numb as she made her way out to the waiting van. She liked that Lindquist had stuck up for her. He'd given her the first sense of comfort she'd had in a long time. But in the end, she knew in juvie was where she would need to be protected. Once inside the van, what she'd done sunk in, and so did her grave future.

***

Later that day, when Jiggy heard that Rainey had pleaded not guilty, he sneered.

"I thought I told you to make sure that kid of yours keeps her mouth shut," he said to Peter.

"Look, man, she pleaded not guilty, but she never said your name to anyone, and she never will either. She knows that Ivy will pay if she does anything stupid."

Jiggy threw back a shot of tequila. "Yeah, you better be right. Because if she does mention my name to anyone . . . your younger daughter will belong to me."

Chapter Fifty-Six

As Rainey walked through the loud corridors of the prison, she spotted several inmates watching her with deadpan eyes. One girl growled as she passed. She knew which girls were members of the Vamps, short for vampires, which was Tootsie's gang.

The Vamps were named by its founder, Drake Sallow. Drake had formed the gang while he was serving time in prison for what he had done to fifteen-year-old Camila Falero, a Latina he abducted in Kensington while she was walking home from school. Drake tortured and raped Camila for five days before a neighbor heard the girl screaming and called the police. Drake had drained the life out of her by slicing through her midsection with a handsaw. By the time the police had arrived Camila's body had been partially dismembered and left on the basement floor. Blood covered the floor and had splattered on the walls. The police found Drake on his sofa, in only his boxers, drinking a beer with his still bloodstained hands.

Twenty-six-year-old Drake had eventually admitted to the police he killed Camila as revenge against her older brother Hernando, who had broken Drake's nose and three ribs in a bar fight over money. In prison, the other inmates, after hearing what he'd done to his victim, feared him. His cellmate nicknamed him Dracula because of the widow's peak of his hairline that made a well-defined point in the center of his forehead. This was a nickname that Drake was proud of.

Six months into his prison sentence, Hernando Falero was incarcerated at the same prison. That's when Drake formed the Vamps; it happened quickly. He had the ease of a man with the mind and charisma of a cult leader. Within a week, Drake killed Hernando leaving the dead man's skin in tatters from the multiple tears from prison-made shanks. Drake's motto was "Our enemies' blood gives us life."

Rainey knew the story of the Vamps, and knowing that Tootsie and others were members of the same gang petrified her. The very idea that Tootsie would do something like what was done to Hernando filled her with terror.

As her cell door slid open, Rainey drew in a deep breath. Her stomach cramped and she took in several deeper breaths to ease the pain. With the bars locked behind her, she dropped to her knees and knelt before the toilet, as though she were praying. Her body hitched forward as she threw up the poisonous truth of her new, dangerous reality behind bars.

Leaning against the far wall, Phoenix's eyes bulged and her mouth hung open. "What the hell happened?" she said, rushing to her side.

Rainey retched again and steadied herself by taking in a few quick breaths. "I pled not guilty."

"What? Why would you do that? The cops caught you. Now the judge is gonna really be a prick," Phoenix shrieked.

Rainey flopped her butt onto the concrete floor and sat Indian-style, staying close to the toilet. "Because I didn't do anything wrong. The drugs weren't mine. I was counting the bags for that asshole . . . they weren't mine."

"It doesn't matter. The cops have a solid case against you. What the fuck, Rainey? You realize you've just made yourself a huge target in here, right?"

Rainey nodded and pointed at the toilet. "Why do you think I'm puking my guts up? It felt so good standing up for myself in the courtroom. But when I got in the van to come back, it hit me hard how bad my life is gonna be in here."

Phoenix sat next to her friend on the floor. "Fucknuts, Rainey! What's wrong with you? Can't you just lie like normal people?"

A moment of silence stretched between them. Phoenix nudged her cellmate's knee with her hand, and Rainey looked into a set of eyes burdened with concern.

"Listen," Rainey said. "You don't have to hang with me just because we share a cell. Staying with me is just gonna make you a target too."

"So I'm just gonna let you get your ass beat from one end of this place to another?"

Rainey cringed. "Do you think it's gonna be that bad?"

"Um, yeah."

Rainey rested her head in her hands. "What am I gonna do? Maybe I should tell Fernandez I'm scared of the other girls."

Phoenix snatched her forearm. "Are you outta your mind? That's a definite no. You don't tell any of the bouncers what the other girls are doing. You keep your goddamn mouth shut and we'll deal with it as it comes."

Phoenix stood and pulled the girl to her feet. "Do you know how to fight?"

"I don't know. Kinda."

Phoenix smirked. "You either know how to fight or you don't."

"Well, I've been in fights before." She looked up shyly. "With my mom."

"Rainey, you're freaking me out right now. I mean, I have your back but I can't fight every fuckin' girl in here for you. So have you ever been in a fistfight with your mom? Please tell me yes."

"Yeah. There's been plenty of times my mom started a brawl with me." Rainey let out a heavy sigh. "One time, while my dad was watching from the bedroom door, my mom lunged at me. Her bony fists were cracking against my jaw and ribs. It hurt like hell. I got so pissed. I managed to push her off, get to my feet, and punched her until my dad pulled me off."

"Okay, I'm happy to hear about that," Phoenix said, smiling. "Any other times?"

"I had to fight her four or five times over the years. She and my dad get outta control sometimes. At first my mom kicked my ass, but once I got to be around eleven or twelve, I got better at fighting back. It's a messed-up way to have to learn how to fight," she explained.

Phoenix shook her head slowly. "Okay, well, I guess it's good you at least know how to fight, kind of."

"Yeah, I guess I'm screwed," Rainey mumbled. "How about you?"

Phoenix let out a curt chuckle. "I prostituted on the streets of Kensington for long enough to see my share of bullshit. So yeah, I know how to fight and I won't back down from anyone. Not even that brute Tootsie. That girl thinks she's hot shit 'cause she runs the Vamps in here. Problem is, if you get on her bad side, she'll have her girls torture you, but I don't give a fuck. I'd rather die fighting than be tormented and bullied into backing down."

"My attorney said there are girls worse than Tootsie in here."

"Your attorney is a lying sack of shit. He's trying to scare you. Everyone knows Tootsie's the most vicious person in this place."

Rainey bit down on her bottom lip and her eyes flicked toward the wall, realizing the danger she had put them both in.

"Hey," Phoenix said reaching for Rainey's hand. "I'm sorry. I don't mean to freak you out."

"No, it's cool. I was thinking just because I know how to fight doesn't mean I *want* to fight. I fought my mom because she gave me no choice, but I don't fight like a girl in a gang," she said thoughtfully.

"Listen, if any of those girls come after you then you'll have to show 'em everything you're made of. Punch, kick, bite, doesn't matter. You do what you gotta do so they think you're not afraid and that you'll stand up to them," Phoenix said.

Rainey wrapped her arms around her knees and lowered her head. "But I *am* afraid of them. I'm scared to death," she muttered.

Chapter Fifty-Seven

The next morning, at breakfast, Tootsie slid into the seat next to Rainey, jarring her. Three other girls stood behind them, blocking the guard's view. Tootsie grabbed a piece of toast from Rainey's tray, took a bite, and spit the chewed-up bits into her food.

"So I heard you told the judge you weren't guilty of nothin'," she said into Rainey's ear. "I thought you and me had an understanding. Now you gotta explain to the judge why you pleaded that way. See, I got word from Jiggy that he ain't cool with what you did, and that doesn't look good on me."

Phoenix's back was erect, her eyes set hard and hands clenched into fists under the table. "She's not looking for any trouble."

Tootsie turned slowly and glared at Phoenix. "Is somebody talking to you? Did you hear my motherfuckin' voice ask you a question? You best roll up your window on this conversation before you find yourself in a heap of shit. If I want to know what you gotta say, I'll invite your sorry ass to say something."

Phoenix's jaw jutted forward, and she remained quiet as she sized up the other girls. It would be an unfair fight for sure, but she wouldn't back down if things swung in that direction.

Tootsie turned back to Rainey. "You had to go and make things real hard for yourself, which means you made things hard for me. I thought you looked smart but I guess you're just as dumb as your bitch over there," she said, gesturing in Phoenix's direction with her chin.

Rainey pushed her hair over her shoulders. "I never told the judge anything about Jiggy."

"That don't matter, girl. All you had to do was plead guilty and say you didn't know the bitch who sold you the drugs. Basically," she said, poking her finger in Rainey's forehead, "this was about you taking responsibility. That's what you ain't getting."

Rainey pulled her head away and straightened her rounded shoulders in an attempt to appear confident. "I'm the one sitting in juvie with a ton of evidence against me. What difference does it make that I pled not guilty?"

Tootsie's hand shot forward and slammed against Rainey's cheek. Her head flew sideways, and she was dazed for a moment. "Because if you took responsibility then all of this would be over. Now that you left things hangin' who knows if the cops will start snoopin' around?"

Rainey held her burning cheek. "I'm sorry, okay? But I didn't do anything to Jiggy. The drugs weren't mine and besides . . . *he was about to rape me*," she said as her chest hitched.

Tootsie turned to the girl standing closest to her. "You hear that, Moody? Little miss innocent was about to get raped."

Moody smiled, cocked her head to the side, and cracked her knuckles. "Yeah," she grunted looking directly at Rainey. "I heard the bitch. We don't care what was gonna happen to you. Ain't none of us care what problems you got. We all got problems. Now you're our problem too."

Tootsie turned back to Rainey stone faced. Slowly she gave her a tight-lipped smile. Rainey's heart was beating so hard in her chest, she thought that surely Tootsie would hear it. She willed herself to breathe and appear brave, but it was no use.

"Anyway," Tootsie said, standing, "we just wanted to stop by and let you know we heard what you done. Oh, and to make sure you understand that what you said in court just started a war, dumb girl."

When Tootsie and the others walked away, Rainey looked down at her shaking hands. She turned her attention to Phoenix. "I screwed up. What the hell am I gonna do?"

Phoenix nodded, picking up her tray, and took a few steps away from the table. She stopped and looked over her shoulder at the scared girl. "You could've made our lives a whole lot easier if you had just pled guilty. You and me are gonna need a plan."

As Rainey watched her friend walk away, she realized the depth of trouble she caused, not only for herself but for Phoenix as well.

***

That night the two teens sat on the bottom bunk together. Rainey had been so worried all day that her head was pounding.

"So here's what we need to do," Phoenix said. "We need to stick together as much as possible. Two is much better than one. I know we can't always do that, like when we're in separate classes and stuff, but let's try to figure it out. We gotta avoid being in the cut too."

"What's the cut?"

"You know, the places where the cameras can't see us." Phoenix paused and gave her a look. "You really don't know?"

Rainey shook her head, feeling more out of the loop than ever.

"I'll point some of them out to you on our way to breakfast in the morning."

Rainey rubbed her temples. "That doesn't sound like much of a plan."

"Hey, you're the one that got us into this mess. You have any ideas?"

Rainey shook her head. "No. Look, Phoenix, I'm sorry you're going through this because of something I did. Maybe someday I'll be able to make it up to you."

"Maybe? Shit, girl. Someday you *are* gonna make it up to me." Phoenix gave her a toothy grin, which eased Rainey's nerves. "It's going to be okay. All we can do is watch our backs, be aware of everything going on around us, and try to stay where the bouncers can see us. Being around them will keep Tootsie and her peeps away; they hate everyone in a uniform."

Phoenix's confident voice was thwarted by the way she rubbed her arms, and her eyes darted around. When Rainey was younger, she had learned from watching people that physical reactions speak much louder than anything said aloud.

That night, Rainey lay on her bunk, raging war against the fear ravaging her insides. She understood the gravity of her mistake as she held onto her regret. Her nerves were frazzled. Telling the truth had made her lonelier than she could have imagined, and she was understanding why people were so willing to lie.

Chapter Fifty-Eight

The next day, Rainey was walking through the door to her first class when someone shoved her from behind. She fell forward and landed face-first on the tile floor. While pushing herself up on her knees, blood poured from her nose and mouth. Twisting around, she saw Moody grinning.

The teacher, Miss Charlotte, yelled, "Everyone down!"

Immediately, all the girls lay flat on their stomachs, with their hands clasped behind their backs.

Miss Charlotte grabbed the handheld radio hanging from her shirt and pressed the side button. "Guards in C block I have an inmate down in room four. Need assistance." Then the teacher rushed forward and got on her knees next to the girl. "Rainey, are you okay?"

The girl looked at her sideways, her nose already swelling.

"Oh, crap," Miss Charlotte breathed, looking at the volume of blood streaming from her nose. She pressed her fingers on the bridge and helped the girl sit up.

Rainey glanced at Moody, who stared back at her with a satisfied smile. Upset from all of the blood and the throbbing pain, Rainey bit the inside of her lip, trying not to cry.

After several minutes and a lot of craziness, Miss Charlotte gently pressed a towel against Rainey's face, and a guard escorted her to medical. The girl laid flat on a gurney, holding ice on her face. All she could focus her attention on was the burning, stabbing pain that pulsed through her nose and mouth.

"Hello, Rainey," a woman standing next to the gurney said. "I'm Nurse Dix. Let's take a look at what you have going on."

Rainey's eyes roved over the woman. Her black hair was smattered with streaks of gray, her brown eyes were surrounded by creases on the outer edges, and her teeth, while pearly white, were slightly crooked in the front. Rainey smiled at her and winced with pain.

Nurse Dix pulled the towel and ice away from the girl's face and studied her for a moment. "Oh, boy. You sure did a number on your nose. I'm going to fix you up, don't worry, sweetheart," she said, and with those simple words of kindness, Rainey's eyes filled with tears.

"Now, honey, you're going to be just fine." The nurse gently touched either side of the girl's nose, lifted her top and bottom lips to ensure no damage to her teeth, and felt along her jawline.

The nurse continued examining Rainey for a while longer. Then she patted her arm. "No, need to cry. There's nothing to be scared of. It doesn't look like anything is broken, but you're going to have some bruising. I'm going to clean you up and get you back to your cell to rest for a day or so."

Rainey pushed herself up on one elbow; she was scared to stay in her cell all day without Phoenix. "Can't I stay here with you?"

The nurse bent closer to Rainey. "Are you afraid to go back to your cell? You can tell me."

Rainey gingerly laid her head back on the small pillow and looked to the wall. "No."

"I see. Well, perhaps it *would* be prudent to keep you in here overnight so I can keep an eye on you . . . just in case the bleeding starts again. Plus, if you're here I can help manage your pain. I suppose I can send you back after breakfast tomorrow morning. How does that sound?"

Rainey glanced back at Dix, her panic subsiding. "That would be good. Thank you."

Nurse Dix ran her hand over the girl's hair. "I'm going to get you something for your pain and a *real* ice bag." The nurse looked over her shoulder at the noise of a door opening and closing. She turned back to Rainey, "In the meantime, Officer Jeffers would like to talk to you."

The officer, with whom Rainey was familiar, stepped forward and looked down at her. "Hello, Rainey. How are you feeling?"

"Not that good. I have a lot of pain," she said, worried that this was nothing compared to what Tootsie had planned for her.

"I'm not surprised; your face is bruised and swollen. I'm here because I have some questions about your injuries. It's very important that you're honest with me, for your safety and the safety of the other girls. Did someone hurt you?"

Rainey closed her eyes to give herself a second to think up a lie. "No. I tripped and fell."

"Are you sure you're telling me the truth? If you're being bullied it will only get worse if it goes unchecked," Officer Jeffers pressed.

"Yeah, I'm sure. I know what happened, okay? It was an accident . . . I tripped over my own feet," the girl said, then turned her head away from the guard.

"Okay, if you say so. If there's something that comes up and you want to talk to me you just let Nurse Dix know," the officer said and walked out of the room.

Over the next twenty-four hours, Rainey savored the peace and comfort of the infirmary, but when Officer Fernandez came for her, her heart beat in triple time. She'd been dreading returning to her cell and facing the horrible things would happen to her next. Her legs wobbled as her bare feet hit the cold tile floor.

Nurse Dix grabbed Rainey's arm and held onto her until she was stable. "Now you listen to me," the nurse said. "You can't let other girls be mean to you. You need to stand up to them." The nurse paused and glanced at Officer Fernandez, whose boot was loudly tapping on the floor. Nurse Dix gently tugged the collar of her shirt. "What I mean to say is if anyone is giving you a hard time you have to tell one of the guards so they can help you."

Rainey looked down at her feet through the slits of her swollen eyes. Just like Phoenix, Nurse Dix was right about standing up to her tormentors. "Yes, ma'am."

The nurse put her arm over Rainey's shoulder. "You can call me Nurse Dix. I'm too young to be a ma'am," she giggled. Then she turned to Fernandez. "I'd like Rainey to stay in her cell for the next two days. I'll be giving her medication that makes her sleepy and we don't want her to hurt herself more."

"You got it," Fernandez said with a smile.

"Now, Officer Fernandez, that includes her meals. She needs have those in her cell too. Will you make sure that's taken care of?"

Fernandez nodded.

"Rainey, it's important that you stay put for a few days until your injuries heal some more. I hope you understand why I need to place these restrictions on you," Nurse Dix said.

Rainey leaned into the woman and gave her a quick hug. "Thank you, Nurse Dix."

Relieved to be confined to her cell for a few more days, Rainey welcomed not having to stand up to her tormentors just yet. But the relief was short-lived. When she got back to her cell, Phoenix stood, giving her a hard stare with her chin held high and her nostrils flared.

Rainey knew something had gone wrong while she lay in the protective cover of the infirmary, and her whole body stiffened as she prepared herself to learn what was coming next. The skin on the back of her neck prickled so firmly it hurt, and she rubbed at it mindlessly while keeping her eyes glued to her cellmate.

Phoenix squeezed her eyes shut and opened them again, blinking several times to focus.

Chapter Fifty-Nine

Rainey ran both hands through her hair. "What happened?" she asked.

Phoenix squinted and her mouth twisted to the side, but she said nothing. She appeared agitated, and Rainey hoped it wasn't with her.

"Tell me what happened. Did someone hurt you?" she asked.

Phoenix moved toward her, and seeing how unsteadily she walked, Rainey realized that she wasn't wearing her glasses. She took a few steps toward her and grabbed her friend's hand.

"Where are your glasses?" she asked "You need to put them on."

Phoenix's upper lip curled. "Those fuckin' bitches . . ."

Rainey sucked in a loud breath. "They took your glasses?"

"Yep. Just like that, they snatched 'em off my face while I was walking down the hall. I can't see anything. I'm pretty much blind without them," Phoenix growled.

Rainey led her over to the bunks and they sat. Then she spoke in a whisper so the other girls wouldn't overhear. "Are you okay? How have you been getting around?"

"The stupid teachers have been walking me to each class, and then, of all the things I didn't want, one of the bouncers came and brought me back here at the end of the day. So I've been surrounded by all the people who work here. Let me tell you something . . . that shit ain't good for my reputation. The bitches in here will think I'm snitching on them," she spewed.

"Well, can one of the bouncers get your glasses back for you?"

Phoenix shrugged. "Are you kidding? They messed that up too. One of the bouncers announced to all the girls today that if my glasses don't show up in the rec area by tomorrow morning, they'll pull the tapes and whoever took them will get time in solitary. Like I need this shit in my life."

"I don't see how that's a bad thing," Rainey said, confused." Whoever took them *should* be put in solitary."

"Whatever." Phoenix rubbed both sides of her forehead with her index and middle fingers. "I have the *worst* fuckin' headache from straining to see."

"Look, you need to just do your own thing," Rainey said. "One of us needs to stay safe and we know it isn't going to be me. It's stupid for both of us to be getting knocked around in this place. Starting tomorrow, we aren't sitting together in the chow hall, and you're not walking to classes with me."

Phoenix shook her head. When she spoke, her voice was raspy and serious. "That ain't how I roll. That shit is for people who don't have a backbone. I've been where you are right now—the person who no one wants to know or take care of. I know how it feels when no one has your back. There was a time when I needed someone to believe in me. It was like I was being thrown off a cliff and there wasn't anyone there to catch me . . . to back me up 'cause it's the right thing to do. I remember that emptiness. Those were dark, motherfuckin' days. As long as I'm alive I'll do whatever I need to make sure you don't have to go through the same thing."

Phoenix pressed her palms against her eyes. "There were some days that were so bad I wished I was dead. Like the day I asked my sister if she'd let me live with her and she said no and closed the door in my face. It ain't easy to live with that shit. But when you do come through the other side, you won't care as much and you'll do everything you can to protect yourself from being hurt again."

Rainey put her hand on her cellmate's shoulder and pressed their cheeks together. She'd never had a true friend before Phoenix, and she was learning what it meant to be selfless. "You're right. We *are* a lot alike. A long time ago I stopped expecting people to act the way I want them to. You're a good friend and I'm happy you're my roomie."

Phoenix giggled and rolled her eyes. "Don't be so touchy-feely. Okay?"

"Whatever. You know you're happy to have me around here," Rainey said, putting her arm around her shoulders. "I've never had a friend before, and now that I do, I like it." She lowered her voice to a delicate whisper. "You're pretty freaking cool. Thanks for being here for me. I ain't used to it."

Rainey looked up as Fernandez approached the bars. "Phoenix, look what turned up," she said, holding up a pair of glasses.

Phoenix breathed a sigh of relief and took them from the guard. "Thank you so much," she said, sliding the glasses onto her face.

"You're welcome," Officer Fernandez said. "Now maybe you can stop referring to all the guards as bouncers."

Phoenix huffed. "Now you're taking things a little too far. We have our place in this dump and you have yours. We're criminals and you're bouncers . . . simple as that." She placed her hands on her hips and smiled. "But I'd say you're the coolest of them all."

The right side of Fernandez's mouth rose into a half smile. "Am I supposed to be flattered?"

Phoenix smiled and nodded.

Fernandez stepped backward. "Phoenix, get yourself together. Doors will be opening for dinner soon." Then she looked at Rainey. "I'll bring your tray back after all the girls are settled."

While Phoenix was in the cafeteria at dinner, Rainey worried about her the entire time. She didn't eat, just paced the small space. An hour later Phoenix, looking unharmed. sauntered back into their cell.

Rainey halted in her tracks. "How was it?" she asked.

Phoenix shook her head softly. "Well, they told all of us that if anything goes missing, like my glasses did today, there wouldn't be any second chances."

"That's good, right?" Rainey asked.

Phoenix laid on her bunk. "Rainey, none of this shit is good. Every time we get more restrictions people get more pissed off. At some point, you or me, or probably both of us, will pay for all the extra rules. Tootsie and her girls are making sure that everyone else gets pissed at us too."

A chill ran up Rainey's spine. She clutched her hands together, climbed onto her bunk, and started her long night of fretting.

Chapter Sixty

On the morning when Rainey was to rejoin the other inmates, she woke suddenly and could feel the quickness of her heartbeat inside her chest. Dread hit her hard as she laid on her bunk and staring at the ceiling, repeating over and over, *You will be fine. Don't let anyone mess with you. Stand up for yourself.*

Rainey's legs were weak as she forced one foot in front of the other to the cafeteria for breakfast. Her senses were heightened, in tune with everything going on around her.

"You need to breathe," Phoenix whispered.

Rainey forced air through her lips. "I hate not knowing what to expect. It's hard waiting for something bad to happen."

"Yeah, I know, but you gotta shake it off. Act like there ain't a thing wrong. These bitches will smell your fear," Phoenix warned.

"So what am I supposed to do? Just pretend like everything is fine? Act like I'm made of steel or something?" Rainey snapped.

"Yeah," Phoenix snapped back. "That's exactly what you need to do."

Several minutes later Rainey sat at the table across from Phoenix with her breakfast. Tootsie and three of her girls approached, holding trays of food. Rainey stiffened as Tootsie and Moody sat on either side of her while the other two girls sat on either side of Phoenix.

Phoenix put her fork down and glowered at Tootsie. "What do you want?"

Tootsie smiled, but her eyes were flat. "Bitch, don't worry. You don't need to ask what we want." She leaned into the center of the table. "'Cause we'll *take* what we want."

Phoenix leaned closer. "I ain't afraid of you." She looked at the girls sitting next to her, "Or either of you."

Tootsie snatched Phoenix's wrist, and Rainey gasped. "I ain't playin' with you. Do you know who the fuck you're talking to? You understand how many Vamps I have in here?"

Phoenix yanked her arm away. "Here's the thing, Tootsie. We ain't bothering you, so just leave us alone. We don't wanna be up against the Vamps, but if we gotta fight, then we'll fight."

Rainey's mouth hung open. *Why was Phoenix threatening her?* She wrung her hands together, staring at her cellmate in disbelief.

Tootsie turned away from Phoenix and gave her attention to Rainey. "How about you? Huh? You willing to fight with your dumbass friend here? Because we don't just fight, we kill. We get power from your blood, remember that."

Rainey's muscles were seized by fear. At first she couldn't move, then she looked at Phoenix and there was a fearlessness in her eyes. She turned back to Tootsie. "If you're going to mess with us then we don't have any choice but to protect ourselves."

"Oh," Tootsie chuckled. "There's only one way you're gonna protect yourself and your little whore over there," she said, pointing to Phoenix. "See, it's real simple. All you gotta do is tell the judge you lied when you go back to court in a few days. Tell him everything that Brice told you to say and this will all be over."

Rainey pushed herself up from the table, but Tootsie took hold of her forearm and pulled her back down into the seat.

"The drugs weren't mine. Yeah, they were in my lap but I was only doing what Jiggy told me to do. If I tell the judge I lied the last time, he might decide to try me as an adult, I can't go to adult prison. But I swear, I'll never tell the judge the drugs belonged to Jiggy," Rainey said.

Tootsie stood and gave her friends a curt nod. "Well, that ain't good enough so I guess you and me still have a problem." Before the gang members walked away, she said, "You just made the wrong decision, bitch."

***

Rainey shuffled into the courtroom the following week. Her eyes roamed, looking for her mother and father, but they weren't there.

Oddly, she had a sense of relief knowing that whenever they were around the two only made things worse for her.

As she made her way to her seat, her eyes met Agent Lindquist's, and he flashed a smile.

Once seated, waiting for her name to be called, Rainey's legs bounced and she couldn't focus. She'd been festering on Tootsie's threat all week. The more she thought about it, the greater her worry and anxiety grew. At the sound of her name being called, Rainey's eyes shot forward and the judge watched her.

She glanced at Stanley, her court-appointed attorney, whom she had spoken to earlier that week. Stanley had passed the Pennsylvania bar exam nine months prior and was still unsure of himself. His legs were unsteady as Rainey followed him to the table in the front of the courtroom.

Rainey watched Agent Lindquist intently as he gave his account of finding her with drugs and a gun the night of her arrest. When Lindquist was finished, he looked over at her.

Rainey's gut tightened, and her hand flew to her mouth. She closed her eyes as tears ran down her cheeks. *Why did I plead not guilty? I made everything so much harder for myself.*

"However," Lindquist continued giving the girl a sympathetic smile, "I'd like to say that even though Rainey Paxton doesn't have much of a defense, from the little I've gotten to know her, she seems like a decent kid. Rainey comes from challenging circumstances; at least that's what I've gathered from what I've been able to observe. I'm certain Rainey will leave juvenile detention one day and become a productive member of society. She is not destined for a life of crime."

The judge looked over the top of his glasses at Rainey. "That was very nice of Agent Lindquist to say, and I'll tell you, he rarely gives anyone sitting in your seat right now, compliments."

Rainey fidgeted in her seat and gave the judge a nervous smile, hoping he wouldn't want to prosecute her as an adult for being dumb with her plea.

"Miss Paxton, when you were in court last, you pleaded not guilty, which was troubling considering all the evidence the prosecution and the DEA office had against you. After hearing Agent Lindquist's account of your arrest, it gives me pause about your honesty and makes me question your motives."

Rainey looked up at the ceiling for a few seconds, then directly at the judge, knowing she couldn't talk her way out of the situation. "I'm sorry," she cried.

The judge focused on her attorney. "Is there anything else you'd like to present to the court for your client? Perhaps something that would support her not guilty plea that can override the testimony that Agent Lindquist provided?"

Stanley stood quickly. "No, Your Honor." He glanced sideways at Rainey. "My client was scared and is sorry for any confusion she may have caused the court. We have nothing further."

The judge scowled at Rainey, and her fear of being tried as an adult mounted. "Well, I have something further, counselor. Miss Paxton, it pains me to see someone your age caught up in this type of criminal activity."

This is my moment to make everything better with Tootsie. I'll tell the judge I bought the drugs from a girl in Center City just like Brice wanted me to and this will all be over, she thought.

Rainey raised her hand in the air. "Can I say one more thing?" she asked.

The judge leaned forward. "No, Miss Paxton, you may not. I've already given you the opportunity to speak the last time you were in my court and that didn't turn out so well for you given what Agent Lindquist described he found at the time of your arrest."

Rainey's eyes burned from scorching tears. "But Your Honor . . . I just wanted to say . . ."

The judge slammed his gavel and gave Rainey's attorney a scornful look.

"I'm sorry about the outburst Your Honor, it won't happen again," Stanley stated. Then he leaned into Rainey's ear, "Don't say anything else or this judge is going to make your situation worse than it already is."

"Okay," the judge said, shaking his head. "Miss Paxton, are your parents here today?"

Rainey shook her head and looked at her attorney.

Stanley stood again. "No, Your Honor. Something important must have happened because they would've been here," he stammered, having argued the day prior with Miranda and Peter about the importance of them attending their daughter's sentencing hearing.

The judge tilted his head. "I'm not sure what could be more important than your fourteen-year-old daughter being sentenced for possession of one hundred grams of heroin."

"Yes, Your Honor," Stanley said.

"Well, young lady," the judge said, looking directly at Rainey, "I understand you may have been scared when you pled not guilty, but given the events that happened the night you were arrested, it's clear what you've done. I'm sorry to say none of this speaks well for your character or credibility with this court. I have decided to sentence you to five years in juvenile detention. You'll be eligible for parole in three years."

The judge stopped when Rainey's gasp echoed throughout the courtroom. "Young lady, I suggest you do what is expected of you in juvenile detention if you wish to get out of jail before you turn eighteen and are sent to an adult prison to finish serving your last year," he said sternly.

She hadn't expected to get off with no proof of her innocence, but the realness of her situation knocked the breath from her lungs. Paralyzed with despair, Rainey stood like a statue forcing herself to breathe.

The judge let his eyes settle on the girl. "You'll be eligible for parole if you work the program. Juvenile detention focuses on rehabilitation rather than imprisonment itself. I wish you the best of luck in the future, and hope that as Agent Lindquist said, when you are released, you will become a productive member of our society."

Rainey's head hung and she flopped down in the chair. Two officers quickly moved beside her lifting her back to her feet. They each held an arm as they led her from the courtroom. Rainey's eyes stayed on the floor and she willed herself to walk as the two officers pulled her along.

I'm stuck in jail and Tootsie is probably going to kill me, she thought. *I'll just tell her the judge wouldn't let me say anything, maybe she'll understand.*

Chapter Sixty-One

Rainey was so fixated on keeping up her defense against Tootsie that she could barely think about the length of her sentence. Within the first few hours of returning to juvie, while walking to class, Tootsie grabbed her hair from behind, halting Rainey in place. Her hands flew up and she tried to pry herself free, but Tootsie knotted her fingers farther into her hair.

"Looks like the fun is about to begin," Tootsie hissed. "You are one dumbass ho."

"No, wait!" Rainey shouted. "The judge wouldn't let me say anything—I didn't get to tell him I bought the drugs from some girl I didn't know. I tried."

Tootsie yanked on her hair harder. "Oh really? That's too fucking bad. It wouldn't have mattered anyway—see, Jiggy can't stand you and wants you to suffer so just for that reason you'll need to pay."

Beads of sweat formed over Rainey's upper lip as she stared into Tootsie's face. Her mouth hung open as she tried to breathe through the pain. On instinct, Rainey pulled her arm back and landed her fist in Tootsie's stomach. Breath shot out of the girl's mouth and she instinctively released her hair.

When Tootsie caught her breath, she charged at Rainey like a bull. She wrapped her arms around the girl's waist, lifted her off her feet, and slammed her onto the ground. Quickly, a group of girls converged, yelling for a fight. Tootsie straddled Rainey's chest, punching her wildly.

"Get up," Moody warned. "A bouncer's comin'."

Tootsie sprung to her feet, and with her crew around her, sauntered away, leaving Rainey on the floor in a heap. Rainey rolled onto her side and brought her knees up to her chest. With the bruises from her previous fight not yet healed, the new injuries pitted the pain deep in her bones and muscles. It was as though someone were holding a blowtorch to her face.

A guard approached with a stern look. "What happened, Paxton?"

"Nothing," Rainey mumbled.

"Well, if nothing happened, then why are you laying on the floor in a fetal position?"

"I fell."

"Really? You fell again?"

Rainey groaned as she pushed herself up to her knees. "Yeah."

"You fall a lot for a girl who appears capable of walking without any issues." The guard stooped closer so no one but Rainey could hear her. "Look, kid. If somebody is harassing you it isn't going to go away on its own." The guard took in Rainey's injuries. "You got yourself bruises on top of bruises. We can protect you, but you have to tell me what's going on."

Rainey slowly rose to her feet and said, "There's nothing going on. I'm gonna be late for class. I gotta go," as she shuffled away slowly.

***

Over the next week, the torture continued. At first it was little things, such as stealing Rainey's bras, or all the girls would gather and stare at her while she showered. There always seemed to be one or two of the gang members following her everywhere. This kept her edgy and on high alert.

"The bitch gets no peace," Tootsie told her girls. "That means someone is always on her. I want her to be so scared that she wants to kill herself instead of me having to do it for her. Understand?"

"Don't worry, we got this," Moody said.

"That's right, you better fuckin' got this." Tootsie turned to the other girls. "I want to harass the bitch every chance we get, keep her worrying. Anyone got a problem with that?"

Critter, one of the smaller, meth-addicted Vamps, shook her head vigorously. "We hear you, Tootsie. Ain't nobody got a problem with nothing you're saying. You don't need to worry about a thing. We's all in this together."

Tootsie took a few steps forward and positioned her face uncomfortably close to Critter's. "Don't let that shit you plug up your nose every fucking minute get in the way of what you're expected to do here. I'll cut you off from your meth in an instant. Remember what happened the last time you screwed up?"

Critter ran her fingertips over the scar on her hip where she'd been held down and cut with a knife for being high and forgetting to show up when she was expected to. "I ain't gonna screw up. I know what I'm doing. And you know what, Tootsie? I ain't the only person on your crew that likes to get high, but I'm the one you're always picking on. How come you do that?"

Tootsie's hands sprang forward and grabbed Critter by the throat. She pressed hard and backed the girl up against a wall. Critter tried to free herself, but Tootsie squeezed tighter. Through clenched teeth she said, "First, don't you *ever* question me. Second, I stay up your ass because you get so high you can't even remember your dumb name. All of us like to party, but you take it too far . . . with your eyes always buggin' outta your head and your jaw grindin' back and forth. You make me sick."

Critter groaned as she tried to take air into her lungs. Finally Tootsie let go and the girl, sucking in air, collapsed to the floor.

"You remember your place, bitch," Tootsie said.

Critter looked up with bloodshot eyes and nodded. "I swear . . . I swear . . . I won't do nothin' to piss you off again."

"Good." Tootsie turned to face the others. "Back to Rainey, we need to make that bitch wish she was never born. Jiggy ain't playin' around with this one. She up and defied him and that ain't cool."

***

The next morning after breakfast, Rainey stopped to use the bathroom before class. When she looked up into the mirror, she was startled to see Moody and Critter standing behind her. Her eyes widened and she frantically looked around for Phoenix. Rainey's stomach flopped when she spotted her friend surrounded by Tootsie's crew at the far side of the room.

Rainey looked back at Moody and Critter. "What do you want?"

Moody stretched her arms out by her sides. "We just came over to say good morning."

"Okay, well you said it. Now I have to go," Rainey said in a shaky voice.

In a flash, Moody's open hand came up and crashed across Rainey's cheek. She staggered sideways, catching her balance on the edge of the sink. Rainey turned with the swiftness of a feline and raked her fingernails over Moody's forehead. Surprised, Moody hesitated for a second, and Rainey's fist pounded into the girl's chest. With adrenaline racing through her body, Rainey took a defensive stance and curled her hands into fists, but before she could take a swing, two other gang members were on top of her.

One girl jumped on Rainey's back and they fell to the floor. The other kicked her while Critter bit Rainey's legs and arms. Phoenix rushed forward and jumped into the mix. Six girls were rolling on the floor, throwing punches, pulling hair, and jamming the tips of their shoes into each other's limbs. The fight had gone on for less than a minute when two guards rushed in and broke it up. Rainey, who was still screaming as the guards pulled her away from Moody, had entered a state of hysteria. The guard grabbed Rainey by the shoulders and shook her hard until she snapped out of it.

"I'm sorry," Rainey cried. "I don't know what happened. I'm upset."

"I think that's an understatement," the guard remarked. "Let's get these girls to the infirmary," she directed the other guard.

"I'm fine," Rainey insisted, panicking at the thought of Tootsie's revenge.

"Well, you might think you're fine, but you have blood oozing down the side of your face so we'll have to find out from Nurse Dix if you're *fine*."

All six girls put their hands behind their backs and the guards secured them with plastic zip ties to keep them restrained. The only sounds they could hear as they walked to the infirmary was the distant voices of the girls in the cafeteria. With a heaviness in her chest, Rainey already wished she had never been born.

Several hours later, Rainey and Phoenix left the nurse's station, walking in silence.

"Thanks for jumping in," Rainey said after a few minutes.

"No problem. You'd do the same for me." Phoenix glanced at Rainey. "We didn't do too bad."

Rainey looked over at her cellmate, who gave her a small smile.

"Moody looks like she was in a fight with a tiger. Did you see those scratches across her face?" Phoenix giggled. "I love it."

Rainey stood up straighter, suddenly proud of fighting back. "Yeah, I surprised myself. I was so pissed I didn't even think and just started swinging."

"Good. Moody got what she deserved. Tootsie's gonna be so annoyed with her."

"Do you think maybe Tootsie will call everyone off now? You know, since we stood up to them?" Rainey asked hopefully.

Phoenix grunted. "Oh, hell, no. All we've done is piss her off more."

Rainey cringed. "But I thought if I stood up for myself it would get better. That's what you told me."

"No. I told you to fight back because if you let them know you're scared it's gonna get worse. I never said if you fight back that they'll leave you alone."

Rainey wiped the sweat from her forehead. "It can't get any worse than it already is."

"Oh, yeah it can. Things can get much worse."

Chapter Sixty-Two

One week later, as the two girls sat in the common room after dinner, Rainey looked around, taking in the murky beige block walls, the dark brown plastic chairs, and the stainless-steel tables bolted into the floor. The room had always seemed bleak and uninviting to her, but now it seemed worse—a place where people wait to die.

"Anything good happen today?" Phoenix asked, breaking Rainey's dreary focus.

"Nope." Rainey dropped her voice to barely a whisper. "I'm just happy that Tootsie and her crew have been keeping a low profile. Not one of them has even given me a dirty look since last week. Maybe fighting back did get them to leave us alone," she said hopefully, bouncing her eyebrows.

"Hmmmm, don't take your victory lap too soon. Gang bitches don't give up that easy."

"Are you trying to scare me?" Rainey leaned forward, annoyed. Her eyes bore into Phoenix. "Why can't you just admit that things have been better? You know how much I hate being in here and that I'm worried all the time, always looking over my shoulder, waiting for someone to hurt me. I need a break from it, okay? I'm tired."

Phoenix rested her chin in the palms of her hands. "Yeah, okay. Sure, it's true that things don't seem that bad. I'm just worried you'll let your guard down and they'll catch you by surprise. I don't want anything bad to happen to you."

Rainey laid her head on the table. "I never would've thought it would be possible to be homesick. I mean, really, I live in a shit hole that's half a step away from living in the streets. And as messed up as my parents are and even all the bad shit they've put me through, not being able to leave here and get away from these girls is even worse. Is that crazy?"

"Bitch, that's bookoo crazy. Your parents whored you out, remember?"

Rainey sighed "Yeah, you're right. I don't know what's wrong with me. It's making me nuts that we can't get away from Tootsie and her stupid friends. I can't change none of this. And to make everything worse, I've been so worried about myself that I've barely given any thought to Ivy. Who knows what those people are doing to her?"

Phoenix smiled at Rainey but didn't speak. A long silence stretched between them.

Rainey drew in a breath. "I'm gonna talk to the cop that arrested me . . . Agent Lindquist. He's been nice; maybe there's something he can do to get me outta here sooner. I swear, I'm gonna do everything I can to get paroled sooner."

Phoenix nibbled on one of her fingernails and averted her gaze, staring intently at the wall.

Rainey placed her hand on Phoenix's arm. Something was up. "What's wrong?" Rainey asked. "You look upset all of a sudden."

Phoenix shrugged. "Ain't nothing. I mean it's something, it's just that I'm an asshole."

Rainey giggled. "Tell me something I don't know."

Phoenix looked into her eyes. "No, seriously. You're talking about asking that cop for help and all I can think about is how alone I'd be if you got out and I was stuck here by myself. It's selfish, but it's been a long time since I had someone who cared about me. I don't wanna lose you. We are just starting to be friends."

Rainey, her heart swelling, clutched Phoenix's hand. "Even if I do get out sooner, I'll still come and see you. I swear. I'll come visit you whenever they let me. Then, after you get out, we can get an apartment together and Ivy will live with us. We'll be like a regular family."

Phoenix looked away and shook her head slowly. "No, that won't happen. Once you're out of here you won't ever want to come back. And you know what? I wouldn't blame you. This place sucks and I hate it and neither of us wants to be here." She paused, then gave a slow smile. "But you know, that thing about us living together as a family that would be awesome. I think that's something we should do."

Rainey smiled back, already picturing it. The two of them living in their own apartment and taking care of Ivy together. "I know. It would be so cool. We'll be able to eat whatever we want and sleep whenever we want. Not like in here or when I lived with my parents." Rainey pulled at the ends of her long hair.

"So you really think being in here is worse than living with your parents?" Phoenix asked, curiously.

Rainey considered the question for a moment. "I'm not sure. They're both shitty places, and like in here, things that happened to me at my house weren't right. Oh, man," she said, calling up a memory. "There was this one time that my dad made me sleep outside."

Phoenix looked at her closely. "Why? What happened?"

Rainey paused, embarrassed, but then realized that if there was anyone who wouldn't judge her it was Phoenix. "When I was eight my dad told me I had to stay in my room. I had already been in there for almost two days. I had to pee in a cup and had no food, nothing to drink. Anyway, when I couldn't take it anymore, I snuck out of my room and sat at the top of the stairs, where I could see into the living room. I was planning to sneak into the kitchen to look for food."

Rainey paused and looked at Phoenix, who was listening intently.

"So my timing sucked, and after a few minutes, I saw my dad in the living room about to shoot drugs into his arm. He had just inserted a needle when he looked up and caught me." Rainey rubbed her forehead with her thumb and index finger. "Man, that was a bad night. He pulled the needle out of his arm midway, ran up the steps, and dragged me downstairs."

The scene vividly ran through Rainey's mind as she remembered the embarrassment and humiliation.

Phoenix tapped her knee as her anger swelled. "Then what did he do?"

"Oh. He opened the front door and pushed me out onto the porch. I was barefoot and got a couple of splinters in the bottoms of my feet, so I started to cry because they hurt."

"What an asshole," Phoenix said, shaking her head.

Rainey scoffed. "Um, you have no idea. He forced me to sleep under the porch that night for not listening to him. He stood there and waited until I went down the steps, around the side, and climbed in through a big hole in the wood. It was pitch black and all I remember was the smell of dirt and feeling things crawl on me."

Phoenix's eyebrows knotted. "Are you serious? He made you stay there all night?"

"Yep, all fucking night."

Rainey brought her feet up on the chair and pulled her knees to her chest and wrapped her arms around them. "There were a lot of bad things my parents did to me. That's what it's like when your parents take drugs all the time. They don't remember half of the stuff they do. Once in a while, when other people were watching them, they pretended to be nice but mostly they were rotten."

"Your mom and dad are shit stains."

Rainey let out a short laugh. "Yeah, whatever. At least they gave me Ivy. That's one thing they did right."

Rainey glanced around the room. Some girls were watching television and others played board games. "This place is so boring. I hate it."

Phoenix yawned. "Yeah, it sucks. You wanna ask one of the guards for cards? We can play a game, you know, to pass the time and not think about all this stuff," she suggested.

Rainey sat up taller. "Yeah, that sounds like fun. You got any candy stashed?"

Her cellmate smirked and Rainey followed her to their cell. Phoenix kneeled in front of the toilet like it was an altar. Then she slid her hand along the bottom of the metal bowl and pulled down a half-eaten candy bar from the tape securing it.

"Did you ask if I had candy?" Phoenix sang quietly.

"Wow," Rainey breathed. "You always have something up your sleeve."

Phoenix blushed. "Yeah, that's just my talent. Always having stuff that other people want."

Rainey gave her a sideways glance and laughed. "You're funny. I wish I had stuff that people wanted."

"No, you don't." Phoenix stuck her hand out and pulled her up from the bunk. "Okay. Let's go play cards."

As the two walked out of the cell, Rainey said, "I would never want to be stuck in here without you."

"I don't think you have to worry about that," Phoenix giggled.

Rainey held out her pinky and Phoenix looped her pinky around it.

"When we get out of here me, you, and Ivy are going to start the best life ever. Pinky swear," Rainey said.

"Pinky swear."

Chapter Sixty-Three

The next morning, Rainey woke to the sound of Phoenix shuffling back and forth in front of their bunks. Rubbing the sleep from her eyes, she saw she was already dressed.

"Why are you ready so early?" Rainey asked, stretching her arms and legs.

"Mr. Bernard wants to see me before breakfast. He wants to talk to me about what I plan to do with my future. It's such a joke."

"What do you mean, 'a joke'? That's great. You should be happy. I'm happy about how well I do in school. My teachers are always telling me how smart I am," Rainey said, beaming.

Phoenix shrugged. "I guess. All I wanna do is get the hell outta here. Oh, and when I do get out of this shithole, I'm gonna move to Center City to hook so my pimp doesn't find me and kill me. Mr. Bernard knows I was a hooker before I landed in here."

Rainey flung her feet over the side of her bunk. "Mr. Bernard wants to help you. You'll still be young when you get out of here. And if we're gonna get a place together and have Ivy live with us, then you *can't* be a hooker."

Phoenix put her hands on her hips. "Why can't I be a hooker? It's not like Ivy would know what I'm doing."

"Of course she'll know. Ivy will be like eleven years old by that time. I knew a ton of shit by the time I was eleven."

"Oh, yeah? Like what?" Phoenix asked.

"I knew how to find my own food. I knew how to take a sink bath with a slow drip of water and an old rag. I knew all about my parents' taking drugs and drinking all the time. I watched them stumble around the house. It's not like they tried to hide it from me. Plus, I was around a lot of strangers who would tell me stuff like they didn't have a home and had to live on the streets or that they would steal from stores so they could eat . . . stuff like that."

"Yeah, that's a lot of stuff for a kid," Phoenix said, nodding.

Rainey's eyes cast down at the memories. "I did things to feel normal. But there ain't no normal when you have no money, water, food, or electricity," she explained. "What was it like for you after your parents died?"

Phoenix leaned against the wall, facing her. "Things were bad and I was all alone. You know, it isn't easy being a hooker. Everybody thinks all you need to do is lay on your back and spread your legs, but it ain't like that. You need to be able to read people real fast before you jump in a car with a john, and you need good people skills. Like how to make a guy feel like he's the only person in the world. And you know what else? You gotta have a strong mind and believe you're worth something because what you're doing is so degrading. Hooking is something I do to survive. You don't think the treat fairy buys us all our stuff from the commissary, do you?"

Rainey's cheeks flushed. "What do you mean?"

"I mean I ain't pickin' money off of trees. Where do you think I get the cash to buy us stuff?"

Rainey shrank away, it became clear that Phoenix was making money in juvie. "I . . . I never thought about it."

Phoenix tilted her chin up. "Relax, it's not a big deal. You didn't believe that bullshit about Mr. Bernard wanting to talk to me about math, did you?"

Rainey looked at her, confused. "Yeah, I did."

Phoenix let out a short cackle. "Nah, that ain't it. I give him what he wants and he gives me some cash. It's a simple transaction."

Rainey wiped her sweaty palms on her pant legs as what Phoenix said sunk in. "You mean Mr. Bernard is a pervert? He can't do that to you. It's not right. You have to report him."

"Report him? I'm the one who offered him sex. I ain't stayin' in here with no money. Besides, he's just one of a million pervs." Phoenix moved closer to her and lowered her voice to barely a whisper. "You listen, you better keep your mouth shut about this. You got it?"

"Yeah, I would never tell anyone." Rainey paused. "I don't know how you do it. After my parents made me have sex to pay for their dope, I thought I would die. It was the worst feeling ever. I was trapped inside my own head for weeks. It's really hard to let it go."

"Being forced to have sex ain't the same thing as what I do. You never agreed to it. That's rape. I made my own decision to sell sex." Phoenix let out a soft sigh. "It's different when you get to decide. I mean, it didn't seem as bad because I was in control. That is, until I was taken over by my pimp . . . he messed things up for me real quick, he snatched my freedom away, I hated him. But even then, when I was alone with a guy, I got to have some say."

"It's all so messed up," Rainey mumbled. "I don't need anything from the commissary anymore. You don't have to do things for Mr. Bernard or anyone else."

Phoenix gave her a quick flip of the wrist. "You may not want shit from the commissary, but I sure as hell do. Anyway, I gotta run. I'll see you at breakfast."

Rainey looked around the small space they shared as if the answer to life would show itself. She thought about the sacrifices Phoenix had made so she could have snacks and personal hygiene products. Her spine prickled as she imagined her friend letting Mr. Bernard do whatever he wanted to her. Deep in thought, she stood before the sink and grabbed her towel from a hook. She looked in the metal mirror and a distorted reflection stared back at her.

Shaking her head, Rainey turned the faucet on, and she leaned over the sink and splashed water onto her face. As she lifted her head, she caught sight of Moody in the mirror just before she twisted her fingers deep inside Rainey's long blond hair and pulled down hard.

She lost her balance, and her tailbone slammed against the floor. Stunned, she gripped the sides of her head with both hands and gaped up at Moody, who nodded at something behind her.

"You didn't think this was over. Did you?"

Rainey, startled by the voice, twisted to see Tootsie.

Tootsie crossed her arms over her chest. "What? You scared? Ain't nothing to say when your friend ain't around to fight for you?"

Rainey flinched as Moody yanked her hair tighter.

"What . . . what . . . do you want?" she stuttered in sheer panic.

Tootsie leaned her shoulder against the upper bunk. "What do I want?" she spat, then squatted next to her. "I told you what I wanted, and like a dumbass, you decided not to give it to me. I figure either you're stupid or you ain't paying attention. Soooo," she sang softly, "now you gotta pay for what you did."

Before Rainey could grasp what was happening, Tootsie reached behind her back and pulled out a pencil that had been split, with a razor blade jammed into its center, held securely with tape. Tootsie jabbed it toward Rainey's face.

Frightened, Rainey frantically tried to wiggle away from Moody. "Get off of me," she croaked and swung at Moody with her fist but missed, making contact with the bottom of the metal sink. The pain registered like fire crawling from her knuckles, up her forearm, and settling in her elbow.

Moody brought her free hand down and punched Rainey in the side of the face. She leaned into her ear. "Shut your fucking mouth. We do what we wanna do."

Tootsie stood and bent over top of her. The girl was still reeling from the sudden attack. Suddenly Tootsie swiped the razor back and forth . . . back and forth . . . back and forth. Rainey squeezed her eyes closed tightly. She didn't want to know when the blade slit her throat. She preferred to die without seeing it coming. Instinctively, Rainey rolled onto her side and brought her elbows up around her head. *This is it. I will die on this cold, cement floor of juvenile detention,* she thought. As the blade was slicing through her hair, her scalp was burning and her mind was set on Ivy. She focused on her sister's face. Unable to control her fear and helplessness, she openly cried, "Please don't kill me. Please," she begged.

Tootsie bent down in front of Rainey. She opened her palm and let the long golden locks she'd cut off fall over the withering girl.

Rainey let out an involuntary moan, still fearful that the worst was yet to come. With her heart racing like a marathon runner's, she lifted handfuls of hair and looked at the clumps as though they were a foreign substance.

Tootsie and Moody laughed as they were leaving her cell. "We're just beginning to have fun with you," Tootsie taunted.

Rainey's breath hitched. Her mind was racing and her life with her parents was crashing in on her. In all the years she'd lived at home, she could never get control over her life. Now, in juvie, it was starting all over again. She wanted to do better by consistently standing up for herself, but fear of making things worse kept her voice trapped deep inside of her. But here she was, lying on the cold floor, too afraid to tell anyone about the hell she was living on the inside of juvie because she learned early on snitches were always punished.

Chapter Sixty-Four

Alone in her cell, Rainey was curled in a ball on the floor and held tightly to the long strands of hair that had been cut from her scalp. Once she was certain she was alone, she hoisted herself up and looked into the murky silver plate on the wall. She stared at the atrocity that glowered back at her. Her red, watery eyes were an eerie contrast to the few inches of hair remaining on her head. Several clumps were left, and five-inch hairs spurted out from the center. She ran her fingers over several places where blood dribbled from the razor blade that had grazed her flesh.

Shame and fear converged inside her. She pulled toilet paper from the roll and dabbed at the blood on her head. She shook uncontrollably as she rinsed her scalp with water. Every noise made her flinch, afraid it was Tootsie and Moody returning to do more damage. With an intense need to flee her cell, Rainey dressed and rushed down to the cafeteria. Along the way, Tootsie's gang members pushed her while others blocked her passage, forcing her to scurry around them.

Inside the cafeteria, girls watched Rainey walk to her table. As she made her way deeper into the noisy room, most girls laughed, some mocked her, while others found gratitude in silent relief that they weren't the target. Some kept their eyes cast down, understanding the unspoken sorrow of being Tootsie's latest victim. It was no secret that she was after Rainey—gossip was a key staple in juvie, and word spread fast. Rainey kept her eyes glued to the floor, wishing she could cover up her head to prevent the others from seeing her pain and humiliation.

Hearing commotion, Phoenix looked up from her tray of food. Her hand flew over her mouth when her eyes landed on her cellmate.

Rainey approached the table and put her tray down gingerly, avoiding eye contact with Phoenix. Then Rainey sat, picked up a roll, and took a nibble.

Phoenix looked around. All eyes were on them. She popped an orange slice into her mouth and chewed a few times. "What the fuck happened to you?" she asked quietly, using every ounce of energy to keep the scowl off of her face.

Rainey shrugged. "Can't talk about it now because I'm afraid I'll cry," she said, already feeling her voice break. "That's the last thing I need to do. Everyone is watching. I'm a freak show."

"A couple of things: stop feeling sorry for yourself because that ain't gonna solve anything, and you better not cry. Understand?" Phoenix took a sharp inhale. "Did Tootsie pay you a visit?"

Rainey nodded. "Moody was there too."

"Fuck!" Phoenix growled through clenched teeth. "Those fucking idiots. Which one of those whores gave you the bruise on the side of your face?"

Rainey kept her head down. "Moody did. Then Tootsie cut off my hair."

"Those bitches gotta pay," Phoenix stated. The words tumbling out in a low, deep-throated vibration.

Panicking, Rainey's head bolted upright. "No. Please. Don't do anything to them. They'll just come after me again. You have to promise me."

Phoenix laid her fork down. "Rainey, you can't—"

"Promise," she begged, with large eyes filled with raw desperation.

Rainey followed Phoenix's stare as she looked over at Tootsie and her gang. Tootsie returned her gaze, pursed her lips, and cocked her head to the side. Then she mouthed "Fuck you." Rainey shuddered and looked away.

"Here's what I'll do," Phoenix said. "I won't start anything, but if they do one more thing, I'm gonna beat the living fuck outta someone. I ain't gonna take—" Phoenix suddenly went silent.

Rainey looked up and saw a guard approaching. It was Officer Elda, notoriously known for being cruel.

"Paxton, what happened to your hair?" Elda asked.

"I . . . I . . . don't know." Rainey wished she had come up with a better answer before now.

Officer Elda put her booted foot up on the stool next to Rainey. "You don't know? Well, you better figure it out. Did you cut it off yourself?"

Rainey shook her head. "No."

"I see. Well, then who did?"

"I have no idea. I woke up like this."

Officer Elda watched her carefully. "Paxton, don't take me for a fool. All you're doing now is asking for time in solitary. You better tell me what happened."

Rainey hung her head, knowing she sounded foolish, but she had no options. "I can't tell you if I don't know."

The guard looked up and noticed the other girls watching with interest. "Okay, Paxton. We'll play it your way for now before this whole cafeteria is in an upheaval. But here's the deal: when I find out what happened to you, and to be clear I *will* find out, you'll be sorry you lied to me. I'll make sure of it. You understand me, Paxton?"

Rainey stared at the guard, unable to muster anything more than a blank expression and sullen eyes.

"This is your last chance to tell me what happened," the officer warned.

"Like I told you," Rainey said, straightening her spine and looking into the guard's eyes, desperate to be left alone. "I don't know what happened."

"We'll see," Officer Elda said as she turned and walked away.

Once the officer was far enough away, Phoenix sputtered, "You woke up that way? Why would you say that?"

Rainey gave her a pained expression. "Well, if I said I did it myself then I'd get in trouble for having something to cut my hair off with."

"Oh," Phoenix breathed. "Good thinking."

Rainey clasped her hands together. "Tootsie isn't going to stop. She told me it's only the beginning. I don't know what that means, but I'm scared. I can't live like this. Look at me. Look what they did to me and I didn't fight back. I just sat on the floor like a lump of shit."

Phoenix stood and lifted her tray. "You ain't got no choice but *to* live like this. *This"*— she looked around her—"is all we got."

Rainey shivered and grabbed her tray as she followed Phoenix out of the cafeteria. She didn't want to live in fear the entire time she was in juvie, always worried that someone would hurt her . . . maybe even kill her. The contents in her belly turned sour and sloshed around, making it hard for her to concentrate on everything around her.

As the two girls walked to their first class, Rainey reached for her friend's hand. It was the only small comfort she had in the world, the touch of someone who cared about her.

Chapter Sixty-Five

Throughout the day, Rainey mindlessly raked her fingers over her scalp, gently exploring the small scabs that had formed where the razor had left behind tiny divots of flesh. She pulled on the few long strands of hair, wishing she could make it all grow back instantly. Periodically, Rainey's mouth filled with the bitter taste of self-loathing.

Before she had arrived in juvie, Rainey saw herself as resourceful and a survivor. Now, she considered herself defenseless prey for the girls out to get her. She wasn't strong enough to stand up to her tormentors, and that bothered her. Her mind drifted back to after the attack and staring at the image of herself in the metal mirror. She despised how her green eyes protruded grotesquely from her high, pale cheekbones and nearly bald head.

Tootsie's threats weighed heavy on her, putting Rainey in a constant state of tension. Rainey lied to every teacher who tried to discover the real story, feeling as ugly on the inside as she thought she looked on the outside. She wasn't the kind of person who told lies easily. Each lie filled her with shame. She told herself that these lies would keep her safe. She hoped that if she didn't tell on Tootsie, they would see she wasn't a snitch and leave her alone.

Other fears took root inside her. Rainey knew some were rational and some were downright nuts. She worried that the girls would throw acid in her face or saw her hand off—not understanding it would be impossible even for Tootsie to get the materials needed to do those horrible things to her.

Later that night, Rainey snapped when Phoenix asked if she'd told any teachers what happened.

"I'm not an idiot or a snitch," Rainey said.

"Whoa. I never accused you of being either of those."

Rainey's chin dropped to her chest. "Yeah, sorry." She lifted her head and met her cellmate's eyes. "Look at me. I look ridiculous. You know what else?"

"What?"

"When those girls came after me, I was scared. I mean really, really scared. I didn't know what to do . . . I just froze and could see my fear feeding their rage. I tried so hard to snap myself out of it—to fight back—but it was like I couldn't get my mind and my body in sync. I couldn't even fake like I wasn't afraid, I was literally shaking uncontrollably. They saw right through me."

"It's not the end of the world." Phoenix put her arm around Rainey.

"I laid on the ground and bawled while they laughed."

"Excuse me? You what?"

"I curled up right in front of them. Like I was a baby . . . with my knees up at my chest. I was begging them to stop beating me. It was humiliating."

"That's pretty fucked up," Phoenix said. "We talked about playing the part."

Rainey let out a loud sigh. "I know; I couldn't stop myself. After Tootsie and Moody left our cell I laid right there," she said, pointing to the floor, "and I cried so hard my body shook. Because I was so scared. They're never going to leave me alone now."

"Come on. So you got scared. Does it suck? Hell, yeah. Is it the worst thing that could happen? No, you could've shitted your pants," she said with a chuckle, but Rainey sat stone-faced, unable to appreciate the humor. "Look, girl, everybody gets scared sometimes. That doesn't mean you give up. Whenever you're scared you have to fight harder. You gotta let those bitches know you ain't gonna lay down and die."

Rainey stood and leaned her back against the cinderblock wall. "Yeah, well, what am I supposed to do when they come for me again? This time they cut my hair off. What if next time they hurt me worse? What if they kill me?"

Rainey squirmed while Phoenix studied her for a moment.

"Look," Phoenix said, "I can only tell you what I've learned on the streets. If you give in to your fears then it'll eat you alive and you just said it—your fear fed those girls. People like Tootsie collect souls. If you let them, they'll take everything good inside of you and leave you an empty shell. You gotta push past it no matter how shitty it feels."

Rainey shook her head, feeling at a total loss. "I don't know how."

Phoenix snapped. "What are you talking about? You know how to hide your fear. You did it the whole time you were living with your parents. I mean, when you told me that your mom and dad let guys have sex with you to pay for their drugs, that scared the hell outta me. I can't imagine having parents who would do that."

Rainey was quiet as she let Phoenix's words sink in. "It's not the same," she whispered.

"You're right," she answered. "It's not the same. Living in your house was way worse than the problem you have with Tootsie. You gotta start to see it that way because it's true. At least in here, there are a few adults who give a fuck whether you live or die. Someone who would stop bad things from happening to you if they knew or saw it. That's more than you had when you lived at your house."

"Maybe you're right," Rainey mumbled with a sense of security having her friend so firmly on her side. "Maybe I'm just letting Tootsie get to me too much. But you know she wants to hurt me. We both know that."

Phoenix nodded. "Yeah, Tootsie wants to mess up your whole world. The thing you need to do is let her know you ain't going to take her bullshit and that you'll go after her harder than she'll ever come after you. It's all a big fucking game. That asshole Jiggy is pulling her strings from the outside. He's pushing her to make your life miserable. So make it hard for her."

"That's easy for you to say," Rainey remarked.

"Actually, it isn't. I never had any bad blood with Tootsie or her gang members, but I'm in this with you, remember? So whatever you do or don't do affects me. I have your back and I'm good with that, but I can't stand behind you if you're gonna let these girls eat you alive." Phoenix paused. "And you need to have my back too—that means you gotta fight 'em back. If not, you're just leaving me to fight them all by myself and that ain't cool."

Rainey took a deep, painful breath and closed her eyes. She better understood the burden of her actions on Phoenix and, the heavy load of guilt dampened her spirit. She ran her fingers over her scalp again. "You're right. It's not fair. I swear, I'll try my best to not be afraid and stand up to them."

"This ain't about trying, Rainey. This is about *not* being afraid. What the hell are you scared of? Are you really afraid some ugly-ass girls are gonna whoop your ass? So, what! That ain't nothing. When your pimp locks you in a room for five days, then him and his crew rape and beat you continuously . . . well, that's something different. That's real fucking fear . . . and pain."

Rainey cringed; an emptiness was in the pit of her belly. She understood the need to change her reaction to her situation with Tootsie or lose the only person willing to stand up for her. Phoenix was right; she was putting them both in harm's way by letting the bullies get the best of her.

I will be fearless . . . I will be fearless, Rainey repeated in her head, trying to convince herself it was true. She admired how Phoenix could be so courageous with a ruthless enemy nipping at her heels. She needed to know how her friend did it, how she could go through every day without obsessing on what could happen to her in juvie.

Chapter Sixty-Six

Several days later, Rainey and Phoenix were talking in their cell. "Tell me about the foster homes you lived in. What was it like?" Rainey asked.

"Jesus, girl. There's nothing subtle about you."

Rainey grinned. "I can't help it. I wanna know. See, my life was crap, and I always thought if Ivy and me could just live with another family we could've been happy."

Phoenix rubbed her temples, knowing Rainey wouldn't stop until she satisfied her curiosity. "What do you wanna know?"

Rainey leaned forward and put her elbows on her thighs. "Tell me about the foster home you were in . . . the one that you liked. You said you had to leave. What happened?"

Phoenix forced out a grunt. "Well, it all started good. You know . . . the parents didn't slap me around or make me their housekeeper, like most of the foster parents did. The McDonnells were nice. I was only eleven when I went there. They had one kid of their own. His name was Robbie and he was already nineteen by the time I moved in. At first everything was great. Mrs. McDonnell told me I was the daughter she never had, and Mr. McDonnell was interested in what I was learning in school. I thought I'd finally found the place where I belonged."

"So what happened?" the girl asked.

Phoenix held her palms up. "I'm getting to that part. So Robbie, their son, started hanging around me all the time. He seemed to be everywhere I was, always putting his arm over my shoulder and pulling me in to hug him for too long. Weird shit that made me uncomfortable. After about nine months, the McDonnells found out their son had a crush on me."

"A nineteen-year-old had a crush on an eleven-year-old? That sounds like my life."

Phoenix raked her fingers through her hair. "Yeah, I know. Anyway, Robbie told my foster parents that he was in love with me and wanted to marry me. So the McDonnells sat me down and told me they requested a new placement to keep me safe."

"Did they tell you what Robbie told them?"

Phoenix shook her head. "Nah-ah. One night, I was already in bed and I heard them all screaming at each other. Robbie was like, 'You don't understand, I love Phoenix and we were meant to be together. I'm going to marry her whether you like it or not. Don't try to stand in the way of us being together.' Then Mr. McDonnell was so mad. I never heard him get angry until that night. He yelled, "You're a sick boy, Robbie. Phoenix is a child and you are a grown man. We promised to take care of that girl and protect her. We will not put her life in jeopardy, not even for you. You need help and Mom and I will make sure that you get it.'"

Phoenix paused, and Rainey could tell it hurt her to relive the memory—to know that she had been wanted, could have been loved, and some deranged nineteen-year-old man had ruined it.

"You have to finish," Rainey said, squeezing her friend's arm.

Phoenix sighed. "So yeah, Robbie yells back, 'I'm not going to hurt her or ruin her life. I love Phoenix and she's going to be the mother of my children.'"

"They made you move out because their son was fucked up in the head?" Rainey asked.

Phoenix threw her hands up. "Yeah, they made me leave 'for my own good.' Robbie was a fuckin' perv. He was into young girls. His parents didn't even know how messed up he was. He would've gone after younger girls whether they lived in their house or not."

"Really?" Rainey pictured Freddy and wondered if Robbie would turn out like him.

"Hell, yeah. Robbie used to talk to me about the girls in my grade . . . 'this one is pretty, that one is a slut, the blonde wants to get laid, the brunette needs to shed some weight.' I didn't even know what he was talking about most of the time. It was weird. And the thing is the McDonnells were Christians, like super religious. When they let me know they contacted social services to take me back because I was too much of a temptation for their son, I was crushed. They were like, 'Look,

Phoenix this isn't your fault. Our son has a sickness, something's wrong in his head and we are afraid that if you stay here, he'll harm you.'"

Rainey grunted. "So instead of kicking their adult son out, they made you leave. That makes no sense."

"Exactly. It was fucked up. It broke my heart. I was really into the McDonnells. They reminded me of my own parents. I felt safe with them and I hated leaving. I hated them for making me leave." Phoenix shrugged. "I didn't understand it back then, and sometimes I worry that Robbie might've done some messed-up shit to other little girls after I was gone."

"How long did you live with them?"

"Just over a year."

The two girls were quiet. Rainey thought about how devastated Phoenix must have been to be given away so easily.

"What happened after you were kicked out of the McDonnells?"

"I got sent to this evil foster home. They didn't sexually abuse me or nothing like that, but they treated me worse than a dog. I wasn't allowed to do much else besides go to school, clean the house, and cook for them and their rotten kids."

"At least school got you out of the house, though," Rainey said.

"Yeah, whatever. That was no break. By the time I was twelve I was letting the ninth graders feel me up . . . and down. They'd give me a buck or let me use their lunch ticket. I started saving my money—I had almost fifty dollars when my foster mom found it and took it from me."

"You let the boys in school touch you?" Rainey looked at her friend with large eyes.

Phoenix shrugged. "I did what I had to do to survive. For a while, I was always able to buy myself stuff. My foster parents didn't buy me nothing with the money they got to take care of me. I got sick of not having notebooks and pens or any of that stupid shit I needed for school. So I figured fuck it, I'll let those little piglets touch my boobs and my crotch, it wasn't a big deal. It didn't mean anything to me and it only lasted like a minute or two. I was making good money for a quick feel."

Rainey's mouth hung open. "How long did you live with those people?"

"Almost two years. I was sick of foster homes. So a year after I got to the next shithole, I snagged money from my foster mom and took off for Kensington. I had already been letting boys touch me for money, so it didn't matter much when a guy approached me the first time for a hand job. I made pretty good money," she said proudly.

"I remember the story you told me about your pimp," Rainey said, nodding.

"Yeah. So that's my whole fucking messed-up life. I went from being an orphan to a whore to an inmate. My life has been hard since I lost my parents." Phoenix rubbed her temples, then looked up at her friend. "Maybe that's why Tootsie doesn't scare me. I already went through the worst thing in my life, losing my mom and dad, then being tossed aside by my sister. So I think the other stuff—you know, hooking, getting knocked around, or neglected by foster parents—didn't bother me as much. I haven't belonged anywhere in a really long time and I guess when you don't belong anywhere things don't seem as important . . . like Tootsie."

"I think you're really brave," Rainey said, touching her hand.

Phoenix gave the girl a small smile. "So . . . what about you? I know your parents suck, but how about the other kids while you were growing up. You weren't letting boys feel you up for cash," she said with a giggle. "So did you ever have a boyfriend?" Phoenix asked.

Rainey shook her head. "No. Are you serious? First off, I quit school when I was twelve, so I wasn't interested in boys. Second, I only left my house to hunt, steal, or beg for food for me and Ivy."

"Your parents made you stay home from school?"

Rainey shook her head. "No, that was my choice. Ivy had been wandering around when I was at school, and some of the teenagers were doing stupid stuff and thought it was funny. My parents would leave her alone and I was afraid for her. I was so freaked out that someone would hurt Ivy and that's when I decided not to go to school anymore."

"Hmm. So are you telling me you never even had a crush on one of the older dudes that hung at your house?"

Rainey blushed. "Um, no, not like that."

Phoenix leaned her upper body toward her. "Really?" she sang. "I think you're lying."

Rainey smiled at a memory. "Well, there was this one guy when I was little, his name was Skeeter. He was cute and he was nice to me. When he came over, he always made it a point to talk to me before he got stoned. Then some bad stuff happened and he was gone for good."

"What bad stuff?"

Rainey's gaze dropped away.

"Oh, come on. I told you all about my shit, but you're not going to tell me yours?"

"Fine." Rainey hooked her fingers behind her head. "He was a narc. I watched my dad and some other guys beat him bad. They threatened him and he never came back to my house again. That's all I can remember. It was just a little-girl crush. But I always wondered what happened to him."

"Like you wonder if he might be dead?"

"As in anything is possible," Rainey admitted. "I knew my parents could be crazy mean to people—I saw that most of my life." She rubbed the back of her neck. "Talking about this stuff makes me worry more about Ivy. I have to know that she's okay. I'm gonna try to talk to Agent Lindquist."

Chapter Sixty-Seven

Immediately following breakfast, Rainey moved swiftly to the guards' office. She tapped lightly on the metal door, and a few seconds later an officer poked her head out.

"Everything okay, Paxton?"

Rainey nodded as she twisted her hands together, feeling suddenly nervous about her next question.

"Something I can do for you?"

"Yeah. Can I talk to Officer Fernandez?"

The officer looked over her shoulder. "Fernandez, Paxton wants to talk to you."

When Officer Fernandez appeared, she let out a quick gasp as her eyes roamed over Rainey's hair and face. "Jeez," she said with concern, "I heard you were pretty banged up but I had no idea."

Rainey slid her hand over the bruise on the side of her face and tried not to wince. "It doesn't hurt that much."

"And this?" Fernandez asked, cupping her practically bald head.

She gave the officer a weak smile. "I told Officer Elda I have no idea how it happened. Besides, it'll grow back." Rainey, feeling tears prick at her eyes, turned away to compose herself.

Fernandez gently took Rainey by the elbow and led her to a small office across the hall. Shutting the door behind them, she said, "Let's get this straight. I'm not Officer Elda. Clearly, someone did this to you. I want you to know you can confide in me. I'll make sure you're safe. Can you tell me who is responsible for hurting you?"

Rainey looked into the woman's face, and for a split second she considered telling the officer the truth because her need for relief and protection was so great. Then she came to her senses—as kind as Fernandez was, she wasn't the one living in juvie.

"I don't know what happened," Rainey said. "Like I said before, I woke up like this."

"Well, that's too bad," Fernandez commented. She sat down and gestured for the girl to sit next to her. "Here's the thing, Rainey. I don't believe you, and I know none of the other guards and faculty do either. I just want you to know I'm here if you need me." She paused, and when Rainey didn't speak, let out a loud sigh. "So since you're not going to give me information about what happened to you, why don't you tell me what you want to discuss."

"I want to talk about my sister, Ivy."

"All right. Well then, let's talk about Ivy. What's going on?"

Rainey's fingers nervously fiddled with the long strands of hair left on her scalp. "I wanted to find out if you could call Agent Lindquist and ask him to come and see me again. I need to talk to him."

Fernandez rubbed her chin with her thumb and index finger. "I can call him for you. But I'm certain he'll ask what you want to talk to him about."

"It's about my little sister." The girl blew out a breath. She was nervous that Fernandez wouldn't call him, since Rainey hadn't given her the information about her attackers.

Fernandez studied her, wanting more, but was happy to try to help her. "Sure. I'll let him know you want to see him right away."

Rainey stood from the chair, eager to leave. "I appreciate your help."

"Sure thing," Fernandez said as the girl walked toward the door. "Paxton?"

Rainey turned back. "Yeah?"

"My offer stands. You can tell me anything. I'll make sure you're safe."

Rainey's heart quickened. She hated that the guards kept pressing her for the information she was never going to give them. "There's nothing to tell you."

***

Three days after her conversation with Officer Fernandez, Rainey sat in a conference room waiting for Agent Lindquist. When he walked through the door a sense of security washed over her. Desperately, she wished he could protect her from the evil that lurked in the halls of juvie.

"Hi," she muttered, now nervous to be sitting in the room with him. "Thanks for coming to see me. I know I'm being a pest."

She shrank away from him as his eyes roved over her scalp and face. "It's not a problem. I keep coming here hoping you'll eventually tell me who your supplier is," he said, giving her a curious look.

She pulled her head back and smirked. "Okay," she mumbled.

"How have you been?" he asked.

"Fine, I guess."

Lindquist sat across from her. "You don't look fine."

Rainey shook her head. "I didn't ask you to come here to talk about me. I wanted to talk to you about Ivy."

Lindquist nodded. "Okay, what's going on?"

Rainey rubbed her forehead, trying to find the right words. "My parents haven't come to see me. I haven't heard from them at all. I'm really worried about my sister. I don't know if she's okay or what's happening to her. I can't sit in this place and not know anything about her."

Before answering, Lindquist reached in his pocket, removed a pack of gum, and pulled out a stick. He held the pack toward Rainey and lifted his chin, but she shook her head.

Lindquist popped a stick of gum in his mouth. "I can tell you this . . . I saw Ivy about ten days ago."

Rainey smiled, thankful that she'd been spotted. "How did she look? What did she say?"

"I didn't talk to her. I sat and watched your house for a few hours," he said.

"Why did you do that? Did something bad happen?"

"No, no, no," Lindquist said. "Everything is fine. I just parked down the street for a few hours and was just about to leave when I saw your mother leaving and dragging Ivy behind her."

"Dragging?" Images of Miranda being mean to Ivy flashed through Rainey's mind. "What does that mean?"

"Well, Ivy was screaming and trying to pull away from her, though I assumed that was fairly normal given what I've seen in the courtroom between you and your parents."

Rainey nodded. "My mom says mean things to us all the time; I just learned how to ignore them. To make myself feel better, I'd tell myself it was the drugs talking. Ivy is different, though—she's always had me to shield her."

She saw Lindquist studying her scalp and the bruise on the side of her face. She was nervous under his gaze.

"Sounds like you've had a rough childhood," he said.

Rainey nodded, then waved her hand as if to clear the air, wanting to get back to the subject of Ivy. "Well, anyway, where did my mom take her?"

"She drove down to the welfare office, which seemed like a good sign."

Rainey gave him a tight smile. "You don't know my mother. I forgot all about welfare and food stamps. Now that I'm in here the state is probably giving her less. My parents aren't married, so she tells them she's a single mom. That bitch will let my sister starve." Rainey closed her eyes, remembering how it was to be hungry all the time. Leaning up on her elbows and looking at him stone-faced, she said, "How did Ivy look? I need you to tell me the truth."

"Well, okay. She looked—um, *weathered*. She was dirty, her hair was tangled, she had dark circles under her eyes—not much has changed since the last time you saw her."

Rainey nodded and looked down at the table, avoiding Lindquist's eyes.

"Are there any other family members that could check on Ivy? I could call them for you."

"No," Rainey said, shaking her head, but then a thought came to her. "Well, there's this girl who used to go to our house a lot. She doesn't shoot up drugs; she just drinks a lot. Anyway, her name is Buddy. My mom kinda likes her and I bet she could get—"

Lindquist put his hands up, and Rainey stopped talking. "I know Buddy," he said, averting her gaze.

"You do? How?"

"I know her from working the streets." He paused. "Unfortunately, Buddy's no longer here."

"What does that mean? Like she moved somewhere else? You could still call her; I know she'd come back. Buddy loves me and Ivy."

"No," Lindquist said firmly. "Buddy died."

"She died?" Rainey lowered her head as a heaping of sorrow filled her. "Buddy died?"

Lindquist was quiet while Rainey processed the new information. She remembered Buddy's kindness to her. She was saddened by her death. After a minute he patted her hand. "I'm sorry about Buddy."

Rainey spoke, but her voice cracked. "Buddy was a nice person. Not only that, but she was probably the only person in the whole world that could help Ivy."

Lindquist nodded. "I understand. And I agree with you, Buddy was a decent person."

Rainey wrapped her arms tightly around herself. "How did she die?"

"She was murdered. We're looking for the person who might've done it."

"How . . . how did they kill her?" she stuttered.

Lindquist looked down at his hands. "She was stabbed."

Rainey covered her face with her hands at the image. "Buddy knew me. She protected me. She knew that Ivy and me needed someone to take care of us. Then she stopped coming around and we ran into her one day and she was drunk."

Rainey paused and stared at Lindquist for a moment, remembering something Buddy had said the last time she saw her. "Wait. Did you know Buddy because she was a narc?"

Lindquist met her eyes but said nothing.

Rainey sighed. "You don't have to tell me. I had a feeling that's what she was doing. She wanted me to help her get information. So you're the cop she was doing it for?"

"I'm not sure what you're talking about," Lindquist said abruptly, clearly signaling that all talk of Buddy was over. "Now I think we should get back to Ivy. Isn't that why you asked me to come here?"

"Yes, it is," Rainey said, refocusing her thoughts. "There's no one else I can ask. Not one person gives a shit about what's happening to her while I'm in here. Please, Agent Lindquist. Please, you have to help her."

Chapter Sixty-Eight

Agent Lindquist met his partner, Patrick Roper, in the parking lot and they left the Juvenile Detention Center, driving into the heart of North Philadelphia. People clustered on the streets, some passing joints in broad daylight and others trolling for drugs or prostitutes.

After weaving his unmarked car through crowds of people walking and stumbling along, Lindquist turned left onto West York Street and parked. He leaned back on the headrest and took in the sight of the house where Rainey had lived. His eyes wandered over the rotting floorboards of the porch and the puke green paint chipping away from the fissured stucco, leaving large areas of exposed cinder block. Agent Lindquist tried to imagine the horrid upbringing Rainey had lived. *So many children are suffocating in severe poverty,* he thought.

"They put more boards on the windows since the last time we were here," Lindquist said.

"Yeah, that's to keep the cops out," Roper said with a laugh.

Lindquist nodded, still staring at the wooden, splintered front door. The once white door now showed the weathered dark wood underneath.

"Do you want to tell me what we're looking for?" Roper asked.

Lindquist glanced over at his partner. "Do you remember when we stormed that shithole not so long ago? The thought of kids living inside that house haunts me. All the dirty walls and those horrible stairs with indoor-outdoor carpet glued on. The retched smells of meth, piss, sweat, and old beer come back every time I even think about this place. It was like stepping through the door of hell."

Roper nodded. "Yeah, okay. It was raunchy. But so are all the other drug houses we bust. Why are you so fixated on this one?"

"Rainey Paxton is why. I believe the girl has a good heart. You know, maybe a victim of her circumstances. I don't know, man, I get a different vibe from this kid. You know, the only thing she asked me for today was to make sure her little sister is doing okay. She's not like the other kids we busted selling drugs."

Roper pulled a candy bar from the glove compartment, ripped open the wrapper, and bit into it. "Lindquist, you know better than that. Just because the girl cares about her kid sister doesn't mean she's a good person. How many drug dealers have we arrested that were worried about their siblings? That isn't anything new."

Lindquist took a swig of his cold coffee and grimaced. "Not the same thing, Pat. I'm telling you, this kid is different. We know when people are lying."

"Yeah, and?"

"Well, Rainey is lying. She knows more than she's willing to tell me. She knows who sold her the drugs. And because she won't tell me, there's nothing I can do to help her."

"Look at that shit," Roper said suddenly, pointing to Rainey's house.

Lindquist looked as Miranda stepped onto the porch in her bra and panties. A lit cigarette dangled from her lips. Her eyelids drooped and she began to stumble-dance. Three men followed her outside to gawk at her, frothing at the mouth. Lindquist looked over to the open doorway and saw Ivy standing just inside, wide-eyed and hugging herself. The child was barefoot and dressed in a dirty, ripped T-shirt and stained pajama bottoms that cut into her scrawny waist.

"What the fuck is wrong with those people? Look at that kid, will you?" Lindquist growled.

Roper turned his attention to Ivy. He slowly laid down the remainder of his candy bar and shook his head. "Jesus Christ. Look how skinny that kid is. I can practically see her whole skull. What the hell is wrong with her hair? Is it caked in mud?"

Lindquist leaned up closer to the front window to get a better look. "I don't know, man." He turned and met Patrick's eyes. "Rainey Paxton was right. She said the kid is being neglected."

The agent's watched in disbelief until finally one man on the porch, longingly watching Miranda, lit a joint.

"Let's go," Lindquist said. "That's our in."

The agents approached the row home quickly and stood a few feet away from the porch. Miranda kept stumble-dancing to the music blaring through the front door, unaware of the agents.

Lindquist and Roper took a few steps closer and held up their badges. "Is that marijuana you're smoking?" Lindquist asked.

The young guy grinned at the officer and nodded.

"What's your name?" Lindquist demanded.

"Joey-J," he said, smiling broadly and revealing his rotted teeth. Joey-J swayed and offered the joint to the agent.

"Have you lost your mind?" Agent Lindquist barked.

"No, but maybe you should take a couple of hits and lose yours, man. You don't need to be such a dick."

Lindquist grabbed the collar of Joey-J's shirt. "Who the hell do you think you're talking to? Are you looking to go to jail?"

Joey-J let out a chuckle. The stale bitterness of his breath hit Lindquist's nose and his head jerked back a few inches. Then Joey-J moved in closer. "So what are you gonna do? Arrest me for having half a joint or for offering you a hit? Oh, maybe because I called you a dick. You don't have a fucking thing on me, man, and you ain't got no reason to arrest me. Just 'cause I'm high don't mean I'm stupid. I know my rights."

His patience boiling over, Agent Lindquist turned Joey-J around and pushed him up against the stucco wall. "You listen, motherfucker, you don't want to bust my balls. I'm in a really bad mood today and I don't like you very much, *Joey-J*. You understand me, *man*?"

Joey-J smirked. "Yeah, dude. I understand."

Lindquist looked at the others in the group. His gaze stopped on Miranda. "This is your house, right?"

Miranda tilted her head to the side. "Yeah. I rent it. What's it to you?"

"What's it to me? Well, don't you think it's messed up that you're out here dancing around in your underwear while your kid stands in the doorway watching you? It's a bad example you're setting for her. Don't you think?"

Miranda moved closer to the agent. "Hey listen, I don't care who you are. You don't get to tell me what I can wear or how to raise my kid! I'm a great mom."

Having heard Miranda yelling outside, Peter pulled Ivy from the doorway and went onto the porch. "What's going on?"

"This asshole," Miranda screamed, pointing at Agent Lindquist, "is trying to tell me I'm a bad mother."

Peter looked at the agent. "What's the deal, man? What the hell do you want here?"

"We were driving by and saw your friend here, lighting up a joint," Lindquist said, pointing at Joey-J.

"So what?"

"So it's still illegal to smoke pot," Roper stated.

Peter turned and stared at Lindquist and a flash of recognition crossed his face. He shook his index finger at the agent. "Oh, now I know who you are. You're that guy that arrested my daughter."

"That's right. I'm *that* guy."

Peter smiled and pulled Miranda into him. "Good thing that you have that little bitch behind bars. She was a real pain in the ass. Big-time drug dealer."

Lindquist kept a poker face, even though he wanted to punch Peter in the throat. "Given the condition of your younger daughter, I have some concerns about her welfare."

Peter pointed his finger at him. "Fuck you, man. You have no right coming here and passing judgment. Ivy is fine; she's better than fine, actually. She ain't nothing like her older, drug-dealing sister. So unless you have a search warrant you better see your way off my porch." Peter turned to the small group. "Let's go. Everyone back inside."

The three men followed Miranda inside, and Peter was the last in line. He turned and glared at the agents, then threw the door shut in their faces.

Lindquist was stunned. He couldn't imagine why people like Peter and Miranda would ever have children. His anger got the better of him and he slammed his fist into the front door. Feeling feeble, he and his partner got in their car and left.

***

Inside the house, Peter grabbed Miranda by the forearm and backhanded her across the face. "Don't be such a dumb bitch. Keep your ass inside the house when you're juiced up."

Miranda tugged away from him. "Well, maybe if you paid any attention to me, I wouldn't need to go outside."

Peter pulled Miranda to him and kissed the top of her greasy hair. "Our pain in the ass daughter is telling that agent shit about us. She thinks she's so fucking clever. Well, I'll show her. I'm gonna have to make sure she keeps her mouth shut. I have an idea . . . we can talk to Jiggy later."

Peter pushed Miranda up the stairs, into their bedroom, and slammed the door behind them. "You want my attention? Fine. You got it. Take off that fucking underwear and come over here and suck me off."

Miranda stared at her boyfriend with weighted eyelids. "What? You're crazy."

Peter pulled off his shirt and pants, dropping them to the floor as Miranda watched curiously. He moved close to her and grabbed a handful of her hair, tugging hard. "I told you to take your underwear off. Didn't I?"

Miranda giggled and Peter slapped her hard in the face, her eyes widening.

"I ain't joking! When I tell you to do something, you do it!"

Miranda fumbled to unlatch her bra and quickly slipped her panties down to her ankles. Peter sat her down on the edge of the bed and stood over her. He pushed his groin forward and pulled her head to him. "Let's go," he demanded.

Miranda, knowing Peter was serious, took him into her mouth.

After a couple of minutes, Peter pushed her away. "You give the worst head when you're too high," he said, pushing her down onto the bed and climbing on top of her. He entered her quickly and hammered away like a rabbit until he finished and his full body weight fell on top of her.

Miranda pushed against his shoulder. "Come on. My turn."

Peter turned his head away. "Yeah, I don't think so." He got up and pulled his pants on.

Miranda put her hands on her crotch. "Come on, baby. Take care of me. Will you?"

Peter finished dressing and left the bedroom as Miranda stared at the empty doorway in disbelief.

***

Later that evening, Peter and Miranda found Jiggy and brought him upstairs into their bedroom.

"What the hell is so important that you have to drag me up here?" Jiggy asked, irritated. "You got something to say to me, so just say it."

Peter put his arm over Miranda and pulled her into him. "Those drug agents were here earlier today."

Jiggy narrowed his eyes. "And?"

"*And*," Peter said, pausing dramatically, "he was asking about you. Rainey is running her mouth in juvie," he lied. "We thought you'd want to know so you can take care of it."

Jiggy clenched his jaw. "See now, that's the kinda shit I want you to tell me. I'll take care of her real good."

Peter was pretty proud of the lie he'd concocted. He knew that if he told Jiggy it was his name that was being thrown around to the cops, his girls on the inside would silence Rainey, maybe for good.

Chapter Sixty-Nine

Two days later, as Rainey was walking to the common room, she was grabbed from behind. With a hand clamped over her mouth and her right arm jacked up behind her back, Tootsie and two other girls dragged her a short distance inside a stairwell.

"You fucked up real good this time," Tootsie said. "Singing to the cops. Tellin' them a bunch of lies about Jiggy. You done messed up for sure."

With a girl's hand still over her mouth, Rainey's eyes bulged as she tried to shake her head. But Tootsie ignored her struggle and stood glaring with the focus of a hungry demon. From behind, one of the other girls landed a solid kick into the center of Rainey's back, sending her flying forward into the wall. Before she could regroup, the three girls were kicking and punching her. Fists and feet flew from all directions. She tried to curl into a fetal position, but Tootsie kicked her in the forehead, leaving her helpless and sprawled out on her back.

After several minutes, the beating stopped, and Rainey drew in a sharp breath. She could feel wetness in her hair, and when she pulled her fingers away, she saw blood.

Looking above her, one of Tootsie's girls was peeing on her head. She didn't jerk away or fight back. Rainey laid there, too broken to move.

Before leaving, Tootsie pulled her foot back and gave Rainey one last kick to the head. The girl lay in the stairway unconscious for close to an hour before she was found by a guard who had been part of a larger group searching for her.

***

When Rainey opened her eyes, Nurse Dix was staring down at her, the corners of her mouth turned down, deep lines curving out at the sides of her eyes. "There you are," she said gently.

Rainey tried to talk but her mouth was bone-dry. The nurse held a Styrofoam cup with a straw in front of her and she took small sips.

"How are you feeling?" Nurse Dix asked.

"Horrible," Rainey croaked, trying to remember what had happened. "Where's Phoenix?"

"Your cellmate?" the nurse asked.

Rainey nodded slightly.

"Did Phoenix do this to you?"

"No. She would never hurt me," she whispered. "Will you get her for me?"

The nurse pinched her lips together. "I'll see what I can do. For now, though, I need you to rest and focus on getting better."

Rainey adjusted her body on the small bed in the infirmary, and pain shot up her legs and into her hips and back. She groaned. "What's wrong with me?"

"Well, your right arm is broken, along with two ribs. And, my dear, you have bruises everywhere. We had to rush you to the emergency room to have your arm set. The doctor sent you back here and said you'll be fine, but you need time to recover. So you'll be staying here with me for a week . . . maybe a few days longer."

Rainey lifted her good arm and moaned.

"On a scale of one to ten, what's your pain level? Ten being unbearable."

Rainey forced her eyes open. "Ten."

Several minutes later, after the nurse had injected morphine into Rainey's IV line, she allowed herself to relax into the thin mattress and drift off to sleep. She dreamed of Tootsie and her friends coming after her again. Her mind raced with frightening thoughts of them killing her. She tried to wake herself up, but the drugs were too powerful. After a while she slipped into a deep, black sleep where there was no light; no hope; no escape; and thankfully, no Tootsie.

Just as Nurse Dix promised, ten days later, Rainey was released and sent back to the crowd of unruly teenage girls. She limped through the hall, her arm in a cast and cradled in a sling. When she looked into her cell and saw Phoenix laying on her bunk, the stress she'd been holding inside broke and tears pricked her eyes.

Phoenix stood quickly and rushed toward her. "Rainey! These assholes told me you were fine, but I didn't believe them. I begged them to let me see you, but they wouldn't," she said, glaring at the guard who had escorted her friend.

"I know. I asked Dix like a million times if you could come to visit and she just kept saying she'd look into it. I'm so happy to see you." Rainey threw her good arm around Phoenix's neck.

Once the guard was gone, Phoenix pulled the girl onto the cot next to her. "So what happened?"

"Come on. You know what happened. Tootsie and her goons beat the crap out of me."

"Did you tell Nurse Dix?"

"Do you think I want to die in here?"

Phoenix shook her head.

Rainey pushed her hair from her eyes. "What has everyone been saying about me?"

Phoenix shifted her eyes away.

"Oh, come on," Rainey pressed. "I know the girls in here are a bunch of gossiping bitches."

Phoenix turned her body slightly away from Rainey, not wanting to upset her friend so soon after being released from the infirmary. "There's been a lot of rumors. Like that you were talking shit on Tootsie . . . you know, that you made up lies about her."

"Lies? What lies? I never talked about Tootsie to anyone."

Phoenix shrugged. "Doesn't matter that you didn't do it if everyone is saying that you did. The rumor was you said you saw Tootsie having sex with Moody and that they found out about it and beat your ass."

Rainey covered her face with her good hand. "That's so stupid."

"Well, if you haven't noticed, that's the one thing we got a lot of in this place . . . stupid."

Rainey looked up at the block ceiling. "What about the guards and teachers? Do they think that Tootsie and Moody did this to me?"

"I'm sure they hear the rumors, but they can't do nothing unless you tell them what happened."

Rainey, already exhausted for the day, laid back on Phoenix's bunk. "Anything else happen while I was away?"

"Yeah. Something you should know, I guess," she said with apprehension.

"What?" Rainey said, sitting up again.

"Moody and that girl, Critter, the one that lives for meth, they cornered me a couple of days ago." Phoenix looked down at her hands. "They told me if I keep hanging out with you that I'll be next."

Rainey's heart tumbled from her chest to her stomach. The idea of not having Phoenix was frightening, intolerable. She stared at her friend with wide eyes.

"Shit, girl," Phoenix said. "Chill the hell out. I ain't gonna ditch you because some raggedy-ass big mouths threaten me. You know I don't give in to bullying. Nope, not me, I'll fight anyone any day of the week."

Rainey laid her head on Phoenix's shoulder, feeling happy to have her as a friend. "Thank you. And . . . and I'm sorry."

"You're sorry for what?"

"I'm sorry that being my friend is so hard. But I swear, someday when we both get out of here, I'm gonna make it up to you."

"Oh, yeah?" Phoenix said, giving her a genuine smile. "I'm gonna hold you to that. It means you got to find us a place to live since you'll be out of here before me."

"Done!" Rainey promised, and she meant it—she would make it happen.

"Since we got that settled, I want to warn you that Tootsie isn't going to let up. The best you can do is never find yourself alone with her or those little brown-nosing creatures that follow her around this place."

Rainey shook her head. "You don't have to worry about that. I'll do my best to stay in the view of every stupid camera in this place. That's the only chance I have of not being jumped again."

"You wanna play a game of cards?" Phoenix asked.

"Nah. Not tonight. I'm really tired. I gotta go back into general pop tomorrow, and I'm gonna need sleep."

Chapter Seventy

Rainey sat in history class, lost in thought as her teacher wrote the names of Native American tribes on the blackboard. She imagined how wonderful it would be to be born into a whole tribe, an entire group of men, women, and children who accepted and cared for her from the moment she was born. While she'd learned of the struggles and abuses Native Americans had suffered, the idea of communal living and having a tribe of her own filled her with longing.

"Rainey?" Ms. Ellis said, and she realized she'd been daydreaming.

She blinked several times. "Sorry, I didn't hear the question."

Some girls in the back of the class giggled, and Thunder, one of Tootsie's gang members, chucked a small balled-up piece of paper at her. Rainey turned her head slightly to take a peek behind her, then back at Ms. Ellis.

The teacher crossed her arms over her chest. "I understand you've been through a rough time recently, Rainey. But I want you to put in a little more effort to pay attention."

The other girls snickered, and the one who'd thrown the paper yelled, "Loser!"

"Girls!" Ms. Ellis snapped. "You stop it. Every one of you needs to pay closer attention to what you're being taught, not just Rainey. Now, the question I asked is, what is one thing that the Plains Indians are known for?"

The room went dead silent. Rainey's good hand found itself on the nape of her neck. She cleared her throat, trying to remember what she'd read. "Their feathered war bonnets."

"Yes," the teacher said, delighted, clapping her hands together. "That's exactly right." She turned to write the answer on the blackboard.

"Fucking brown-nosed bitch!" someone yelled from the back of the room.

The teacher spun around quickly. "Who said that?"

Met by silence, the teacher's eyes narrowed and passed over the group of girls before she went back to teaching her lesson.

At the end of class, Ms. Ellis asked Rainey to stay behind. The girl stood to the side of her desk, watching the others talk among themselves as their voices mixed into the din of the hallway. Once everyone was gone, Ms. Ellis gestured for Rainey to sit.

"How are you doing?" she asked, touching Rainey's shoulder.

Rainey forced a smile. "I'm good. My arm is getting better, and Nurse Dix said the bruises on my face will be gone in about a week."

Ms. Ellis shook her head. "That's not what I meant. I'm asking how things are going with the other girls in here. I feel pretty certain that what happened to you wasn't an accident."

Rainey looked down at her good hand, tasting the truth sitting on the tip of her tongue but swallowing the words back down her throat.

"Well?" Ms. Ellis said gently.

"Well, what?" Rainey said, knowing she was avoiding the question.

"Look. You're a nice girl and you're very smart. I believe that when you get out of here, you're going to do something good with your life. But first we need you to make it out of here. You've been here less than six months and already you've had several injuries. I think it's time you talk to someone about what's going on. If not me, then there must be a guard that you trust."

Rainey stood and grabbed her notebook. "I don't know what you're talking about, but I appreciate that you care about me."

Rainey started toward the classroom door, but Ms. Ellis called her name.

"Yeah?" Rainey said, pausing.

"I'm here if you need me. If you ever need to talk. Okay?"

Rainey nodded and walked into the hallway. As she made her way to her next class, she thought about how great it would be if she *could* talk to someone who could help her, someone in authority, about what Tootsie and her gang members were doing to her, but she knew that if she did, her odds of being killed were likely.

At the end of the day, as Rainey was making her way back to her cell, Moody came up from behind and slapped her in the back of the head.

Fed up with being bullied and weary of being scared, Rainey spun around. "What's your problem?"

Moody puffed out her chest. "*You're* my motherfuckin' problem."

Rainey's face flushed with red-hot anger. "I want you to leave me alone. I haven't done anything to you or Tootsie. I'm sick of you picking on me and busting on me for no reason."

Moody seemed taken back for a moment, and Rainey was satisfied to see the bewildered look on the girl's face.

Then Moody gave her a cruel smile filled with hatred. "See, that's where you got it all wrong. The fact that you still exist is a good reason to despise you." Moody lifted her fist, and Rainey involuntarily flinched and stepped back. "Yeah," Moody said. "You better stay afraid too."

Her heart racing and anger filling every crevice of her being, Rainey turned and quickly walked away. Inside her cell, Phoenix was counting the money she kept hidden inside a book on their shelf.

"What's wrong with you?" Phoenix asked.

"Moody stopped me on my way back here."

Phoenix huffed. "You can't be afraid of her."

Rainey clenched her teeth. "This isn't fear; it's anger. I'm sick and tired of this bullshit. I didn't do anything to those pieces of shit. So what if I pled not guilty? And so what if I didn't say I bought the drugs from some random chick in Center City? Fuck Jiggy and fuck Tootsie and fuck all those Vamp bitches. I'm sick of them."

Phoenix gave her an unexpected hug. "That's good that you're mad. If one of them messes with you again, you need to flatten them. Lay 'em out right where they stand."

Rainey nodded, feeling more fired up than she had in weeks. She had decided, while she laid in the infirmary, that it was time to defend herself. Time to get over her fear and be brave enough to end this nonsense. "What gives them the right to bully and abuse people? They're all so insecure. You should've seen the look on Moody's face when I stood up to her. For a split second, she looked like she was gonna shit her pants. The only time they're cocky is when they're all together."

"Yep, that's why they call it a gang and that's exactly why people join them. Most of them are too afraid to stand alone."

"Yeah, well, I think we should make our own gang," Rainey said, her brain spinning a mile a minute. "You know, see if other girls want to join us. We can be a tribe like the Native Americans."

"No thanks. You can't trust people in here. I keep telling you that. What you and I have is special. Besides, if we tried to put together a gang, someone would tell Tootsie, and the Vamps would take us down before we even got started."

Rainey gave her a curt nod. "Yeah, you're right."

"That doesn't mean we shouldn't prepare for battle. We need to focus on what Tootsie and her girls have planned next. It's important to be in front of them. Never let ourselves be taken by surprise. We need to think of a way to get to them first."

Filled with the courage she hadn't had before; Rainey hugged her friend. "You're right. That's what we're gonna do."

Chapter Seventy-One

Over the next two months, there were no incidents with Tootsie or her gang members. Rainey believed it was because she had a different attitude, but Phoenix insisted the Vamps were planning an attack.

It was Halloween night; Rainey and Phoenix were in the common room watching a scary movie with a bunch of other girls from their cell block. They sat on a sofa covered in brown fabric that smelled like hair gel and rose-scented lotion. Their stocking feet flung over the sides of the sofa arms as they munched on potato chips, a special Halloween treat. Unlike other evenings, the holidays brought out the best in the guards, who had supplied candy, pretzels, and potato chips and let them stay up later to watch a movie.

Rainey leaned close to Phoenix's ear. "I wish it was like this all the time. You know, the guards are nice and the girls aren't all in a bad mood."

"Yeah, just imagine how good it's gonna be on Christmas."

Rainey tilted her head and gave her friend a blank stare. Finally she said, "I never give much thought to Christmas. It was never a thing in our house. I mean, I have these far-off memories of my aunt Sophie buying me presents and taking me out to lunch, but once she was gone, anything related to Christmas was lost."

"For real?" Phoenix gasped.

Rainey nodded. "For real. Christmastime wasn't like the stuff I saw on TV. It was never happy and nothing fun happened at my house. There was no cookie baking and hot chocolate."

"Then what was it like?"

Rainey shrugged. "I don't know. It was like any other time of year. Except that there were way more people stoned in our house. Those idiots partied from Thanksgiving to New Year's. They took a lot more drugs and drank way too much booze. My parents and everyone there would be blitzed for a couple of weeks. I'm talking out of control."

Phoenix put her hand over her mouth. "Jeez, that's heavy shit. My parents always made Christmas so much fun. For a couple of weeks my whole family was closer . . . it made me feel safe and happy and like I belonged to some magical family. But once I got to the first foster home it wasn't the same. I mean, some of my foster parents tried, but their real kids always got better gifts. I guess they knew I wasn't going to be there forever and didn't want to waste the money."

Rainey adjusted on the sofa and placed a leg under her. "I think we should try to do something special for each other this Christmas."

"Oh, yeah? Like what?"

Rainey shrugged. "I don't know. Maybe we can make each other gifts so we have something to open on Christmas morning."

"Whatever," Phoenix said with a smirk. "Getting gifts doesn't mean shit to me. I can care less about stuff. I used to think the best part about Christmas was the presents . . . then my parents died. There's nothing that can compare to my mom and dad."

"Okay. Then we can sing Christmas songs together," she offered.

"Ugh. Cut me a break. The only thing I want for Christmas is to get the fuck outta this place and go live on an island somewhere."

Rainey giggled. "Oh, me too. That would be so cool. We could bring Ivy."

The two girls sat together quietly for a few moments, dreaming of a place and time when their lives would be their own. Rainey pictured them all together, happy and healthy.

It was just before lights out, and the girls were in a good mood.

Phoenix got up from the sofa and put her sneakers on. "I have to take a squirt. I'll see you back in our lovely cell," she joked and headed off.

Inside the bathroom, Phoenix exited the stall and stood in front of the sink. She studied herself for a minute, imagining what she'd look like with a deep, tropical tan. She finished washing her hands, and when she looked into the mirror again, her whole body twitched at seeing Moody's reflection behind her. Before she could react, Moody put a towel around her face, securing it behind her head while Critter and another gang member, Fibber, threw their fists into the girl's face and upper body.

After several punches to the face, Phoenix collapsed to her knees, then curled herself on the ground, nearly suffocating in the towel so tightly held over her face. As she lay on the cold tile floor, breathless, Critter untied one of Phoenix's sneakers and pulled the shoelace free. Phoenix was too startled and injured to move as they tied her hands behind her back. Coming to her senses, she sat up, attempting to yank her wrists free, but that only made the laces dig deeper into her flesh. After a minute or two of wrenching her head from side to side trying to get free, she was pushed down onto her back and Critter plopped down on the girl's legs. Unable to fight off her assailants, she laid still. Finally, mercifully, Moody released the towel from her face and Phoenix saw the two girls, just inches away, glaring at her.

"Open your mouth," Moody demanded, holding up a small plastic medicine bottle with the bottom cut out to create a homemade funnel.

Phoenix tried to squirm away from them, but Moody stuck her knee in her stomach.

Phoenix growled, "Fuck you, Moody," locked her lips tightly, and shook her head.

"Open your mouth or I'll open it for you."

Phoenix glared at the girl, feeling more defiant now that she'd been unmasked.

Moody pinched Phoenix's nose closed until she couldn't hold her breath any longer and had to open her mouth. In that instant, Moody shoved the homemade funnel between her teeth and pressed hard to keep it in place. The sawed-off edge of the plastic medicine bottle burrowed into Phoenix's tongue, causing excruciating pain, and the taste of blood filled her mouth.

Moody looked at Fibber and jerked her chin upward. Phoenix watched in horror as Fibber walked into a stall and grabbed a white plastic bottle hidden behind the toilet. She waltzed back to the other girls and knelt beside Moody.

Moody took the plastic bottle in her empty hand. "See this? I bet you have no idea what's in here."

Phoenix, suddenly understanding how vulnerable she was with a makeshift funnel in her mouth, felt her stomach flip-flop. Her eyes bulged and her nostrils flared as she tried again to escape from the girls who held her hostage.

"Well, I'll tell you what's in it because I don't want to keep you guessing. This is a bottle of bleach. Do you know what happens when you drink bleach?"

Phoenix tried to fight the pure terror that rose inside her. With wide, unblinking eyes, her heart thudded and beads of sweat formed on her brow. Her chest heaved up and down in quick, jerky succession. She looked from Moody to Critter to Fibber, wanting more than anything to see empathy from the girls—any of them—but was met with silence so deafening all she could hear was her own heart drumming in her ears.

Moody gave Phoenix a punishing smile. "I guess you *don't* know what happens when you drink bleach. Do ya, bitch?"

The skin on Phoenix's arms prickled like red ants biting at her.

Critter snorted out a laugh while Fibber, a smile fixed on her lips, glared at Phoenix.

Moody looked back down at Phoenix. "Here's what you're gonna do. You're gonna drink bleach and tell us what happens," she cackled.

Protesting noises burst from Phoenix's throat. She'd never been this vulnerable before. It was like standing on the edge of a cliff and one foot shoots out too far, and right before you fall, you have the realization it's too late to stop it. Overwhelmed with the seriousness of her situation, she let out a guttural moan. With the homemade funnel wedged between her teeth, Phoenix grunted as tears slid down the sides of her face. She was trapped. There was no amount of grunting, groaning, or wiggling that would get her out of the grave situation.

She watched in horror as Moody poured the half gallon of bleach into the homemade funnel. Bleach splashed into Phoenix's eyes. The searing heat of the harsh chemical caused so much internal and external pain it put her into shock. The skin around her eyes was red, and within several seconds her eyeballs were covered with cloudy tissue. Phoenix squeezed her eyes closed and thought about her parents as the bleach burned the back of her throat and she involuntarily choked on the liquid and vomit as it passed through her esophagus and into her stomach.

Phoenix was barely aware as Moody snatched the empty bleach bottle, shoved the homemade funnel in her pocket and said, "Let's get outta here."

As if from far, far away, she heard Critter say, "She ain't dead yet."

Moody replied, "Yeah, well, it ain't gonna be long now."

A moment later the three girls were gone, leaving Phoenix on the bathroom floor, alone and crawling toward death.

Chapter Seventy-Two

The minutes passed slowly as Phoenix withstood the agonizing effects of the bleach burning and blistering her insides. Her eyes were now wide open and she tried to focus them, but she had gone blind. She felt as though she laid there for an eternity, and then sweet mercy crept in. As death came for Phoenix, she realized she had no regrets or shame. She embraced her demise with honor and grace. Peace washed over her when she accepted that her struggles were over. It was a welcome relief from the pain, the foster homes, prostitution, and being left an orphan. Phoenix lowered her chin to her chest, eased her eyes closed, and allowed herself to leave this life.

***

Back in the cell, Rainey laid on her bunk waiting for Phoenix to return from the bathroom. She had just drifted off to sleep and awoke to the sound of Officer Fernandez at her door.

Rainey sat up. "What's going on?" she asked, disoriented. She looked below her into Phoenix's bunk, but it was empty. "Where's Phoenix?"

Fernandez took in a long breath and looked away, and something about her reaction made Rainey nervous.

"Where's Phoenix? Did something happen to her?" she asked frantically.

"Come with me, Paxton," Fernandez said. "Let's take a walk."

"Where?"

"To my office."

"Why do we need to go to your office?"

"So, we can talk privately," the officer said softly.

Rainey knew that something bad had to have happened and she blamed herself because surely Tootsie had been involved. As she followed the guard, Rainey's thoughts were consumed with how she would take care of Phoenix once she came back from Nurse Dix's clinic. As she stepped into the office, Officer Fernandez gently closed the door behind them.

"Let's sit down," the guard said.

Rainey sat in a chair at a round table. Fernandez sat across from her.

"So what happened? Is everything okay?" Rainey asked.

"No, everything isn't okay."

"Where's Phoenix?" Rainey demanded.

"Rainey, I'm so sorry to have to tell you that Phoenix . . . Phoenix is dead. She was found a short time ago."

"What? No. You're wrong. Phoenix and me were just watching a movie together. She went to take a piss. That's it."

As the room went quiet, Rainey's thoughts ping-ponged between sorrow for losing her only friend and anger at herself for putting her in danger. She consumed herself with guilt. She knew, before even understanding the details, that Phoenix died because of her and she already hated herself for it.

Rainey stood and walked to the door.

"Take a seat, Paxton. I know you're upset, but you have to calm down."

I'm sorry, Officer Fernandez," Rainey said, desperate not to lose her chance at getting more information. "But I don't understand."

The officer reached for Rainey's hand. "I know this is difficult for you. I know you and Phoenix were close. But she *is* dead. I saw her . . . after she was found."

Rainey's mouth dropped open as grief filled her. She dropped to the floor and lowered her head. Her shoulders raised and fell as she mourned the loss of Phoenix. She had so many regrets. If she could just turn back time. Maybe if she'd gone to the bathroom with her. Maybe if she'd said everything that Brice told her to say that first time in court. Maybe if she had fought harder when the gang came after her. And maybe if she hadn't been stupid enough to think that Tootsie was done torturing her, Phoenix would still be alive.

Fernandez stooped and placed her hand on the girl's back. "Come on, now. Everything is going to be okay. I recognize this is very hard for you."

"How did she die?" she muttered through her drenching tears.

Fernandez rubbed her eyes. "It appears that she was poisoned."

"How?" Rainey bellowed with a heavy heart.

"We aren't certain yet, but we think someone forced her to drink bleach," Fernandez said. "Now I must ask—do you know who would want to hurt her?"

Ignoring the officer's question, Rainey folded her body over, face to the floor, and wailed. Fernandez stepped away and allowed her to grieve properly.

"She was my only friend and she died a horrible death . . . all alone," Rainey blubbered. "I have no idea how I can stay in here without her. We loved each other. We were gonna get a place together when we got outta here, start our lives over, be a real family," she bawled.

When Rainey finished crying, a hollowness filled her. The loss was great and she knew she'd never get over it. With her eyes red and swollen, Rainey hoisted herself from the floor and sat in the chair across from Fernandez.

Officer Fernandez leaned forward and patted Rainey's shoulder. "I'm going to give you a little time to pull yourself together. I'll go grab you a soda. I'll be right back."

After the officer left, locking the deadbolt on the door behind her, Rainey's breathing was labored as she tried to digest what she'd just learned. Numbness took over her body and she looked up to the ceiling, trying to clear her head. "Why did you leave me, Phoenix?" she moaned. Her chest heaved and she aggressively wiped her wet cheeks with the back of her hand. "I'll find out what happened to you. I swear."

When Officer Fernandez returned, she sat down and slid a can of soda across the table, but it remained untouched. Rainey was too lost in anguish to put anything into her body without it coming back up.

"How are you doing?" the officer asked.

Rainey shrugged. "It's like I'm in a nightmare and I can't wake up. I just want this to all go away. I want Phoenix to be alive again."

"I know. And I'm sorry this happened."

Rainey looked at the guard with her red, puffy eyes, and allowed herself a small glimmer of hope. "Are you sure it was her?"

Fernandez nodded. “Yes, I’m sure. I’ll give you some time, but then you’ll need to tell me anything that might help us figure out who did this to her.”

“I don’t know who did it. I was in my cell, sleeping. You came and woke me up.”

Fernandez cleared her throat. “Do you know who would want to hurt Phoenix?”

Rainey shook her head. “No one I can think of. Everything was going great. Like I said, we watched a movie and she went to the bathroom. That was it.”

***

As Rainey lay alone in her cell that night, her thoughts remained on Phoenix. Regret, remorse, and sorrow occupied the space once filled by the love of her only friend.

Chapter Seventy-Three

The next morning, the halls of juvie were buzzing with the news of Phoenix. Rainey, still in shock, plodded into the cafeteria, holding a tray with two slices of toast and a carton of orange juice. All the girls turned to watch her as she made her way to the place where she and Phoenix had eaten their meals together. Keeping her head down as she walked, she could sense that all eyes were on her. She placed her tray down gently and plopped down in the seat, immediately covering her face with her hands. She was lost in grief, unable to comprehend the realness of never talking to Phoenix again. Her death was sudden. It was jarring. Heartbreaking.

Realizing she couldn't eat; Rainey flicked the toast around the tray with her index finger before pushing the tray to the other side of the table. A tap on the shoulder shook her from her dreary existence. Looking up, her lips were pressed together in a straight line and her eyes narrowed at the sight of Tootsie.

"Get the fuck away from me," Rainey said in a flat, steady voice.

Tootsie clenched her teeth as she sat next to her. Rainey remained still, too devastated to be scared or even care anymore.

"I hear your girl got wasted last night. That's a damn shame," Tootsie said with a grin. "Looks like you're all alone now to fight your own shit."

Rainey turned and faced Tootsie and saw her not as a girl, but as a thing, a monster, a ghoul, the devil . . . anything other than a human. "You can't even imagine how much I hate you. Let me tell you something, *Tootsie*," she said, enunciating her name like it was poisonous. "I'm never gonna forget that you killed Phoenix. Ever."

Tootsie tilted her head back and laughed. "Bitch, I don't know nothing about what happened to Phoenix. I ain't had no beef with her other than she thought she needed to protect you. You're outta your fuckin' mind."

Tootsie moved so she was only a few inches from Rainey. So close that Rainey could smell the rank sweetness on Tootsie's breath from not brushing her teeth. "Listen here, princess," Tootsie hissed. "Don't you talk shit on me. Who the fuck do you think you are? You're threatening me? Is that what you're trying to do?"

Rainey's eyes narrowed, and all the fear she once had hardened into a flaming ball of hatred. "You don't scare me anymore. You make me sick to my stomach."

Tootsie grinned. "Oh, I get it. You're some badass all of a sudden. Trust me, you keep talking to me like you are and you'll end up worse than your dead, whore friend." Tootsie stood. "If you think things were bad before, you better really watch your back now, Paxton."

When Tootsie walked away, Rainey grabbed a slice of her toast and flung it into the wall. Then she stood, took her tray, and stormed out of the cafeteria.

Officer Fernandez was quickly behind her. "Paxton! Stop!"

Rainey stopped but kept her back to the officer.

"Are you okay?" Fernandez asked.

Rainey spun around. "No, I'm not okay. Why do you even care? Just leave me alone."

"Calm down. Not everyone is out to hurt you, Rainey."

With leftover rage still circulating through her body, the teen put her hands on her hips, "What's gonna happen to Phoenix now? Did her sister come for her?"

Fernandez shoved her hands into her pant pockets. "Look, I've been considerate to tell you some of the things going on because I know you and Phoenix were close, but don't get flippant with me. Her sister *has* been contacted and they're waiting to hear back. You know, I think it would be nice if you organized a small memorial for Phoenix. Maybe you and a couple of the other girls can plan something. I'm sure I can get permission to do something tasteful in her memory."

Rainey shook her head slowly and choked out the words, "Phoenix didn't have anyone but me. She didn't bother with the other girls. No one was friends with her and she didn't like any of them. That's just how she was . . . that's the way Phoenix liked it."

Fernandez grabbed Rainey's hand. "Come on. That can't be true. She's been here for a while—as long as you have. Surely other girls were friendly with her."

Rainey pulled her hand away and stumbled back a step. "No, she didn't have any friends, just like I don't have any. But if you find someone that gives a shit about Phoenix, you let me know. Otherwise I'll have a memorial by myself. That's the way Phoenix would've wanted it. She never pretended to like people she couldn't trust."

Rainey turned and walked away as the officer watched after her.

***

In the common room that night, Rainey sat alone at a table in the back corner. She was staring off into space when Officer Jeffers approached her.

"How are you, Paxton?" Jeffers said, sounding sincere.

Rainey's eyes followed the voice. "I'm fine. Did Phoenix's sister call?"

Officer Jeffers shook her head. "No. Sorry, no one has heard from her."

"What happens if she doesn't call back? I mean, what will happen to Phoenix?"

Jeffers shifted uncomfortably. "Well, if Phoenix isn't claimed then she'll be buried by the state."

"Will there be a funeral?" Rainey asked in a barely audible tone.

"Well, not one specifically for her. The state will have a mass funeral—"

"What does that mean?"

The officer sighed. "The state will have a funeral for all the people who died and weren't claimed within a given time."

Rainey's eyelids stretched open. "Are you saying they would bury her with other people?"

"Yes. Unfortunately, that's how it works."

"But that's not what she would've wanted. She has to be buried with her parents. That's the right thing to do. She loved them," Rainey stated.

"They cremate the remains," Jeffers said, thinking it would ease some of the girl's pain. It didn't.

"There has to be something this place can do to help her," she moaned.

"Sorry, Paxton. The Juvenile Detention System doesn't oversee these matters. The guards know this is hard on you, but you have to keep your head up."

Officer Jeffers continued to speak, but Rainey had stopped listening. All she could think about was how sad Phoenix would have been to be separated from her parents in her death.

Later, inside her cell, Rainey curled onto Phoenix's bunk and wept. She cried for all that she had lost, she cried for Phoenix being cheated out of the life she deserved, and she cried for the emptiness that filled the space inside her that once belonged to Phoenix.

Chapter Seventy-Four

Several weeks after Phoenix was murdered, her ashes, along with those of other unclaimed souls, were placed in a mass grave by the City of Philadelphia. On the afternoon of the funeral, Agent Lindquist visited Rainey.

The agent was waiting when Rainey walked into the room. She rushed to the table and sat down on the edge of the chair. "Did you go to the funeral?"

"Yes, I went. You asked me to go and I promised you that I would."

"How was it?" she asked somberly.

"It was sad. Very sad."

"Did Phoenix's sister show up?"

Lindquist shook his head. "No one showed up. It was only me, my partner, and a few people from the state who handle the process. One of them recited a very thoughtful prayer, though."

"Oh, good. Well, if someone said a prayer then I guess everything is great," Rainey snapped, rolling her eyes. Then she caught herself. This wasn't Lindquist's fault. "I'm sorry, I didn't mean to be a jerk. Thank you for going. It means a lot to me. I know there's nothing Phoenix would have loved more than for me to send a cop to her funeral," she said, chuckling.

"Well, technically, I was there in your place since you couldn't go, so I'd say Phoenix would be happy."

Rainey's smile dwindled, giving herself a moment to remember how much she loved and missed Phoenix. They sat together in silence for several seconds.

Agent Lindquist leaned forward. "How have you been?"

Rainey shrugged. "Fine. Most of the other girls have been avoiding me even more, ever since Phoenix died. I guess they're afraid if they hang with me, they'll get killed too."

At this, Lindquist's eyebrows shot up. "Why would anyone think that hanging out with you would get them killed?"

Realizing too late she had said too much, Rainey sat back in her chair, waved her hand in the air, and forced a smile. "Sheesh, it was a joke. Lighten up."

"Are you sure you're okay?" Lindquist pressed.

"What the heck? Yes, I'm fine," she lied.

Lindquist glanced at his watch, then at Rainey. "I understand the detention center doesn't have any leads on who killed Phoenix."

Rainey shrugged. "I haven't heard anything. The guards would never give us that kind of information. It would cause a lot of trouble. So instead, all the girls make up rumors."

Lindquist grimaced. "Sorry. I shouldn't have mentioned that to you. Forget I said anything."

"Already forgotten," Rainey confirmed. "You did me a big favor going to the funeral, so now I totally owe you."

Lindquist sipped the water from the Styrofoam cup in front of him. "Do you know who hurt Phoenix?"

"They didn't *hurt* Phoenix. They *killed* her. And no, I have no idea who would've wanted to kill her." Rainey wiggled on the chair. She realized lying to the guards was hard, but lying to Lindquist was much more difficult. They had built a rapport, and he had done nice things for her.

"Why don't I believe you?" he asked.

Rainey stood, unable to look the man in the eyes and defend her lies. She put her hands on her hips. "Because you're a cop and you never believe anybody." She lowered her intensity and changed the subject. "Hey, have you seen Ivy?"

Lindquist shook his head. "No, not recently."

"Can you go there and make sure she's okay?" Rainey asked.

"It's not that easy. Cops can't walk into someone's house because they want to, and believe me, I want to, but I need a good reason," he explained. "Is there anything you can tell me?"

"I don't know anything. I haven't been living there and they don't come to visit me here," Rainey said as she walked toward the door but turned back and gave him a sad smile. "Thanks for going to the funeral and coming to see me, though. Will you try to check on Ivy?"

"Yeah, I'll try."

***

Alone in her cell again, Rainey stood against the back wall. Lowering her head, she let out a noiseless cry. "No one you knew showed up at your funeral," Rainey whispered to Phoenix's spirit. "I'm sorry. I'm so sorry this happened to you because of me. My mother always told me I was a hard person to love . . . and she was right." When Rainey was done crying, she lay on her bunk. The long, intense cry made her eyes feel heavy and her whole body weak. It was as though she were sick with fever. Rainey pulled the scratchy wool blanket over herself and shivered in the darkness. She had finally fallen into a deep sleep when the lock on her door clicked open and she looked up to see Officer Fernandez.

Still in a stupor, Rainey garbled, "What's wrong?"

"Nothing's wrong, Paxton," the officer said. "This is your new cellmate, Franny." She stepped aside so Rainey could see the tall girl with broad shoulders and a shaved head standing behind her.

Franny stepped into the cell. "Nobody calls me Franny," she said, scowling at Officer Fernandez, "And you better not call me that either," she said, turning to Rainey. "My name is Frankie."

Rainey stared at the new girl for a few seconds, willing herself to accept this sudden change, and sat up. "I'm Rainey."

Frankie stared at her. "Yeah. Okay. I'm beat. It took forever to get processed into this dump. I wanna get some sleep."

Fernandez glared at Frankie. "Sure, *Frankie*. You rest up. Tomorrow morning Rainey will show you where the cafeteria is."

Frankie turned away and laid on top of the thin sheet. Once Fernandez was gone Frankie kicked the bottom of Rainey's bunk from below.

Rainey leaned over the side. "What's up?"

"I wanna be clear, I won't be hanging with you. I know plenty of other people in here so don't go trying to be my friend. Got it?"

Rainey rolled onto her back and laid her head on the small, flat pillow. "Yeah. I got it."

Rainey was already sick of Frankie. The girl was overbearing and rubbed her the wrong way. She pushed her thoughts to Phoenix. She realized how lucky she was to have her in her life, even for only a moment.

Chapter Seventy-Five

True to her word, Frankie darted away from Rainey the second they reached the cafeteria. She found her way over to Martina, the girl who'd threatened Phoenix when Rainey had first arrived at juvie. Rainey sat at her table alone, picking through her food, wondering if Martina could have had anything to do with Phoenix's death. She'd never considered Martina before now. But it had been months since Martina and Phoenix argued. It was as though the two enemies had called a truce.

Rainey glanced up and saw Tootsie and Moody making their way to her. She sighed, not in the mood to hear anything they had to say. She hated them now more than ever.

Laying her food tray down, Tootsie sat straddling the seat next to her, glaring at Rainey, "We see you got yourself a new cellmate. She ain't nothing like your last one. Frankie doesn't give a fuck about fuck and she certainly ain't gonna give two fucks about you."

Rainey sat silently, almost bored with the garbage that came out of Tootsie's mouth.

"What? You ain't got nothing to say?" Moody added.

Rainey shook her head. "Nope."

Tootsie gave her a sinister smile. "Maybe you got something to say about your little sister, then. I hear that Jiggy's going over to your house soon to make sure the kid is happy."

Rainey's eyes bulged and her hands curled into fists. "What are you talking about?" she said, holding her breath. She wanted to run through the concrete wall, all the way to her house, and save her sister.

Tootsie chuckled. "I'm talking about Jiggy, and him not liking you. He still wants you to pay for not doing what Brice told you to do. How old is your little sister, anyway? What's her name again? Daisy?" Tauntingly,

Tootsie tapped her chin with her index finger. "Oh yeah, Ivy. It's the second stupidest name I've ever heard, right after Rainey."

"How do you know my sister's name?" Rainey said.

Tootsie glanced at Moody. "We know everything. There ain't nothing in your life that's a secret from us. From what Jiggy says, your parents are even more fucked up than you are. They're willing to do anything for a little dope."

Rainey bit back tears. "What are you trying to say? Is there something I can do to help Ivy?"

Tootsie shrugged. "Not sure. What do you have to offer me?"

Rainey closed her eyes for a prolonged second. "I don't have *anything* to offer you."

"Oh, yeah? What about your commissary?" Tootsie asked.

"My parents don't put money on my commissary account."

"Oh, boo hoo hoo," Tootsie mocked. "Nobody cares about your problems."

Rainey's thoughts were racing about what Jiggy might do to Ivy.

"Ivy is only five years old." The words burst from her mouth. "She can't take care of herself. She doesn't have anyone to protect her." Rainey jabbed her index finger toward Tootsie. "Nothing better happen to her or I swear I'll tell someone that you told me Jiggy was going to hurt Ivy."

Tootsie's nostrils flared. She grabbed ahold of Rainey's finger and bent it back sharply, and the girl's body lowered itself to offset the pain.

In a low, slow growl Tootsie said, "Girl, I don't think you understand who you're dealing with. Threaten me again and you'll find yourself in the same place as Phoenix. We ain't the kind of people who tolerates a snitch."

Tootsie let go of Rainey's finger and took off to the other side of the cafeteria, with Moody following close behind her.

For the rest of the day, Rainey's thoughts remained on Ivy and the helplessness that devoured her entire being. Desperate for anything to help her sister, she set off to find Officer Fernandez.

"Officer Fernandez, do you have time to talk?" Rainey asked, when she found her.

Surprised by the question, the officer looked her up and down, curiosity running through her. "Sure. Let's go over there," she said, pointing to a quiet table in the common room.

"What's up?" Fernandez asked once they were seated.

"It's about commissary. Well, my parents, they don't come to see me or anything. And, um, I never have money on my account. Well, I was wondering if there was a way that I could get somebody to put money on it for me. You know, maybe the state would give money to someone like me," letting the words rush from her lips before she lost the nerve.

Fernandez rubbed her forehead. "The problem is that your parents are living and they are well aware that you're in here. The state doesn't help inmates just because their parents won't."

"Oh," Rainey said, looking down at her hands.

"Though, I'd be willing to put some money on your commissary one time if that would help," Fernandez offered.

Rainey's head lifted and she smiled. "That would be nice. Thank you."

While Rainey knew the money from Fernandez was only a temporary solution, she was already considering another option. One she had to think about a lot more. A solution that could get her into a heap of shit, but she'd do anything for her little sister. Anything.

Chapter Seventy-Six

That night, after dinner, Rainey approached Martina while she and her group were watching television. She tapped the girl on the shoulder, and Martina spun around.

"Hey, um, do you think I could talk to you for a minute?" Rainey asked, trying to keep her voice from cracking.

Martina tilted her head and squinted at her. "You wanna talk to me now? When your girl Phoenix was alive you didn't talk to me at all. I asked you to join us—guess you made the wrong decision, huh?"

Rainey wrung her hands together, trying not to let Martina see that she could care less about her little group. "I know. I'm sorry."

"You got that right—you're a sorry scab," Martina stated.

"Look, I was hoping I could run something by you." Rainey glanced at her cellmate, Frankie, who was sitting among the other girls.

Martina flipped her long hair over her shoulder. "Yeah, I guess. Go ahead and talk."

Rainey leaned in closer. "I want to talk alone. Over there," she said, pointing to the far corner of the room.

Martina cackled. "I don't think so. If you wanna talk to me you can do it right here in front of my girls. I'm not going anywhere with you. I ain't stupid."

"Fine. I wanted to see if there's anything I can help you with so that I could earn some money. I'm good at math and history. Or . . . or . . . I could take your cleaning assignments. I don't know. I'll do whatever," Rainey said, cringing at how desperate and pathetic she sounded.

Martina raised her eyebrows and looked around at her friends, all of whom exchanged menacing smirks. Then she turned back to Rainey. "Well, now that you put it that way, maybe there *is* shit you can do to earn some money. I'll tell you what—you let me think about it and I'll find you tomorrow."

Rainey, ashamed and mortified to have to bow down to Martina, nodded. "Okay. I'll talk to you later."

***

"There's something wrong with you," Frankie said in an accusatory tone as she walked into their cell later that night. "You went crawling to another chick in this joint so you can get some money. Girl, you ain't connected at all. Are ya?"

"What?" Rainey asked, confused.

"Martina told me that shit you told her about knowing Jiggy . . . and that you were with him the night you were busted. Everybody knows if you're hooked up with Jiggy you would have money on your fucking commissary. You lied, and now Martina knows it. Anyway, I'm embarrassed to have to share a cell with you."

"What was I supposed to do?" Rainey bellowed, losing her composure. "I told her about Jiggy because she was threatening my friend. And it wasn't a total lie, I *was* with him when I got arrested."

Frankie pursed her lips and snickered. "You're nothing but a June bug, begging for money like a drug-addicted whore, and I hate being stuck in here with you."

Rainey jumped from her bunk and faced Frankie, with fearlessness flowing freely. "If you wanna hate me because I'm willing to do whatever I have to do for commissary, then I don't care. Be that way."

Frankie grinned at her. "Sure. Whatever you say . . . as long as you know what you're getting yourself into, *June bug*."

"Stop calling me that," Rainey huffed. "I don't even know what it is, but you sound stupid."

Frankie slipped her feet out of her shoes. "A June bug is someone weak, someone like you. You just signed up to become a slave to our group. Now do you see how stupid you are?"

"I'm not gonna be a slave to anyone. I'm going to do some things to make money. Slaves didn't get paid for their work, but I'm pretty sure you missed that day in school," Rainey said.

Frankie stood tall, towering over Rainey. "I'm pretty sure that school doesn't know how to teach the shit that goes on in places like this. Don't think you're some kinda hard-ass. You better remember that Martina is a friend of mine and you'll be doing shit for me too."

"I don't think so. I offered it to Martina, not you," Rainey said, turning her back to Frankie.

Frankie grabbed the flesh on the back of Rainey's arm and twisted, sending her to her knees, and said, "Well, you better think again. When you ask Martina if you could do things for her, that meant for her *and* all of her girls. That's the way it works."

Frankie pushed her forward, but Rainey caught herself before she fell. Rubbing the back of her arm where she'd been pinched, she said, "Well then I'll just tell Martina to forget it."

Frankie chuckled and gave an exaggerated scratch of her forehead. "Oh, really? I thought you'd do *anything* for commissary money."

"I would," Rainey insisted, realizing she was contradicting herself.

Frankie took a few steps toward the girl. "Well, that's good to hear because now that you made Martina the offer you can't back down. That would be bad form and then we'd all have to punish you for it."

"That's not true. You're just saying that," Rainey argued. Her face filled with waves of fiery heat. She was embarrassed, angry, and scared. Her insides were jittery and her skin prickled, knowing that there probably would be a price to pay for reneging on her offer.

"I ain't playing and I ain't lying. My advice? Don't back out. It won't be good for you."

As Rainey lay on her bunk, she decided the only way to control the situation was to go through with her offer but to place limits on what she'd be willing to do for the girls. She knew it was a long shot, but she needed to manage herself out of the mess that she'd put herself in.

Chapter Seventy-Seven

In the morning, when Rainey walked in with her breakfast tray, Martina waved her over to where she was sitting.

"Hi," Rainey said, feeling on edge as she approached.

"Sit down," Martina said, pointing to the spot across from her. "So I decided to take you up on your offer. Here's what I'll do, I'll get someone on the outside to put twenty-five bucks a week on your commissary account, but you're gonna have to work for it."

Rainey took several short quick breaths and put her hands on her lap so Martina wouldn't see them shaking. "Well, like, what kind of work?"

Martina turned to the girl next to her. "Is this girl kidding me? She comes and asks me to help her, then she's gonna try and make it like she'll only do certain shit." She turned back and glared at Rainey.

"I didn't mean it like that," Rainey said quickly. "But I just wanna make sure you know I won't do anything illegal. I'm not staying in here one more minute than I have to."

"Listen, *Rainey,*" Martina said sarcastically. "If I need something illegal done I ain't gonna be trusting you to do it. But you're gonna do everything else."

Rainey pushed her hair behind her ears. "Okay. When do we start?"

Martina snapped. "Um, like now. The first thing you're gonna do is put all of our trays away. We'll sit here while you do it so that the guards don't think we left you with a mess."

Easy enough, Rainey thought. She nodded, then picked up a muffin from her tray and peeled back the paper.

"Wait," Martina said. "I want that muffin."

Rainey looked at it and handed it over, figuring that Martina was just testing her. All of this was doable.

Frankie said, "I'll take your orange juice."

Rainey looked at her cellmate with a scowl and handed her the juice.

Martina looked around at the others. "Anyone else want something?"

In less than a minute, Rainey's breakfast tray was emptied. Not having eaten since dinner the night before, her stomach rumbled. Juvie provided three meals a day, but snacks were considered luxury items and had to be bought, so she'd have to wait until lunch to eat.

Rainey watched as Martina put her arms around the girl next to her and hugged her. She turned to Rainey, who was staring at them.

"What the hell are you looking at?" Martina snapped.

Rainey zapped out of her daze. "Nothing. I'm just sitting here."

"Well, get your lazy ass up and start clearing our trays. We don't have all day. We gotta get to class."

As Rainey walked back and forth with the trays, she felt eyes on her—what she was doing wasn't going unnoticed. When she emptied the last tray, she went back to Martina's table.

"Why are you sitting here?" Martina snarled.

All the girls around her laughed, and Rainey's face and chest turned a deep crimson.

"Get lost," Martina said and snapped her fingers.

Rainey got up quickly and looked around, avoiding probing stares as she walked over to where she usually ate.

Tootsie followed behind her quickly. "You Martina's pet now?"

"What? No."

"Did you find a way to pay me with commissary?"

"Yeah," Rainey said. "But you have to promise me that nothing bad will happen to Ivy."

Tootsie chuckled. "Yeah. Sure. I promise."

"No. I mean it. How are you gonna make sure Jiggy leaves her alone?

"You're just gonna have to trust me," Tootsie said. "I have my ways, but they ain't none of your business."

Rainey looked directly at Tootsie. "Okay. We have a deal. You protect Ivy from Jiggy and I'll make sure you get fifteen bucks a week in commissary stuff."

Tootsie didn't expect her empty threat to provide such a lucrative outcome. Playing it cool, she shrugged her shoulders. "I was thinking more like twenty bucks a week," she countered.

Rainey hesitated on purpose, trying to save some of the money for herself. "Twenty? What the hell? That's a lot of money."

"Twenty bucks doesn't sound like a lot to me for your sister's safety. It's gonna be hard work to keep Jiggy away from her." She stared down at the girl, her eyes large and piercing.

After a long pause, Rainey sighed. "I don't know how I'm gonna get that much money, but I'll figure something out. Fine, twenty bucks a week in commissary stuff. You can let me know what you want and I'll order it."

"Great. The first thing you can get me are large cotton T-shirts. The long-sleeved kind. And I want some of those cotton underwear too—the soft ones. Oh, and order me corn chips and a few sodas, the cola kind."

Rainey nodded. "Okay, I have to wait until my person from the outside puts money on my commissary, and then I'll get you everything."

Tootsie turned away and took a few steps, but Rainey called out to her. Tootsie turned back and raised her eyebrows.

"You'll take care of everything with Ivy, right?"

Tootsie smiled. "Nah. I'll take care of everything with your sister when you give me my shit," she said before strutting away.

There was a searing burn in Rainey's stomach, and not eating breakfast was making it worse. As she made her way out of the cafeteria to her first class, she stopped at the water fountain and filled her belly with the only thing that wouldn't cost her any money.

Opening a book in class, she smiled internally, thinking about the extra five dollars a week she'd have left over to buy a few commissary items for herself. She was proud of how she played it with Tootsie, giving the bully what she wanted to keep Ivy safe and still saving a little for herself. Five dollars a week wasn't much, but it was more than she had yesterday, and that little win made her happy. It was turning out to be a better day for Rainey Paxton.

Chapter Seventy-Eight

At dinner, that night, Martina and her friends repeated what they'd done at breakfast. Rainey stood in front of her bunk later, her belly aching with hunger pains. Then a loud growl crept from her empty belly into the cell.

Frankie smirked. "Hungry, huh?"

Rainey nodded. "Yeah, a little."

"Ha! Well, that's too bad, June bug. You signed up for this shit. Just remember that as you go to bed hungry tonight."

Rainey sat on the stool. "That's nothing new for me. I went to bed hungry lots of nights before I got here."

"And why would you think I care about that?"

Rainey flashed back to the nights in her bed when her stomach would burn from the emptiness. Her lower lip trembled. "I know that you don't care about my life. I just thought if I shared something about myself that maybe we could get to know each other a little bit. It's been hard since Phoenix died . . . you know, there aren't many nice people in here and I wanted you and me to get along."

Frankie sat up on her bunk. "Listen, Blondie. I already told you that I ain't looking to be friends. Keep all that crybaby shit to yourself. I don't feel bad for you, okay? You think you're the only one in here who's had a hard life? You think you're the only one who knows what it's like to suffer? To be hungry? Or lonely? Or lose someone? Well, think again." Frankie laid back on her bunk and rolled on her side, with her back toward Rainey.

A flush crept across Rainey's face, and she played with the collar of her shirt. Frankie was right—every girl in juvie had suffered. She knew better to think that anyone locked up would care about what happened to her.

Without Phoenix, Rainey felt vulnerable and powerless, in debt to two powerful teenagers. She had volunteered to be Martina's servant while living with the threat that Tootsie presented.

Rainey climbed onto her bunk gently and laid her head on the pillow. "I'm sorry," she said aloud. "You're right. I'll never bring up my problems again."

Frankie didn't respond, but Rainey was sure she'd heard her. She pulled the blanket up to her chin and drifted off to sleep.

***

The next morning, Rainey walked out of the shower stall and was startled to find Martina, Frankie, and one other girl waiting for her. She tightened her grip on the thin towel covering her body, trying to pretend like everything was all right, but she instinctively knew this was trouble. The three girls were silent as they followed Rainey into a small dressing area. Still wet from the shower, Rainey pulled her shirt over her head and swiftly stepped into her underwear before tossing her towel aside. She glanced at the girls, who stood with their arms crossed over their chests, watching her. Quickly, she stepped into her jumpsuit and sat on the wooden bench. She pulled her socks on and grabbed her sneakers.

Martina cleared her throat loudly and Rainey eyed her cautiously.

"I really like your sneakers," Martina said. "You're about a seven-and-a-half, right?"

She nodded, sensing the conversation was already moving in a bad direction.

"Well," Martina said, leaning her shoulder against the open doorway, "I like those sneakers and I really want to have them."

Her skin prickled. "They're just ugly state-issued sneakers."

"So?" Martina said.

She looked down at her shoes. "They're the only pair of shoes I got."

Martina smiled. "Again, so?"

Rainey glanced at Frankie, who looked away.

"You know," Rainey said, "I have two extra pairs of socks. They're the good kind, you know, the ones that are cotton. Anyway, they belonged to Phoenix, and when she died, I snagged them. How about if I give you a pair of those instead?"

Martina moved into the room and sat next to Rainey. "Oh, I know which ones you're talking about. What colors do you have?"

Rainey's heart slowed slightly. "Pink and orange."

"Wow," Martina breathed. "Pink and orange. Isn't that just fucking awesome? I'll tell you what," she said, twirling her hair with her fingers, "You can give me your sneakers now, and later you can bring those two pairs of socks to me in the common room. How's that sound?" Martina smiled and patted Rainey's leg. Then she held out her hand.

Reluctantly, Rainey picked up her only pair of shoes and gave them to the girl, who waltzed away without another word followed by the other girl, as Frankie lagged.

"You need to stop telling people shit," Frankie said. "You don't know how to keep your mouth shut and that's gonna be your biggest problem. Martina wanted your sneakers, but if you hadn't sniveled and moaned you would've been able to keep those socks from your girlfriend. Now you lost both."

Rainey sat alone and thought about what she'd done. She needed to keep her mouth shut. She had lost the only thing she had left of Phoenix: two pairs of socks. With shame, she slipped her feet into her plastic flip-flops used for showering and made her way to class.

In the common room later, after Rainey handed over the socks, she walked to the back and sat at a table alone. Martina and her friends kept turning around, looking at her, and all bursting into laughter. She forced herself to ignore them, focusing instead on her strength. She realized that if she could stand up to the cruel girls, she would make it through her time in juvie.

She replaced dread with hope—sadness with anger—weakness with strength. She remembered the things that Phoenix had taught her about standing up to the bullies and not backing down no matter how scared she might be.

As Rainey made her way back to her cell, she held her head high. She resigned herself to the fact that she had to please Martina so she could bribe Tootsie to keep Ivy safe. She would do anything for Ivy and this was just a small price to pay.

By the weekend, twenty-five dollars had been placed into her commissary account. Victory surged through Rainey's body as she filled out the paperwork to order the first items for Tootsie.

Chapter Seventy-Nine

Over the next three weeks, Martina and her friends belittled and degraded Rainey. They sprayed red food coloring on her while she was showering, which turned her hair pink, and made her do their homework into the early hours of the morning, as well as their chores. By the end of the third week, Rainey was drained, but she kept the thought that this was keeping Ivy safe at the top of her mind.

The following week, while Rainey was sleeping, she woke coughing and hacking. She looked around her and after a few seconds realized there was smoke in her cell. Her mattress was smoldering. She jumped off and screamed for help. Frankie joined her, seeming equally alarmed.

The guards extinguished the mattress quickly, but the cell was left in disarray and covered in white foam, so Rainey and Frankie were moved to a temporary cell.

Once they were alone, Rainey glared at Frankie. "Did you try to set my bunk on fire?"

Frankie huffed. "Bitch, no. Why would I do that while I'm in the same cell?"

"Well, if you didn't do it, then who did?" Rainey asked.

"I saw Tootsie's whore, what's her name, Moody? I saw her throw something onto your bunk," she lied.

Rainey's eyes narrowed. "How did Moody get out of her cell in the middle of the night?" she asked.

"How the fuck do I know?" Frankie said, going on the defensive a little too quickly. "Do you and me have a problem? I don't like all these questions you're asking."

Rainey backed up. "No. We're cool. But Tootsie hasn't bothered me in a long time, so it doesn't make any sense that Moody would come after me now."

Frankie laughed. "You are dumb. Tootsie made your girl Phoenix drink bleach—gave her a backdoor parole and you let her get away with it."

Rainey squinted her eyes and lowered her voice. "How do you know that Tootsie killed Phoenix?"

"Oh, please. Stop acting like you don't know it, too. Everybody in here knows it was Tootsie who offed the girl," Frankie stated. "She made Moody do it. Martina heard Moody and her friends laughing about it the next day."

"I'll make her pay if she did," Rainey growled. While she suspected Phoenix's death involved Tootsie, actually hearing it from another inmate made it real.

"Oh, shut up. You ain't nothing but a cell warrior. You're that chick who talks and acts all badass while you're in your cell but doesn't do shit when you get in general pop."

"You don't know anything about me," Rainey said, but she knew in her heart that Frankie was right. Trying to preserve some of her dignity, she sat on the floor with her back against the wall. "So you think because I didn't go after Tootsie for killing Phoenix that she's trying to kill me?"

"Fuck, yeah. And I ain't gonna be caught in your crossfire. Hell, no. I'm asking for a transfer. I ain't getting killed for your shit. If someone was coming after me, then I'd fight. I ain't like you. You're afraid of everyone."

"No, I'm not," Rainey lobbed back halfheartedly. At least it wasn't *all* fear; she just didn't have that thing inside her to hurt people.

"Yeah. Okay. Whatever. Just stay the hell away from me," Frankie said.

Frankie laid on her bunk and remained silent. She was proud of the way she'd manipulated Rainey. She was certain the girl was convinced that Tootsie killed Phoenix and had just tried to kill her too. It was an effortless setup. All Frankie had to do was start a small fire on the side of her mattress, and the rest fell into place.

Frankie had no guilt about the game she was playing, remembering how Tootsie had threatened Martina the day prior over a missing bracelet. Martina had told Tootsie to go fuck herself, and the two went at it like two stray cats—hissing threats and promises of violence at each other. That's when Martina hatched the plan to use Rainey to get even with Tootsie.

Now all Martina and her friends had to do was sit back and watch the show.

***

The following weekend, when Rainey checked her commissary, there was no money. Thinking something must have gone wrong, she went to Martina's cell. "Hi. Can I come in?" she asked.

Martina shot a glance to her cellmate. "Sure. Carla doesn't mind. Do you?"

Carla gave Rainey a half-cocked smile.

"I just checked my commissary," Rainey hesitated, "and, your person didn't put any money on it."

"And?"

Rainey's shoulders rose to her chin. "And that was our deal. I've been doing every single thing you and your friends want me to do."

Martina let out a soft laugh.

"Girl, you'll do everything we tell you whether or not I pay you," she said.

"What are you talking about? Are you saying our deal is off?" Rainey asked.

"Well, if you mean the part of the deal where you do shit for me and my girls, then no. But if you're talking about the part where I give you money to be a June bug, then yes, that part of the deal is off," she said smugly.

Rainey's thoughts immediately went to Ivy, and her heartbeat quickened. "You can't do this to me. I need that money."

"I can do this to you and I just did. You think I'm dumb?"

Rainey nervously raked her fingers through her hair. She had to figure out how to play this right. "No. I never said you're dumb. What are you talking about?"

Martina stepped toward Rainey and jabbed her index finger into her sternum. "You haven't been doing all of our chores. You've been letting them go, and some of the girls got in trouble with the guards."

Rainey smacked her hand away. "That's a lie. I've done everything that I promised."

Martina grabbed Rainey's wrist and held it tightly. "That's not what Tootsie told me. She saw one of my girls get in trouble. Are you saying she's lying?" she hissed.

Rainey, filled with adrenaline and ready for a fight, ripped her wrist away. "Yeah, she's lying."

Rainey turned and left Martina's cell quickly. As she walked down the hallway, she could hear Martina and her cellmate calling her names and threatening to get even with her. She was almost back to her cell when Tootsie stepped in front of her.

"Where's my commissary shit?" she growled.

"I don't have it today," she said, losing her patience.

"You don't have it?" Tootsie roared. "Well, when are ya gonna get it?"

"I don't know. Why don't you go ask Martina, since you're telling her a bunch of lies about me?"

Tootsie grabbed the side of Rainey's face and smashed it against the wall. "I ain't got no idea what you're talking about—I didn't tell Martina shit. Now, let's try this again. When are you gonna get my commissary?"

Rainey skinned the side of her face pulling out of the wedge between the concrete wall and Tootsie's hand. "I'll get it. I just need time. My . . . my outside source fell through," she said, trying to steady her voice.

"Not my problem," Tootsie said.

With shaking hands and rage pulsing through her body, Rainey blurted, "No, you have a lot of other problems, too, like lighting my bunk on fire and killing Phoenix." Seeing the rage that contorted Tootsie's face, Rainey braced herself for a fistfight.

Tootsie's feet parted and her hands rolled into fists. "I already told ya that I didn't off your bitch. As for that fire, I heard about it, but it wasn't me." She pressed her nose against Rainey's. "If I lit that fire in your bunk you can bet your ass you wouldn't be here to talk about it. I don't do shit halfway."

Rainey's teeth were locked together. "You're a liar. I know that you made Moody kill Phoenix. Frankie told me all about it."

Tootsie grabbed her shirt and shoved Rainey against the wall, knocking the wind out of her. In that second, Rainey knew she had to do the best fighting of her life.

Chapter Eighty

Tootsie's fists flew through the air at lightning speed, being stopped only by Rainey's jaw. Rainey knew she was no match for the girl, but punched at the air in front of her wildly, kicking, scratching, and slapping at Tootsie, anger fueling her jerky, unprecise, nonstop movements. She unleashed her anger for her mother and father, anger for Freddy and Jiggy, anger for the life she'd been given, and anger for the mean people who surrounded her in juvie.

Tootsie fired back with tight fists, hitting Rainey in the face, stomach, and back, but Rainey didn't give up. Seizing a handful of Tootsie's hair, she used her weight to push the girl's face forward into the wall, feeling a sense of satisfaction at seeing blood splatter from Tootsie's nose. Tootsie wheeled around on her and tackled her to the floor, where they rolled around. The other girls surrounded them, screaming, chanting, and egging on more violence. Somehow in the scuffle, Rainey spotted Martina standing in the back of the group, arms crossed over her chest and wearing a big smile, which further fueled the fight in her.

"Stop it immediately!" Officer Fernandez yelled. Rainey and Tootsie were tangled in a mess of arms, legs, and hands full of hair when the guards broke them apart. Fernandez shook Rainey from her hate stupor.

Rainey dropped her hands to her sides. Fernandez placed her up against the wall gently, spread Rainey's legs with her feet, and patted her down, while another officer did the same to Tootsie. Both girls were put into handcuffs and shuffled out of the general population area.

Tootsie turned to look at Rainey and said, "You're fucking dead. You understand me? Your time here is over. You don't have to worry about getting out or seeing your stupid little sister. You're finished, Paxton."

But Rainey still had too much adrenaline for the threats to sink in.

"Eyes forward, Tootsie!" Fernandez yelled. "Keep your trap shut before you find yourself in more trouble than you're already in."

Rainey looked at Fernandez as if seeing her for the first time. It was as though Rainey were in a raging time bubble that just now burst. Blood dripped from Rainey's forehead and onto her cheek. Fernandez pulled a rag from her back pocket and held it to the wound.

"We're taking you two troublemakers to see Nurse Dix. You both need medical attention," she said.

Nurse Dix examined Rainey first, since she had more visible wounds and was covered in a lot of blood. It took three stitches to close the slash across her forehead, but other than that, she was just heavily bruised.

"You're lucky that you didn't break any bones," Nurse Dix told Rainey.

"Yes, ma'am," she said, beaming with pride about surviving a brawl with the supposedly meanest girl in juvie.

The nurse placed her hands firmly on her round hips. "You better keep out of trouble. Anything could happen when you young girls start hitting each other. Accidents happen. You could fall and hit your head, break bones, there's no telling. I suggest you and Tootsie find a way to get along."

Rainey stared at the nurse blankly, hearing the words but not accepting them.

"Did you hear me?" Nurse Dix pressed.

"Yes, ma'am. We need to learn to get along," she whispered, but her mind and mouth weren't in the same place. Rainey no longer cared what Tootsie had planned for her, now that she understood that fighting back was her only weapon.

As Fernandez guided Rainey off of the gurney and toward the door, they passed Tootsie in a room to the left. Rainey glanced in the open door and saw that the nurse was packing Tootsie's nose with cotton. Her lips raised slightly at the corners realizing she'd done some damage.

Rainey was surprised when Fernandez took her to solitary confinement. Inside, the guard had her stand facing the wall as she unlocked her handcuffs. "All right, you need to take your clothes off. You can leave your panties on."

"What? Why do I have to take my clothes off?"

"Rules. Can't leave you with anything but your underwear and this," the officer said, holding up an undershirt. "Get a move on, everything comes off, I need you to hurry."

Mortified, Rainey undressed quickly. After she pulled the undershirt over her head, she looked at Fernandez.

"Welcome to your new home for the next three weeks," the officer said, gesturing toward the narrow cell with a bed, mattress with no sheet, and a metal toilet.

Rainey walked in slowly. Once inside, Fernandez gave her a roll of toilet paper.

"Settle in," she said.

"Wait," Rainey breathed. "What about a blanket? I'll be cold at night."

"No blankets or sheets allowed in solitary. Don't worry, Paxton. You'll manage. Lots of girls have been through this before you."

"But, but, why? It's just stupid that I can't have a blanket."

"Well, that's because we don't want you to hurt yourself. Three weeks in here all alone is a long time for you to think about what you did. You'll come out every three days for a five-minute shower and then right back to this cell. After a while, it'll wear on your mind. Try to remember that. When it gets bad, and believe me it will, think about getting back to general pop. That's my best advice."

"Is Tootsie staying in solitary confinement too?"

"Sure is. She'll be right next door. Now settle in. Someone will bring you dinner after the other girls are finished in the cafeteria."

Rainey nodded. The weight of her situation crashed in on her. She was partly relieved that she would be confined where Tootsie couldn't get to her. But she was worried that being alone for so long would make her go crazy; plus, the things that Jiggy would do to Ivy now that Tootsie couldn't keep him from hurting the child gnawed at her.

Alone, Rainey curled onto the bare mattress and pulled her knees to her chest. She listened to the quiet around her. She hadn't heard silence since she arrived at juvie. A peacefulness settled over her, interrupted now and again by the distant sound of the clanging of metal doors. In those moments, her peace was replaced with darkness at the reminder of where she was.

Rainey had been in her cell for about an hour when she heard Fernandez giving instructions to undress. She heard Tootsie say, "This is bullshit. You ain't got no right to make me take off my clothes."

"I have all the rights in here. You're the one who doesn't have any rights, Tootsie. The only thing you get in juvie is privileges, and you've lost yours because you can't seem to behave."

"Whatever," Tootsie grumbled.

Rainey listened to the lock being thrown on Tootsie's door. She could hear the girl fuss around on the mattress. Finally Tootsie went quiet, and for the first time since knowing her, Rainey wondered what Tootsie thought about when she was forced to be alone. She imagined that Tootsie was thinking about killing her as soon as they got released back into the general population.

Chapter Eighty-One

The first night in solitary confinement, Rainey was on her back with her eyes open, staring into the blackness of her cell. She didn't know how much time had passed since she'd eaten dinner. In the quiet of the night, she heard a soft buzzing in her ears; as though she were submerged in water. Her eyelids grew heavy and just as she was about to fall asleep, she heard a sound. At first she thought it was a mouse, so she listened more intently. She knew what chirping and squeaking mice sounded like—plenty of them had lived in her house. She stood and put her ear to the opening of the metal door and strained to hear the sound again.

Rainey wrapped her arms around herself, shivering from the cold, and listened closer. She focused every part of her body on the sound but heard nothing in the stillness. *Had she imagined it?* As soon as she laid back down, she heard it again, only clearer this time—a whimper followed by hushed sniffling. She stood and walked back to the door, placing her ear at the rectangular opening.

"Hello?" Rainey said in a low voice. "Tootsie? Are you okay?"

An empty silence followed, but she stood, waiting. When she heard Tootsie sniffling, she sighed softly and said, "Tootsie, I can hear you. Are you okay?"

"I'm fine," Tootsie croaked finally.

"Are you crying?"

"No. Why would I?" Tootsie said, her voice cracking.

"I don't know, maybe because you're stuck in here?"

"Mind your own business."

"Are you hurt? Should I call for the guard?"

"No," Tootsie huffed. "Keep your fucking mouth shut."

"Okay," Rainey mumbled. She was about to turn away when she heard the girl suck in a loud breath as she broke into tears. She couldn't believe she pitied the girl.

"You can talk to me. I won't tell anybody, I swear," Rainey said, but there was no response.

Rainey was quiet for a while, then pressed her face against the metal of her cell door. "You know, when I was a little girl, my parents would punish me for crying. Most of the time I cried because I was hungry. Sometimes because I was scared or lonely. I know what it's like to have to hide your tears."

"Why would they punish you for crying?" Tootsie asked in a garbled voice.

"Because I was interrupting them from getting high. They didn't want to waste their time making me feel better—they told me that a million times. So they said if they heard me crying, I would be spanked until my ass was raw." Rainey closed her eyes, remembering the void inside her as a little girl. "Yeah, I knew they'd do it too. There were lots of times my dad pulled down my pants and whipped my butt with his belt."

A sob broke from Tootsie's throat, and Rainey allowed the girl privacy to bawl. Once she calmed down, Rainey said, "Maybe talking about it would help?"

"I ain't no fucking idiot. You're just looking for something to tell those other bitches in here about me," Tootsie hissed.

"No, I'm not," Rainey said calmly, realizing she meant it. "I'm offering to listen. I would never tell anyone about someone else crying. That's not how I am."

A silence stretched between them.

"Besides," Rainey finally said, "if I told anyone what you tell me, you'd kick the shit outta me," she joked.

Tootsie giggled through her tears. "Yeah, that's true."

"Did your parents beat you if you cried?" Rainey asked.

"Nah. It was only my mom and her nasty boyfriend. My dad split when I was four. He promised to come and visit me, but he never did."

"Oh. That sucks."

"Yeah, and my mom's boyfriend, Roy, he was a lot younger than her. He put a lock on the outside of my bedroom door and nailed my window shut. He would lock me in there while my mom was at work. He'd have parties and I could hear him having sex with other girls in my mom's bed. Man, I wanted him to die so much," Tootsie seethed.

"Did he die?" Rainey asked.

"Nah, the prick just kept freeloading off my mom and she let him. He'd tell her lies about me, and my mom believed everything he said. She used to tell me to make myself scarce when I was home alone with him because I annoyed him," Tootsie said. "But that wasn't true. It was *that* motherfucker who annoyed *me*."

Rainey contemplated the next question that had come to her mind. She knew she'd probably pay for it later, but she'd never known Tootsie to be vulnerable before, and if she didn't ask now, maybe she never could. "Did your mom's boyfriend bother you like Jiggy bothered me?" she asked, then held her breath, hoping she hadn't crossed a line.

"I don't know nothing about what Jiggy did to you, but Roy came in my room one night when I was thirteen, beat me, and raped me. That's when I ran away from home and never went back," Tootsie said, sounding strangely distant as she spoke.

"Is that why you joined a gang?"

"Hell, yeah. My brothers and sisters have my back."

Rainey could tell she was trying to sound confident, but she detected the weakness in her words. "I'm gonna try and get some sleep. I'll talk to you tomorrow," she said, feeling hopeful that they'd had the beginning of a connection.

She pulled the bare mattress from the metal bunk onto the floor. Crawling on top, Rainey rested her head on the mattress, the traumatic events of the day catching up to her. She could hear Tootsie crying softly in the background as she drifted into the release of merciful sleep.

Chapter Eighty-Two

The next morning, Rainey woke to her breakfast being delivered. She sat on the floor with her back against the wall and picked up a piece of cold, hard toast, took a bite, and set it back down.

"How can toast suck?" Rainey said to herself.

"Because we're getting all the leftover shit."

Rainey was startled for a moment, having forgotten that Tootsie could hear her. Still, she was delighted that Tootsie had answered. "How are you feeling this morning?" Rainey asked.

"Why do you gotta ask so many questions?"

"I can't help it. I'm curious. I care about people."

"That's another one of your problems. You say you care about people you don't even know. Why the hell would you care about me anyway? If I were you, I'd hate my guts."

Rainey sighed, then a small smile played on her lips. "I did hate your guts before last night. I mean, you're always so mean to me."

"Well, that's because I'm loyal to my gang. That's how it works. It wasn't nothing personal . . . I just carry out the orders I'm given. Doesn't make much of a difference to me."

"How can hurting people who didn't do anything to you not bother you? I could never do something like that to anyone," Rainey said.

"Girl, you ain't got no idea what you'd be willing to do to survive. Just because your parents were fucked up and treated you like shit doesn't mean you know anything about what it's like to be on your own on the streets."

Rainey shuffled on her hands and knees to the door. "You're right. I don't know what it's like, but Phoenix did. Her parents died when she was little and she got passed around from one foster parent to the next.

She ended up running away, just like you and living on the streets. She was a prostitute."

Tootsie cackled. "Everyone knows that Phoenix was a whore. What's your point?"

"My point is you killed her and she went through the same kind of things that you did."

Tootsie pounded her fist on the metal door of her cell, and Rainey jumped, startled. "I fucking told you that I didn't kill Phoenix. Why do you keep saying that?"

"Martina told Frankie, who told me that you made Moody kill her. I believe her, too."

"Well, if Moody killed her, she didn't do it because I gave her the order."

Rainey was stunned. Tootsie had no reason to lie at this point. Rainey thought she had it all figured out . . . had Tootsie all figured out, but maybe she'd been played by Frankie.

In those same quiet moments, Tootsie thought back to the night when Phoenix died. Moody acted strangely euphoric that night. Tootsie only remembered because the next day, when they heard Phoenix was dead, Moody wasn't surprised about the news. At the time, Tootsie thought it was odd but never questioned it. Now she wondered if Moody carried out a hit on Phoenix she didn't know about. Jiggy would not likely go straight to Moody; he didn't have an ax to grind against Phoenix.

"How did Martina say she found out?" Tootsie asked.

"Martina said she overheard Moody, Critter, and Fibber talking about it the next day."

"I don't know nothing about it," Tootsie said angrily. "If I find out one of my girls did something without me giving the order, there'll be hell to pay. Jiggy don't play that game and neither do I. I earned my position and I get respect because of that. Period."

"Hey, I'm just telling you what Frankie told me. When we get outta here you can ask Moody yourself. Besides, all I was saying is that you and Phoenix had a lot in common, that's all."

"Bitch!" Tootsie roared and Rainey froze. "I wasn't no whore. I ain't sucking nobody's dick for a couple of dollars. I earned my way on the streets doing shit that people like you and Phoenix would be too scared to do."

"You mean like killing people?" Rainey asked, agitated.

"Yeah, like killing people," she snapped.

"Well, I'd rather do anything for money than take someone's life."

"You don't know what you're talking about."

"Maybe, but at least I know that I could never hurt someone who didn't do something to me first." Rainey looked at the dried blood under her fingernails from the fight the day before. "Remember when we first met and you kept beating my ass?" she said, an edge of annoyance creeping into her voice.

Tootsie chuckled. "Yeah, the good old days."

"Anyway," Rainey continued, ignoring the comment, "you told me that you suffocated your little sister to death because she told the neighbors about what you were doing for Jiggy. Is that true?"

"Nah. But it could've been true if I had a sister who was that stupid."

Rainey gasped, irritated with herself for being gullible. "Do you?"

"Do I what?" Tootsie barked.

"Do you have a sister?"

"Yeah, sort of. My father had another kid with the slut he lives with. Anyway, I have a stepsister. I never met her, though. I only know about her because I heard my mom on the phone screaming at my dad that she needed money to raise me and that he was spending it all on his other kid—the one from his whore."

"Why would you tell me that you killed your sister then?"

"The same reason I told you I only had a year left in this place. Did it scare you? Make you not want to be around me?"

"Um, yeah. I thought you were crazy," Rainey admitted.

"That's why. Part of being in control is always keeping your enemy on edge."

"I'm not your enemy."

"That's what you think. You'll be my enemy until Jiggy says you're not," Tootsie warned.

"That's messed up," Rainey mumbled, disappointed. She moved to the other side of the small space and stared at the ceiling. She wondered if when they were released from solitary confinement Tootsie would still consider her an enemy, and given that Jiggy would never let up on her—she knew it was likely.

Chapter Eighty-Three

Early the next morning, before breakfast arrived, Rainey hurried to her cell door.

"Tootsie? Are you awake?" she said, having stayed up late thinking about being considered her enemy.

Tootsie moaned. "I am now. What the hell do you want?"

"Sorry, I've been up for a while thinking—it's hard to sleep in this hellhole without a blanket or pillow or a sheet. It's freezing in here."

"Yeah, it's cold. Do some exercises or something and quit bothering me."

"I'm sorry if I woke you but I have a question."

Tootsie sighed. "You always have a question, Paxton. Is it any wonder you get your ass beat all the time?"

Ouch, Rainey thought, *that hurt.*

"You're right. Never mind," Rainey said, moving back to her mattress.

Tootsie never had a friend; someone she could talk to and share secrets with. But in the privacy of solitary confinement and talking through the small opening of her door, she let her guard down, and for the first time, it seemed natural to talk to Rainey about her life.

"Well, I'm awake now. Just ask me the stupid fucking question," she said gruffly.

"Okay," Rainey said, a rush of excitement running through her. "I was wondering . . . if that whole story about killing your sister is a lie, then why are you here? Like, what did you do?"

"Damn, girl. You go ahead and open your mouth and don't give a shit what falls out. You got balls," Tootsie said, amused.

Rainey smiled remembering how Phoenix also gave her a hard time at first for asking too many personal questions.

Tootsie let out a loud sigh. "I robbed a store with a gun, and when I got busted, I had a shit ton of crack and heroin on me that I was *supposed* to be selling."

"Oh." Rainey paused. "What does that mean—'*supposed* to be selling'?"

"Look, that's all you need to know about the drug shit. Let's just say I started using and when it came time to pay, I didn't have the money, so I got a gun and robbed a store."

"You were addicted to drugs?" Rainey asked, incredulous. "You're like the last person I would ever think would do drugs. You're always so . . . in control."

Tootsie scooted over to her door. "Yeah. It was fucked up how it all went down. I sold a lot of dope. Watched way too many people get wasted, never touched the stuff. Then I went to this party one night and there was this guy in our gang, I had been crushing on him for a while. Anyway, he came over to me and we were doing shots of tequila and he asked me if I wanted to try some meth."

"And you did?"

"Well, I was hot for him, and didn't want him to lose interest, you know? So, we go into this room and he pulls out a spoon, dumps some crank in it, squirts water in, and heats it up. The next thing I know I have a belt around my arm and he shoots me up."

"Were you scared?" Rainey asked. The scene Tootsie had described was familiar to her; it was the same things she saw her parents do.

"I mean, sorta, I wasn't a fan of needles, you know? But, after a few minutes I was too stoned to be anything but happy." Tootsie paused and thought back to the moment that changed her life and took away her freedom. When she spoke again, her voice was quiet. "A little pinprick changed my whole life. That's all it takes—it's that quick."

Now Rainey understood how little time it took for someone to become an addict. She realized the fine balance between sober and stoned, and while it didn't change her opinion of her parents, it did give her some perspective. "My parents are drug addicts. I was never able to understand why they like it."

Tootsie leaned her head back and closed her eyes, remembering the rush from that first hit of meth. "The first time you shoot up, man, it's like this freedom you've never experienced. In an instant, I believed everything was going to be great and it made me think I could do anything with my life. It made me forget about all the bad things that happened to me—all the shit with Roy and my dad."

Rainey listened intently, trying to make the correlation between what Tootsie explained and what she had seen of her parents. "My parents weren't like that. They never seemed happy or positive or anything. They were just messed up and angry all the time. Almost like they lived in constant panic mode."

"That's because they are always trying to get the same rush like they did the first time they shot up. But that never happens, no matter what you do, it's impossible to get that same rush. I was always chasing that initial high too. I kept doing more and then I did more, more often. It was like a big spider web that I couldn't climb my way out of. And then I started stealing and doing whatever it took to buy my dope. I didn't prostitute, but I did sleep with guys who would share their crank." Tootsie paused again. "Yeah, I loved me some crank."

"It sounds awful. To want something so bad that you'll do horrible things to get it," Rainey said, still reflecting on her parents.

"Yeah, that's how it goes. And let me tell you, sometimes the hunt for the dope and the needles was half the fucking high. It all blurred together."

Tootsie took a long pause, thinking back on the madness and driving need involved in drug addiction.

"Anyway," Tootsie said a minute or so later, "I was lucky when I landed in this dumb place 'cause I had already moved up in the gang. Gave me an upper hand when I got here." She sighed heavily. "Listen, no more questions now. It's ruining my appetite for the disgusting breakfast we're gonna get soon."

"Sure. Whatever you want," Rainey said with a small smile. "Um, one more thing. I'm sorry about what happened to you when you were a kid."

"Yeah," Tootsie whispered. "Me too."

Chapter Eighty-Four

Over the next two weeks, the girls shared pieces of their lives. Tootsie was surprised to be so interested in what the girl had to say. Rainey's story was no better or worse than the people Tootsie knew, but she was most impressed with how she didn't live with hate or resentment. Tootsie had given in to the anger of having a rough childhood—where the fight and bitterness drove criminal priorities over the rights of others.

"You know, you're weird," Tootsie said at the end of their second week in solitary.

Rainey grunted. "Really? You think *I'm* weird? Compared to you, I don't think so."

"What I mean is you grew up with as much shit as I did, but you're still nice. That makes no sense to me. Sometimes I think it's all an act."

"I'm not acting. I told you about my aunt Sophie. I always hoped to be a lot like her. She was great to me. When she stopped coming to my house, I was so lonely I wanted to die. I would stay in my bedroom most of the time. After a while the silence was disturbing. Not being able to talk to anyone tore me up . . . there were times I thought I was losing my mind. Even in solitary, I have you to talk to." Rainey paused and laughed a little that in a strange but interesting way, Tootsie was now her comfort. "When I was with my aunt it was like no one else in the world existed. I guess I got through things better because of her."

"Okay, then you were lucky."

Rainey rubbed her arms to fight the coldness of the cell. "Yeah, I guess I was. Then I got lucky to be friends with Phoenix. I loved her."

"Mmm," Tootsie hummed.

"No, really. She would've done anything for me—she actually did. Anyway, I know you hate when I say it, but Phoenix was a lot like you in some ways."

"I don't think so," Tootsie grumbled.

"Well, it's true. Phoenix was tough on the outside, but once I got to know her, I found out she was cool.

Tootsie lay on her side in front of her door. "Oh, yeah? What was so cool about her?"

Rainey ran her index finger around the edges of the door, the image of Phoenix lodged in her memory. "Phoenix lived in a lot of foster homes. She told me she was either stuck getting beat on or being their maid . . . it was sad. After a while, she gave up and ran away. But she was cool because through all of that shit she still knew how to be a real friend . . . she had my back no matter what happened."

Tootsie grunted. "Yeah, lots of us lived on the streets. That ain't nothing new."

Rainey cleared her throat. "I know that, it's just—she didn't deserve to die. Her only crime was being friends with me. Makes me feel like shit."

Tootsie sat quietly, not knowing what to say to make things better for her.

Then Rainey filled the silence. "I miss her a lot. Anyway, here we are, you and me having fun in solitary together."

"Yeah, just so you know, this ain't fun to me. I can't wait to get outta here."

Secretly, though she would never admit it, Tootsie did find that talking to Rainey was interesting and gave her comfort—a chance to be calm and not on guard.

Tootsie's eyes were sad when she said, "It must've been nice to have a friend like Phoenix. I never had any friends before I joined the Vamps. Even in a gang, nobody is friends with me because they like me. They only hang with me 'cause I'm a member." Tootsie paused for several seconds. "I hate to say it. It's weird, I've told you more about my life than anyone else, ever. If you tell anyone I swear I'll kill you."

"Jeez, Tootsie," Rainey huffed, insulted. "You don't have to threaten me to keep my mouth shut. I told you when we got here that I'm not like that. It's annoying when you don't believe me."

"Yeah, well, I ain't used to trusting people . . . I don't believe nobody."

"That's because you hang out with a bunch of girls who only care about themselves. Your friends are a pack of morons," Rainey ranted.

"Hey! Be careful—they're my sisters you're talking about," Tootsie warned.

"Right. Your sisters," she huffed, making it clear that she thought it was ridiculous.

"That's right, girl. Don't push me. You don't know anything about my bitches, so keep your mouth shut," Tootsie growled.

"Fine," Rainey said, deflated and ready to change the subject. "We get out of here in a week. That's good, right?"

"Yeah."

Rainey dreaded her time alone with Tootsie ending and this made her restless. She lost her appetite and could barely sleep in the days leading to their release back into the general population. Even though Rainey knew her better, she couldn't completely trust that Tootsie didn't have Phoenix killed. It was bittersweet. She'd grown to believe they'd leave solitary confinement friends, but she couldn't let go of what happened to Phoenix. It was a dilemma Rainey couldn't figure her way out of. She hoped that if Tootsie had anything to do with Phoenix's murder, she would get her to admit it before they were released from solitary confinement.

Chapter Eighty-Five

The night before the girls were released back to their regular cells, Rainey's arms and legs tingled with a fiery sensation, worrying about what would happen between her and Tootsie. She was restless and couldn't sit for long. She tried her best to focus only on the things she was looking forward to in the general population, especially showering every day and eating hot food. In solitary confinement, the girls were only fed cold food they could eat without utensils, "for safety reasons," the guards had explained.

"Hey Tootsie?" Rainey said, sounding nervous, "we're going back to general pop tomorrow. I hope we can stay friends."

"I never said we were friends," Tootsie grumbled.

Rainey grinned. "That's a rotten thing to say. Stop acting like you don't like me now." In an excess of restless energy, she started pacing in the small space as she waited for Tootsie to respond.

"I gotta do what I gotta do. Just because we spent some time together doesn't mean that I can let up on you."

There was a callousness in Tootsie's tone that brought Rainey back to before they were confined together. Surprised by the change Rainey's anger was triggered.

"So killing Phoenix wasn't enough punishment for me? Why can't you just tell Jiggy you couldn't hurt me any more than you already did by taking away the only friend I had in here," Rainey spat at the wall between them.

Tootsie stood and banged on her door several times. "I told you already, I didn't have nothing to do with your friend getting killed."

Rainey, under the weight of Tootsie's anger, took a deep breath and pressed on against all her instincts. "No, you're right. You didn't kill Phoenix. You made Moody do it."

"Bitch, you're wearing my nerves," Tootsie warned.

"Well, if you didn't tell Moody to kill her. Then who did?"

"Moody didn't kill nobody. She can't do nothing without my permission. Period."

"Well, then I believe that Moody, Critter, and Fibber killed Phoenix without your permission. Did you ever think about that? Not everyone does what they're supposed to do."

"Just shut the fuck up, okay?" Tootsie yelled. But questions and doubts reeled through her thoughts ever since Rainey had first mentioned it.

It was silent between them for the next ten minutes, until Rainey spoke. "Just so you know," she stated, "the drugs weren't mine. It's true I had bags in my lap and I was holding a gun, but all of it belonged to Jiggy. He ran like a girl when he knew the cops were coming. I wasn't smart enough to understand what was happening. I'm only in here because of him."

"Yeah, whatever."

"No, Tootsie," Rainey squealed, "I'm serious. You're out to make my life miserable for no good reason."

"It ain't for no good reason—it's because you didn't tell the judge what Brice told you to say the first time you went to court. Instead, all those cops are still sniffing around Jiggy, looking for a reason to pop him. That's why I got a problem with you. It was so easy, all you had to do was lie to the judge."

Tootsie knew the girl had taken the fall to keep Jiggy from hurting her little sister. The odd thing was, Tootsie had become fond of Rainey. If she was honest with herself, which wasn't something she practiced often, she would miss Rainey once they moved out of isolation.

"Tootsie?" Rainey said.

"Yeah, what?"

"When we get out of here are you gonna keep coming after me?"

"It ain't that easy," Tootsie said, though Rainey thought she detected a hint of remorse.

"Why?"

"Because when it comes to you, I take my orders from Jiggy. I ain't sure what it is, but he's got a special kind of hate for you. I don't understand it and I don't need to understand it. All I need to do is carry out his orders."

"I can guess why he hates me. He was about to rape me when the cops raided our house. I was fighting him off right before he stopped and told me to count out the bags of heroin. He acted like he owned me—because he owns my mom and dad. He got mad when I wouldn't lie to the judge for him . . . it wasn't enough that I didn't tell anyone that the drugs and the gun were his."

"Fuck," Tootsie said with such a slight breath that Rainey almost didn't hear her. "You already told me all of this. I don't want to know about you being involved with Jiggy," she said louder.

"We weren't *involved,* I said he was going to rape me. Besides, why would he tell you anything? I bet Jiggy knows that Roy raped you, right?"

"Yeah, of course," Tootsie said. "When I first joined the gang, I told him what happened."

"Well, that's probably why he didn't tell you that he was *involved* with me, as you put it. He knows how you feel about girls getting sexually assaulted," Rainey reasoned. "I know this girl in Kensington . . . she's a prostitute. Anyway, she told me that Jiggy has a thing for pain—you know when he has sex. I was so scared the night he came after me. If it weren't for Ivy I would've run away and never come back."

"Your friend was right about Jiggy. I had sex with him after I joined the gang," she said in a strained tone.

Shocked that Tootsie would say anything bad about Jiggy, Rainey asked in a high-pitched voice, "Did he hurt you?"

Tootsie thought about her question, not knowing how much to share. When she spoke, her voice was shaky. "Well, first off, I agreed to have sex with him; he didn't rape me. But, umm, yeah, he did stuff that hurt. Stuff that most guys wouldn't do."

"Like what?" Rainey asked curious to know and fearful of what she would hear.

"I don't know. Why do you have to ask so many fucking questions?" Tootsie growled.

"I can't help it sometimes," Rainey said.

"Well, when you grow up you ought to be a damn detective. You never run out of shit that you wanna know."

Rainey let out a nervous giggle. "So are you gonna tell me then?"

"Fuck, girl. He did things," she grunted. "He stuck stuff in there that hurt . . . things that don't belong in there. And he likes to pinch and bite . . . hard, long pinches and bites that leave marks and make you scream. It turned him on when I screamed. He's sick when it comes to sex and I did everything I could to never have sex with him again. That's kinda how I became his go-to chick because I'd ruin anyone he told me to, I'd cut a person to the bone not to ever have to lay down with that motherfucker again."

Rainey's blood ran cold at the thought of what she'd narrowly avoided.

"Who's the prosti that told you about him?" Tootsie asked.

"Oh, umm, I never knew her name," Rainey lied. There was no way she would rat out Mona. "So you didn't answer my question—when we get outta here are you and me still gonna be enemies?"

"Depends," Tootsie said.

"On what?"

Tootsie smiled slyly in her cell. "On how nice you are to me."

"Nice to you. Okay, I've never *not* been nice to you."

Tootsie's smile broadened behind the cinderblock that separated the two young teens. Well, then we won't have a problem," Tootsie said, still smiling.

"What about Jiggy?"

"Not sure yet, but I'll figure something out."

Rainey's heart quickened. "I told you about Martina and what she did to me. I won't have any money to buy you commissary—but I'll do whatever I need to do to keep Ivy safe."

"Yeah, I know you will. Listen real good . . . when we get outta here tomorrow don't go running around telling everyone we're friends. That'll just bring bad shit my way. I'll handle my girls, and as for Martina, I'll handle that backstabbing whore too."

"What do you mean by 'handle'?" Rainey didn't want to be the cause of anyone getting hurt.

"Shut the hell up and go to sleep. Keep your trap shut when we get outta here and find yourself a friend to hang out with. I know your cellmate, Frankie, doesn't want nothing to do with you—hell, she lit your bunk on fire."

"What?" Rainey gasped. "How do you know that?"

"Because I got sources everywhere. Even inside Martina's camp. Now, keep your eyes open and your pie hole shut. Got it?"

"Yeah, I got it," Rainey breathed. Intense stomach pain ripped through her as she thought about returning to the cell, she was sharing with a girl who had tried to kill her.

Chapter Eighty-Six

Upon release, Rainey and Tootsie stood outside their cells in solitary confinement and stared at each other like they were seeing each other for the first time. They'd spent three weeks talking day and night without actually looking into each other's eyes. Rainey couldn't help but smile.

"You look like shit," Tootsie said with a smirk.

Rainey chuckled. "And my mouth tastes like shit too."

"Let's move it, girls," Fernandez said. She and another guard led them to a cell neither in Rainey's nor Tootsie's block. Fernandez stopped in front of an empty cell and turned to the girls. "All right, here we are. Welcome to your new home," she announced.

"Who are you talking to?" Tootsie growled. "This ain't my block."

Fernandez gently grabbed Rainey's shoulder and turned her toward the opening of the cell. "Get moving. This is where you're both staying from now on. You two will need to learn to get along if you have to live together."

Fernandez and the other guards knew of the relationship that had blossomed while the two spent time together in solitary. The staff thought it would be a good idea to place them in the same cell upon release, hoping that they could continue to cultivate their friendship. They believed it would soften Tootsie and give Rainey some needed relief.

"Hey, Fernandez. You know this is fucked up," Tootsie said.

"I don't know any such thing, Tootsie. I don't see what the problem is. You're in juvie, not summer camp; you don't get to pick your cellmate."

Rainey saw Tootsie's jaw tighten and jumped in before Tootsie made it worse. "Stop making a big deal out of it, Tootsie. You think you're some prize to have to share a cell with."

Breaking her death glare, Tootsie glanced at Rainey.

"I'm serious," Rainey said, giving Tootsie a wink and hoping that the bond they'd formed in solitary would hold.

Tootsie walked into the cell and plopped down on the lower bunk. "Fine. I'll stay in here but I want you to know I don't like it."

Rainey crossed her arms over her chest. "Me neither."

Fernandez leaned against the bars that framed the door. "No one asked you what you like. Now settle in. Chow is in half an hour."

"What time is it?" Rainey asked.

"Almost seven. The rest of the girls will be up soon. Get yourselves together. There are two boxes over there with your names on them," Fernandez said, pointing to the corner of their cell. "We brought your stuff over."

When the guards were gone, Rainey sat on the edge of Tootsie's bunk. "This isn't so bad, right?" she said, secretly pleased by the development. At least the two of them could still talk.

Tootsie, who was laying with her hands behind her head, just glanced at her and said nothing.

"Well," Rainey said, "I'm happy that I don't have to go back to my old cell with that asshole Frankie. I was kinda worried that she'd try to kill me again . . . maybe set my hair on fire." Rainey chanced a joke, and to her delight, Tootsie laughed a little.

"So, what now?" Rainey asked, hating the silence.

"See, I don't even know why you ask shit like that. There is nothing we need to do. I told you before we got here that I'll handle everything. We didn't plan on this, but it might work out to be better," she said.

"Better how?"

Tootsie rolled her eyes. "The only way you and me are gonna live together is if you stop asking so many questions."

Rainey sat on the floor and faced Tootsie. "I'll try to do better, I swear, but I can't promise anything. The silence bothers me."

"Why? Your parents keep you in a box when you were little?" she snickered.

"No, but they would lock me in a closet in the attic when they wanted to punish me—you know, because I wanted their attention. I didn't have anyone to talk to. Sometimes they'd leave me there for a day or two. I was only five the first time they did that. I remember it was winter and I was so cold I thought my fingers and toes would freeze and fall off." Rainey looked down at her hands. "I never told my aunt Sophie. Maybe if I had she would've taken me away from my mom and dad."

"That's messed up," Tootsie said.

"Yeah, so I hated the silence when I was all alone in the attic. But that was nothing. Once Aunt Sophie was gone, my whole life was so dark, like I was swimming through mud. Then my parent's brought Ivy home, and it was like shining a bright light into the pitch-black night.

Rainey looked up and caught Tootsie watching her with tear filled eyes.

Inside, Tootsie's chest ached. She never would have imagined that the little blond girl had such a rough life—she had assumed Rainey was just another spoiled girl. But now, after knowing so much, Tootsie recognized the similarities between the two.

"Okay, well, we better get our shit together," Tootsie said. "It's our first day back in general and all my girls are gonna want to know everything that happened over the past three weeks."

"What are you going to tell them?"

Tootsie shook her head. "We already talked about this, remember? I'm just gonna tell them I was stuck in the hole and when they let us out the guards put us in the same cell. That's it."

"Right," Rainey said.

"If anyone asks, that's what you say," Tootsie instructed. "It's not even a lie."

"Sure, but I'm not worried about anyone wanting to know what happened. I'm worried about what Martina is gonna do to me now," Rainey confided. "I mean, if it's true that she had Frankie set my bed on fire, well, I'd say she's probably got something else planned for me."

Tootsie rose from her bunk and kneeled next to Rainey. "You listen real good. When we go down for chow, you find an empty table and plant yourself. I can't be dealing with your shit right now. Stay as far away from Martina as you can. Got it?"

Tootsie stared at Rainey so hard she shrank away. But still, she knew it was the right thing to do.

"Yeah, damn, I got it."

Chapter Eighty-Seven

The Vamp members closed in on Tootsie like a swarm of wasps. They fist-pumped, she punched their arms, and they pushed each other around. Rainey was fascinated watching the barbaric ritual of greeting each other.

As Tootsie had instructed, Rainey took her breakfast tray to an empty table, as far away as she could get from where Martina and her friends sat. When she picked up a fork, she was surprised at how good it was to hold it in her hands. Something as simple as using an eating utensil seemed like a luxury. She put a forkful of eggs into her mouth and closed her eyes briefly, savoring the flavor. She was almost done with her meal when Martina sat down across from her.

Rainey looked up at the girl and Martina was sneering.

"What?" Rainey asked, bracing herself for the worst.

Martina gave her an ugly grin. "How was solitary?"

"What do you want?" Rainey repeated.

"Oh, I see. Is this how you're gonna be?"

Rainey's grip around her fork tightened. She tilted her head and narrowed her eyes. "You mean like I don't wanna be bothered with you? Yes, that's how it's gonna be."

Martina took a grape from Rainey's tray and popped it into her mouth. "Oh, yeah?"

"Yeah, Martina. I know you had Frankie set my bunk on fire. Don't deny it," Rainey huffed.

Martina put her head back and wailed a crazy laugh. "You're pretty fucking brave for someone who was my bitch three weeks ago."

Rainey stood and picked up her tray. "Well, I guess three weeks in solitary confinement gave me a lot of time to think about what a nasty, rotten person you are."

Watching Rainey walk away, Martina seethed, thinking that she'd make her pay for being disobedient. After a minute, Martina got up and started back to her table, but before she got there, Tootsie stepped out in front of her. She tried to walk around her, but Tootsie sidestepped and blocked her way again. Martina was respected in her circle, but she still knew better than to get on Tootsie's bad side.

"Can I help you?" Martina said, hating how her voice squeaked.

"Hmmm. Let me see. Yeah, maybe you can," Tootsie said.

Martina cocked out her right hip and placed her hands at her waist, trying her best not to let Tootsie see her fear. "Okay. What?"

"Well, I guess you heard about the fight I had with that little pug Rainey. Anyway, that fight landed me in solitary for three weeks."

"Yeah? So? Why do I care about you and Rainey?" Martina quipped.

"You should care because the fight I had with her was because somebody spread a rumor that I killed her bitch, Phoenix," Tootsie said.

Martina leaned closer to Tootsie. "Well, you did. Everyone knows that you had Moody take care of Phoenix," she said, waving her bony hand around to the others in the cafeteria.

Tootsie smirked. "Everyone except me. You see, I think you know you're wrong, and you're spreading lies to cover your ass."

Martina couldn't believe that Tootsie was denying it or, worse yet, that she didn't know about it. "Hey, go ask your girl, Moody. I only passed on what I knew to my friend Rainey."

"Oh, I see, so you're friends with her?" Tootsie asked.

"Yeah. So what?"

"Well, I've seen her stepping and fetching for you and those dimwits you hang around with. I don't think you and Rainey are friends. I think you use her as entertainment."

"What's it to you, anyway? What? Is Rainey your lover now or something?"

Tootsie shook her head and grabbed Martina's boney wrist. Through clenched teeth, she said, "You and me—we aren't the same. I'm a Vamp and we don't play little-girl games. Let me be clear. I'm stuck with Rainey—we're sharing a cell now and I won't have any trouble where I live. So, here's the deal, you and your asshole buddies over there," she said, lifting her chin toward Martina's friends, "you stay the fuck away from Rainey until I get moved to another cell. You hear me?"

Martina's eyes bulged. She hadn't anticipated that Tootsie would defend Rainey—all the girls in juvie knew that she had it out for her. She snapped her wrist from Tootsie's grip. "Yeah, I hear you."

"Good. Then we have an understanding. That's a start. Now, if you wanna keep things peaceful I'm gonna need you to get money on my commissary—you know, the money that you were supposed to be giving to Rainey," Tootsie stated.

"You're kidding me, right?" Martina balked.

Tootsie looked at the girls in her gang behind them, and Martina followed her eyes. The gang members were practically frothing at the mouth as they eyed her up. She broke into a cold sweat; this was a war she and the girls she hung with couldn't handle.

"Does it look like I'm kidding?"

Martina shook her head. "I'll see what I can do. No promises," she said, trying not to appear rattled.

"You're still confused. I ain't asking you, I'm *telling* you. Consider this a warning."

Martina's face went deadly pale. She spun and walked away on shaky legs.

As Tootsie walked toward her gang, she glanced to the other side of the cafeteria and caught Rainey staring at her with her mouth hanging open. Tootsie gave her the slightest head nod, and that small gesture let Rainey know that Martina had been put on notice. With a huge smile spread across her face, Rainey waltzed out of the cafeteria and down the hall to her first class of the day.

Chapter Eighty-Eight

After Rainey's last class she went back to her cell to lay down. She was so tired and wanted to take a quick nap before dinner.

At the same time, Tootsie was forcing Critter closer to the stairwell. "Come here, bitch,"

Critter stood still and her eyes darted around the hall.

"Did you hear me?" Tootsie said, filling her voice with as much authority as she could muster.

Critter stared straight ahead.

Tootsie grabbed her arm and dragged her into the stairwell, then spun on her. "I have some questions for you, and if you're smart, you'll tell me the truth."

"O . . . okay," Critter stuttered.

"I heard that you, Moody, and Fibber killed Phoenix. Is that true?"

Critter wrung her hands together, looking like she was about to melt into a puddle.

"Are you deaf? I asked you a question," Tootsie growled, knocking her fist against the girl's shoulder.

Critter's arms and legs shook. "It wasn't my idea," she stammered. "Moody said you gave the order."

"Oh, yeah? And when have I *ever* given an order to off somebody through Moody? What's the fucking rule?" Tootsie demanded through clenched teeth.

"Nev . . . never take an offing order from anyone but you," she stuttered, pressing her back to the wall to put space between them.

"That's right, never!" Tootsie persisted. "Was Fibber there too?"

Critter nodded.

Tootsie lifted her fist and placed it on the girl's mouth. "Right. Here's what you're gonna do. You're gonna keep your mouth shut about this conversation. If I find out you breathed a *word*, I will kill you. Do you understand?"

"Yeah," Critter said, protecting her face with her hands. "I won't say anything. I swear."

In response, Tootsie pulled back her arm and nailed Critter in the gut.

Critter bent over, spewing and gasping for breath, eking out an "I'm sorry."

"Not yet, but you're going to be sorry. You know there'll be a price to pay," Tootsie promised.

"Please," Critter cried, "I'll do anything. I won't tell the other girls."

Tootsie eyed the girl up and down, satisfied she would keep her mouth shut. She turned to walk away and, looking over her shoulder, said, "Remember what I told you. Not a word."

After Tootsie left the stairwell, Critter collapsed to the ground, holding her stomach. She sobbed with regret. "I knew it wasn't right . . . I knew I shouldn't have done it," she whispered.

Tootsie made her way to the phones and placed a call to her commander on the outside. "Hey, Grinder. I got news."

She listened as Grinder, the leader of the soldiers, took a long drag from his cigarette. "What you got?"

"Moody broke rank. Offed a girl without my permission."

"Oh," Grinder said, butting his cigarette into an ashtray. "That ain't good. What do you wanna do?"

"Take her out. I have to send a message to the other Vamps in here."

"Hmm. I don't think that's a good idea. No members get taken out while they're still locked up. But I'll tell you what—you can oust her from the inner circle. Tell her she's gotta respect all the rules like she is an active member, but keep her in the dark."

"Fine, I guess," Tootsie said.

"Fine? Look, Toots, you gotta worry about taking care of that little bitch that didn't do what Jiggy told her to do."

"Things have changed, Grinder." Tootsie hesitated, collecting her courage. "They put the two of us in a cell together. I'd never get away with it."

"That's fucked up. Okay, have one of the other girls do it for you," Grinder said.

"Well, I wanted to talk to you about that. You see, the chick that Moody killed was the only person in here that Rainey got on with. I think it might be the worst thing we could've done to the bitch. I was thinking I'd just keep riding her. You know?"

"Nah, I ain't picking up what you're laying down. Seems funny to me. You wanted to off Moody for killing Rainey's friend and now you think your new little cellmate has had enough? I ain't following what you're trying to do here. What exactly *are* you trying to do?"

"Two different things, Grinder," Tootsie said, keeping her voice as even as possible. "First, Moody has to pay for doing shit that is against the rules. Second, I need to deal with Rainey."

"I still ain't following, bitch. You wanted to kill Moody two minutes ago, but in the end, she helped you punish that girl Jiggy wants you to deal with. Explain that to me," Grinder said.

Tootsie's heart hammered in her chest. She hadn't anticipated that Grinder would challenge her—that wasn't the norm for him. Now she needed to talk her way out of it.

"Look, my head is kinda messed up. I got sent to solitary for three weeks, just got out. I shouldn't have said I wanted to off Moody. That was over the top. As for Rainey Paxton, she's paid a big price by losing her friend—the stupid girl is all alone in here and there ain't nobody to protect her now. All I'm saying is seeing that I'm her cellmate, I can't do anything to blow my cover. I'm just trying to think of a way to make her pay without killing the bitch. You know, like busting her up or something."

"There ain't nothing permanent about breaking a bone. You know that. I'll tell you what. I have an idea. Let me check with Jiggy about it. Give me a call back tomorrow night."

Tootsie's mouth was so dry she could barely reply. "Sure," she managed.

When she hung up the phone, she scanned the room, and her eyes settled on Moody. She smiled, and Tootsie lifted her chin in response, holding back the urge to rush over to her and rip her heart out. Walking back to her cell, she realized that she handled Grinder all wrong. Now she had to wait to see what Jiggy would decide about Rainey. The truth was, Tootsie actually had grown to like the girl.

***

The worst part about dealing with Jiggy is he takes his good old time to decide. The next twenty-four hours were painstakingly slow for Tootsie as she waited to call Grinder.

The next day, right after dinner, Tootsie headed for the phones.

Grinder picked up on the second ring. "Yeah?"

"It's me," Tootsie said, trying to swallow the lump in her throat. "You talk to Jiggy?"

"Yeah, I did. He wasn't too happy about everything that's happening. You're lucky, though: he's got some new whores he's breaking in and he's preoccupied."

"Oh," Tootsie said. She hated when Jiggy turned girls in dire straits into prostitutes. The slug exploited everyone for his own benefit. Still, if it saved her and Rainey, it was a good thing.

"Yeah, so here's what you're gonna do . . ."

Chapter Eighty-Nine

Tootsie struggled. Jiggy's order made her uncomfortable. It wasn't like she hadn't done it before, but she'd never had to harm someone she cared for. She couldn't believe she liked the runt, but she did.

"Rainey, we need to talk," Tootsie said, walking into their cell.

Rainey shimmied up on the bed. "Okay. What's going on?"

"Remember I told you that I'd handle Jiggy?"

"Yeah. What did he say?" Rainey asked, fearing the worst.

"Well, he's willing to give you a pass for now," she said.

"Whew. Oh, thank God. I was so freaked out."

Tootsie held up her hand. "Let me finish. When Jiggy gives a pass, he just means he's gonna let you live."

The intense heat in Rainey's chest quickly rose to her face. "What does that mean?"

"There's this thing we do in gangs," Tootsie started. She considered trying to find a softer way to say it to her, but in the end, decided it was best to be upfront. "Okay. When you've done something really bad, instead of being killed, the member who fucked up has to cut off their pinky finger."

Rainey instinctively balled up her hands. "No. What do you mean? Are you saying he wants me to cut off my pinky?"

"No," Tootsie said, looking away so Rainey couldn't see her sadness. "I have to cut it off for you."

Rainey shoved her hands in the waistband of her pants. "I can't. I mean, you can't. I'll bleed to death."

Tootsie tried to reassure her. "Nah, you won't. I've done it before. I know it sounds horrible, and I ain't gonna lie, I hear it hurts like hell. But I can get something sharp enough to take it off real quick."

Tears pressed out from Rainey's eyes and streamed down her cheeks. "Can't you just *tell* Jiggy that you cut off my finger? He'll never know."

Tootsie shook her head slowly, wishing that were an option. "It doesn't work that way. I gotta do it in front of a couple of gang members."

Rainey dropped to her knees and looked up at Tootsie. "Please don't do this to me. Please."

Tootsie wanted to give her a pass, show her mercy, but it was out of her hands. She took hold of Rainey's shoulders and helped her stand. "You don't understand," she said, looking into her eyes and keeping her voice as even as possible. "He wanted you dead. This is the compromise. If I don't do this, he *will* have you killed. And trust me, if it isn't in juvie, he'll snuff you out the minute you get out—right after he tortures you. Jiggy doesn't play. That dude ain't got no heart."

"I don't think I can let you do it," Rainey said in a weak voice.

"You don't have no choice. And I gotta do it in the next twenty-four hours."

Rainey climbed into her bunk quickly. "No, Tootsie, you can't. I won't let you."

Tootsie watched the girl curl into herself, trying hard to deny her reality. There was a pain in Tootsie's heart as she watched how helpless she'd become. She had a need to protect Rainey, but not knowing how to comfort her, she just placed her hand gently on her back.

"Try not to think about it," she said. "You'll only make it worse."

***

After dinner, Tootsie caught up to Rainey as she was rushing back to their cell. The time had come to take care of business.

"We need to make a stop," she said gently.

"No. I can't let you do it," Rainey squealed in a defeated tone.

Tootsie grabbed Rainey's arm and stopped walking. "I ain't playing right now. You have to come with me. If not, you're gonna end up dead," she said seriously.

Rainey shook her head, and Tootsie tried to hide her mounting frustration. Telling Rainey, the grave consequences of not having her pinky removed wasn't working—she was still too afraid. So, Tootsie did what she did best. She lied.

"Look, I didn't want to tell you, but Jiggy said if this doesn't happen, he's going after Ivy," she said, hating that she'd resorted to this. "He told me he doesn't have an issue messing up a little girl."

Rainey gasped and her expression immediately changed to one of acceptance. She was trapped. Her legs were rubbery as she numbly gave Tootsie a slow nod before following her to the bathroom, where Moody stood just inside one of the shower stalls. When Tootsie and Rainey entered, she turned on the water. Moody leaned down and pulled a knife from her sock that she had stolen from the food prep kitchen and handed it to Tootsie.

Tootsie pulled Rainey into the stall, slamming her hand against the tile wall. From behind, Moody held her hand over Rainey's mouth while Tootsie quickly sliced through her pinky right above the second knuckle. Rainey railed and bucked against Moody, but it was done. Searing pain ran from her finger to the top of her shoulder. Tootsie quickly wrapped the stub in paper towels. She couldn't console the girl, knowing it wouldn't be lost on Moody.

Tootsie handed the finger to Moody. "Go. Hurry up. We gotta get out of here. Do your thing and leave."

After Moody flushed the severed finger down the toilet, she left the bathroom, leaving Tootsie and Rainey alone. Tootsie dropped the gangster act and helped the girl to her feet, supporting her so she could stand. Then she led her over to the toilet stall that Moody had just left, took her hand, pulled the paper towels away, and let the blood drip down the hinged side of the door. With Rainey watching in horror, she wrapped her finger back up and sat her on the toilet while she cleaned up the mess in the shower.

When Tootsie finished, she bent down and looked into Rainey's eyes. Her gaze was distant and she knew the girl was in shock. "You doing okay?"

Rainey's face was ashen, and her lips had taken on a blue hue. Tootsie shook her shoulder gently. "Hey, hey."

Finally, Rainey's eyes met Tootsie's.

"Come on," Tootsie said. "You're losing blood, but you'll be fine. You gotta go see Nurse Dix."

Rainey stood and immediately grabbed onto the wall to steady herself.

"I need you to pay attention," Tootsie said, taking the girl's face in her hands. "Now, you're gonna tell Nurse Dix that you took a piss and your finger got caught in the door hinge and you pulled it away and almost ripped it off—there was only a thin layer of skin keeping it on. You panicked because blood was everywhere and so you held your hand over the toilet and that small piece of skin gave way just as you flushed."

Rainey's expression turned frantic. "What? I don't know what you're talking about. I gotta get to Dix."

Tootsie grew darkly serious. This was important. "No," she said, leveling Rainey with a hard stare. "You ain't going anywhere. Not until you get this right."

Tootsie made Rainey repeat the story three times before she pulled the bathroom door open to let her out. Rainey gave her a nod and turned right, holding the blood-soaked paper towels where her pinky finger used to be while Tootsie turned left to return to her cell.

Chapter Ninety

Rainey underwent surgery to salvage the remainder of her finger and spent three nights in the hospital before she was sent back to juvenile detention. While in the hospital, Rainey's anger grew that Jiggy would require her to lose a finger. He had caused her so much pain and forced her to take jail time by holding her sister's well-being over her decisions. Now she had one less finger but a lot more anger and determination to get even with him and her parents.

Upon her return, she was sent directly to Nurse Dix's office, where she sat on a gurney.

The nurse went over Rainey's instructions. "The doctor gave you ten days of antibiotics, which you must finish, as well as pain medication, which I see you're not taking."

Rainey sat, hunched over, her arms hanging limply by her sides. She was still exhausted from the surgery and the pain she had endured. "I don't like that stuff. It makes me tired."

The nurse nodded. "I understand, and normally I wouldn't make you take it. But the doctor was very clear about staying in front of your pain, so I'd like you to take some now. You'll be due for another dose in two hours. One of the guards will get you and bring you here."

Rainey looked up at the nurse and could see she was honestly concerned for her. "It doesn't hurt that much right now."

"Well, that's because the hospital stayed on top of the pain. For now, you'll need to take the pills every four hours as prescribed and we can reassess your pain in a couple of days."

"Fine," Rainey mumbled, knowing she didn't have a choice.

"I'd like to understand how you did this to your finger, Rainey."

Rainey relayed the story that Tootsie had given her to the nurse. She didn't care anymore. She'd given a finger, and now she just wanted to move on.

Nurse Dix raised her eyebrows. "Rainey, if someone harmed you, I need to know . . . for your safety."

"I swear that's what happened," Rainey said. She knew the nurse didn't believe her, but she'd stuck to the story for Ivy's sake.

"I see," Nurse Dix said. "Well, that's quite a tragic accident. And unfortunately, you'll have challenges without that finger," she said, placing her hands on her hips and staring hard at the girl. "Are you sure there's nothing you want to talk to me about?"

Rainey squirmed under the nurse's penetrating gaze. "No," she managed. "There's nothing else. I told you everything."

The nurse let out a loud sigh. "Okay, you can go then. Officer Fernandez is waiting to escort you back to your cell. If you don't feel well, please let one of the guards know and they'll bring you back to see me."

Back at the cell, Tootsie anxiously waited for the guard to leave before she rushed to Rainey.

"How'd it go?" Tootsie asked, sounding upset.

Depleted, Rainey held up her bandaged hand. "Just great."

"Did you tell them what I told you to say?"

Rainey nodded but turned her back to Tootsie. "Yeah, sure. I told them that stupid story you made up. They think I'm an idiot or a liar . . . but I'm both."

Tootsie stepped closer. "What the hell is your problem?"

Sick and tired of thinking about Jiggy and how he controlled her friend, Rainey whispered through clenched teeth, "You cut my fucking finger off. They had to take skin from my thigh and sew it onto the top of my finger. And now, I'm not gonna be able to use my hand like I used to so I have to learn stuff all over again. That's my problem!"

"Cutting your pinky off saved your life," Tootsie said. "I told you already—Jiggy wanted me to kill you. I had a choice to make."

"Yeah, you decided that cutting off my finger was the right punishment. Couldn't you just tell him you beat my ass a bunch of times already?"

"Look, you need to check yourself. You don't know anything about how the Vamps work. I made a good fucking deal for you," Tootsie said, nostrils flaring. "I put my ass on the line for you so you better rethink the shit you say to me. I never back people, ever. Don't make me sorry I did."

This statement from Tootsie hit Rainey in the heart, and she was grateful to have her as a good friend. She looked down at her bandaged hand. "So you *do* like me then," she sang, giving Tootsie a sly smile.

Tootsie grinned. "Yeah, and I don't know why, and don't let me see you gloating about it either."

Rainey moved closer. "Oh, come on. You know why, it's because I'm such a fun girl."

"Ha!" Tootsie huffed. "You are the least fun person I've ever known. But I feel like I can trust you. That ain't something I had before, a person I could trust."

Rainey gave Tootsie a genuine smile, then sat on Tootsie's bunk and leaned her back against the wall as her hatred for Jiggy faded into the background. "You can trust me. I won't disappoint you either."

"I'll hold you to that."

"By the way," Rainey broke the serious moment, holding her bandaged hand toward Tootsie, "in case you're wondering, it sucks not to have my pinky finger. I don't even know what it's really gonna be like without it, not until I get this bandage off. Nurse Dix said it's gonna be hard for me to do a lot of things."

"Nurse Dix doesn't know her ass from a hole in the ground. I know lots of people who lost their pinky. And just so you know, if you were a Vamp you would've had to cut that finger off yourself," Tootsie said.

"Oh. There's no way I could've done that to myself."

Tootsie took Rainey's bandaged hand in her own and looked it over. "You'd be surprised at what you'll do when your life is on the line. The gang can make it miserable; you know? Like I'm talking to the point where you wish you were dead. And the fucked-up part is, most of my Vamp brothers and sisters don't have anywhere else to go. No one to call family. Once you find people who have your back, it's hard to give up. You just do whatever is expected of you."

Rainey rested her head on the girl's shoulder, feeling a wave of affection for her.

Tootsie was touched by the gesture, and a warm sensation ran through her. Instead of pushing Rainey off, she pretended as though the moment were normal. She suspected that for other people, not people like her, the gesture *would* be normal.

"I'm not going to thank you for cutting my pinky off," she said, laughing a little.

Tootsie chuckled. "I didn't think that you would."

"I didn't get to ask you. What about Moody? Did you find out if she killed Phoenix?"

Tootsie nodded.

"And?" Rainey asked hesitantly, bracing herself for the answer.

"And she did it with the other two, just like you told me."

"Well, we have the truth. What happens to her now?"

Tootsie moved from the bunk and stood at the door, with her back to Rainey. "You don't need to worry about any of that—it's been taken care of."

"Taken care of? What are you, the Godfather now?"

Tootsie turned, and her glare let Rainey know she crossed the line. "This isn't a joke. So, like I said, it's been taken care of. Moody isn't a problem."

Rainey's breath caught in her throat. "Shit! What did you do to her?"

Tootsie shook her head. "You remember when we were in solitary and I told you that you ask too many questions?"

Rainey nodded.

"Well, this is one of those times. You and I need to have an understanding if we're gonna live in here together. When I say something has been taken care of, that means you stop asking questions. If you can do that, we'll be good."

"You're serious? Rainey asked, confused as to how their conversation turned so cold.

"Dead serious."

"Okay," Rainey said, suddenly feeling heavy exhaustion settle over her. "I'm going to lay down for a while." Gripping the upper bunk with one hand, she tried to hoist herself up, but it was no use—she slipped and fell to the floor.

Tootsie helped her up. "You sleep in my bunk and I'll sleep up top."

Rainey slid onto the bottom bunk, smiling. "Thanks, Tootsie. I mean for trading bunks, not for cutting off my finger."

"Yeah, yeah, I know."

As Rainey drifted to sleep, she thought about Phoenix. Tootsie and Phoenix had more in common than either girl knew. They were both fearless and never backed down from danger. Rainey had learned a lot about standing up for herself from each of them and realized she had grown as a person. She was thankful to both and, like Phoenix, Tootsie had also saved her life—even if it did cost her a finger.

Chapter Ninety-One

When Nurse Dix removed Rainey's bandage for the last time, the girl stared hard at the bright red stump protruding from her hand. She watched it with all her might, willing it to grow back.

"The doctor did a nice job," Nurse Dix said, interrupting Rainey's useless conjuring of a new pinky.

Rainey's mouth dropped open in shock. "A *nice job*?"

The nurse nodded. "Yes, he sure did. See how smooth those lines are where they covered the tip with new skin? It's not always that pleasing to the eyes."

Rainey raised her finger to eye level, examining the ugly nib. "Looks like complete crap to me. I have a stump growing out of my hand."

"Well, be grateful that nothing more serious happened. So tell me, how have things been since you got back?"

Rainey glanced at the nurse and back at the remains of her finger. "Things have been good, I guess. I mean, I'm in juvie so it's as good as can be."

"I understand Tootsie is your cellmate now. That one is a mean little thing. How's that going?"

Rainey smiled softly. "Tootsie isn't as bad as everybody thinks. Now, don't get me wrong, she doesn't take crap from anyone, but she's been nice to me."

Nurse Dix pursed her lips, "Well," she said, pausing, "I'm happy to hear that. She's quite the hoodlum. It wasn't too long ago you and she were in solitary confinement for fighting."

Rainey flinched. "If by hoodlum you mean she grew up poor and didn't get everything she needed, then yeah, I guess I'm a hoodlum too," she said defensively.

"What I said had nothing to do with how much money she had growing up. Most of the girls here come from poor families. I'm talking about her boyish ways. Strutting around here like she's a tough guy, acting more like a grown man. Living her life thinking that brute force is the only way to treat people."

"Nurse Dix," Rainey said quietly, "It's really hard to live in the center of this place. Tootsie is just taking care of herself like the rest of us."

The nurse turned away. "Okay, Rainey. I see you don't understand my point. All I'm trying to say is that Tootsie isn't the person you think she is, and you should be careful. We're all done here."

Annoyed, Rainey was about to leave, but wanted to get one final word in. "Nurse Dix, Tootsie is kind and gentle and sometimes fiercely defensive. There's a soft side to her that people will never see . . . because, well, maybe they don't want to see it. Maybe all they can see is that she acts like a man," she said, then left the office.

***

Over time, Rainey and Tootsie became close friends. Rainey believed they were even closer than she'd been with Phoenix, perhaps because she was with Tootsie much longer, and she was much more open than Phoenix about her past.

The girls remained cellmates for the rest of Rainey's time at juvie, and, other than the occasional fight with a catty girl, Rainey's life was relatively peaceful. Living with Tootsie gave her special protection, but greater than her safety was the sense of home Rainey had with her. Tootsie felt like a blood sister, and the two girls grew to love and respect each other.

Even Martina, who had vowed to get even with Rainey, backed down from trying to make her life miserable. Over time, it was clear to Rainey why so many girls joined a gang—there was a certain camaraderie and the comfort of knowing that other people could be counted on in a time of need. This was Rainey's third chance at sisterhood, first with Ivy, then Phoenix, and now with Tootsie. All were wonderful, special, and different.

Chapter Ninety-Two: Two Years Later

After spending three years in juvie, and to Rainey's delight, she was awarded her freedom at her first parole hearing. Over that time, aside from the fight with Tootsie, she had done everything the way the system expected, and her good behavior had paid off.

After learning of Rainey's upcoming release, Tootsie made a deal with Jiggy. He would make sure that Miranda fetched Rainey from juvie, because at seventeen she could only be released into the custody of a parent or legal guardian. In return, Tootsie sold her soul to the devil.

The night before Rainey's release, the mood in their cell was somber—loneliness clung to each of them as they fought the separation that would come in the morning. An unmanageable empty void took center stage. Deep down, Rainey was excited about seeing Ivy again and having her freedom, but she was also frightened to leave the controlled environment. The memories of hunger and fear from her life before flooded back. She was returning to an unpredictable life that tore at her insides like an untreated terminal illness. The fear and anguish grew by the minute.

"Well?" Tootsie said. "How are you feeling? You must be stoked to get outta this place."

Rainey shrugged. "Yeah, I'm excited to see Ivy, but that's about it." Something that had been tugging at her mind rose to the surface, and she figured it was now or never. "Hey, just curious . . ." she said, feeling oddly nervous. "What did you have to do to make Jiggy get my mom to come get me? I mean, I don't have to cut off my thumb or anything, right?" she half joked.

Tootsie smirked. "Nah. You're good to go. No strings attached."

Tootsie wouldn't ever tell Rainey she had agreed to sell smuggled drugs to inmates when she got moved to state prison the following month to serve her last three years. Tootsie knew that Rainey wouldn't approve and would be disappointed in her.

"So, you're gonna go home when you get out?" Tootsie said, changing the subject.

Rainey nodded. "Yeah, that's the plan. Honestly, I'm not sure what to expect—my mom and dad are unpredictable. They probably set up a dog house for me in the backyard." She sighed, "Three years is a long time. I'm more worried about what my stupid parents have done to Ivy since I've been in here."

In response, Tootsie grabbed a piece of paper and a marker. She scribbled an address down, folded it, and handed it to Rainey. "You keep this. If you find yourself on the streets, you call Winnie. She's someone on the outside I know—I told her about you."

Rainey pushed Tootsie's hand away. "I told you a million times I'm not built for gang life."

Tootsie's eyes turned serious and she looked at Rainey intently. "Winnie ain't in a gang. She was my best friend all through junior high. Her dad was an alcoholic, and when he lived with them, he yelled at her all the time. Man, that wrinkly old jerkoff treated her like shit—called her a slut, told her she was worthless and that he wished her mother had aborted her. He died, and when her mom died a few years later, she was torn up. Winnie is good people, you keep this address," Tootsie said, shoving the paper into Rainey's pocket. "Just in case you need it."

Rainey wrapped her arms around Tootsie's waist. "Thank you."

"For Winnie's address?" Tootsie chuckled.

"No." Rainey shook her head fiercely.

Tootsie grinned. "For cutting off your pinky, right?"

"Oh, hell no," Rainey said. "Thank you for trusting me. For being kind to me. For letting me get to know the real you. For being like a sister."

Tootsie's eyes welled. This stirred emotions in Rainey to see the girl always so stoic and tense lose herself for a moment.

"Crybaby, cry, my eyes are dry," Rainey sang jokingly.

"I ain't no crybaby. These are tears of joy that you're gonna get the hell outta here tomorrow and I'll finally have some damn peace," Tootsie said, playing along.

"I'll miss you, Tootsie."

Tootsie turned away and grunted.

"I know you'll miss me too. Someday, when you get out, I expect you to look for me. By then, maybe I'll have my own place and you can stay with me for a while."

Tootsie smiled. "Yeah, that would be nice. Except I have somewhere to go when I get released."

Of course: the Vamps. Rainey nodded. "Maybe you'll decide to leave the gang once you're out of prison."

"Girl, you don't leave the Vamps . . . the Vamps leave you. And, trust me, if they leave you, that isn't a good thing. It means you're leaving this world," Tootsie said.

"Doesn't that scare you?"

Tootsie shook her head. "What scares me is not being able to stay off of dope when I get out of here."

"What are you talking about? You haven't done drugs in forever," she said.

"Yeah, well, everything changes when all the shit you couldn't get is suddenly everywhere you turn. There's temptation all around. People are partying and happy, and it's so fucking easy to get sucked right back into it," Tootsie admitted, worried about using again when she has to sell for Jiggy.

"Well, then you remember how miserable my parents made my life by choosing drugs over their kids. You remember that I was born addicted to heroin. Anytime you even think about doing drugs I want you to hear my voice in your ears: What are you doing that for? Why would you want to do drugs again? Why do you even *like* drugs?" Rainey said.

"Yeah, you're right. And you're a total buzzkill with all of those questions," Tootsie said, patting Rainey's back. "But seriously, when you leave here tomorrow, remember to be a bad bitch. Don't take any shit from anyone, and whatever you do, stay the hell away from Jiggy. Got it?"

This time it was Rainey's eyes that welled. "Yeah, I got it."

***

The next morning, when Fernandez arrived to get Rainey, the two girls huddled together and clung onto each other.

"You remember everything I taught you," Tootsie said.

"Only if you remember everything *I* taught *you*," Rainey said. "What's the most important thing?"

Tootsie put her hand on Rainey's cheek. "Don't be a dick."

"Exactly," Rainey stated. "You look for me when you're out of prison. Promise?"

Tootsie's breathing was shaky. She looked into Rainey's eyes. "Yeah, girl," she said as her voice cracked and she tensed her muscles to keep from crying. "We'll see each other again."

Rainey hugged Tootsie tighter. "I'll see you."

Rainey turned away quickly as tears flowed down her cheeks. Outside the cell, she turned around and took one last look at Tootsie, who gave her a small wave.

As Rainey walked away from the heart of the detention center, the structure that had kept her intact faded. It was as though she were passing through a dark portal with no idea of what or who would be waiting for her on the other side. The acid churning in her stomach bubbled up to her chest and she clutched at her stomach to cope with the burn deep inside of her. She'd recognized this feeling, the unknown, and knew the only way to conquer it was to fight her way out and find something better . . . something that would give her the life she'd dreamed of.

Chapter Ninety-Three

It was a warm morning in early June as Rainey walked into the exit room to be processed out of the detention center. Her eyes landed on her mother, Miranda, the woman who'd betrayed her in so many ways throughout her short life. Taking in the features and flaws of the woman who she called Mom, Rainey looked at her objectively for maybe the first time. Miranda's braless chest was covered by a thin spaghetti strap shirt. Her breasts jiggled as she followed a guard into the room. Her jeans were stretched out and baggy from being overworn and under washed, stained from spills and cigarette ashes. The hem of her jeans was ripped at the back from her walking on them with the grungy yellow flip-flops she wore. Her mom had aged in the past three years. She was sickeningly skinny. The translucent skin on her face was crater-like. Miranda's eyes grotesquely bulged from her gaunt face. Her addiction ravaged what little beauty was left of her.

Rainey's flesh crawled at her having once been inside her mother's body and had fed from her mother's breasts. Repulsed, she stared hard as Miranda approached.

"How soon can we get out of here?" Rainey said in a flat voice.

Miranda kept a distance between them and lifted her chin. "How the fuck should I know? I never had to spend time in prison, remember? I'll tell you what, though: it better be quick, 'cause this shithole gives me the willies."

After Miranda and one of the detention administrators went through the paperwork, which took a surprisingly short amount of time, Rainey followed her out of the jail.

Once outside, Miranda turned to her. "You got fat."

Rainey sucked in a breath. Every inch of her had to hold back from tackling Miranda to the ground and choking the life out of her. "I'm not fat, my weight is normal. It's called eating. You should try it sometime."

Miranda cackled. "Yeah, well, from what I can see, you need to shed a few pounds, fatty."

Rainey's jaw was set hard as she followed her mother to their car. Her desire to get away from the detention center outweighed her urge to bash her mother in the face.

Inside the car, when Miranda turned the key and revved the engine, black smoke billowed from the muffler as she took off toward Kensington. Six blocks before reaching the street Rainey had grown up on, Miranda pulled over and shut the car off. Her fingers tapped on the steering wheel as she stared through the front windshield. After a minute of this, Rainey turned to her, confused.

"What are we doing here?"

"This is the end of the line for you," Miranda said.

"What?" Rainey asked, thinking she must have heard her wrong.

Miranda pulled a cigarette from the console and lit it. "Yeah. What'd you think? We were gonna let you live with us after all you put us through?"

That comment set Rainey off. "After what I put *you* through? I just spent three years in juvie for something I had nothing to do with so you and Dad could protect Jiggy. Do you have any idea how fucked up that is?"

Miranda took a drag of her cigarette and blew the smoke in Rainey's face. "Wah, wah, wah! Get the fuck outta my car."

Rainey, more stunned than angry, grabbed for the door handle, then paused. "I don't have any money."

Miranda reached in her jeans pocket and pulled out a twenty-dollar bill. She balled the bill in her fist and tossed it at her daughter's face. "Now you have money. Get out."

Rainey shook her head slightly. "I'm your kid. How can you live with yourself throwing me out on the streets? What's wrong with you?"

Miranda pulled a long drag from her cigarette. "I don't care who you are," she said, her bulging eyes watching her daughter intently. "You stopped being my kid when you didn't do what your father and I wanted. You gotta learn there are consequences for your actions, and now you have. So, for the last time, get the fuck outta my car."

Rainey turned and looked at her mother with fiery eyes. She leaned back in the passenger seat and crossed her arms over her chest. "If you don't want me to go home, that's fine. But I want to see Ivy first."

Miranda smirked and lowered her chin to glare at her elder daughter. "Yeah, so about that . . . your dad and me don't think that's a good idea. Ivy has been doing great without you and it'll only upset her to see you. That's what you do . . . you bring people down."

"That's bullshit! I've taken care of Ivy since she was born!" Rainey yelled.

"Well, you haven't been around for three years. Things changed."

The passenger-side car door opened suddenly and Rainey looked up, startled. Peter leaned down and looked into the car at Miranda. "Did you tell her?"

"Yeah, I told her," Miranda said bitterly. "The little bitch wants to argue with me."

Peter reached in and grabbed Rainey's wrist. "Let's go, girl. Get out."

Rainey yanked her wrist away from her father and put the palms of her hands out in front of her. "Don't touch me. I don't need your help."

She stepped out of the car in a swift motion. Standing on the sidewalk, Rainey looked into her father's bloodshot eyes. "What are you two doing?" she asked, softening her tone. "You have to let me see Ivy. I can watch her so she isn't hanging around the house all day. I . . . I can take care of her. You know, keep her busy for you."

Peter grabbed Rainey by her shirt and shoved her down to the sidewalk. Instantly thrown into fight mode, she popped up and charged at her father.

Peter's eyes grew wide. *His daughter had changed over the past three years. Prison hardened her, made her more confident. Good thing she isn't coming back home.*

"You rotten bastard!" she screamed, swinging her fists at him. "I hate you! I hate both of you!"

Rainey had landed a punch to the right side of Peter's chin, and he was momentarily dazed. Clearing his head, he grabbed a handful of her hair and dragged her away from the car. He put his face close to hers, both of them huffing and puffing from the scuffle.

"You stay the hell away from us or I swear you'll be sorry."

"Why?" Rainey asked, trying to pry her hair out of his fist. "What are you gonna do? Kill me?"

Peter hacked up phlegm and spit in Rainey's face. Degraded, she stumbled backward and caught herself on a dilapidated chain-linked fence. She stood, dumbfounded, watching as her father scurried, like a rat, to the car and slithered inside.

After the car sped away, Rainey took in her surroundings. There were two hookers across the street staring, but everyone else in and around the area went about their lives. She noticed people sitting on the steps of their row homes getting high and chugging quarts of beer with nowhere to go in the middle of the day. No one seemed to notice what just happened to her . . . in Kensington, a fight on the sidewalk was an hourly occurrence.

Seeing Ivy was more necessary now than ever. She was convinced her parents had done something awful to the child. In her mind, the only reason her parents would keep Ivy from her was if she was hurt. Then her stomach clenched as she thought that maybe Ivy was dead.

Rainey stood alone on the sidewalk with nowhere to go, abandoned once again by the people who brought her into the world addicted to heroin. On the overcrowded street, loneliness seeped into her belly and the paralyzing isolation controlled her. Rainey gave her head a sturdy shake to clear her agonizing thoughts. She focused on the only thing she knew for certain; she wouldn't rest until she had ahold of her little sister. Rainey made Ivy a promise to come back for her someday, and she intended to keep it.

Continue reading . . .

A Little High (Rainey Paxton Series) Book Two

Read the first chapter of the next Rainey Paxton book.

Chapter One

Clinging to the dilapidated chain-link fence, Rainey watched dumbfounded as her father scurried like a rat to the car. Without a backward glance, Peter pulled the door closed on the passenger side and her mother, Miranda, sped away, leaving the confused seventeen-year-old on the streets of North Philadelphia with nowhere to go.

A hooker across the street who had watched the fight lifted her chin and yelled over the traffic, "You okay, doll? You need a sugar daddy to kiss your boo-boos?" she mocked, then broke into laughter.

Ignoring the girl, Rainey looked around frantically. Flustered, she wished she was back in juvie. While she hated being in prison, at least when she was locked up, she had Tootsie to count on. Gathering her courage, she straightened her rumpled shirt and flattened her hair, trying to put her dignity back together. Then she walked toward one end of the block, and right before reaching the corner, a man approached her.

"Hey, you!" he said, scampering toward her. "Come here. I want to talk to you."

She turned around cautiously and watched the tall black man close the distance between them. Her eyes roamed over him as she tried to assess how much of a danger he'd be to her. The man had a medium build and wore baggy jeans and a tight T-shirt. He had a barbed wire tattoo running the length of his right arm. As he slithered a few steps closer, a set of keys dangling from his finger jingled. Stopping a foot away from her, his eyes got dark and serious, looking at her as though they were long-lost lovers.

"Do I know you?" Rainey asked, wondering if he was a squatter from her childhood home.

"I ain't sure," he said with a slow smile. "Do I look familiar, baby?"

The hairs on the back of her neck stiffened.

He continued in a creepy tone, "Everybody in this town knows me. I'm Brewer. What's your name, baby doll?"

Rainey's intuition told her that Brewer was trouble. She stood taller, trying to hide her uneasiness. "Listen, I need to get home before my mom and dad get upset and call the cops," she lied, trying to deter him.

She turned to walk away but the man grabbed her shoulder, twisting her around to face him. "Whoa. Not so fast!" Brewer bellowed. "I wasn't done talking to you. I think you better calm down."

Rainey's apprehension hardened into annoyance. "I am calm. Look, I have to go. I don't have time for this," she said, narrowing her eyes at him.

"All right, hold on now. Let me say this first, I saw that man push you down and spit in your face. I only wanted to make sure you were okay. See, that's what I'm all about, taking care of women. That's right, there are no finer creatures on this earth."

She hiked her hands to her hips. "Great, I'm fine. Thanks for checking."

"But wait," he said firmly, grabbing her arm and holding on. "I saw that asshole get in the car that drove away and leave you standing here looking lost. I ain't sure why someone would treat a girl as beautiful as you like that—he must be outta his damn mind. I would never do that to my woman . . . someone as fine as you," Brewer schmoozed, leaning in closer.

Rainey tried to hide her disgust, wanting to get away from him without setting him off. "I'm not his *woman*. I'm not anyone's woman," she stated, stone-faced.

Brewer let out a cackle. "I see. You're one of those independent types." He touched the ends of her hair and she jerked her head away.

His comment caused a fresh surge of aggravation, which further fueled her bad mood. "Yeah, that's right." She stared at Brewer for a few seconds, then looked around. A few feet away two hookers hung onto each other, watching her interaction with him. The way they were staring and smiling at her—whispering things she couldn't hear confirmed what she already knew.

Brewer followed her gaze to the hookers, baring his teeth at them and they walked off together. He turned his attention back to Rainey. "Okay baby, I feel you on that one. You like your independence, but that comes with a price. See, I know you ain't got no mommy and daddy waitin' for you to get home."

Rainey crossed her arms over her chest, and her shoulders slumped slightly. Neither action went unnoticed by Brewer.

He moved in closer. "But here's the deal. I can offer you things. See that car over there?" He pointed to a silver Mercedes. "That's the car you'd be driving in if you were my girl."

Losing her patience and having given him too much of her time, Rainey glared at him. "That's your car, huh?" she asked, looking him up and down. "Are you a pimp?"

Brewer forced out a fake laugh. "Baby doll, you sound like you're a hundred years old. *Pimp, pimp.* Who uses that word anymore?"

"*I do, Brewer,*" she said, spitting out his name like it was poisonous. "*I* use the word 'pimp.' Here's the thing. I'm having a really shitty day and I think it's better if you leave me alone," she said, turning and walking away.

"Bitch, you don't walk away from Brewer!" he yelled after her.

But Rainey picked up her pace and didn't turn back.

Enraged, Brewer screamed, "That's right, whore. Keep walking. You ain't good enough to be one of my bitches. You can come back and beg me to take you in when your white ass is sleeping in the streets and your belly is hollering at you for food. That's right . . . that's when I'll see you. You'll be sorry. Just wait and see!"

Once Rainey was far enough away and couldn't see Brewer anymore, she leaned against a brick wall to catch her breath. The only thing on her mind was to find a place to stay where she would be safe for the night. She needed time to figure out where she could go next. Shoving her hands into her front pockets, she felt the twenty-dollar bill her mother had thrown in her face before she kicked her out of the car. She wrapped her fingers around the bill and balled it up in the palm of her hand, grateful to have the meager amount of money to fall back on. As Rainey roamed the streets trying to figure out what to do, dark clouds formed over her head. As the day quickly turned stormy, she ducked into a doorway and looked up at the sky. It started to drizzle, but a few minutes later the dark clouds released and the water came down in sheets.

With almost no visibility, Rainey closed her eyes and drew in a breath through her nose. The rain hitting the hot sidewalk gave off a distinct scent that brought her back to her childhood . . . playing at a park on hot summer days with her aunt Sophie. She remembered one time they had gotten soaking wet as they ran for the cover of the car. Inside, they watched the rain coming down as they ate cookies and listened to the sound of raindrops hitting the car roof and windshield. As the storm formed around them, lightning flashed and thunder banged and all she could recall was being safe inside the car together.

Rainey hated that those days with her aunt were long gone and was left to face the world on her own. She was determined to find her way in the world, and with her courage mounting, Rainey was ready to do what was needed to make a better life for herself and her sister, Ivy.

More books by Paige

Believe Like A Child
When Smiles Fade
One Among Us
Mean Little People
Never Be Alone
My Final Breath

Rainey Paxton Series:
A Little Pinprick
A Little High

A Note From Paige

Dear Dearth Reader,

I want to take a moment to thank you for reading and supporting my work. I appreciate you spreading the word about my books to family, friends and co-workers. If you enjoyed this book please go to Amazon and leave a short review so that other readers can determine if this is the right book for them . . . great reviews mean so much to me and keep me writing. Thank you!

~Paige

Made in the USA
Coppell, TX
16 August 2022